Three Cats Publishing

This book has been written in an attempt to provide accurate and authoritative information regarding the subject matter contained herein. It is a work of fiction. It is therefore offered for sale on the understanding that neither author nor publisher can be rendered responsible for any errors, whether cultural, political, legal, factual, or statistical. The reader should seek the legal and professional assistance of appropriate experts when dealing with some of the situations that are covered in the book.

All statistics and facts quoted are those that were relevant and available at the time of writing. All research was made with the intention of presenting an unbiased portrayal of the various subjects as seen through the eyes of the author. Some of the content of this book is the personal opinion of the author and should be treated as such. Any misrepresentation or offence that may be made or caused is completely unintended and is therefore apologized for, unreservedly.

No part of this book may be reproduced in any form, except for the inclusion of brief quotations in a review, without the prior permission in writing from the author or publisher.

First Edition
(September 2024)

Publisher:
Three Cats Publishing

Printed in the United Kingdom

Available in hardback, paperback & Kindle from Amazon

Nick Robson can be contacted by email at:
nick@nickrobsonbooks.com
www.nickrobsonbooks.com

Cover design by Nick Robson
Interior design by Nick Robson
Lucy's Cats by Lucy Robson

Author Photos by Amanda Everett

© Nick Robson 2024
All rights reserved.

TICK TOCK

A NOVEL

Nick Robson

I'm not a prophet or a stone-age man
Just a mortal with the potential of a superman
I'm sinking in the quicksand of my thought
And I ain't got the power anymore
Don't believe in yourself, don't deceive with belief
Knowledge comes with death's release...

(David Bowie, 1971)

Prologue

I'm a writer, I write novels, to be precise. I'm also a part-time private investigator. I was a cop for fourteen years but got pensioned off after being shot, and then restricted to desk duty, which just wasn't something I had envisioned for my future.

So, I started in the PI business as a way of coming up with ideas for stories. The idea was to leave some kind of legacy, such as it is. The problem is, I've just been murdered. But I'll get to that shortly.

Now, private investigating isn't fun. I know how it seems in movies and books and television series, but it's tiresome, unrewarding, and incredibly dull. And there's never anywhere to take a leak. Writing's no better, although the bathroom facilities are less of an issue.

And although the actual process of stringing fragments of ideas together to make a story that fills a book is incredibly rewarding, it requires a Herculean effort to get to the end where you discover that you have a finished tome, worthy or unworthy.

And then comes the next phase, the arduous effort of convincing your agent to believe that what you've written is somehow special, something that should be unleashed onto an unsuspecting book-buying public. And if you've ever tried to get published, you'll know what I mean.

In order to get published, you need an agent to open the doors in the first place. An agent has the contacts and the ability to take an author to something greater, and I do have an agent, Nora, so I'm lucky I guess. I don't like her very much, and she doesn't particularly like me, but at least I can call her my own.

But back to my murder for a moment, I'd almost forgotten about that. Don't get all mushy and sad about the fact that my life is ending now, because I have no regrets on my side. I've done all the things I've ever wanted to do, I've had all the things I've ever wanted, I've loved and have been loved, and I can leave this world without remorse.

I guess at this point, you're probably wondering what the heck is going on and I should explain. I've discovered that life is merely a series of sins, forgiven and unforgivable. But there's only one sin that won't ever really go away.

The original sin. And that's where we begin…

Chapter 1

She figured she had maybe a two-minute lead on him, but her limbs ached from running, legs and forearms slashed and bleeding from the forest's plant life; brambles, branches, and thorny stems blocking her path as she raced toward the house. He was still distant, but she had heard shots ring out so she picked up the pace, her athletic legs powering her forward, desperate to escape what might befall her if she was captured.

She'd had no time to pack, it was fight or flight and she knew she wouldn't have had a chance unless she ran. Her knowledge of the wooded area was her one savior as she continued to run deep into it, knowing that she could lead him in a circle that would take them back to the house. Her agility and fitness, plus the twenty-year age difference meant that her husband had no chance of catching her. She just prayed that he hadn't worked out her plan.

Four hundred yards ahead, she could finally see the perimeter of the grounds where they lived, but she was hoping that none of his goons were on the property. She could still hear him yelling and wondered if he had somehow managed to close the gap on her, because the venom in his voice seemed much louder and more grotesque now.

As she vaulted the post and rail fence, she fell onto the ground on the other side, her ankle taking the brunt of the fall. She screamed in agony, pushing herself to her feet, half jogging, half limping toward the car barn, realizing that her two-minute gap may be down to as low as sixty seconds now.

There were six vehicles in the barn, and she knew that the keys were always left inside them. She quickly grabbed the bag that she had secreted in a cupboard for a moment like this, one that she knew he'd never look in.

There was no time to think of which vehicle to take so she jumped into the closest one, a stealth, matte-black Range Rover, cranking it and gunning the engine as soon as she was inside, forgetting the seat belt as she lit up the tires toward the main gate of the house.

She was thankful that it had been left open for the party guests, and as the Rover hit the highway outside, her foot slammed the gas pedal knowing exactly where she was headed.

Chapter 2

I looked up from above the rim of my coffee cup, steam still rising from the glorious caffeinated brew, fogging my sunglasses, or maybe it was the dawdling remains of the summer's humidity that was steaming up my lenses. No matter, the vision being displayed onboard the neighboring superyacht was a pleasant one, particularly for this early in the morning.

The gulls were enjoying themselves, swooping into the water and then landing back on the dock, occasionally with a fish in tow. The water made slow and laborious lapping sounds against my boat's hull, and the sunlight dappled the shiny white paint in an almost hypnotic manner.

I never tire of the sky in Florida, they have stunningly unique cloud formations here that almost look like they came straight from *The Simpsons* opening title sequence. I could stare at the sky all day watching the shapes and transformations. And occasionally, I do.

I live on the boat and I know that sounds pretty cool but honestly, it isn't. I live alone, but sometimes my twenty-one-year-old daughter comes to stay at the weekends which is, for a father, the deepest joy one can have. It doesn't happen often enough, but I cherish those moments and look forward to them immensely and I also realize that as Molly grows older, her father will figure less in her life. It's just the way it is, so I tell myself to get over it and enjoy it while it lasts.

~ ~ ~

"Are you done with this pizza?" trilled a voice from inside the cabin.

"Has it developed a life of its own yet?" I answer, not really wanting to avert my gaze from the aforementioned vision in the next slip.

"It's got mold on it and you've already had two rounds with it in the microwave," the voice replies.

"Well, put it in the fridge and see if we can rescue one more go around," I counter.

"No. It's done, it's in the garbage now. Try eating a little better, would you?"

"Duly noted," I reply.

The sweet and melodic voice coming from within my boat is my PA, my Personal Assistant, as they say. Although I'm not entirely sure why I have one or need one, or even how I came to have one in the first place. Pippa, or Pip as I have come to know her, just showed up one day and announced that she could be my assistant.

And that's what she became. I didn't really have much input into her self-proclaimed position, although I suppose I should be grateful. And really, I am. I like Pip, mostly. Except on serene days like this, when my peace is interrupted over concerns about three-day-old pizza. She arrives at the boat each morning, and she is pretty efficient, albeit unpaid. I should probably pay her someday.

So, the vision. You're probably wondering what had my rapt attention on this extraordinarily picturesque morning in Palm Beach,

Florida. Well, it was a green thong, not very much of it, but it was just enough to cover the naughty parts of an almost perfect, tanned body. I say almost perfect, because the owner of this magnificent body had seen fit to apply a non-essential tattoo to one of her buttocks, thereby ruining what God, or whoever, had deemed to be his masterpiece.

"Cooper Hemingway," I said to myself, assuming I was out of staff earshot, "You really need to grow up…"

"Yes, you do, Coop, and you need to keep that galley cleaner, it's disgusting. And you need to take better care of yourself too, you're going to get old quickly," instructed my assistant as she emerged from the cabin below.

"I know, Pip, I just hadn't gotten around to it before you showed up this morning. Quit nagging, you're like a wife without the nocturnal activity. Anyway, I'm busy," I replied.

Pip is tall, almost willowy, with strawberry-blonde long hair, hippy-ish figure, and the greenest of green, sparkling wide eyes. I think she's around twenty-five, but I've never asked.

She reminds me of that girl in the Coca-Cola ad in the 70s, you know, the one with the girl on a Californian hilltop singing, *"I'd like to teach the world to sing"*. I'd always liked that girl's sense of purity which is why I like Pip, although I don't let her know that. You have to keep staff on their toes, even the unpaid ones.

I know what you're thinking. You think that maybe occasionally, I have a quick fumble between the sheets with Pip, a brief excursion into the land of twenty-something sex. But it's not true, and I prefer reasonably age-appropriate ladies, and I also make a rule of not philandering with the staff, particularly the unpaid employees in my staff of one.

Pip was now standing deliberately in my vision.

"Can I help you?" I asked.

"I need some cash for supplies."

"Why?"

"Because you're eating processed garbage and I need you to stay fit, or I won't have a job soon when you finally croak it," she replied.

You won't have an unpaid job?

"Sure, okay, how much?"

"A hundred should cover it."

"How about fifty?"

"Not happening, Coop, come on, hand over the money."

Pip is not someone to be placated so easily, so I pulled a recently acquired shiny C-note from my wallet, pressed it into the palm of her hand, and watched her gambol off down the dock toward the pier. I love making people happy.

"Don't spend it all at once," I yelled after her, "There's not much more from where that came from."

If she heard me, then she was ignoring me, but at least she was busy and happy. Pip's place was quickly taken by the arrival on deck of my cat. He'd had a late night so I could understand why he'd only just finally surfaced at eleven in the morning.

"Want some pizza?" I asked.

But like most cats, he ignored me. When I say he's my cat, that's not strictly true. In the same way that Pip just arrived one day, as if beamed down from another planet, Kinky had also mysteriously appeared one afternoon and made my boat his own. He's Siamese and a bit overweight on account of the fact that he rarely moves. He's called Kinky because I accidentally trapped his tail in the cabin door one day, soon after he materialized, and I guess it must have broken his tail because it stayed in a kinked right-angled shape from thereon in. And so, Kinky he became.

I also have a German Shepherd and as usual, Diablo was sitting by my side, quietly watching the same spectacle as me, whilst simultaneously working out how he could eliminate Kinky altogether. That's the thing about Shepherds, they make plans, they're silent, and they're deadly once a plan is hatched.

So now you know my crew, Pip, Kinky, and Diablo, and there's not a lot else to say, I suppose. Oh yes, my name is Cooper Hemingway, private investigator and author. On a good day anyway.

I live on my unimpressive boat, *Lost Soul,* in an impressive slip in the ritzy Riviera Yacht Club in Palm Beach, courtesy of my good friend Remy Washington, who manages the marina where I reside. I pay him a peppercorn rent, and he kindly massages the remainder of the mooring fees across the accounts of the owners who can actually afford to be here, which of course, doesn't include yours truly.

Fortunately for me, the yachts and boats here are rarely used, because the owners are busy making money to buy their next status symbols, which suits me fine because I like my peace and harmony. These owners usually visit on Independence Day, Labor Day, or occasional birthday celebrations, and so Remy and I spend countless evenings on my boat drinking beer and talking nonsense for the most part.

Anyway, back to the business at hand. The vision of immaculate thonged beauty was now stretched out on the enormous sunbathing platform at the 'front' of the motor yacht, (I've never really gotten to grips with nautical jargon, it's probably called the bow). She'd now been joined by a balding and morbidly obese gentleman, smoking an even fatter cigar, whilst commanding that the aforementioned thonged ingénue apply suntan oil to his large and hairy body. More hair suit than hirsute.

The temptress waved, apparently unseen by her older companion and so I waved back, forever the knight in a damsel's distress.

"I saw you."

Pip.

"I wasn't doing anything, just being neighborly," I replied.

"Fuck you, Coop."

Chapter 3

She eventually pulled onto the used car forecourt, parking the Range Rover to the left of the small office building where Wayne ran his business. She prayed that he could help her and that she hadn't made a huge mistake by coming here. Wayne knew of her husband, but hadn't actually ever met him, because Carlo never bought used cars. Only new ones.

But when she had first arrived in Miami from Wisconsin, she'd struck up a friendship with Wayne and his wife, Greta, at a cousin's wedding. She'd grown close to them, particularly Greta, and she would miss them. The likelihood was that she'd never see them again, which at this moment deepened her melancholy at her horrendous situation.

Walking into the ramshackle sales office, she immediately spotted Wayne, deep in earnest conversation on the phone with what must have been a potential buyer, so much so that he didn't acknowledge her as she pulled up a seat in front of his immaculately arranged desk.

The brass plaque, although now in need of a polish, pronounced the name and title of the occupant, *Wayne Randolph, Proprietor – RandyWayneAutos Inc.* Next to it, sat an A4 size picture-frame with a photo of his beloved wife, Greta. The two were inseparable, joined at the hip.

Wayne was old-school Florida, he carried a mild paunch, but still had longish wavy hair as a reminder of his surfing days in his youth. He tied it back in a ponytail now, the grey seeping into his dark brown thatch. He was dressed head to foot in denim; jacket, shirt and jeans, coupled with spotless tan Timberland boots.

Notwithstanding the obligatory gold chain around his neck, Wayne was far from grubby, he was immaculate in denim, smelled good, and for someone who had to occasionally tinker with car mechanics, his hands and nails were equally well maintained.

Wayne was a true Southern boy, born in Atlanta, Georgia, but the pull of the ocean down south in Miami was too much to ignore. By the time he was twenty years old, he'd migrated south, tried his luck at surfing, and realized he was likely to make far more money by buying, fixing and selling automobiles, so surfing became an occasional hobby.

But it was through that passion for cars and trucks, that he met a girl who would become his life partner, one Greta Dibromo, who waltzed into his then small forecourt of just a few cars, in search of a new ride, and Wayne was smitten immediately. Still is.

Eventually, he looked up at her, smiled, and began to close the deal he was making with the customer. Putting the receiver back on its cradle, he beamed,

"Well, ain't you the prettiest highlight of my day, Cassidy?" he said, coming around the desk to hug her, "To what do I owe this great pleasure, darlin'?"

Tears ran immediately down her cheeks as she realized the quickly arriving finality of her friendship with Wayne and Greta, the tears rapidly evolving into uncontrollable sobbing.

"Whoa!" said Wayne, "What the heck's going on with you, girl, tell me what's upsetting you so bad?"

Once she had managed to get control of herself, Cassidy blurted out, "I nee... I need... I need help, Wayne, I'm so sorry but you were the only one I could come to, the only man I can trust," she cried, her make-up now a mess around her eyes.

"What's that husband of yours been up to now?" he soothed, "Man, that fucker is a monster."

"He wants to kill me, Wayne, I can't explain right now because I know he's already set his goons out after me, I just need to get away, as quickly as possible."

"Okay, I'm here baby girl, what do you need from me, just say it and I'll fix it."

"Oh God, I wish I had time to tell you everything but all I need is a car that can't be traced. I've taken one of his cars, the Range Rover parked outside, to make a trade. Can you help?"

"Consider it done, Cass, I can vanish the Rover and give you something anonymous that can't be traced. Come on outside."

Once they had left the office, Wayne quickly hid the Range Rover temporarily in the adjacent barn, the SUV would be out of the country by midnight. And once he had returned from the barn, he took her to the back of the lot, led her to a green Mini Cooper, and fished the keys out from on top of the driver's side front wheel.

"Can you drive a stick?" he asked.

"Yeah, that's not a problem, I grew up with stick shifts in Wisconsin, but this is a nice car, Wayne, won't it be easy to trace?"

"Well, bearing in mind it's not even registered in the US, no, no chance at all. I bring in cars from Mexico and Europe all the time, keep the original titles, and re-register them for my customers as U.S. cars," he explained, "But this beauty ain't been registered so it's totally under the radar. If you get pulled over, just show the original title to the cop and tell them you're waiting on the Florida title to come through."

"Jeez, I don't know what I'd do without you, Wayne, you're literally a Godsend," she said, tears again cascading down her face.

"Look Cass, just let me 'n Greta know when you find somewhere safe. The car's gassed and ready to go, and it's only got six thousand miles on the odometer. Now get along and don't look back."

She wrapped her arms around him, kissed him on the cheek, slung her bag in the back seat and got behind the wheel of the Mini.

Winding down the window, she said, "I won't ever forget this, Wayne, I promise you, and tell Greta I love her and I'm going to miss you both so much."

"You take care, girl," said Wayne, as she quickly slipped off the lot and out onto the highway.

Chapter 4

My daughter, Molly, used to live on the boat with me, but when she turned eighteen and went to college at Palm Beach State, she decided that she could no longer cope with my lifestyle, so she moved in with her boyfriend in his apartment in West Palm Beach. Billy is a nice kid, a bit older than Molly, he's twenty-four, but he loves her, adores her, so I'm happy. And since Molly moved off the boat, our relationship has grown better, almost exponentially.

When Molly was born, and my wife was still around, she was a cute, beautiful bundle of blonde and brown-eyed joy. When she smiled, it made us melt; we had to pinch ourselves that we'd brought this child into the world. Well, I pinched myself anyway, my wife not so much, given her own natural beauty.

Molly's a lot different visually now, her hair is long and dyed jet black, she wears short black skirts and a leather jacket, usually finished off with a pair of Dr. Marten's lace-up boots. She has an unusual look in a world where the standard teenage attire is flip-flops and cutoff shorts. But she's still my Molly, and always will be.

In my reverie, I thought I heard a footfall on the boat's stern and a subdued growl from Diablo. Looking up, I realized that I hadn't been mistaken.

"Coop?"

Remy.

"You're a man deep in thought, what ails you, my friend?"

Who uses the word ail *these days?*

"Not much, Rem, just wondering what life is all about, I guess, perusing where it will take us."

"I've got the antidote, Coop, you need a beer," he replied, setting down a case of Yuengling on the tabletop.

Remy Washington is one of those rare people you are lucky to meet in life, blessed to call your friend. He's huge, 6'5", and built like a bull. His smile is the whitest and widest, brilliant and immaculate teeth lighting up a beautiful ebony face. His only mild imperfection was the lack of a left forearm, lost in an explosion whilst serving as a military medic on the front line.

But other than that, he had the shape and power of a modern heavyweight boxer. Remy is my best friend, has been since the moment he intervened in a one-sided bar fight seven years ago, which was the closest I'd ever come to buying the farm.

"You look tired, man, up all night again?" he asked.

"Yeah, I'm getting too old for this shit," I replied.

I'd spent the whole night and some of the morning camped out in my trusty '62 Cadillac Coupe DeVille, supposedly the one Don Draper bought in the famous car showroom scene in *Mad Men*. But probably not.

Remy leaned back in the tattered half recliner, his muscles seemingly trying to escape the tautness of his white shirt, his huge hand dwarfing the cold bottle of beer, as he relieved it of half its nectar.

"You still working that thing for Joe?" he asked, intent on pulling me out of my slumberous low, "But you're getting paid, right?"

Remy was clearly in the mood for a long evening of talking and drinking.

"Yes, and yes. And actually, the money's good, might even pay Pip something this week. But being holed up in the Caddy the whole night, taking photographs and waiting for something to happen, whilst eating cold KFC, and always desperate for another leak, is not how I saw my life blossoming."

It's Flick, right?" asked Remy, "What's that girl been up to this time?"

"Same old, same old," I replied, "Except this time, Joe's done with it. He needs out of his toxic marriage and I've been working on his exit strategy for the last couple of weeks or so. But actually, I think I'm going to nail his little wildcat this time."

"Pray tell," said Remy, swigging back on his second Yuengling.

Pray tell? He's been mixing too much with my old buddy, Talbot, a devout Shakespearian...

"Well, you and I both know that Flick has been bedding young guys ever since she first arrived at Joe's house and moved in with the hapless sap. And I think Joe has always known too, kind of accepted it because there's a huge age difference and in Joe's words, she's apparently 'a whore in the bedroom'," I explained.

Remy didn't respond, because he's not Flick's biggest fan.

"But she goes missing far too often now and he's kind of over it, and wants out of the marriage, but has never caught her in the act, as it were."

"I'll give her one thing, she's smart, cunning almost," Remy replied.

"But," I continued, "By complete coincidence, Molly's boyfriend, Billy, saw Flick with a young guy recently, maybe twenty-one, twenty-two, and they were snuggled up in a nightclub where Billy works a few nights a week. Pretty brazen really, for her anyway."

"Sounds like she's got her end game planned," said Remy, "Flick's nothing if not calculating."

"Exactly," I replied, "So I told Joe about it and he's been paying me to work a nocturnal schedule to finally begin gathering evidence, so he can legally and easily divorce her, without getting taken to the cleaners."

"How's that panning out?"

"I've got nothing yet that's going to incriminate the girl, but she's begun making mistakes, so I think it's going to turn out a result for Joe soon, I'm just beat from seventeen nights of it.

"I'm not sure I'd have the patience or the will to do what you do, Coop, I'd go crazy camped out in my truck all night."

"Gotta eat, I guess, but enough about my whining, what's going on with you? How's Memphis, are you guys official now?"

"It's all good, man, but it's early days yet, we've only been dating a few weeks but yeah, he's something else."

"That's longer than I usually last with anyone," I laughed, as we settled down in the warm spring evening to finish off the six-pack.

Chapter 5

There are two types of rock stars, those who are born gifted and clever, and those who are just born gifted. Joe Jarvie is one of the latter, and he's also a pretty good friend. He's never been too clever in choosing the women with whom he spends his life, but he has a heart of gold and an interminable lust for life.

Joe is rail thin, an almost athletic body that has ignored his excesses of junk food and drugs. His mane of tousled hair is testament to my notion that a life nourished by cocaine is a walking advertisement that rock stars who snort it daily, are guaranteed to never lose their locks. Steve Tyler, Axl Rose and Tommy Lee, are perfect examples of this philosophy.

Joe is an extraordinary guitarist, the complete old-school rock 'n roller, not quite in the legend or icon frame, but he's incredibly respected for his talent and has played with the best of them. Joe could never foresee a time when he would hang up his axe and retire from music, because music lived in him, and apart from sex, it was the main reason for which he existed.

And right now, in what can only be deemed as the twilight of his career, he is lead guitarist and vocalist with a young band called *Shamenless*. He's 48, and his band members have an average age of twenty-one. Go figure.

Joe's current flame, a dancer called Flick, is someone he met whilst spaced out on Quaaludes in Las Vegas a number of years back.

For no reason, apart from the fact that he's a hopeless and gullible romantic, he woke up one morning in his Caesar's Palace suite, married to the multiple-tattooed Flick, who was lying comatose next to him.

At that precise moment, he wasn't actually aware that they were now married. It was only when he reached over to take a gulp from the almost empty bottle of Wild Turkey on his nightstand, that he noticed a marriage certificate from the Elvis Chapel on 3rd St.

Now, Flick isn't exactly the type of girl you take home to meet Mom, if you get my drift. She's never going to be that apple pie and white-picket-fence kind of gal that mama is going to approve of as a daughter-in-law, and she's never going to teach the world to sing either.

Flick's only 26, but she's been around the block, and frequently back again, but when she happened upon poor Joe, she saw an opportunity. So, she fucked him senseless, had his driver take them to the chapel, and somehow managed to coerce a signature from him on a marriage certificate.

If she hadn't taken him back to Caesar's immediately afterward and fucked his brain out once again to consummate the aforementioned vows, and if Joe had stayed sober for just one of the following sex, drugs, and alcohol-fueled days, he might have had just one chance to annul the marriage obligation. But he didn't.

Chapter 6

I enjoy taking a trip further inland occasionally, because you can quickly grow tired of the incessant, money-fueled wealth of Palm Beach. I usually get away a couple of evenings a week, and mostly, I would find myself at *Nate's Bar & Grill*.

Tonight, was no exception. The bar was old school, no high-net-worths amongst the clientele, just old-fashioned native Floridians gathered in the timber and log building that nestled out in sleepy Okeeheelee. I'd known Nate for over twenty-five years, since meeting at the police academy.

Nate had taken his pension just as soon as he'd put his time in, and bought what was a wreck of a building and turned it into one of the most hospitable and comfortable bars for miles around. No big TVs on the walls with sports playing, just a mellow thrum of good conversation, the old timers recounting their life stories to anyone who'd listen.

As I took my usual stool at the bar, the girl who made a beeline toward me to take my order, wasn't someone I recognized. I assumed that Nate had had someone quit on him and taken on a replacement.

"What can I get you?' she asked, putting down a coaster in front of me with a bowl of peanuts and a napkin.

"Hey, you must be new here, don't think I've seen you around before?" I replied, "But I'll take a Michelob, please."

"Just moved here this week, saw an ad for a barkeep out here and Nate gave me the job."

"Well, welcome… sorry, I'm Coop, I didn't catch your name?"

"Layla, it's Layla," she replied, putting down a glass and a bottle of Michelob on the coaster.

"Layla…?"

"Just Layla," she replied.

"Well… you got me on my knees, Layla," I crooned badly and somewhat clumsily.

I'm such a schmuck, I'm even embarrassing myself…

"I beg your pardon?"

"You know, the Eric Clapton song?"

"I don't know it, I'm afraid. Do you want to run a tab?"

Seriously? Clapton's biggest hit?

"Sure, yes… run a tab, thank you," I replied, as she went to the till and wrote a ticket.

It was strange though, how can you be called Layla and not know that song? It was iconic Clapton, everyone knew that song. Didn't they?

I took my beer to a corner table in the bar's lounge area and cozily secreted myself whilst idly scanning the evening's clientele, along with an occasional passing gaze toward the mysterious Layla. She was a pretty girl, slim and sleek, long blonde hair, eyes like Indian sapphires. She wore blue jeans that sat easily on her hips, white sneakers and a Hard Rock t-shirt. And she made the simple outfit look perfectly designed, just for her.

It wasn't long before Nate made his way over to my table and slumped into the chair next to me. His wrinkled blue jeans, country shirt and Stetson, bore homage to his ambition as a kid to become a cowboy. He reminded me of Bernie Taupin, Elton John's lyricist, who dreamed of becoming a cowboy as a kid whilst growing up in a village in the north of England. Although Mr. Taupin eventually realized that dream, Nate never did, but he still lived the spirit of it, and embraced it every day.

I had known Nate for the best part of my life, we were kindred spirits. Nate used to be a big guy, always worked out, but since buying the bar and working on it until it was ready to open, I think he pretty much wore himself out doing the work all on his own. The gym was a distant memory now, but you could see that his leanness and musculature, still shone a light to his hyper fitness days.

"New girl?" I asked.

"'She showed up a couple of days ago, asking if I had any work for her."

"And you did, obviously."

"Yeah, well, Babs quit Monday and Layla kinda just walked through the door at the right moment. She's good though, no problem with that girl. And if I'm honest, her looks don't do any harm with the locals here, she seems to have them pretty much charmed."

"What do you know about her," I asked, trying not to sound too inquisitive.

"Not much really, her name is Layla, she's from out of state, and she's always on time," he replied, "It's pretty much all I need to know, and I don't need to tell you how staff never hang around too long, so I don't expect much different with her."

"Did she say where she's from?" I asked, "I kinda sensed a Midwest accent going on there, maybe Indiana or Iowa, even Wisconsin."

"Yeah, I got the same vibe too, but honestly, I've no clue and I don't think she was about to tell me anyway. You know what it's like here, people come and go, some have secrets, some are open books."

"Where's she staying while she's here?" I asked, intent on getting at least a nugget of information from my friend, but at the same time realizing I might sound like I was grilling him.

"Well, that's the strange thing, I asked her the same question and she said she'd been traveling and had been sleeping in her car."

"Seriously?" I said, a little surprised.

"As a heart attack," he replied, "But considering the type of girl she seems to be, I couldn't have imagined her living out of her car for too long."

"Me too, she's kinda classy, even in the whole jeans & T look," I said.

"Well, I didn't want her working here and having to sleep in her car, so I told her that the little bedsit above the bar was available if she wanted to use it temporarily. It ain't much, but man, she almost bit my hand off when I mentioned it. She's already moved in. So maybe up until she arrived here, she'd been sleeping in her car awhile, or maybe she's been on a road trip staying at guesthouses or motels, who knows?"

"So, you've got live-in help, good to know," I replied.

"I've known you a long time, Coop, and something tells me she has your interest?"

"I'm probably too old for her, but she seems nice."

"I think she's older than you realize, my friend, just blessed with good genes, I think."

"Really?"

"Yes. Now, you wanna refill?"

"You already know it, partner," I replied, grinning.

As Nate went off to get another round in, I glanced once again at the mysterious Layla, who was moving swiftly along the bar taking care of customers. Nate was right, she had them eating out of her hands, the girl was cuteness and charisma on a stick.

Chapter 7

Later that evening, as I settled in for another long night in the Caddy, I knew that I needed a break on Joe's case, that is if you can call it a case, watching and waiting for his wife to make a nocturnal mistake. I felt guilty for taking money from my friend just to watch what Flick was up to for endless hours, at five hundred bucks a night. But as Remy had said to me earlier, Joe wasn't short of money, in fact Joe was loaded, so what can I do?

My tacos were still hot, having just picked them up from the Taco Bell two blocks from where I was camped out. As I bit into the first of four, I kept my eyes on Flick's new paramour's dwelling, a small ranch home in the Wellington suburbs. There was some activity inside, because I saw that a couple of lights had gone off and then back on again, but it was probably still too early to expect either one of the nightbirds to make an appearance outside.

So far, I had racked up a little north of eight thousand bucks during my nightly watches, which seemed to me an appropriate figure to maybe pay Pip a few dollars for her services. She was a good kid, she actually looked after me and if I was honest with myself, I'd kinda got used to her coming around each day. And the real truth is that I would miss her if she wasn't there.

Okay then, note to self, five hundred bucks to Pip, come the morning.

Six hours later, tacos dispatched and coffee tepid at best, I saw lights come on at the front entrance. Time to get some shots of the couple, finally. I had spied them together of course, on a couple of occasions, but never in a full embrace, let alone practicing the beast with two backs scenario. If I didn't get something soon to build a slam-dunk adultery case for Joe, I would need to take some risks. Which, to be honest, I wasn't averse to doing.

I opened my driver's side window, perched my telephoto lens on the door frame, and looked through the viewfinder, my camera aimed squarely at the portico which was now fully lit up by the outside light.

It was another twenty minutes until the entrance door finally opened and the two of them came outside to the driveway, where Flick's recently acquired 2023 white Jaguar F-Type had been parked, since around 10pm the previous evening.

My index finger began pressing the shutter button, keen not to miss a guilty photograph from what was now a long night's stakeout. Image after image were stored to my memory card, in my desperation to get just one damning piece of evidence against Joe's two-timing wife.

But as I clicked away, waiting for that goodnight meshing of tongues, I realized she was far smarter than I'd given her credit for, because she simply gave the young man a gentle hug, and scampered off to her car. And that certainly ain't gonna hold up in court.

I watched, incredulous that I'd wasted yet another night on this skank of a woman, as she hit the gas and the Jaguar roared away from the house, leaving me hungry, thirsty and so goddamned tired.

So, I made up my mind that the next time would be the end game, because it was time to finally reel in this bed-swapping alley cat.

Chapter 8

It had been a long night tonight, a pretty good crowd, and tips had been good too. But as the hot water streamed down her, soothing her aching body, she felt exhausted, her mind already feeling the lure of sleep. She washed her hair, grateful to no longer be feeling the pain from it being practically yanked from her skull.

She wouldn't miss Carlo, and at times she'd thought about cropping her hair close, so he wouldn't be able to drag her around by it. But then she also knew that her face would become a punching bag instead.

Since she had left Carlo, almost five months ago now, she had zigzagged her way up and down and across the state, sometimes staying in her tent, sometimes grabbing a motel for the night, something that had become a small luxury to her. Well, not a small luxury at all, but a huge one that she looked forward to whenever it came around. But the beautiful thing about camping in Florida, is that it has the longest coastline of any state, so she could always get shower-clean just by jumping into the ocean.

She just didn't know how long she could stay incognito from Carlo, before it would be time to disappear again. But since she'd arrived in this sleepy little part of Florida, she had become comfortable with where she was, and saw the opportunity of work and a place to stay at Nate's, an extraordinary slice of good fortune in her otherwise disconsolate world.

After drying her hair, she had crawled into her bed, checked her phone, and realized that it was already one o'clock in the morning. She thought back on the evening, and remembered what the guy had said to her earlier on, that thing about… what was it… "You got me on my knees, Layla." She'd only chosen the name Layla because a girl she'd known in high school had had the name.

She opened Safari on her phone, and typed in the words she had recalled, and immediately the results came back with the lyrics of a song called *Layla* by the musician, Eric Clapton. As she read the words, she began to understand that the guy in the bar was just being pleasant, a regular who was just breaking the ice with a new barkeep.

I tried to give you consolation

When your old man had let you down

Like a fool, I fell in love with you

You turned my whole world upside down

She found a YouTube video and played the song she'd never heard of before. Wow, this was a beautiful love song. How did she not know this track? Although according to the YouTube notes, it had been released in 1970, pushing fifteen years before she was born.

Maybe she'd been a bit cold with the guy, what did he say his name was? Mac or Coop or something? But the last thing she needed was someone prying into her world, which was neither safe for her nor anyone else.

Stumbling over Nate's place had been like a gift to her, when she realized that the previous barkeep had upped and disappeared the day before she had stopped off on her journey, in need of a burger & fries and a Coke. When she had taken a stool at the bar and made her order, it was Nate who had written it down and taken it to the kitchen, and at that moment, she didn't realize that he owned the place because she hadn't known his name.

But when Nate introduced himself, she quickly realized he was the owner and she'd made light conversation on and off with him, as he tended to other customers' needs. In between those snatches of conversation, she had spied a 'HELP WANTED' notice at the far end of the bar.

She had worked in restaurants and bars many times while she was in college, so when Nate asked her if she wanted a Coke refill, she'd asked, "What's the job?" pointing at the notice.

"Oh, that? As of yesterday, I need help behind the bar. You looking for work?"

Without thinking too much about whether or not she was actually looking for a job right now, she had replied,

"I am, but I'll have to find a place to stay as I'm not from around here."

"You've done bar work before?" he had asked.

"Been doing it for as long as I can remember," she had lied, "The name's Layla, when do I start?"

Nate had laughed at her cockiness.

"Pleased to meet you, Layla. Where are you living right now, are you close by?"

"Ha! You could say that, I'm kinda living out of my car right now."

Nate looked at her, astounded that this stylish and smart-sounding girl was living in her car, but he liked her and had an idea.

"Look, I've got a tiny little apartment upstairs if you're interested, more of a studio really, start tonight and I'll throw it in for free."

"You serious?"

"Absolutely. Twelve bucks an hour, free grub and you keep your tips, all cash," he'd said, "And I'll get one of my guys to give the place a lick of paint in the next week, you know, freshen it up a little."

"It's a deal," she'd replied, "Looks like you're busy right now, why don't I pitch in and help and I'll unload my stuff later tonight?"

And that was how she happened to be lying in bed in this cramped but cute little studio apartment, thinking as her eyes began to close,

My bad, Mac or Coop, I'll try to be a bit friendlier next time…

Chapter 9

I enjoy the tranquility of the very early hours, that time of the day just before the sun cries morning. I like to listen to the birds waking up, the gentle lapping on the sides of the boat from an otherwise calm ocean, as I snuggle under the sheets in rapt attention and awe of Mother Nature. I treasure these moments, with the vain hope that I can put off the inevitable, when the world decides to invade my life once more.

But now, as impatient footsteps sounded on the stern's deck, growing louder and less palatable as they neared my cabin, I realized that any hope of floating languorously in my secret and silent bliss was about to be rudely interrupted, just as my door was kicked open without invitation.

"What the fuck do you think you're doing?" said a voice I knew too well, a sudden bead of perspiration appearing on my forehead.

This was Rainee, my friend… well, I think she's my friend, but with Rainee, you can never be certain. But mostly, I count her as a friend, although a sometimes unrequired, and utterly non-sexual dominatrix. You get the drift. And it's difficult to describe Rainee in terms that most men, or even women, might understand. She's an attractive woman, no argument there, and she magnetizes men to her, like moths to a flame, or more accurately, like bugs to a spider's web.

You've seen those old movies when the Private Investigator is sitting at his desk in his darkened office, wondering where his next case will come from, when suddenly his door is abruptly opened, and standing in front of him is the classic femme fatale, raven hair, beautiful, scarlet-lipped, a long white coat hiding what only schoolboys can dream about. Well, this is Rainee, a femme fatale with the emphasis hovering equally on both femme and fatale.

But, and this is what is so contrary about Rainee and what makes her my personal conundrum, she has the softest heart I've ever encountered. Rainee can metaphorically castrate you, and then moments later hold you tenderly in her arms like a newborn baby, the very model of love and compassion.

"Get up, Coop, you and I need to have a conversation," she commanded, "And put some fucking clothes on, for Christ's sake."

Rainee Showers wasn't entirely born with that particular name. Her mom, a spaced-out commune dweller, named Pattie Showers, who was perpetually cocooned in the 1960s flower-power, peace and love movement, christened her new baby, Janis Lorraine Showers.

Pattie was keen to acknowledge the commune's heroine, Janis Joplin, and constantly cooed about her good fortune to have given birth to this tousled, blonde-haired, gray-eyed little girl, her golden child. God only knows where Lorraine came from though. And, as young Janis grew up amongst the other commune friends and neighbors, she became known as Golden to everyone.

But as she reached her teenage years, during which she became more and more feisty, sullen, and fiercely independent, with a rapt dislike for the commune music, particularly the aforementioned Ms. Joplin, she decided that the time had come to abandon her given name and nickname, use an abbreviated version of her middle name, Lorraine, and Rainee Showers she became. It killed two birds with one stone, if you see what I mean…

Rainee sighed. But not a sigh of passion when seeing me partially naked in dawn's flattering early light. This was a sigh she gave, just before she verbally sliced through me, the proverbial quiet before her raging and brutal storm.

"Cooper Hemingway, why are you meddling in my business? I thought we had a fucking agreement?"

See? You know she's going to bury me when she uses my full name, because mostly, people call me Coop. But I kind of knew my actions last night would come back to haunt me, and I was right, Rainee was going to rip me a new one, even before the morning's ablutions…

Chapter 10

I'm not really American. I wasn't born here, and my first name was derived from the tiny British motor car in which my American mother and English father engaged in an aerobic sex act at the point of my creation. I guess I should be thankful not to be called Mini.

I was born in Knightsbridge, in December 1976, (yeah, the posh and glamourous part of London Town) just as The Sex Pistols became infamous on the Bill Grundy Show, although the two events are sadly unconnected. I think that makes me forty-six at the last count.

I get along with most people I come across, but I always had the thought that my mother wasn't a fan. I mean, I think she probably quite liked me when I was born, but her dislike of me grew at an exponential rate as I grew older. She was doing a lot of Charlie in my formative years though, which explained her aversity to what might have been natural maternal instinct, so I'm guessing that underneath it all, she probably wasn't all bad.

And I guess it's why I got screamed at every other day, until I decided I'd had enough and left. I was only sixteen at the time, but to be free of the anger and hatred was a welcome change, even when endeavoring to survive on the streets of London as a young teenager.

My mother died of an overdose when I was seventeen, a sad ending for the life of someone who was the epitome of the London Party Girl. She was just forty-one years old. I remember vividly, standing by my father's side at her funeral, his hand gripping mine so tightly, as though if by letting go, he'd fall through the earth.

Angus Hemingway fell in love with Arabella Winslow on his very first sight of her. He was somewhat older than my mother, fifteen years older, to be precise. She was at every party from Chelsea to Notting Hill, Kensington to Holland Park, and invariably, hers was the first name on the guest list. She literally partied like it was 1999, as Prince would sing, although she never made it to that particular year.

My father met her at one of said frolics, and two weeks later they were married at The Royal Borough of Kensington & Chelsea Old Town Hall in the King's Road. A typically impromptu exchange of vows that was endemic of the era in London.

But my father never wavered, even as he watched my mother spiral out of control on alcohol and drugs, she remained the constant center of his attention, the only love he'd ever known, and sadly, the only love he would ever know.

My dad is a good man, actually a great man, a scientist who'd made a small fortune entirely from a brain that could think, predict and rationalize, in a way that mere mortals like us can only dream about.

Of course, his super intelligence was not passed down to his only child. Hey ho. And although our relationship has never been a close one, because he has never been able to express love and emotion to me, he's still my dad. And I love him, because he's the only dad I have.

I think I mentioned previously that I kind of split my time these days, being a part-time private investigator and keen, but lazy writer. The novels I write are mostly love stories, and my output would be far more impressive if I adhered to the task more frequently.

The thing about writing novels, is that when I look around me, when I see people on television or writers of other books, I realize that there are so many more naturally gifted people than me in the world. So, it takes some degree of effort to just get up in the morning and stare at a blank page on my Mac and believe that I can write something that anyone would actually want to read.

But, I do, and it's because I enjoy doing it. The pleasure for me is the achievement and the pleasing of oneself, and if only one other person gets a kick out of what you've done, then the mountain climb has been worth it. And to be fair, when I look at the sales of my novels, there may only be one other person who likes what I write.

Chapter 11

"Would you like me to make coffee before you dismember me?" I asked, aware that although Rainee was still pissed at me, it was no longer at the murderous level when she'd first kicked open my door this morning.

"Sure, but I'm still fucking mad at you," she replied, now lying on her back on my cabin floor.

I pulled on my dressing gown, stepped around her outstretched body and made my way into the galley, quickly preparing a couple of cortados to take back to my cabin.

By this time, Rainee was sitting up on the floor, her back against my bed. I sat down beside her and offered her the small cup of nectar which she drank fervently, as I sipped gratefully on mine.

"So how much trouble am I in?" I asked.

"You're not in trouble, Coop, I'm just so fucking frustrated, is all," she replied, much more softly now, her anger now having passed like a fleeting tropical storm.

"Have I missed something? What's going on?" I asked.

"It's fucking Flick, I've been working for her," she replied, "I mean, I was, before you barged in."

"Whoa!" I exclaimed, "You're working for *her*?"

"Yeah yeah, I know she's persona non grata with you and Remy, but I saw a nice little side hustle because I knew she was good for the money. So blow me."

"No, no, that's fine, but why would she need you to help her, she's more dangerous than a cottonmouth snake," I said, still wondering what the hell was going on.

"She says that Joe is going to kill her and she wants protection," Rainee replied, "So I've been working around the clock just keeping an eye on her. But then I saw your car anchored outside her new boyfriend's place last night, and I guessed she'd traded me in for you. Are you telling me that's not true?"

My car is not something that blends easily into the background, so the Caddy probably wasn't the smartest thing to use whilst on a clandestine surveillance.

"It couldn't be further from the truth, Rainee, I'm working for Joe, not her."

"What the fuck?" she yelled, dropping her cup to the floor.

Fortunately, she'd finished glugging the cortado before dropping the vessel.

"Yeah, I have been for the best part of almost three weeks now. Joe knows she's fucking someone, just wants to nail her ass with some photo evidence before he files for divorce," I explained, "Although last night was another bust again. Anyway, how did I not see you if you saw me?"

"We both know I'm just better than you, dipshit, get over yourself," she said, now finally giggling at the dilemma.

"Yeah, I think you've mentioned that a couple of times," I said, laughing too at the ridiculous situation we'd found ourselves in.

"So, what do you want to do?" she asked.

"We could go get breakfast," I offered.

"That's the best idea you've had this morning."

"Good to know."

Chapter 12

With Rainee suitably fed, and now departed, I decided that sleep was no longer an option today, so after my morning ablutions I decided to have another cup of coffee on deck and see what chance I might have of glimpsing the previously mentioned art on the ridiculously large superyacht next door.

I wasn't to be disappointed, although this morning's thong was a new shade that I might describe as mango. Look, I know what you're thinking, and it's not true. This example of pure feminine art was maybe twenty, twenty-two tops, pretty much the same age as Molly, and that's not in my wheelhouse. But when pure loveliness is put on show for the entire world to see, who am I to not appreciate it?

But putting the aforementioned feminine beauty aside, and looking down at Diablo, who I'd just fed, I suddenly realized that whenever Rainee comes onboard in a huff, Diablo doesn't bat an eyelid. He's meant to be a guard dog, not just my companion. But to be fair to him, I can kind of understand with Rainee, he knows what she's like.

I didn't feed Kinky though. I'm not cruel, it's just that Kinky seems to eat elsewhere and only has bowel movements on my boat. Seems fair. Right now, he was doing that cat thing, where you think they love you because they're curled up on your lap, gently extending their claws into your thighs, but actually, it's just their way of finding a warm crotch to sleep on for the time being.

And then he was off of me in a split second as he spied Pip approaching, my lovely unpaid assistant ambling down the dock in a diaphanous summer dress, the very picture of innocence and youth. But this morning, I'd decided to be the man and make her presence relevant at Hemingway Investigations. We call the company HI for short, not sure if that works though, but it does mean that you can legitimately answer the phone with "Hi."

"Good morning, Pip, did you have a pleasant weekend?" I asked, certain that everything in Pip's life was bound to be wonderful, except for the five days a week when she comes to work for this middle-aged ingrate.

"It's Pippa, not Pip. You're up early, what's wrong?" she replied, ignoring my pleasantries.

"I wanted to be risen and shining by the time you came to work."

"Why? What's wrong?"

"Nothing's wrong, Pip, can't a man be caring about his staff?" I responded.

"Unpaid staff, you mean?"

"Exactly. That's what I want to talk about," I said.

"Unpaid staff?"

"I would like to make a change," I said.

"You're firing me?"

"On the contrary, Pippa, I want to make you underpaid staff instead of unpaid staff."

"Why?"

"Because, believe it or not, and I know I'm an ungrateful boss sometimes, but I do appreciate you and everything that you do for me," I replied.

"Boss? Since when?"

"I can't win, can I?" I said, feeling a little exasperated.

"The thing is, Coop, I know you don't make much, but coming here, sorting you out each day, is more for my benefit than yours," she laughed.

"Seriously?" I replied, not particularly expecting these words from her.

"My parents are wealthy, very wealthy in fact, and all they want is for me to get married off at one of the numerous, stupidly expensive and elaborate debutante balls they donate to, and I'm just not ready for that."

"I learn something new about you every day, I should definitely spend more time with my staff," I said.

She laughed at my humor this time, a rare and special thing.

"So," she continued, "I don't come here for the money, I like it here, I kinda like you too, and Diablo and Kinky of course. I have all the money I need, although it would be nice to be appreciated once in a blue moon, that's all."

"Okay then, that answers a lot of questions. However, I have your first pay packet right here," I said, handing her an envelope, "If we're working together, it can't only be me that benefits from paying clients."

Pip was astonished, and for the first time since I'd known her, she was lost for words. I think in the old days, the word *dumbfounded* might have been the appropriate adjective.

"This is a thousand dollars, Coop, you can't afford that!" she exclaimed, as she looked at the ten one-hundred-dollar bills inside, "Take it back, I don't need it."

I know I previously said I was going to give her five hundred bucks, but I suddenly realized that I was being an asshole, and not only did I like her being here, I needed her too. Even a thousand wasn't enough.

"Look, I've made a few grand watching Joe's missus playing her young fiddle, and you deserve it. It's not much, but if I can get more nice cash jobs like this, I intend to make staff payroll a regular thing," I explained, realizing now, that I clearly needed the thousand bucks more than she did.

"I never saw this coming, Coop, I've got to admit that today's the first time you've amazed me. So thank you, and I will gracefully and gratefully accept," she cooed, her smile the brightest I'd ever seen in the time she'd been working here.

I watched as she hopped onto the boat, happy with my minuscule effort at philanthropy for the week.

Chapter 13

Rainee and I had decided to pool resources in the Joe/Flick operation, which gave me some welcome breathing space before I changed shift with her at 4am. I was planning an excursion this evening at Nate's bar to have supper and a couple of drinks, before I grabbed some shuteye prior to my shift.

I was also secretly hoping that Layla would be working, maybe get to know her a little better, although in all honesty, I felt it unlikely, because I knew I was probably punching above my weight with her.

So, in the interim, while Pip did what she did, I nodded off. All of which was going rather well, until I realized that Remy had slumped down in the chair next to me.

"You still ass staring?" he asked in his deep baritone.

"Trying to sleep, actually," I replied, opening my tired eyes.

"You look whipped, man," he said, "Long night again?"

"Long night followed by an unscheduled angry visit from Rainee before sunup. You can probably imagine how that played out," I explained wearily.

"Yeah, that would scare the shit out of me too, good luck with that," he replied in agreement.

"It wasn't just working the graveyard shift and Rainee's early visit though, there was something going on over there," I said, casually nodding toward the neighboring superyacht.

"How do you mean?" Remy asked.

"It must have been around 5am, and I woke up because I heard voices next door, and when I looked out through the porthole, it was a bunch of guys unloading something off the boat. And the language from the voices sounded like it was maybe Russian, or Eastern Bloc anyway."

"They're a strange bunch," he replied, "I've had no actual interaction with the owners whatsoever, it's all done by email and bank transfers for the mooring rental, but to be honest, they always pay in advance and I've had absolutely no issues with them."

"Do you know anything about their business, what they're doing here anyway?" I asked.

"Like I say, they give me no problems, so I ask no questions. Anyway, what I skim off their account makes a decent contribution to your berth fee," he laughed.

When Remy erupts into laughter, it feels as if the earth itself quivers, such is the depth and resonance of his baritone. And of course, this particular burst of mirth was at my expense, so he was enjoying it.

"Okay, okay, you got your jab in, can we shift the conversation?" I asked.

"Sure," he said, still laughing, "How's your love life, brother?"

I responded with a hint of resignation, "Same old, same old, nothing much to report on that front."

But Layla had been on my mind recently, a fleeting intrigue I couldn't resist acknowledging and sharing.

"There is, however, a new girl working at Nate's," I ventured with a hint of excitement lacing my words, "But she's gotta be at least a decade younger than me and probably out of my league."

I could see immediately what was going through Remy's mind, given the amused smirk that graced his countenance.

"So, does this girl have a name?"

"Yeah, it's Layla. And I know what you're thinking Remy, but the truth is that she fascinates me on a different level than just the potential opportunity of a quick fling. And I think I'm over one-night-stands."

"Maybe your approach to dating has been all wrong in the past?"

"You're probably right," I agreed, "But in my rather unremarkable existence on this planet, this is what I've deduced. Women claim to want a 'good guy', but when they find one, they tend to walk all over them and then make a quick exit, stage right."

"Can't disagree with you on that one, brother," replied Remy, "Women are a strange and perplexing breed."

"They certainly are."

"So?"

"So what?"

"Layla, you dumbass."

"Remy, do you mind if we change the subject again? So far, I know nothing about her and I get the feeling that she's not interested in me anyway."

"How's the current novel going?" Remy asked.

"Let me tell you," I explained, "Trying to write the last twenty thousand words of a novel, is like wrestling in Jell-O with a slippery mistress, it ain't easy."

"So, you're not currently writing then, correct?" asked Remy, knowing that I needed a kick up the ass occasionally.

"A little bit of writer's block right now, can't figure things out," I said, fully aware that I hadn't been giving my other profession much time recently, "But it'll come, it always does."

"There's no such thing as writer's block," he replied, "As long as your fingers move over the keyboard, eventually it'll segue into something."

"Where did that come from?" I asked.

"Something Mary Kay Andrews once said," he replied, nonchalantly.

"I didn't know you were a fan of hers."

"I've read everything she's written, she's badass," he said, "I read a lot more than you do, Coop, maybe you should try it someday?"

And there it was again, the deep baritone laugh kicking in, once again at my expense.

But to be truthful, he had a point. Maybe I did need to get some reading in with some authors I'd not yet tried, it actually might even kickstart my own writing again. Although that wasn't going to begin tonight, as I had other plans.

Chapter 14

Greta Randolph loved her life. Ever since she had stumbled onto her husband's forecourt almost twenty years ago, she had fallen in love and remained, totally besotted with Wayne.

They had wanted to start a family, have a couple of kids, but sadly, life dictated that this couple would never produce children. It didn't change anything in their love for one another though, and they were blessed to have nephews and nieces to spoil. They had a good life, a nice home in the quiet and peaceful neighborhood of Coral Gables, no money problems, and they were grateful.

She'd been to Publix that morning to get groceries, now eager to get the frozen items, including Wayne's *Gelato Fiasco Sunken Treasure* ice-cream, tucked away into the freezer before they melted from the car's searing heat.

After putting all of the groceries away, she realized in her rush to get the frozen items stowed in the kitchen's freezer, she'd forgotten to close the garage door. The last thing she wanted was a raccoon getting inside and tearing up everything in there. Much as she adored the creatures, she knew from experience that they could cause mayhem in just a few short minutes.

She hurried back to the garage, passing through the property's internal door to gain access, and pressed the garage remote button on the wall by the door. She heard the immediate and reassuring noise of the electric motor sliding the door back to the closed position.

Raccoon-proofed…

She was still lightly sweating from what was an unusually hot and humid day for the time of year. And although her body had acclimatized over the twenty plus years of living in Miami, and had gotten used to the crazy summer and fall humidity in Florida, she still tried to avoid being too far from air-conditioning at these times. She needed an iced tea, soon as.

Opening the internal door to go back to the kitchen, she felt the relief of the 68-degree air-conditioning suddenly rush over her. And that was the last thing she remembered.

~ ~ ~

"Jeez," Wayne muttered to himself, "It's almost winter, and it feels like friggin' summer."

He too was grateful for the small refrigeration unit that kept his forecourt office cool at times like this. And unlike the sales guys on the vast new-car dealerships that surrounded him, desperate to make last-minute sales at the end of the month to boost their figures, he had no desire to be standing on a hot and sticky car lot today.

It had always surprised him that not only was he able to stay in business, nestled amongst the mega dealerships of Ford, Toyota, Chrysler, Cadillac and Chevrolet, he actually found his sales improving each year. He put it down to the fact that although he sold used vehicles, he was always responsive to customer issues after a sale. He was a skilled mechanic in his own right, so customers respected him more for that than as a salesman.

Today wasn't going to be much of a selling day, so Wayne had decided to concentrate on the clerical side of the business, although sitting in front of a computer screen wasn't his idea of heaven. And as he stared at the Excel document in front of him, he was surprised to see a vehicle drive onto the forecourt as it passed his office window.

They could just be drive-thru lookie-loos, he thought, as he continued to enter numbers on the spreadsheet, certain that if they had spotted something they liked, they'd make their way over to the office.

After another ten minutes, he got up from his padded, leather swivel chair, stretched, and traveled the much-used path to the coffee station. Refilling his mug from the glass container of four-hour-old coffee, he still savored that caffeine aroma, although he had to admit, it was probably due for a fresh brew.

As he turned to go back to his chair to continue the ennui of his task today, he was startled at the door opening, three men immediately appearing inside his office.

A shiver went down his spine when he recognized the deeply tanned face of the man in the center of the group. Carlo Galotti.

"Gentlemen, how may I be of assistance?" he asked.

"Just browsing," replied Galotti, "Anything interesting in stock?"

"Sure, let's take a look outside and I'll show you the new stuff I have," said Wayne, not knowing if this was a genuine visit in search of a rare vehicle, or if it had something to do with Cassidy's recent disappearance.

"Please," replied Galotti, smiling and gesturing politely toward the door, "Lead the way."

The four men, led by Wayne, slowly toured the lot, Wayne pointing out particular vehicles that he thought may have been of interest.

"We had a brief look at the vehicles on your forecourt when we arrived," said Galotti, "Are you sure you don't have anything that has arrived more recently that you think might pique my interest?"

There was something disturbingly chilling about the man, thought Wayne. Sure, he was charming enough, immaculately dressed in what looked like a hand-made Italian suit and black leather Prada loafers, but a wolf always finds it hard to hide the menace within.

"Yeah, sure, maybe I can show you something that just came in," said Wayne, pointing at a small barn at the back of the lot, "It's in the detailing building just over there."

"Please," said Galotti, again smiling with those immaculate and unfeasibly white teeth, "Show me, I'm very interested to see what you have in there."

Once again, the group, led by Wayne, walked to the rear of the lot, and on arrival at the building, he pulled open the giant doors to reveal what was inside.

"Ahh," said Galotti, now smiling, "You have your crown jewel hidden from view, my friend."

"It's not, as I am sure you can understand, the type of vehicle I want to have out on the lot overnight," Wayne replied, "You don't come across many Mil-Spec H1 Hummers, this is one of only twelve made in the world."

"She's a beauty, Mr. Randolph, said Galotti, "And I would think rather expensive too, no?"

"Well, this ain't no ordinary Humvee," said Wayne, aware that the two men accompanying Galotti, hadn't spoken a single word throughout the visit, "It has a 500hp turbo-diesel motor, Kevlar-infused body panels, military axles, carbon brakes and an interior that would satisfy a Rolls-Royce buyer."

"I like it, Mr. Randolph, I like it very much in fact," said Galotti, genuinely impressed by the enormous vehicle, "But you didn't say what the price is?"

"Sure, well as you might know, it was built in 2020, although originally a 2009 model, only has 1,500 miles on the odometer, and the price when rebuilt as a Mil-Spec H1 was just short of $230,000. But again, as I'm sure you're aware, all Hummers have become appreciating investments since production ended in 2010."

"I am fully aware, although the electric version is currently in production, Mr. Randolph, as I'm sure you already know?"

"Yes, of course, but that will not affect the appreciation of the last of the original H1 models, even they fetch more than the original sticker price," Wayne replied, "You would also know that as well as I do."

"So, again we return to the price of this particular beast," said Galotti, "What do you have in mind?"

"Mr. Galotti, I don't look to make huge returns on my stock, I prefer to have frequent turnover, rather than to have vehicles sit on my lot," said Wayne, "And when I acquired this vehicle, I was fortunate to buy it from a man who had severe liquidity issues, and who needed quick cash."

"I understand," said Galotti, his accomplices still mute, "But I am sure we can come to an agreement, no?"

Wayne had paid just $100,000 in cash for the Hummer, and he knew he had 'stolen' it from the guy, but the seller needed cash quickly. Get-outa-town cash, Wayne had thought at the time, because the guy was more than desperate. Pretty common in Miami.

"The price is $150,000, sir, and I'd buy it back for the same price in six months' time if you find you don't fall in love with her."

"Then I believe we have a deal," replied Galotti, "May I hear the engine run?"

"Sure," said Wayne, "Let me find the keys."

Wayne went to a bench at the side of the building and pulled a set of keys from the hook-bar above it. Climbing up into the brutish vehicle, he inserted and turned the key and the engine boomed into life, its noise reverberating throughout the small building.

Galotti, after only twenty seconds or so, put up a hand, indicating to Wayne that he'd heard enough, and Wayne shut the engine down and climbed back down from the vehicle.

"I'm very impressed, Mr. Randolph, how would you like payment? Bank transfer, perhaps?"

"That would be perfect, sir, let's head back to the office and do the paperwork," Wayne replied, amazed that he was about to sell the prized vehicle to Galotti, "But I'd like to have it fully detailed for you before you take it away. How about Saturday for collection?"

"Of course, I'm in no hurry," said Galotti as the four men strode back to Wayne's office.

Once inside, Wayne sat down at his desk and began the process of printing the copious plethora of sale documents, as Galotti and the two other men stood and looked on.

"Tell me," asked Galotti, "Have you had any other high-end vehicles cross your path in recent weeks?"

"One or two in the past couple of months," Wayne replied, "Was there something in particular you wanted?"

"I'm always in the market for rare Range Rovers," said Galotti, "Have you come across anything recently?"

Wayne visibly gulped, but maintained a stoic appearance.

"No, not recently, I don't get too many of those here. Mostly, Range Rovers get traded over at the Jaguar/Land Rover dealership down the street. I've got a contact number for a guy who works there, I can call him if you like, but no, I haven't had a Rover in here for maybe a year or so."

"Are you sure?" asked Galotti, the smile returning.

"Yes, I really don't remember a Range Rover in here for maybe a couple of years when I stop to think about it," said Wayne, fully aware of the stealth black Range Rover he'd hustled out of the country for Cassidy.

"Perhaps I can jolt your memory," said Galotti, turning to one of his men, who pulled an iPhone from his jacket.

The man put the phone upright against Wayne's computer monitor, a video image immediately appearing on the screen.

Wayne gasped. Fear immediately coursed through his veins when he saw the live video feed in front of him. Greta was standing on a chair in their house, a rope taut around her neck.

"Wh… wha… what do you want, Galotti, cut her down, my wife has nothing to do with anything!"

"Of course, Mr. Randolph, and I mean to cause you no concern, but let's look at Mrs. Randolph as, how shall we put it, a bargaining chip?"

"Please Mr. Galotti, please leave her out of it, I'll tell you anything you want to know," said Wayne, breathing hard and quickly, now petrified for his wife.

"Please do not concern yourself, Mr. Randolph, you have nothing to fear," Galotti replied, "Now, the Range Rover if you would be so kind?"

"Cassidy came in a few weeks ago, scared, said she wanted to escape," said Wayne, still wanting to protect both Cassidy and his wife, and deciding on a small lie, "I traded the Range Rover for a Ford Explorer."

"Did you now, and where was she headed, Mr. Randolph? Galotti asked, still completely unreadable.

"I don't know, but I think she was headed west, no idea where though."

"In a Ford Explorer, you say?" smiled Galotti, "Do you recall the color and license plate, perhaps?"

"It was dark blue, but she drove it away unlicensed. I gave her the Title and told her she could register it when she found a destination."

"Very naughty, Mr. Randolph, but thank you for the information, it's most welcome."

"Are we good?" asked Wayne, perspiration now streaming down his face despite the chill of the air-conditioning, "Can you cut my wife down, please, Mr. Galotti."

"Yes, I think so," replied Galotti, "And I think we'll take the Humvee now, rather than wait until Saturday."

Wayne couldn't afford to lose his investment on the Humvee, but right now he was grateful for all of their lives.

"Just one more thing," said Galotti turning to leave, "I can't allow our visit here today to be known by anyone else, do you understand?"

"I won't say a word, Mr. Galotti," said Wayne, still glued to his chair, "You can trust me on that."

Galotti turned back and slowly walked toward Wayne's desk.

"I would love to believe you, Mr. Randolph, but you see, I have such a terribly untrusting mind."

"Please, you have to believe me, your secret is safe with me!"

"I think it's a little late for that," said Galotti, as he removed a SIG-Sauer P320 pistol from his jacket, shooting Wayne twice, once in the center of his forehead, the other in his heart. The age-old professional double-tap. The shots were almost silent, due to the suppressor mounted on the gun's barrel.

Wayne knew little about what had just happened, death arriving almost instantly, his body barely moving from his sitting position. The first shot to Wayne's forehead had been a through & through, only stopping in the chairback, once it had exited Wayne's head.

The fact that Galotti had used hollow-points, a type of bullet that expands on impact, meant that the bullet literally tore Wayne's brain to pieces on its vicious journey. The same had happened with his heart, once the hollow-point had completely shattered it, physically, rather than emotionally.

His wide-open eyes simply stared lifelessly at Galotti, as the man walked forward to see the carnage he'd inflicted on Wayne.

"Tsk tsk, so messy, Mr. Randolph. If only you had kept your nose out of my business."

He walked around the desk to peer at the cell phone still standing upright.

He looked at the video image of Greta Randolph, still standing on the dining chair, the rope taut around her neck. Randolph was right, Mrs. Randolph had done nothing wrong. She was completely innocent of everything.

"Boss?" said the voice of a man who suddenly appeared on the screen, behind where Greta was standing.

"Do it," Galotti commanded. The chair was kicked from beneath Greta almost as soon as he had uttered the words.

Galotti stared at the video image of Greta, as she flailed wildly and helplessly, hanging from the rope, slowly losing life without the knowledge of why her nightmare was happening.

Galotti continued staring for a full minute, until finally, the woman's body stopped moving, hanging lifelessly in the air.

"The clock is now ticking, Cassidy, tick tock," Galotti whispered, as he turned toward the open door.

Chapter 15

Driving my old Caddy this evening, was one of my great life pleasures, its 6.4-liter V8 just idling as I navigated out of the marina onto Flagler Drive, headed west toward Okeeheelee. My car is in mint condition. I take more care of her than I do myself. I spare no cost in keeping her as pristine as she was on the day she left the showroom in 1962.

She's finished in what I believe to be the ultimate color combination, Newport Blue exterior with a white roof, and the interior features a fabric that Cadillac judged to be 'Chelsea Cloth'. And although I've had her reupholstered over the years, adhering strictly to the original pattern, my car has only covered a mere 63,000 miles since the day she was built.

I always have that wonderful feeling when I'm driving, that I'm actually the first owner, taking her on her first outing. I feel utterly privileged to own this vehicle from another era, often wanting to wear a suit and a hat that bears homage to a time when people were properly attired. It's the same with air travel now, no one sees it as special. Salad days, as Shakespeare once said.

But tonight, was another beautiful fall evening, the daytime glare of the Florida sun now faded to a golden glow to the west. Simple pleasures, picturesque moments, as the Caddy burbled along. Even the glitzy brashness of West Palm Beach town seemed more laconic as evening set in, the throng of tourists and daytime workers now reduced to a trickle, as the former found solace and comfort for cocktails and dinner, and the latter scurried home to relax in their own sanctuaries.

And right at this moment, Layla had tiptoed once again into my thoughts. I don't know what it was about her from our first brief meeting, but I wasn't thinking about her in the way I might do in my normal pursuit of joy. Layla was something very special.

Chapter 16

I was grateful that Pip had allowed me to catch up on some sleep in the afternoon, unusual really, but maybe now that she was a paid staff member, she was affording me a new level of respect as her boss. Probably not, though.

But I did need the sleep, and as I inched my way into a parking spot at Nate's, I felt nicely rested, knowing that I would be ready for a shift change with Rainee after my evening here.

Closing the Caddy's door, the heavy reassuring thunk as it found its resting place, never failing to make me smile, I walked across the parking lot toward the Grille, noting a British Racing Green Mini Cooper nestled in the corner by the steps that led up to the studio apartment above the main building.

The bar was buzzing nicely tonight, the muted but soulfully blissful lighting hovering all around the lounge and bar, with many of the regulars already halfway through their suppers. Nate had impeccable taste in décor and lighting, as well as in music.

His bar was not something you'd expect in this particular area, one might imagine more of a Jock-style sports bar with loud music and huge TV screens on the wall. But that wasn't Nate's style, and that's why these people, including myself, chose to come here, and often from some distance away. They even loved the jazz that Nate selected, the music always playing at a level where the clientele could still have a good conversation. And the food, well the food was always excellent.

And there she was. The mysterious Layla. She made ripped jeans and a plain white t-shirt look insanely fabulous.

I found my usual barstool unoccupied, and as I sat down, I could see her finish up serving a customer at the end of the bar, and now moving hypnotically toward me. I say hypnotically because I was hypnotized by the elegance in which she traveled.

"What can I get you," she asked, "You were here the other day, weren't you?"

"I was indeed," I replied, "But I think you had your hands full, being new here and everything. But it's a pleasure to see you again, Layla."

"Likewise," she said, "Sorry if I was a bit off, but I had a lot of things going on that day. It's Michelob, if I remember correctly?"

"No, it's Coop," I said, laughing at my own cringeworthy humor.

"Now I remember, you're the funny man," she said, grinning this time, "Michelob coming right up."

Her smile was sensational, it literally lit up the room. She was even more gorgeous than when she'd verbally put me down the first time. And after she had delivered my beer, and I'd ordered steak and ale pie with mashed potatoes, I decided to once again retreat to the rear of the bar's lounge for the moment, just so I could take her in from a respectful distance.

Chapter 17

Rainee Showers was bored. Sure, she could use the money, but she was the type of individual who needed a little more stimulation than to be camped outside a love nest waiting on something to go down.

She had felt bad about ripping Coop a new one the previous morning. Damn it, the guy needed the bucks more than she did. She knew she could fly off the handle easily, at the drop of a hat if she was honest with herself, but it pained her that she chose Coop as her whipping boy sometimes.

It wasn't fair because he never got pissed at her, and he was just about the best friend she could have, that anyone could have. He just soaked it up, never got angry.

As she sat slumped in her shit-box surveillance car, a 1998 Chevy Impala, and sucking on another quart of Diet Coke, she thought back to the time when she and Coop had first met.

~ ~ ~

They were young, she a lot younger in fact, just eighteen years old, and Coop was maybe twenty-seven. It was in Los Angeles, at a strip club where she was working to make some quick cash after she'd split from the commune where she'd been raised by her mother. Cooper had reluctantly come down from San Francisco for a bachelor party that was being held for a good friend of his, who was tying the knot two days later.

At around midnight, she was on the pole, once again doing her schtick to the Def Leppard song, *Pour Some Sugar on Me*, already stripped down to her G-string, when a drunk had clambered up onto the stage and begun manhandling her. She struggled against the big man as he grabbed at her breasts and tried to put his hand between her legs while most of the patrons looked on and made no attempt to come to her aid.

Coop, although not watching the show, immediately saw what was going down in his peripheral vision, and leapt up onto the podium and ripped the guy away from her, landing a punch on him, resulting in the man hitting the viewing floor incapacitated, and most definitely unconscious. Coop just nodded to her and climbed down as though nothing had happened, and rejoined his friends at the bar.

Later that evening, after she'd finished her shift, she got dressed back into her civvies, and made her way over to where Coop and his buddies were still drinking at the bar.

"Thank you for what you did earlier," she said, squeezing his arm, "I really appreciate it."

He turned to her, realizing it was the same girl he'd previously rescued, and just said, "Well, if my daughter ever found herself working in a dive like this, I would hope that someone would do the same thing for her."

"Wow, you must be one of the last gentlemen left on this planet," she replied, "But I'd still like to thank you properly. Can I buy you a drink?"

"I'm a cop, and if I'm correct in my thinking, I'm not sure you're even legal to buy a drink, but sure, let me get you a Shirley Temple, and I'll join you for one, I'm the designated driver tonight," he laughed, pulling his wallet from his coat pocket.

"Then you're even more of a gentleman than I thought," she said, "I'm Rainee, by the way."

"I'm Coop," he replied, "It's a pleasure to meet you, miss."

They sat down at a small table once the drinks had arrived, and he asked her what she was doing working there. She'd explained that she'd come to Los Angeles with a small suitcase and not much cash, and had been taken on as a stripper at the club, three nights a week.

"But you're what, eighteen, nineteen years old?" he asked, "Surely there are better ways to earn a living than in a shithole like this?"

"Probably," she replied, "But growing up on a commune meant that I never had a formal education, so who would employ someone like me? And the tips are pretty good."

"You grew up on a commune?" he asked.

"It's a long story, Coop, but yeah, it was pretty cultish and I guess, pretty controlling. It wasn't quite like the Charles Manson stuff of the 60s, but as I matured on the commune, I realized it wasn't the life I wanted to lead, so I left."

"You left? Sounds more like you escaped."

"That's actually a more accurate way of saying it," she said, "But I'm glad I'm out of it."

"You seem like a nice kid, Rainee, and it's just a shame that you're having to work here, that's all."

What amazed Rainee about the man was that he wasn't even hitting on her. Just about every man she'd ever encountered in her still young life, had just wanted to get inside her pants.

"You're a cop, you said?"

"Yeah, but not here in LA, I'm up in San Francisco," he replied, "It's a lot nicer up there."

"You said you have a daughter?" she asked.

"I do, her name is Molly and she's just had her first birthday," he beamed, pride written large across his face.

"Proud daddy," she replied.

"Indeed I am," he said, smiling.

"Is your wife taking care of Molly while you're here?"

"Sadly, no. But I have a very reliable sitter who looks after her while I'm away at times like this. I'm very fortunate, although I hate being away from my daughter, especially when I'm forced to be on a stag weekend like this. It's something I could do without."

Rainee decided not to ask about his wife as she thought it was too personal, and there seemed to be an issue there. So, they chatted for another half an hour or so, before his buddies decided it was time to move on to another bar, and he stood up to say goodbye to her.

"If you're ever up in San Francisco, look me up and I'll find you work that pays a decent wage, without sexual assault," he said.

"You're serious?' she asked.

"Very much so," he replied, handing her his SFPD business card, "Just be super careful if you decide to stay in Los Angeles, it's not one of the safest cities to live in at your age, especially on your own."

A week later, Rainee boarded a Greyhound bus and headed north to San Francisco. When Coop had met her off the bus, a friendship began that would never be broken. He had a two-bed apartment in the city, put her up for as long as she needed and found her a job working for a PI friend of his, to begin learning about private investigation.

And an excellent PI she became. Rainee was a born athlete, and Coop had suggested she train herself in Martial arts, knowing that the PI business wasn't always the cakewalk people assumed it to be. So, she spent four nights a week at a dojo in the city, the same one where Coop also trained.

And in all the time she had stayed at his apartment, he'd never once asked her for rent, just told her to save a deposit for a place of her own. Over time, Coop had pretty much become the father-figure she'd never had. She trusted him, and he made her feel safe and relevant.

Chapter 18

It was ten-thirty now, and many of the customers had begun to leave. Seeing that the bar was no longer busy, I idled up to it and sat down on a bar stool. Layla was drying beer glasses, but when she noticed that I was back at the bar again, she discarded her towel and wandered up to where I was sitting.

"I think Nate chose well, business seems to have been booming since you arrived," I remarked.

"Such a flatterer, is that one of your chat-up lines?" she replied, but smiling as she said it.

"No, not at all, but I think the patrons here like you."

"That's sweet of you, so I'll take it as a compliment. Where are you from, anyway?"

"That's a long story, but I grew up in London, and went on a gap year trip to San Francisco when I was eighteen and never left," I replied, "But I never began my degree anyway, so I took more than a gap year, more of a gap life."

"So, you're British?" she asked.

"Yes, but I'm actually English," I replied, laughing.

"Is there a difference?" she asked, confused.

"Yeah, a pretty big one, in fact. Don't ask a Scotsman if he's English," I said, laughing again, "It's kinda like assuming that

Americans and Canadians are the same nationality, and in fact, Great Britain is made up of three very different countries, England, Scotland and Wales."

"Gotcha. Well, that's my geography lesson done for the day. So, do you live here now or are you over on a visit from San Francisco?" she asked.

"No, not visiting, I've lived in Florida for the past ten years or so, I like it here. And my daughter lives here too, so this is home now."

"Oh… you're married then?"

"No, I lost my wife soon after my daughter was born," I replied.

"Oh God, that's terrible, Coop, I'm so sorry."

"No, no, it's really okay. When I say lost, I mean I literally lost her. I couldn't find her anywhere," I replied.

"You are so bad, Coop, is this an example of your regular daily humor?" she asked, slightly grinning now.

"Not really, but it's actually true. When my daughter, Molly, was around three months old, my wife literally just disappeared," I explained, "I think she suffered pretty badly from postpartum depression, and decided that motherhood wasn't for her. Or marriage, for that matter."

"Oh Lord, I'm really sorry, Coop. So, you raised your daughter on your own, or did you remarry?" she asked.

"Never remarried, had some relationships, but honestly, most girls I met, really didn't like the idea of helping raise someone else's child. And I get it, a stepparent will never be seen as a mom or dad, no matter how good or how bad a job they do."

"So, it's always been just you and Molly then?" she asked.

"Absolutely, although she doesn't live with me now. She's twenty-one and lives with her boyfriend, not too far from where I am."

"And where is that?" she asked.

Layla seemed to be a changed woman from our first meeting, almost as if she had found a place where she could be far more relaxed.

"I live on my little boat in Riviera Yacht Club," I replied.

"Where's that?" She asked.

"It's the expensive part of Palm Beach," I said.

"Is it swanky? If it's the expensive part, I'm pretty sure they don't have little boats."

"Trust me, my boat is small, I'm just very lucky to be moored there, and no, I definitely couldn't afford the rent if I had to pay," I replied, laughing at my own good fortune, courtesy of one Remy Washington.

"Okaaay…" she said, a little confused, "Maybe you can explain that to me when I next see you."

"Oh, you mean we're going on a date?" I asked, impishly, "Shouldn't I find out a little more about you before we commit to each other?"

"You crack me up, Coop, who said anything about a date?"

"A man can but try," I said, "But, in all seriousness, it would be my honor to take you out sometime, maybe show you around a little as you're new to these parts. We wouldn't even need to call it a date."

"We'll see, but I've already wasted enough time with you tonight, and I need to think about closing up for the night," she replied.

Wasted?

"I'll take that as a mild possibility then, but in the meantime, I'll look forward to making your acquaintance again," I replied, reaching for my jacket, "Soon, I hope."

"Maybe," she said, turning to walk back to the end of the bar to close out the till for the night, "Who knows, you might just be one of the normal ones."

Normal?

I walked to the end of the bar, placing my business card down onto its surface.

"Call me," I said, "If you ever want to take me up on the offer."

"Thanks, Coop, I might just do that."

As I put my jacket on, I knew there was a lot more to discover about Layla, that is, if I ever got the chance to find out. And right at this moment, I realized that she knew quite a lot about me now, but she had been very astute in revealing absolutely nothing about herself.

But exiting the bar, I felt something I hadn't felt in a very long time, a feeling of lightheaded giddiness, that actually, I really missed.

Chapter 19

Something sharp plunged into the back of my neck. I watched as the ground closed in on my face and winced as my head hit the ground.

An hour earlier, at just after midnight that evening, I'd decided to make some herbal 'sleepy tea', as I knew I had a shift change at 4am with Rainee. It wasn't very long after I'd got into bed, sipping my hot brew, that I'd heard noises from the slip next door, where the megayacht was moored.

Diablo hadn't barked, so I had thought that maybe I'd just been imagining things. But I decided to get back up out of bed and take a look, just in case it was some kids looking to pilfer something off my deck.

Initially, everything seemed quiet. It was a beautiful warm night, practically silent outside, save for the gentle lapping of the water on the boat hulls, and one or two dolphins making brief and almost silent appearances above the water in this area of the marina.

But just when I was about to head back to bed to catch three hours or so of much needed sleep, I once again, exactly as I had seen the previous early morning, noticed some shadows moving toward the bow of the huge yacht.

I quietly stepped off my boat onto the dock, and I walked slowly toward them, cautious that there might be a robbery going on, and equally conscious that I was unarmed. But as I approached the shadows, which now seemed to be more erratic and hurried, I could also make out hushed voices in a language that definitely wasn't English.

With the knowledge that my neighbors weren't American, I made the assumption that it probably wasn't a burglary unfolding, and that these neighbors were just a little nocturnal in their activities.

But I found myself unable to turn away, such is my annoyingly, inquisitive nature. And what I saw was a group of men, still unrecognizable due to the blackness of night, shifting what appeared to be large metal boxes into the hold of the ship.

Interesting…

And it was at that precise moment that my world came crashing down, quite literally in fact, as I felt a sharp pain in the back of my neck. The last thing I remembered were just a few strange words, maybe Eastern European, before I blacked out completely.

It must have been around an hour later that I began to emerge from my reverie, because as I pulled myself up to a sitting position on the dock, I looked down at my watch and it told me it was just after one o'clock in the morning. I looked up into Diablo's eyes and saw the concern in them. I felt my face and realized that he must have been licking me to wake me up, because it was still damp.

My head hurt like hell and my vision wasn't exactly double, but I felt as though I was in a drunken stupor. I reached out to Diablo's giant frame and pulled him close to me, to which his reaction was to lick me even more.

"Thank you, buddy, what the hell happened out here tonight?"

As I held on to him, nuzzling deep into his fur, a vague memory of the previous events began to slip back into my mind. And just as those memories returned, I looked behind me at where the yacht had been moored, and realized that under the cover of night, it had disappeared.

~ ~ ~

Rainee did enjoy the quiet of the night when she was doing observation, it gave her time to think about things that weren't connected with what she did for a living. She also allowed her mind to open up to the fact that she didn't have much of a social life, let alone a significant other. She countered that by convincing herself that she hadn't yet met a man who would put up with how her life and schedule seemed to be orchestrated solely around work.

Coop was much the same, apart from his role as a father, his work was a priority with him too. Even his writing took a back seat most of the time. Although she had noted that he'd taken a couple more trips out to Nate's in the last few days, so maybe he was trying to get a life too. But then again, Nate did do pretty damned good food, and Coop had never been one to cook too often.

The Diet Coke was becoming heavy on Rainee's bladder now, and during the last six hours, she'd probably downed four pints of it. So, she quietly got out of the Impala, made her way toward the undergrowth fifty yards away, pulled down her pants and peed, relief finally flooding through her.

As she hoisted her pants back up, it was closing in on 4am, and just then, she spotted Coop's Cadillac slowly cruising up the street and parking behind her battered Impala.

"My savior, right on time as usual."

Chapter 20

Layla hadn't missed sex. She'd missed making love, but with Carlo, it had been more like rape when he decided he wanted her for sex. And she definitely didn't miss Carlo. In fact, she didn't miss anything about her former life, except for Wayne and Greta. She had even begun to be accustomed to her new name, Cassidy seemingly long forgotten now, after only a few months or so.

She'd taken a Cobb salad from the kitchen up to her room, hungrily feasting on it, as she pondered how the rest of her life might pan out. She figured she was safe for the moment, that even Carlo wouldn't be able to locate her in Okeeheelee, and maybe he would just give up trying.

At the moment, as long as she was reasonably economical, she was okay for money. The bag she'd hidden in the garage before she'd fled Miami, was stuffed with just over twenty thousand dollars, and she was also getting paid by Nate now, as well as earning some pretty healthy tips too.

She wondered how her parents would have viewed how her life had turned out, had they still been alive. Would she have disappointed them, getting hitched with a lothario who turned out not only to be a gangster, but a murderer too? Yeah, she was pretty sure they would be turning in their graves right now.

She never really understood why she had chosen to head to Miami after leaving Wisconsin. Maybe because it was the polar opposite of her life on a farm that had made her want to taste the bright lights of a crazy city. And Miami didn't get much crazier.

But being an only child, and having lost her parents just four months previously, there seemed to be nothing left to stay for in Wisconsin. Most of her relatives were up in Minnesota and her home town, population 927, wasn't exactly the place where she would find that perfect husband to start a new life with. She'd never even left the state, except for a couple of rodeos in Texas and a trip to Disney in Florida when she was thirteen, so she figured it was time. Time to explore what the world had to offer.

So, after she had sold up in Wisconsin, and the farm's debts had been repaid, she loaded up her Jeep and headed south-east toward Florida's party capital. She had some money from the remainder of the farm sale proceeds, so now it was just her, the Jeep and a couple of suitcases. In hindsight, she probably should've headed west to Los Angeles.

She had arrived in Miami in late November, 2010, booked a room at the Cardozo on South Beach, and decided to make this her vacation spot for a couple of weeks or so. After that, who knew where her life would take her?

She was barely twenty-four years old, and quickly became intoxicated by the color, ebullience, and vivacity of the place, pretty much as soon as she had crossed into the city limits. But after only a couple of days, she had heard about an annual event due to take place at the end of her first week there. It was called The White Party.

The White Party was a winter event that had been staged annually since the mid-1980s, essentially launched as a fundraiser for the gay community when AIDS and HIV had infiltrated their world. In the ensuing years, the party, where guests only wore white, had raised millions of dollars toward research for what was being dubbed 'the gay plague', a death knell for so many in that era.

She had decided to go to the event, along with a young group of similarly aged boys and girls she had met at the Cardoza. And this was probably the biggest mistake she had ever made in her still-young life.

She had never seen anything like this before, a week-long event of parties at sublime venues, and feasts and festivities on South Beach, Miami Beach and Nikki Beach. Music, color, dancing, fire eaters, artists, trapezes and bands, as well as every party fantasy one could ever imagine. She was amazed by the throngs of people, extraordinary costumes, and the sexy bodies of the 'beautiful people' abounding everywhere.

She'd never danced on the sand before, but it was as though she had done it for her entire life, as the partying continued on into the night in the discotheques and gay clubs that surrounded the epicenter of the event; the staggeringly beautiful and magnificent estate known as the Vizcaya Museum and Gardens.

The Vizcaya estate was built almost a century ago by one James Deering, a member of one of America's wealthiest families. Deering, a lifelong bachelor and publicly-unconfirmed gay man, chose Biscayne Bay in Miami as the location to build what would be his dream home, not just for the area's natural beauty, but also as a warm climate in which to live, to help with Deering's pernicious anemia.

Deering also had a fascination with landscaping and vegetation, the original 180 acres thus easily able to allot ten acres of formal gardens for the house. Vizcaya was built as a thirty-four-room, Italian Renaissance-style villa, where during the construction, it is said that more than ten percent of Miami's total population was employed to complete the project, the main house being completed in just two years by 1916.

And that was exactly where this farm girl from Wisconsin found herself on this glorious and balmy Saturday evening.

Carlo Galotti was an attractive man, golden Mediterranean skin, punctuated by the most perfect and whitest of teeth. Other guests rushed to greet him, and his smile and double-cheek pecks charmed all of them, particularly the female admirers. And as with all of the party guests at Vizcaya, he was dressed completely in white.

Her makeup was simple, her dark blonde hair hanging to a level just below her shoulder blades. She wore a simple white toga-style dress, paired with gold sandals, and the simplest of jewelry, a thin gold necklace and diamante earrings, that her mother had given to her when she graduated college.

He had spotted her from far across the room, and his eyes had immediately found hers. But at that exact moment, her group of friends had suggested they tour the Renaissance gardens for which Vizcaya was famed, and the small group left the main reception of the building to go and explore.

Galotti had disappeared from her vision now, as her group marveled at the breathtaking scenes in each of the gardens, followed by tastings from some of the best Miami restaurants, whose sample tables surrounded the interior and exterior of the opulent building.

The event was chic, exciting, fashionable, and sophisticated, apparently with every beautiful person on the planet attending. And although she knew there were probably tens of thousands of visitors in Miami for the week, she also appreciated that she was lucky to have a ticket for this particular venue, with its strict limit of 1,600 attendees.

It was only because her newly-found friends had a spare ticket available for a friend who was unable to attend, that she was able to be there at all. And although it had cost her $150, it was money very well spent, because it also happened to be Thanksgiving during the event week, and she was relieved she wasn't alone and miserable, living back home on the farm in Wisconsin.

After watching a performance by Cirque Dreams, the group then ventured into the Viva Las Divas Casino Lounge for cocktails. She had no interest in gambling but still sat awestruck at the enormous sums of money being circulated on the various gaming tables in the casino, obviously pocket change to those who were placing bets.

So she found herself sitting alone at the bar, and very much out of her comfort zone; her friends having decided to try the idea of making a big win with their limited wallets.

"Is this seat taken?" a voice asked.

She whirled around to see who was asking the question, and she came face to face with those same eyes she'd seen a couple of hours earlier.

"No, no, pl… pl… please help yourself," she stuttered, suddenly off guard at the man sitting so close to her.

"Your glass is almost empty… may I get you another?" he asked.

The man was even more dazzling close up, a truly handsome guy with a sexy Italian accent to match. And she was kind of shocked that he'd offered to buy her a drink. This wasn't something she had ever been accustomed to when dating back in Wisconsin.

"Er, well, um, thank you," she stuttered again, "That would be great."

"Well, it's not exactly an imposition," Galotti had replied laughing, "The drinks at this bar are complimentary."

"Yes, yes, of course, sorry, my bad," she'd replied, feeling stupid, "In that case, I'd love to try something uniquely Miami, what would you suggest?"

"Well… the Rum Runner is probably Miami's signature cocktail, but having met you, I suspect you'd prefer a Miami Vice," he replied.

"Oh, that might be a bit too much for me, it sounds like a drink that ends with a hangover, and I have no wish to get drunk tonight, I can assure you."

"No, no, no," the man laughed, "The Miami Vice is a wonderful marriage of Piña Colada and Strawberry Daiquiri, perfect for you."

"That does sound perfect, and I do have a sweet tooth."

"I wouldn't doubt that for a moment," he said, "You seem like a very sweet, albeit alarmingly beautiful girl."

"Well, aren't you the charmer?" she replied to the man who was somewhat older than her, but to whom age had been more than kind.

The requested cocktail appeared almost immediately, a half-red, half-white concoction with a slice of pineapple on the glass's rim. She marveled at the speed and efficiency of the bartender, perhaps this Italian man was someone important?

"You like?" he asked, as she took her first sip.

"I love," she replied, "I don't usually drink fancy cocktails, but this is so me."

"And who *are* you, lovely girl?" he asked, his light brown eyes gleaming with what seemed like tiny crystals sparkling within them.

"Cassidy," she replied, "Cassidy Swain."

"Then it's my absolute pleasure to meet you, Cassidy Swain," he said, taking her fingertips in his palm, "I'm Carlo, Carlo Galotti."

Chapter 21

My head and neck still hurt like hell as I parked the Caddy further down the street behind Rainee's Chevy. When I'd examined my neck that morning, remembering the sharp pain I'd experienced, I found what looked like a puncture wound from a large syringe needle. I should have gone to bed and slept it off, but there was no way I could let Rainee down.

And no sooner had I switched off the car's engine, than the passenger door opened and she slid in next to me.

"What happened to you, girl kick you out of bed?"

"No, someone tranquilized me with a needle."

"Shit, Coop, I'm sorry, are you in pain?" she said, clutching my hand.

"Nah, just a bit of a thick head, I'll be fine," I replied, and continued to relate my previous activities to her.

"I told you that watching teenage ass would get you into trouble," she said.

"Oh, stop it, and she's not a teenager anyway. But something bad was going down on that yacht last night, and now it's disappeared."

"What's disappeared?"

"The yacht, dummy."

"So, no more ass-watching," she said, chuckling.

"Be serious for a minute, Rainee, I don't know what I may have inadvertently stepped into. The boxes I saw being loaded last night were large and metal, and extremely heavy-looking, because they were using the yacht's crane to get them on board."

"Well, you're the ex-cop, what do people smuggle?"

"Top of my head, I'd say gold bullion, weapons, drugs, money, art, and nowadays, people," I replied.

"The first five options sound plausible," said Rainee, "But I doubt it's people. Traffickers don't use yachts, they use trucks."

"I'm not sure what other possibilities there are, not even sure if it's any of my business either."

"It happened on your doorstep, Coop, and they clearly didn't want you to be witnessing anything, so yeah, it kinda is your business."

"I get that, but right now there's nothing I can do because the yacht's gone. Anyway, fill me in, any activity here?"

"Nothing much," she replied, "Although the boy's got a pretty expensive habit, going on the amount of blow he's put up his nose so far tonight."

"I guess Flick's paying for that," I replied, "What time did she arrive?"

"Around midnight, and right now, they're both in the house. Haven't seen lights go on all night, so I'm guessing for once, that they're actually sleeping."

"Suits me," I said, "We're both still getting paid, might try and get my head down for a couple of hours until they wake up."

"Okay partner, you're on your own, and for fuck's sake, be a little more careful with what you stick your nose into, some of us still need you around," Rainee said, touching my arm as she slid out of the car as quickly as she'd slid in.

As I looked across to the darkened and silent ranch home down the street from me, I poured myself a cup of coffee from the flask, savoring its healing qualities.

Putting the flask back into my cup holder, I reached across the seat to open the glove compartment on the passenger side and after a quick rummage, found what I was looking for.

I'm not really a smoker, can't stand the things really, but tonight was an exception. I pulled a cancer stick from the pack and lit it with a match, drawing the hot contents into my lungs, the foul mixture of nicotine and smoke burning my throat.

I held it in for a few seconds, then slowly exhaled, before I opened the car's door and stomped the cigarette out with the heel of my boot.

Time for a little shuteye.

Chapter 22

I opened my eyes, realizing that it must be mid-afternoon because of where the sunlight was entering the cabin. I could hear Pip topside, doing whatever it is she does, and yelled up to her to ask the time, in the faint hope of getting a cup of coffee for my troubles.

"It's 3pm," she shouted back down to me, "You want some coffee, boss?"

Boss?

"Yes please, but only if it's not too much of a problem," I lied, "I don't want to interrupt you."

I checked my phone calendar and suddenly realized that Molly was coming for afternoon tea today, so I needed to be shaved, showered and changed by the time she arrived at 4pm.

"Remy came by this morning, looking for you," said Pip as she handed me a steaming latte, "Asked if you can call him when you surface."

"Noted," I replied, "Tell me, is the yacht next door back in its slip now?"

"Cooper Hemingway, when are you going to stop behaving like a schoolboy?" Pip replied, "It's embarrassing."

"I like the view," I said, "Anyway, the last I saw was that it had disappeared in the early hours this morning. Is it back?"

"Nope, I guess your voyeurism is a non-starter today, so get your ass out of bed and clean yourself up, Molly will be here soon," she replied, waltzing out of the cabin to continue, you know, whatever it is she does.

I drained the last of my coffee, and finally decided to drag myself out of bed and into the shower. Feeling refreshed and regenerated, and having pulled on a pair of clean jeans and a polo, I slipped back onto the bed, and dialed Remy's number.

"Hola, partner," the familiar baritone boomed, "What's up?"

"Pip said you'd dropped by today, so I was going to ask you the same thing," I replied.

"It was nothing really, only that your neighbors have skipped town and won't be back for a while."

"Really?" I replied, "Did they do a runner?"

"No, on the contrary, they paid up in full this morning by email and bank transfer, but there was something odd in the total payment," he said.

"What was odd?" I asked.

"Well, for some weird reason, they added ten thousand bucks to be applied to your marina account, so I guess you're in credit. Which suits me, to be honest. They also added a note, to send thanks to you for being an excellent and understanding neighbor."

"What??" I exclaimed, "Ten Gs on my account?"

"Yeah, why d'you think that they'd do that? Do they think you're the marina charity case?"

"I have an idea why," I replied, and continued to tell him about the events of the early hours of that morning.

Chapter 23

Molly arrived just after four. I waved as I watched her strut down the dock toward me. Her reciprocal wave and radiant smile were enough to make my heart skip a beat, just as it did every time I saw her.

Molly cuts an imposing figure at five foot nine inches tall, dressed in black leather pants, black Dr. Martens and black singlet. She has a commanding presence and mature appearance, and the black attire she wore was emblematic of her personality, a blend of confidence and her own individuality.

The bond between us has grown deeper and deeper over the years, but at its core, she remains my cherished daughter, and no matter how much she grows or how far she ventures in life, I'm still the dad who will always be there for her. The one who had been there from the moment her tiny, fragile body took its first breath.

"Hey Dad," she said, wrapping her arms around me and giving me a hug, "What trouble are you in at the moment?"

Wiseass…

"You know me, Molly, I don't go looking for trouble but it has a knack of finding me," I said, laughing at my daughter's intrinsic knowledge of me.

"Come on," I continued, "Let's go sit on deck and have us a little feast."

We tucked into our afternoon tea, Pip having had the grace and foresight to run out and buy hot salt beef sandwiches, lox and cream cheese bagels, and a mixture of Sufganiyot, Chocolate Matzos and an old favorite from our local Jewish deli, the fabled Molly's Sweet and Spicy Tzimmes Cake.

"Oh, you got the Molly's cake," she said, brimming with delight.

"Well, you can thank Pip, she went out this afternoon and picked up everything for us," I replied, knowing that I wouldn't get away with taking the credit for the spread.

"Doesn't matter," she said, "I love our weekly afternoon teas together."

"Good," I said, "Long may they continue."

We began devouring Pip's purchases, each of us salivating at the deli's fare. After a minute or so, Molly had dispensed with half a salt beef sandwich, and sat back with a bagel in her hand.

"There's something I've thought about for a while now that I want to ask you about," she said.

"You need money?"

"No, I'm working part-time, so no, but thank you."

"Well, no need to hold back, you know you can ask me anything," I reiterated, realizing that she might want to talk about her mom.

"It's about Rainee," she began, "I love Rainee, you know that, right? And she's kinda like a big sister to me, but…"

Molly's voice trailed off as she nervously nibbled on the bagel, gathering the courage to ask the question that had been weighing on her mind.

"Listen, Molly, we've never had any secrets from each other, have we?"

"No, never."

"So just ask, I'll always answer truthfully, you know that."

"Okay… did you have an affair with her, Dad, is that why Mom left?"

It was a question I wasn't expecting, but it was also an important one.

"I can tell you truthfully, that absolutely nothing has ever happened between Rainee and I, but it needs more explanation."

"I'm listening," she said, taking another bite of her bagel.

"When I first met Rainee, she was in what I saw as a potentially perilous situation, and she was still a kid, only eighteen years old," I continued, "And apart from there being a big age difference, I was eight or nine years older than her, I just never viewed her in a sexual way."

"Why? She's super-hot, Dad, although I get that the ten-year age difference when she was a teenager would be weird."

"Exactly," I confirmed, "But there's also something else."

"You were a monk?" she asked, laughing.

"No, but it's not far from the truth, Molly. You see, I was in love with your mom, and when she suddenly disappeared, you became my sole focus so I had zero interest or time for other women."

"Wow!" she exclaimed, "How long did that go on for?"

"Probably for maybe four or five years, I just had no interest at all, and the only thing that mattered in my life, was you."

"Mom hurt you, didn't she?" my daughter said quietly, moving over and gently nestling her hand into mine.

"She did, but it was a long time ago, and I will always thank her for giving me you. Without your mom, we wouldn't be sitting here right now, so I'm eternally grateful."

"You're so soppy, Dad, but I wouldn't want you any other way," she replied, squeezing my hand harder, "But, do you see Rainee in any kind of romantic way now?"

"No, far from it. She's a beautiful girl, we both know that, and an amazing partner, but I think I'm probably destined for a single life now."

"Why do you even say things like that, Dad?" Molly said, clearly exasperated with me, "You'd be a catch for some women."

"Tell that to someone who'll listen," I replied.

"I'm serious!" she continued, "Have you tried dating apps, like most people do these days?"

"Oh Lord, no, Molly!" I said, incredulous that my daughter was suggesting it, "I've heard about Tinder, and it's not a cauldron I want to dip my toe into."

"I'm not talking about Tinder, that's a hook-up site," she replied, "But there are loads of other sites that have worked for people looking for a relationship."

"Like what?" I asked, realizing that dating apps seemed to have passed me by in my life.

"Match, Hinge, Bumble," she replied, "You just need to sign up with a brief profile and a few photos, it's easy, and I'd bet you would get instant likes."

The websites, Match, Hinge and Bumble, were things I'd never come across before.

"Likes?"

"Oh Dad, you crack me up. You literally know nothing about online dating, do you?"

"I know it exists."

"Okay, so when you post your profile online, if people think you're hot, you get a like. If you like them back, then you start a text conversation."

"Text isn't really my bag," I replied.

"Then send a few texts and ask if you can have a phone call. Jeez, Dad! Come on, it's 2023," she exclaimed, laughing, but clearly frustrated by my ignorance of dating technology.

"Okay, my wise one, maybe I'll give it a shot," I replied, knowing that I wouldn't.

"Good, do it tonight."

"I see you're still entrenched in Goth fashion," I said, changing the subject, "Don't you find it too hot to be wearing so much black?"

"Yep, and I think I might be growing out of it, to be honest, it is SOOO friggin hot, particularly the leather stuff."

"You gonna go all girlie on me?" I said, laughing at the idea, "Maybe turn up in a dress one day?"

"Who knows, I might surprise you, Papa H."

I laughed and said, "Yeah sure, is that a pig I see up in that sky?"

"You laugh now, but I've been thinking recently about what I'm going to do after college, and the Goth look ain't gonna win in job interviews," she replied, a little morose now.

"*Isn't* going to win," I replied.

"Yeah, that too," she said.

"So, what's the plan?"

"I thought I might join the police," she replied, "It didn't turn out so badly for you."

"Oh please, Molly, I don't want to see you camped out all night in a black & white, you're way too bright for that. Why don't you pick a career that's safe and will actually earn you a decent living? And besides, being a detective didn't make me wealthy, did it?"

"I wasn't thinking about being a foot soldier, I was more hoping I could get into forensics."

"Now you're talking," I agreed, "Why don't you grill Coke on it? If anyone, he's the man to talk to."

Colin Caine, known to his friends as Cocaine or Coke, along with my buddy Nate, is a man I'd completed training with when I first joined the SFPD. He's solid, one of the cops in Palm Beach who isn't bent, which is kind of rare. We often discuss cases, his and mine, to get a better perspective of things.

"Yeah, I could do that, and he's my godfather after all, so I guess he owes me," she said, laughing, all smiles now.

"Yep, and he's got a soft spot for you, Molly, he might even bend some rules to get you an opportunity. But joking apart, I like the idea because I'm not sure I could live with the thought of you being in any dangerous situations. You're all I have."

"You're so dramatic, Dad, stop worrying, I'm not about to go out on patrol. Now, can we please have pudding, I'm still hungry."

I looked at my daughter as she began unwrapping the desserts that Pip had brought, realizing that she never spoke of her mother. In

Molly's world, she had never known her mom, so as far as she was concerned, she never really existed. I was mom and dad rolled up into one. And I was good with that, because she is my whole world.

Chapter 24

Hurricane season in Florida begins on June 1st and ends November 30th. Rarely, do hurricanes occur outside these dates, but for this six-month segment of the year, most of us have an eye on the radar, hoping that the season will be kind to us and not bring carnage and devastation. I've lived through enough hurricanes myself to share the same annual fear as every other Floridian.

"You worried?" asked Remy.

"Not too much, we've both been through hurricanes before," I replied, "And we're still here."

"True, but to be honest man, I'm not sure if my little house is as safe as your boat. These freakin' 'canes just scare the shit out of me."

It was unimaginable that Remy, this extraordinary specimen of a man, could even know what fear was. But as I looked at him now, I could see abject terror once again, coursing through him. Hurricanes just freak him out. It's the same with German Shepherds, he's terrified of them, although he's okay with Diablo. But then again, Diablo is asleep most of the time.

"Has it turned into a hurricane yet?" I asked, aware that a tropical storm had been battering the Dominican Republic and Haiti.

"Not yet," Remy replied, "And it appears to be a slow-moving storm at the moment. Might not hit Cuba for another four or five days. Just gotta hope it keeps south and burns out somewhere in the Caribbean."

"Look man, we've done the routine countless times before, we can always head inland again 'til it's safe to come back," I said, hoping that I could appease the big guy.

"Yeah, I guess…" he replied, his fear barely dampened, let alone assuaged.

The truth was, I hadn't been paying my normal rapt attention to the radar. And the storm's path that Remy was describing, brought back too many memories of other hurricanes that had begun as tropical storms, but had then quickly become full-blown hurricanes once they passed over Cuba.

And I knew that the reason for this has *everything* to do with climate change. The Atlantic Ocean is now several degrees warmer than in previous decades, the water's warmth allowing hurricanes to maintain their strength, and in most cases, become even stronger, sometimes to Category 4 or 5. And Cat 5 is the most powerful, and the most devastating.

"Have they given it a name yet, if it does become a hurricane?" I asked.

"Who gives a shit what it's friggin name is? Can't believe that they give 'em dumbass names like Richard and Walter," he replied tetchily, "Pretty sure this one begins with 'J' though … it will probably be Jemima or Jonathan".

It wasn't. It was Jacques.

Chapter 25

A couple of days and a couple of long nights later, I found myself immersed in a deep comfortable sofa in Joe Jarvie's spectacular lounge. I'd been summoned to update him on the Flick situation.

Joe's oceanside, Florida home is best described as abnormally excessive, almost gaudy. It's rockstar all the way, a sprawling two-story pink edifice of tacky opulence, with lawns stretching down to a private beach, which lay a couple of hundred yards away from the patio.

The lounge I was currently sitting in was vast, an electric blue shag-pile-carpeted throwback to the 1970s, complete with purple and yellow wallpaper, endless rows of framed gold and platinum records adorning the walls, and a plethora of unrelated art and statues muddying the space.

Between the wall art and the awards, Joe had fourteen of his favorite guitars hanging on the walls, and rich, gold, red and turquoise Moroccan and Arabian tapestries and rugs, filling every available space. A pair of matching vintage brass and glass bongs adorned the huge, square, low-level, rustic Indian coffee table, that was centered between the four gauche, albeit sumptuous pink sofas.

I could probably get used to pink…

He even had the obligatory ashtray full of guitar plectrums, just as I had on my boat. Although sadly, my much used and much-loved

Gibson Hummingbird was not in Joe's guitar collection league. But every time I played that acoustic guitar, I loved her even more.

I sat patiently, the not unusual wait while Joe readied himself upstairs. It wasn't that Joe was deliberately rude, it was just that his clock didn't synchronize with normal people's activities. He hadn't forgotten that I was meeting with him today, it was just that he had still been asleep when I arrived.

His 'manservant', Felipe, had let me in and cordially directed me to the room which I currently occupied, had kindly brought coffee and fresh pastries to me, and continued on upstairs in his daily ritual of dragging Joe out of bed.

I realized that Joe would soon make an extravagant entrance when I noticed two well-known Palm Beach groupies stumbling down the vast curving stairway, both of them half-dressed and somewhat unkempt. I'd met them before on several occasions in Joe's company. Primrose and Daisy, a pair of very attractive identical twins, but they traded penises like pork bellies.

I circled the room, to have a closer look at Joe's magnificent guitar collection, although these fourteen beauties were probably only half of his entire collection. There were others in the rehearsal rooms at the other end of the property, and even more stunning instruments in the recording studio.

I've seen, and played most of Joe's guitars over the years, but my eye was taken by a particular vintage item I'd never seen before on my visits here.

I recognized the model immediately, a 1954 Fender Stratocaster, this one a white ash body, maple neck, gold pickguard, original white Fender pickups and a gold tremolo system. And although I could see that this example had been used excessively during its seven decades, it was still gorgeous. I think I was in love the moment I saw her.

Anyone who has a mild interest in guitars would know that this was identical to the legendary Strat that Dave Gilmour had used on many of Pink Floyd's songs, including *Another Brick in The Wall*. I have a particular penchant for rare and classic guitars, so I was aware of the serial number of Gilmour's Stratocaster.

And although his one was not the first Strat ever built when it debuted in 1954, (that model was oddly given the serial number, 0100), Gilmour's was unique in its own serial number. The only way I would find out, would be to check the serial plate on the back of the guitar.

Realizing that Joe was probably still in slumber mode, I gingerly lifted the well-worn instrument from its hanger, and turned it over to examine it. And there it was, as I'd thought, a small plaque screwed to the back of the guitar, denoting the most iconic and legendary Fender Stratocaster serial number of all time, 0001.

I stood in awe of what was in my hands at this moment, which for me was the golden fleece of guitars, storied also to have been originally owned by Leo Fender himself, the man who created the iconic Fender Stratocaster. I carefully replaced it on its hanger, my stomach churning with something I never usually experience. Envy.

How did Joe acquire this beauty? This had to be a $2m guitar at minimum…

Two Danishes, an almond croissant and three expressos later, Joe made his typical flamboyant appearance at the entrance of the room, brandishing his outstretched arms above his fabulously maned head. Welcoming me as though I hadn't seen him in ten years.

"Coooooooper!!" he yelled, "My man!"

"Hey Joe," I said, "I see you've been busy."

"Hahahaha!" he continued, still loudly, "So you saw the twins leave then?"

"Hard to miss, really," I said as he vaulted over the back of the pink sofa that sat at right-angles to me.

"You should have come joined us," he said, actually quite seriously.

"Felipe served me something equally delightful, but thank you for the invitation, and in any case, I wouldn't want to show you up, little fella."

And then that laugh just howled again, almost deafening in the cavernous room.

You can't not love Joe, I thought, as the satin-panted, bare-chested and sinewy little guy threw back his long, brown and wavy hair in joy. He's infectious, and not in a Covid way. I'm not sure I've ever seen him upset, but then rock 'n roll stars don't have much reason to be pissed about anything I guess, unless they can't get their next high, in whichever form it arrives.

"Can we talk about Flick," I asked, not wanting to waste the entire day at the pink palace.

"Do we have to?" he whined, "I've had such a good day so far."

"It won't take long, because there's not a lot to tell," I replied, "But did you have any idea that Flick has put a tail on you?"

"Really? Who?"

"Rainee," I said.

"Oh fuck, Coop, she's better than *you*."

107

"Well, thank you for that, no hard feelings, but it's not so much working as a tail that Rainee's being paid, more for protection against you, strange as that may seem."

"Rainee's better in that department too, Coop, sorry man, no offense. But why would Flick need protection from me, I've never harmed a fly."

"It's not really about that, Joe, she's trying to create this idea that you're some kind of wife-beating, controlling narcissist, for when you eventually get to court," I replied, knowing that Joe was genuinely the most placid and peaceful guy I'd ever met. Flick knew it too, but she was an alley-cat, a savage one too.

"But that ain't who I am," he replied, "I'm a lover, not a fighter, man."

"I know, but she can try, and she's gotta have some kind of evidence that you're a terrible husband. Might be an idea to keep some things on the downlow for the time being?"

"You mean the twins?" he asked, a little sadness now showing on his face.

"Not for long, Joe, I just need to get some damning shots of Flick and lover-boy, and we'll be good to go," I replied, knowing that Joe's teenage-like sex drive was his biggest passion in life, after music.

"Shit, man, that's a real bummer. I love those chicks. Damn."

"I need to remind you that the reason you hired me is because Flick is playing around, so right now, it's kind of hypocritical to be bedding endless girls, no?"

"I know, man, I just want Flick out of my life so I can be free of the bitch. How long before you can get some evidence, d'you think?"

I hesitated, because I didn't want to reveal that we had Rainee on our team now, even though she was being paid by Flick, ergo Joe.

"I think the gig will be up in the next few days, Joe, just go write some songs or practice with your band this week, keep the twins at arm's length, can you?"

"Sure I can, yeah… maybe I could get Pinky to come over for entertainment? Love Pinky."

"Joe! For fuck's sake, Pinky's even worse! Just keep it in your pants for the rest of the week, okay??"

"Okay boss."

Joe sat there like a scolded schoolkid, his week having grown darker in his mind.

But then suddenly, he chirped up and became excitedly animated.

"Did you see her?" he asked, pointing at the wall of guitars.

"Is she for real?" I replied.

"Fuck yeah, she's triple-0 one, dude!"

"Oh, man…" I replied, when he confirmed my suspicions.

"You wanna play her?"

"Seriously?' I asked, my mouth salivating at the prospect.

"Yeah, come on," he said, once again vaulting the sofa and grabbing the Strat from the wall, "Let's go, partner."

I followed sheep-like as Joe led the way to the rehearsal studio.

So much for a quick meeting…

Chapter 26

It had been six days since he'd been at Nate's Bar & Grill. Would it be so bad to make the call? It was more of an equal world now anyway, wasn't it? She had a day off coming up on Saturday, could be a pleasant outing if the weather played nice.

It was just past eleven in the evening now, too late to call?

Probably...

Rolling over on the bed, reaching out for the cell phone lying on the bedside table, she began to type in his number on the screen. She was strangely embarrassed that she was wearing only underwear, and made sure that when she hit *Call*, it was voice and not video.

He answered on the fourth ring. And she did like his voice, probably the thing she found most attractive about him.

"Hello, this is Cooper Hemingway. If you're receiving this message, then I must be busy. Please call again during daylight hours, or leave a detailed message. Thank you for calling Hemingway Investigations, I look forward to hearing from you."

Layla froze for a moment, not knowing what to do. She had assumed he would pick up. Leave a detailed message?

"Coop, it's Layla."

Chapter 27

It had been another long and pretty uneventful night, watching the Flick show. I was already beat, and fed up with the monotony of the endless night work. Sure, the money was fine, but I was feeling a little guilt from not being able to deliver the goods to Joe.

I briefly glanced at my phone to see the time, and noticed a missed call from an anonymous number. I played back my messages and was surprised that it was from Layla. Despite a little innocuous flirting, mostly initiated by me, and also having given her my business card, I hadn't really expected her to call.

Even if I had wanted to, I couldn't return her call as she hadn't reciprocated by sharing her number, and she had evidently activated the caller ID blocking feature on her phone. My thoughts were then abruptly interrupted by Rainee.

"What do you wanna do, numbnuts?" she asked, sitting in the Caddy's passenger seat, enjoying the comfort far more than she ever did in her beat-up Chevy.

At that moment, I could see a light come on at the rear of the property.

Aha…

"Well, it's just past four and it looks like they might be awake," I replied, pointing toward the house.

"A little early-morning slamming, you think?" asked Rainee, a grin spreading wide across her face.

"Our minds think alike," I replied, "You want to go take a look with the Nikon?"

"You coming with?" she asked.

"Nah, there's probably nothing to see, so I'll wait here and watch your back. Have at it."

Rainee slowly eased out of the car, and crept silently across the street.

～～～

She continued toward the mostly darkened house, momentarily crouching down when she came to the yard's pedestrian entrance on the left side of the building.

She paused briefly, listening for any sounds that might be coming from inside, and decided that she was clear to make her way down the side path toward the rear yard. She was grateful that the guy hadn't installed motion detector lights around the property, although it was a bit of a shithole, and the kid was probably flat broke anyway.

Concealed behind a well-established Firebush shrub at the rear left corner of the property, Rainee had an ideal vantage point overlooking what Coop had pinpointed as the guy's bedroom. He had pulled up county records earlier in the day, which provided information about the house layout, confirming that the room she was now fixated on, was indeed the largest bedroom in the house.

Twenty minutes went by, the silence only punctuated by the relentless drone of cicadas, until she felt the muted vibration of her phone nestling in her front chest pocket.

Anything? vas the text message on the screen from Coop.

She quickly texted him back, Nothing yet

In reality, although Rainee was skilled in martial arts, she was glad that Coop was just a couple of hundred yards away tonight. If anything did go off, she had the best backup at hand in Coop. She'd never admit that to him, of course.

She settled back behind the Firebush, a shrub that held a special place in her heart. It wasn't just the beauty of the fiery red blossoms that emitted a fragrance imperceptible to humans, but rather because it possessed a unique allure for hummingbirds. These tiny creatures were inexplicably drawn to the scent, discernible only to them, a feature that deepened her affection for hummingbirds above all other winged creatures.

~ ~ ~

I stretched out my body inside the Caddy, and took another gulp of coffee to make sure I stayed alert while Rainee was over at the house. Not because Rainee needed a man to fight her battles, she could kick most men's asses anyway, but Florida's dumb 'conceal/carry' permits meant that most any jackass could pull a gun anywhere, at a supermarket, a dime store, or even in a bar.

Florida's doomed, I thought, as I focused solely on the property, still thinking about the voicemail that Layla had left earlier on. I hadn't mentioned the message to Rainee because I knew she'd be twisting my melon about it all night long. And when she starts, she just doesn't stop.

My cellphone rumbled again, another text from Rainee,

> We're on

I typed back a reply, and then I felt for the reassuring cold steel of my Glock G21 .45Auto tucked away inside my jacket pocket, a respected friend when the going got tough. Although *my* gun was registered and I'm fully licensed to carry it at all times.

~ ~ ~

Rainee could now see the two lovers in partial view from her concealed position. Clearly, they liked to have the light on when they were playing hide-the-cannoli, she thought.

> Go get 'em, partner

came back the message from Coop.

With Coop's camera pushed over her shoulder, Rainee slid from the undergrowth and crab-walked across the lawn's harsh Zoysia grass, until she was perched just beneath the bedroom's main window.

With her new and closer proximity, she could suddenly hear the sounds emanating from the room, and quickly switched the camera function to *Movie* mode. She kind've thought that a sex clip with full guttural audio would be better in court than just a few photos. And the shrieks and grunts she was hearing right now, told her that the beast was indeed making two backs, noisy ones at that.

~ ~ ~

I hadn't heard any commotion of any kind, so I was presuming that, either Rainee was waiting to get the shots of Flick and her toy boy, or she was already on her way back to the car with the mucky evidence. But I remained on maximum alert, just in case.

After a few minutes, having seen nothing erupting from the property, I decided that it might be prudent to get closer to the house to listen in on the situation, so I got out of the warm confines of the Caddy, silently closed the door, and crept up the sidewalk on the opposite side of the road to where the house was located.

~ ~ ~

Rainee simultaneously decided that this would be her chance to get the best footage, because she deduced from the escalating moans inside, that mutual orgasms were getting headily closer now.

Gingerly, she raised her head to the window pane, Nikon already filming, the lens concentrated on the two sweaty and naked figures going at it like oversexed jackhammers on the bed.

But just when she decided that she had shot enough divorce-damning, bulletproof footage and was about to switch off the camera, a screeching *"Fuuuuuckkkk"* came from Flick's mouth. But it wasn't the 'fuck' of orgasm occurring, it was the 'fuck' that Flick had just laid eyes on Rainee.

And then all hell kicked off.

Throwing the camera back over her shoulder once more, Rainee abruptly jumped up from her position below the window and began to sprint across the yard and then back up the path at the side of the house.

The front door crashed open as she neared the front yard, and two naked bodies were coming down the steps, yelling cuss words. The boy was already sprinting hard out of the front yard and down the street, just as Rainee collided with Flick, and the girl went down hard on the asphalt drive, cursing at Rainee, every swear-word leveled directly at her.

Rainee looked down at Flick, blood now seeping from the wounds on her naked ass and arms where skin had proven no match for the black asphalt. She almost laughed at the comedy of the scene, but stopped short when she heard two, no three, gunshots from further down the street. But she knew Coop was armed and deadly, and the kid would be no match for him.

"You cunt, you fucking cunt, you're meant to be fucking working for me, you bitch!" Flick yelled, sputum now spraying from her mouth as she delivered the vile expletives toward Rainee.

"Bad luck, girl, I never did like you, and honestly, you ain't paying my invoice, your soon-to-be ex-husband is. So, fuck you, have a nice day," said Rainee, almost laughing at the situation as Flick lay on the ground, her eyes seeming to double in size in their sockets.

Rainee was almost caught off-guard as Flick leapt up and threw herself at her, a whirling dervish with murder in her eyes, clawing at Rainee, desperate to get the camera that was still behind Rainee's back.

But Rainee wasn't moved, she simply drew back her arm and punched Flick squarely in the face, delivering a knockout blow in an instant. She pulled a cable tie from her pocket, and quickly lashed the now unconscious girl's hands together, wondering now what had happened to the boyfriend.

~ ~ ~

From my position on the other side of the road, I had caught the whole episode, wondering where on earth the kid was going, naked as the day he was born, and I stupidly decided to give chase.

Sprinting down the eerily quiet suburban street, I didn't know if I could collar the kid, but surprisingly for my age, double that of the kid, I seemed to be closing the distance.

And that was when he did something that I could never have expected.

The boy halted abruptly, pivoted to confront my approaching silhouette, brandished a gun that had remained unseen in the darkness of the night, and discharged three shots in my direction.

What the fuck?

The first two missed me, but the searing, instantaneous pain that followed with the third shot, was a jarring contrast with the stark reality that this was not the day I had chosen to die. My body staggered, and tumbled to the ground, my own gun clattering loudly as it skittered across the road's surface, its echoes resounding through the obsidian night.

I grunted from the pain of my knees crunching on the asphalt, its ruthless, sharp, and gnarly texture ripping through my pant legs until it found blood.

As I lay prone in the center of the road, I gingerly explored the area on my torso where the bullet had torn into me, pulling up my hand in the mild hope that it wasn't a bad hit, but realizing it was already completely covered in blood.

"For fuck's sake..." I said out loud, watching as the boy continued running down the street until he was completely out of sight.

It's in these moments when you have the strangest thoughts roaming aimlessly through your mind, not whether or not I was about to meet my maker, but more about where a naked kid would go, wielding a weapon in his hand. It's odd.

I moved my head an inch or so on the abrasive tarmac, to a position where I could vaguely see in the distance, a fight breaking out back at the house between Rainee and a naked Flick, everything now happening in slow motion, no longer a barrage of meteoric imagery.

I was beginning to weaken as the blood from my wound continued to leak out onto the road's surface, and I knew as I lay in that crimson puddle, that I had taken one too many risks in my life.

And as I whisper a silent apology to my beautiful, my perfect Molly, my vision begins to blur and my eyes close until there is no more light...

Chapter 28

It's probably the eternal sunshine and hot weather that has made Florida the motorcycle capital of America. But not the capital in the commuting sense of motorcycling. It has far more to do with the nostalgia of the American history of motorcycling, that began with the birth of the Indian and the Harley-Davidson brands in 1901 and 1903, respectively.

In just about every Florida town, and most often in those small ones that track the never-ending Florida coast, Sunday will see thousands of motorcycle clubs arrive in clusters of dozens of enthusiasts on their bikes. On initial sighting, most people who aren't au fait with these motorcycling groups, may think that what they are seeing, is a gang of Hell's Angels coming to tear up the place.

But that couldn't be further from the truth. These 'gangs' are true enthusiasts, men and women who never want to forget the history and the beauty of these old, but classic machines. The fact that these bikes are huge and loud, with every single glistening chrome or painted part, polished to the maximum by their leather-jacketed, bandana-wearing owners, shows the pride they have for the brands of the bikes they ride, albeit mostly Harleys. These are good people, and they ain't scary at all.

Memphis Tennessee was one of those guys, not just on a glorious Sunday, but every day of the week. He lived the whole motorbike life, 365 days a year.

Yes, the man looked scary as hell, his shorter frame, highlighted by the powerful and huge arm muscles that were crudely exposed from his 'wife beater' t-shirt, coupled with the leather biker pants and *Wolverine Los Altos* boots he wore every day. And the endless tattoos of snakes, dragons, daggers and vampish ghouls that covered his entire body, did nothing to alleviate the image of fear that he struck within most people when they saw him.

He was born in Tennessee to a drug-addicted prostitute mother, who lazily decided to call him Memphis, just so the hospital would leave her alone so she could get out and score some crack or chunk. Memphis never really knew his mother that well, she was rarely lucid enough to realize that he had come to visit on the infrequent occasions he made the journey. And the family that had adopted him as a baby were pretty cool, so they became his parents.

After deciding he wanted closure from his pitiful birth mother when she died, Memphis legally changed his last name from Fontaine to Tennessee, and Memphis Tennessee he became.

These days, after having made a small and unexpected fortune with a one-off investment recommended by two friends of his, Vaughn Perryman and Gaylord Talbot, Memphis ran a shelter for abused women. The company that his two buddies had recommended, well mostly Talbot in actuality, was the then-nascent company that over time became the global juggernaut we know today, called Amazon.

At the time, Memphis had a motorcycle repair business down in Jensen Beach and was making good money from customizing and repairing Indians and Harleys, as well as reaping in the money he made from the merchandise and parts shop that his sister ran for him. When Talbot had given him the tip to invest as much as he could afford to lose in this new company, Memphis, who respected Talbot enormously, bought $10,000 worth of Amazon stock. It turned out to be the best decision he ever made.

But it was only due to the fact that his investment had created a sizeable windfall for him, that Memphis was able to open, and then expand the women's shelter he ran up in Palm Beach. He was well known locally in Jensen and up in Palm Beach, for what they termed his 'philanthropy', but the simple reason he had decided to open the shelter was to ensure that there were fewer kids born into a world where their mothers were either victims of abuse, or who were just unable to care for a child because of addiction.

Memphis wasn't one for the limelight, he shunned public exposure to his guarded privacy. He didn't want to be featured in Palm Beach coffee-table magazines, the savior to so many women and girls who had arrived at his shelter's door looking for food and a bed for the night. He was a very private man and just wanted to be left alone.

However, the Palm Beach glitterati loved him despite his request for anonymity, because he was an anomaly. The man born to a drug-addicted mother, abandoned at birth, who looked like a Hell's Angel, wealthy in his own right, and who only cared about the awful fates of women in distress.

And so, he became the poster boy for their well-heeled charity events. And Palm Beach's socialites paid a heavy entrance fee to attend, so who was Memphis to deny their patronage and the cash that constantly flowed into the shelter's expansion? He was literally hailed as Palm Beach's knight in shining armor, so what was he to do about it?

But today, as with every Sunday, was the only day he allowed himself to let his other employees run the shelter and the parts shop in his absence. And on this stunningly pretty morning, he was riding his sparkling and immaculate Indian motorcycle up the coastal A1A to Palm Beach to see the new man in his life, Remy Washington. He might even drop by and check in on the man who'd introduced them to each other, his old buddy, Cooper Hemingway.

Chapter 29

Layla's uncertainty gnawed at her as she contemplated making the call. She couldn't fathom why Coop hadn't replied to her message, but she knew he was in the midst of working nights on a case.

Perhaps he was preoccupied, or maybe he had a girlfriend. Regardless, she desperately wanted to take him up on his offer to show her around the area. Partly because he came across as a genuinely nice guy, and partly because she was growing increasingly restless, cooped up at Nate's place.

Yet, as she lay on her bed staring out of her small room's window, drinking in the picturesque countryside that surrounded her, it suddenly struck her. She snatched her cell phone, a recently purchased burner she'd acquired just three days ago from a Radio Shack in a dingy plaza nearby, and hastily opened the Settings menu.

The puzzle pieces began to align in her mind. It dawned on her that Coop might not have returned her call because her phone had caller ID withheld, pre-activated. She understood the logic behind it – most people buying burner phones wished to remain anonymous. It was a tactic she'd seen Carlo employ countless times, using disposable phones for a few calls before immediately discarding them.

She turned off the anonymity mode and, without thinking, dialed Coop's number.

After a few rings, the call was answered.

"Hello?' said the woman's voice on the other end of the line, "This is Cooper Hemingway's phone, can I help you?"

Layla froze. He *did* have a girlfriend.

"Hello?" said the voice again, "Anyone there?"

But before the voice spoke again, Layla had hung up.

Chapter 30

Carlo Galotti was pissed. The execution of the Randolphs hadn't exactly resulted in pay dirt. Not that he cared about them, and it hadn't been a total waste of his time because he had acquired an interesting new vehicle that added seamlessly to his ever-growing collection at his home. And it had passed to him free of charge. A quarter-million-dollar ride for just a couple of dead bodies. Nice work if you can get it.

But hunting down Cassidy, who had become the biggest thorn in his side, was his number one priority, and he was damned if an ungrateful bitch from Hicksville was going to bring down a feared and respected Miami Mafia boss like Carlo. She had to be found, and she had to be dead. Soon as.

"You think you can find your wife?" said the man sitting opposite him, in his distinct Russian accent, looking at the menu rather than at Carlo.

"Of course I can find her," replied Carlo, somewhat agitatedly, "Have you so quickly forgotten who I am? I didn't get to run Miami without having eyes everywhere."

The restaurant was completely full today, although Galotti had no need of a reservation here. It was his favorite, and if someone was at his regular table in the far corner in a spot where he had full view of everyone who entered and left, those patrons would be ejected immediately on his arrival. This was Carlo Galotti kingdom, here and across the south of Florida.

"But here we are, five months on, and your eyes everywhere seem to be somewhat blind at the moment, no?" asked the man, again in an icy cool, accented voice.

Carlo didn't care for this foreign ingrate, and he was becoming tired of the accusatory line of questioning. Under any other circumstance, this Muscovite would be receiving the contents of the suppressed Glock that he had hidden under the table.

"I'm a Galotti, no one escapes," he replied, "She'll be found. She'll be executed. She'll be an ex-problem. Don't worry. Tell your boss not to concern himself, she'll be taken care of."

"*Da*, but you see, Mr. Galotti, I do worry. I worry that you no longer have the tentacles in this city that you once had. There is a time limit on what my boss will accommodate, and his patience is running thin."

Galotti despised this man, and right at this moment was having nagging regrets about having gotten into business with the Russian mob. But the positive financial return was far too satisfying to ignore.

"Trust me, Sergei, Cassidy will pay for what she's done, but the wheels are already turning, and we now know the exact vehicle that she left in," Galotti replied, his tone measured and composed, hoping that this would gain him some valuable and much needed time to find Cassidy.

"And what vehicle is that, may I ask?"

"We know she traded one of my Range Rovers for a blue Ford Explorer, and that she was headed north-west, probably back to her home town in Wisconsin. I've already sent a couple of my guys over to the small town she lived in. It won't take long to get information."

"And how do you have this information regarding the vehicle?" asked the Russian, really starting to piss Carlo off with his dumb and now boring questioning, "And I suspect that there are a great many blue Ford Explorers littering the entire country, no?"

"You and I both know I have ways of making people tell me what I need to know," Galotti replied, "We even have the registration of the truck."

"And tell me, how did you come across this nugget of information, Mr. Galotti?"

The prick was really pissing Carlo off now, but as the knuckles of his fists grew white on his tanned hands beneath the table, he knew that this was not the time to pull his gun and shoot the Russian, much as he'd like to. He knew exactly who Sergei's boss was, a Russian mafia oligarch, who was very close to Putin.

"My men tore apart the building of the auto dealership where we extracted the information," replied Galotti, working hard now to control his anger, "And once we'd found what we wanted, we took the computers and paper files, so yeah, we're ahead of the game now."

"Then I will leave this affair in your capable hands, Mr. Galotti, my boss has the utmost faith that you will not let him down again."

Again?

Carlo was seething, he'd only ever made one unfortunate error in the last three years he'd been in business with them, and even that wasn't entirely his fault.

Motherfuckers…

"Now, what do you suggest?" said Sergei.

"Suggest?" asked Galotti, anger raging within him.

"On the menu," said Sergei, "I hear that this restaurant has exceptional delicacies."

Chapter 31

"I'm fine," I said, "Stop fussing, it was a through and through."

"You're not, so quit carping," said Rainee, lifting my head and plumping the pillows under it, "The bullet might have gone right through you, but it still tore you up."

My cabin had never been so full, and in addition to Rainee, Pip was fussing around, Molly was lying next to me with her arm over my chest, Diablo was lying faithfully by the bed and even Kinky had dug out a spot between myself and Molly to take a nap.

Memphis had just arrived and was embracing Remy, which is kinda funny when you see two muscle-bound men who look like heavyweight boxers, having a bit of a cuddle. But yeah, it was almost a party at Coop's. That is, if I hadn't been hindered earlier that morning by the intrusion of a bullet hurtling through my body.

I didn't remember much about that almost fateful night, but Rainee had given me the full lowdown of events earlier that morning. While she had been dealing with an apoplectic Flick, she'd heard some shots but had assumed that it was me doing the shooting. When she finally ran to where I lay, losing blood at a rate of knots, she had somehow loaded me into the backseat of the Caddy and driven me straight to Remy's, on my garbled and semi-conscious insistence.

When we arrived, Remy, a qualified military medic, went straight into warzone mode, examining the wound, cleaning it and stitching me up. I was fortunate that once the blood flow had been stemmed, he knew that all I needed was bed rest, rather than a hospital stay.

"You're so friggin' stubborn, Cooper Hemingway, I shouldn't have listened to you, should've taken you straight to the Emergency Room, but you damned insisted that Remy would fix you," said Rainee.

"Well, he did, didn't he?" I replied.

"Yeah, he did, he's brilliant, but what if it had been much worse? You wouldn't be here in your cabin with your family around you, you'd be six feet under and we'd be eating canapes after your funeral, you dumb fuck. Sorry, Molly."

"I would've hated to have missed the canapes," I said.

"Just stop it."

As Rainee tenderly set my head down on the freshly plumped pillows, I asked,

"Just tell me, was the bullet worth our while?"

"Oh, more than," she replied, now finally laughing, "We got the full scoop, Coop, I've already emailed the clip to Joe. Oh, and he's dropping by to see you later this afternoon once he's finished band practice."

"Not gonna get much sleep today then, I guess," I replied, knowing that Joe loved to chat and strum my Hummingbird when he occasionally came to the boat.

"Well, he's incredibly upset that you got shot working for him, so give him a break, Coop."

"Of course, he'll be guilt-ridden, I know what Joe's like. Anyway, how did he take it when he saw the video?"

"Interesting really," she said, "On the one hand he was grateful because he finally had the ammo he needed to get rid of Flick, and on the other hand, I kinda got the feeling he was a bit miffed because the kid could do more for Flick than he could."

"Rockstar vanity mentality," I replied, now chuckling myself, "Even Joe has that interminable desire and arrogant need to be the best at everything."

"But you could have been killed, Dad," said Molly, clutching me even tighter, "I'm not ready to be an orphan yet, you idiot."

"Yeah, and who am I going to find to replace you in this berth to continue making a loss on it? added Remy, now unlocked from the bearlike arms of Memphis.

"You'll find someone," I replied, now aware that every time I laughed, my left side shrieked in pain, "You found *me*, didn't you?"

"Yeah," Memphis chipped in, "And I wouldn't've met this guy if it hadn't been for you, so you'd better be more careful in future."

"How bad was it," I asked, a serious question directly aimed at Remy.

"As Rainee said, it went right through you," Remy replied, "All I had to do was clean it out, stitch it up and apply a dressing. But if it had gone just a coupla inches to the left, you'd be looking at losing your kidney."

"Ouch," I said, "I've only got one left," realizing that I'd actually dodged a bullet.

"Exactly," said Rainee, "But at least you've got another war wound to show off to the ladies."

"What ladies?" I said, "I don't see them banging down my door!" I joked, but deep down knowing that Remy was right. I was already down to a single kidney from another complicated situation like the one that had unfolded only hours earlier.

"Would anyone like tea?" Pip asked above the laughter, "I'm parched."

And so it went on, my little family spooning out the love I needed, to help me heal and return to action.

Chapter 32

When all of my friends and my daughter had finally left the boat, apart from Pip who was staff, I finally took a nap in my bed, grateful for the peace and tranquility of the harbor. It was a wonderful solace to realize that I was still alive, still able to taste the ocean's breeze that ambled through my cabin's porthole, and to hear again, the unencumbered bustle of nature that sang from the birds just outside my room.

As I drifted off to sleep, my mind allowed me to dream, but this time vividly in full color, which is not something I had ever remembered doing before. Images and scenes floated through my slumber, of Molly, my greatest achievement in life who I could never again jeopardize because of my stupid and ill-thought-out recklessness. I also realized in this fleeting moment, that I needed her far more than she needed me.

I dreamed of Remy, my compatriot, my brother-in-arms, my drinking partner, my emotional comfort blanket, my friend for life. In my dream, I promised Remy that I'd be there for him whenever he needed me. I was genuinely happy that I had introduced Memphis to Remy, because I knew there was a budding romance and a rosy future for those two. Sometimes, you just feel it in your bones.

And there was Joe, my larger than life music buddy, with whom I had shared countless jamming sessions and nightclub outings, a man who made everything seem like life was just a blast to enjoy while you still had it. And in his own inimitable way, he was probably right, although Joe didn't have a kid to worry about like I did. Not one that he was aware of, anyway.

Nate would miss my patronage and our late-night chats, but he had so much on his plate with the bar and his ongoing medical conditions, to spend too much time missing me. Life in the Army and the Police would always leave their physical, as well as mental scars on you. I knew it from my own experiences.

Then the dream suddenly flipped to Rainee, the young kid I'd rescued from what might have ended in a life of prostitution, but instead, she'd become my greatest and most loyal female friend. I loved her almost like a daughter, and of course, she did have those "Fuck you, Coop" retorts that reminded me of having an unruly teenager.

But she was properly grown up now, and I knew the derogatory comments were delivered with love, and always with my best interests at heart. And she had saved my life on that anonymous neighborhood street when she'd delivered me back to Remy, to administer his life-saving medical skills.

Images of Diablo and Kinky fluttered into the dream too. Diablo would probably miss me, but Kinky? Fat chance.

And then Pip came into view as my mind kept rebounding from image to image, scene to scene, my faithful and ever-perky assistant who organizes my very existence. I guiltily thought that she'd genuinely miss coming to the boat each day. Well, she'd definitely miss Diablo and Kinky.

And then Pip literally came into view in real life.

"How are you feeling, boss?" she asked in her pure and very gentle tones.

"I was having a dream," I replied, my eyes now half open and awakened from my reverie, "Dreamt about you, in fact."

"Don't go getting any ideas, Coop, you might be laid up right now, but we will never be laying up," she said, "You're old enough to be my father."

"Oh, stop it, Pip," I quickly responded, "You're staff anyway, and you know what they say, don't shit…"

"Where you eat. Exactly," she said. finishing the phrase for me.

"So, what brings you down to my lair anyway?" I asked.

"You had another phone call earlier on," she said.

"A case?"

"I've no clue."

"Did they say what they wanted?"

"Just left a message for you to call her. She'd called before when Rainee had answered your cell, but had hung up. When I answered the phone this time, she asked if I was your girlfriend. How I laughed," she said, smiling at the notion, "Anyway, she left a number."

"Did she have a name, perchance?"

"Oh yeah, someone called Layla," Pip replied, handing me a Post-it note, "Here's her number."

Chapter 33

Joe Jarvie was anxious, maybe even a little nervous. After Rainee had sent the video clip and given him the rundown on what had happened at Flick's boyfriend's place, he hadn't heard neither hide nor hair from her. And that was never a good thing with Flick.

Although their marriage had never been featured in Husband & Wife magazine on how to make a perfect relationship, they had kinda got along. Joe wasn't stupid enough to think that the only reason Flick had tricked him into marrying her, was love and adoration, he knew she was in it solely for the money.

And that was fine, because they did have great sex, and she left him alone most of the time and she didn't seem to care much that he often had girls come back to the house. It was what he termed as a 'quid pro quo' way of living inside a marriage. It suited him.

Until it didn't. He always guessed that Flick was getting laid occasionally elsewhere, but then so was he, so he couldn't really cry foul. But since she had met the new toy boy, Flick began to care less about what Joe thought, often brazen about it and kind've shoving it in his face. And, she was spending more and more of his money now, as though it was an endless supply, which it wasn't. The big punch in the stomach, was that the kid was flat broke and that he, Joe, was now paying for the boy's lifestyle.

Ergo, the sudden need to get Flick out of his life. And Coop and Rainee had indeed delivered, the video he had seen was the most damning evidence he could possibly need to finally smoke the marriage. He should be exhilarated, not anxious.

But sitting here at midnight, he realized that the rented recording studio he was in, was costing him six hundred bucks an hour and beginning to become a drain on his wallet. Sure, he was enjoying writing and laying down tracks with his new band, *Shamenless*, but he was the lone fall guy when it came to paying the bill.

He could move the album sessions to his own studio at home, which was lying idle most of the time, but the kids in the band wanted to taste what it would be like to record in a legendary commercial studio. He'd been there, so he couldn't blame them.

And it was a tight band that he'd put together, young and eager too. None of them had any experience of writing songs, so Joe was happy to take on that task. He also realized in his sober moments that if the album did take off, he'd be getting a fat lot of writing-royalty checks.

As he sat next to his sound engineer inside the control room, he watched through the glass that separated the mixing desk from the studio, as his four apprentices punched out another of his songs. His engineer/mixer, Troy Beauchamp, was pulling on a vape, exhaling mango flavored clouds of 'smoke'. When did studios change the rules on smoking? Back in the day, he and his engineer would have had a hundred cigarette butts in the ashtrays by now. And nowadays, there weren't even any ashtrays in studios.

His band might be young, but man, they could play. He would add his own guitar solos and riffs later when he laid down his vocals. And the truth was, that right here, right now, in this studio doing what he loved most, Joe Jarvie was in his element. For him, there was nothing better or sexier.

But Flick was unleashed and pissed now, and she wasn't someone you wanted to fuck with. And his business manager wanted to have a meeting later in the week to discuss finances. He looked forward to that like a hole in the head.

"Guys? I'm calling it a day now, get outta here and we'll regroup in a coupla days at my place," he said, instantly turning off the cash cow.

Chapter 34

That evening, I felt well enough to give Layla a call. I must admit, hearing her voice stirred something in me that caught me off guard. After relaying a dumbed-down version of the shooting, she sounded genuinely horrified, and was ready to jump in her car and drive over to see me. I assured her that I was fine, just a little fragile, but definitely on the mend.

We chatted for a bit about the bar, and she explained that Nate had given her Thursday off, so we made plans for her to come over to the boat in the early afternoon and I would take her out in the Caddy and show her around town, maybe even grab an early supper.

I heal well, not exactly sure why that is, but I've been shot a few times and I've recovered quite quickly on each occasion. Which is why on this Saturday evening, I had moved from my bed to a chair on the dock, where if you recall, is where you and I first met at the beginning of this journey.

And I wasn't alone, because sat next to me in an identical chair, was Remy, having already dispatched three bottles of Yuengling.

"You're moving better," he said, "You're recovering almost as quickly as the last time."

"You should feel what it's like inside this old body of mine," I replied.

"I know, we've both been through it, it fucking hurts for a week," he replied, taking another gulp from his almost empty bottle.

"Anyway, I owe you one for patching me up, partner, I'll drink to that, so thank you."

"No worries, kemo sabe, glad that I could help."

"So, you and Memphis looked pretty loved-up the other day, do I hear wedding bells in the near future?"

"It's good, man, I mean, it's real good," said Remy, "We've been taking it slow since we met, and I'm not sure about us hitching up together yet, but we did finally make it to fourth base this week. Fifth base, to be more exact."

"I don't need to know, so I'm not gonna ask," I replied, "But quickly changing the subject, I haven't looked at the radar since before the night you stitched me up, what's happening?"

"It ain't good, man, it ain't gonna take long for that tropical storm to become a full blown 'cane."

I shivered myself, at the thought of yet another powerful hurricane making landfall in South Florida, it was all I needed right now.

"Okay, subject change then, have you heard anything more about our neighbors since they suddenly took off?" I asked.

"I have actually, they emailed me this very morning," Remy replied.

"Are they coming back so I can get back to watching thongs? I replied, jokingly, "I'm kind've missing the show."

"Actually, they are coming back, although I'm pretty damned sure you don't miss being tranquilized in the middle of the night," he joked.

"Well, the ten grand was worth it," I laughed, "So when are they due in?"

"Any day now, as a matter of fact."

Chapter 35

Flick hated Joe now, not just because she had a dinner plate sized bruise on her ass, but also because she'd broken four nails in the process and she'd only just been to the manicure parlor the day before.

She wasn't so much as hiding out at The Breakers hotel that lay nestled on the beach facing the Mediterranean on Palm Beach Island, more that she had no desire to go back to Joe's house now. And damn, The Breakers was nice, and it was being charged to her black Centurion American Express card, so Joe would be picking up the bill whether he realized it or not. Fuck him.

Divorce wasn't a potential now, it was a certainty. She felt stupid that they hadn't pulled the drapes that night, and that that two-timing bitch, Rainee, had managed to record one of her many recent sex sessions with Tommy. And of course, Joe's lawyer had emailed the video to her the very next day. She was going to miss Tommy, hell, the kid even looked like Tommy-Lee, and the boy could fuck for America.

But she had a plan now, and although everything had been quickly brought forward because of that video, she knew it was time to implement it. Once it was done, she'd have to lose Tommy boy, which she thought, really was a huge shame.

She had a little time though, so she might as well use it productively in preparation for her next adventure. And the thing about her, is that she always had a fallback plan, her safety net, as she called it.

And as long as she remained a visual catch to the stupid, rich dumbasses that littered the state of Florida, she could always score. That was the beauty of the global male population, men were so gullible, led entirely by their dicks. Flick didn't even have to be smart for these men, they only wanted one thing. However, concealed behind the mask of feigned ignorance she wore for them, lurked a remarkably intelligent and callous woman.

Lying on the sun lounger by the pool in her luxury surroundings, she examined her sun-kissed physique. Her legs retained their statuesque, slender form, her waist trim and her tummy flat. Her augmented breasts stood firm and youthful, a testament to the implants she'd received six months prior. It was a satisfying transformation.

She pulled a compact from her beach bag, removed her sunglasses, and flipped it open to look in the mirror.

"Time's a great healer, but it's no beautician," she muttered to herself, "Guess I'll need some touch-ups if I wanna reel in another rich dumbass."

She lay back, tossing the compact back into her bag, and once again continued to relax in the sun on Joe's dime, singing along to Sade's *Smooth Operator* which was wafting in the background via the hotel's audio system.

"You're singing my song, Sade, you go, girl."

Chapter 36

Layla had kind of imagined that Coop was a 'keep it on the downlow' PI, who took on the easier private investigation cases, to pretty much keep his head above water. She pondered the pun for a moment when she remembered that he lived on a boat. But she had been utterly shocked to find out that he was recovering from a near fatal gunshot wound from one of his assumedly innocuous cases.

But as she thought more about him, she surprised herself that she was actually looking forward to seeing him today. Because since leaving Carlo, the idea of any relationship in the future was the furthest thing from her mind. She thought about her current existence once more, an economical life in a one-room bedsit, no credit card, no bank card even, just her savings hidden in a security box at a small bank in a local plaza.

But the thing was, she realized that she had finally found some form of happiness and a balanced equilibrium, where she didn't have to worry about what awful pain she might next experience. If ever Carlo found her, he would make her disappear as nonchalantly as stepping on a cockroach. And in a way, she understood his anger and desire to see her dead, but that reason needed to remain a secret for now. Being married to a Mafia boss was not a badge for any girl to wear.

She fussed around the apartment, putting together a beach bag of towels and sun lotion, with a bottle of wine included along with a couple of plastic glasses she'd borrowed from Nate. She knew that when she met Coop today, he was still going to be pretty fragile, so she hoped she'd included everything for what she thought would just be a nice day of sunshine and discovery.

~~~

I was moving more easily today, assisted by copious ingestions of ibuprofen tablets. The wound had also healed sufficiently enough that Remy was able to remove the stitches, so I was eager to escape the confines of my cabin to spend a pleasant day with a not unpleasant girl.

"Are you sure you should be going out?" asked Pip, ever fussing over me, "I don't want you splitting open."

I laughed, the more time I spent around Pip, the more I realized how much I enjoyed it.

"I'm fine," I replied, "And anyway, I need a change of scenery, even if it's only for a few hours."

"Who's this woman anyway," she asked again, "Layla? Who these days has a name like that?"

"I'm guessing that her mom and dad had a particular penchant for the legendary Mr. Clapton," I replied, as I gently pulled on a clean t-shirt, to go with my freshly ironed khaki shorts.

"Who's Mr. Clapton?"

Oh jeez…

"Doesn't matter, before your time, Pip," I replied, "But she's nice, I think you'd approve."

"Where'd you meet her?"

"At Nate's"

"She's a barmaid, then?"

"They're called mixologists now."

"Whatever. Is she age appropriate?"

"Yes."

"How old?"

"Maybe thirty-five. I never asked. It's rude to ask, no?"

"So not age appropriate, then, but age acceptable."

"So you approve?"

"Haven't met her. Might be a gold-digger."

"Then she'd be shit outta luck, wouldn't she?"

"Yep. You want me to iron a decent shirt to wear?"

"Would you?"

"Sure, you can't meet someone dressed in that old thing. Give me a minute."

My old t-shirt ploy had worked.

As I came up the steps from my cabin, and gratefully sniffed the air that I knew I might not have been breathing this morning, if events had unfolded differently a week ago, I spotted a green Mini Cooper pulling up into a parking space at the water's edge.

Chapter 37

Around an hour after Layla had arrived at Coop's boat, an altogether different meeting was taking place at Sergei Fedorov's rented, but palatial home on Munroe Drive in Coconut Grove. The Great Room, itself the size of most middle-class homes in their entire square footage, looked out over Biscayne Bay, its endless dock coping effortlessly with the motor yacht moored there.

Five men sat in the vast and opulent, marble, gold and crystal bedazzled room, locked in conversation under Sergei's watchful eyes. He fully understood the issue being discussed, but Sergei had never been a man to be fazed by problems. Problems could always be solved, and Sergei Fedorov was the ultimate problem solver.

"*Mne vse ravno, chto vy dumayete, Miroslav, devushka vse yeshche problema...*" raged Volkov, the smallest of the group.

As Sergei sat stoically in his grand Louis Quatorze armchair, listening to the bickering amongst his five guests, he decided that he was growing tired of the conversation.

"*Yesli Galotti ne mozhet s ney spravit'sya, v etoy komnate yest' odin chelovek, kotoryy mozhet sdelat' etu rabotu za nas prosto i effektivno,*" added Kuznetsov, a bear of a man, forcibly arguing with Volkov.

"Enough!" yelled Sergei, making his point, his fist slamming down on the table next to him.

The room grew instantly silent. The five men faced Sergei, all utterly aware that when Sergei spoke, it was time to listen.

"Gentlemen," he said, his low, calm and commanding voice belying his notorious credentials, "Might I suggest we continue in English for our guest?"

The silenced men now stared at the large monitor in the center of the room that displayed the Zoom app. Although they could see themselves in the smaller picture on the screen, the main picture was black because the person at the other end had switched off their camera.

The guest hadn't uttered a word since the meeting began, mainly because she neither spoke, nor understood, a single word of Russian. But the silent Israeli woman did indeed speak English, fluently.

"I apologize for my comrades, it would appear that we have forgotten our manners," continued Sergei, directing his voice to the screen.

Shira Kadosh was unmoved, almost bored with the heated exchanges she'd been witnessing, from what she saw as children in an adult playground.

Sergei had contacted Kadosh's handler on the standard encrypted military messaging service used by her company, and had secured her services for two million dollars. It was not a sum of money to be sniffed at.

But as she had sat silently and listened to an irrelevant conversation in a language she did not understand or care for, the long and the short of it was that she was there for one thing only, and that was a name and an address.

"Who is the target?" she asked quietly, her electronic voice-changer disguising the fact that she was female.

"It's a girl," replied Sergei.

"That is of no interest to me," she replied.

"I understand," said Sergei, already knowing that Cassidy's gender was irrelevant to this killing machine.

"A name?"

"Cassidy Swain," replied Sergei, "She needs to be eradicated."

"It's what I do."

"Of course."

"And where might I find this Cassidy Swain?" asked Kadosh, the calm of the assassin oozing through every part of her unmoving body.

"We will have that information for you, soon," said Sergei, armed with the knowledge that Kadosh had an emotionless killer instinct more savage than even his own.

"Call me when you have located the target."

And in that moment, she was gone, the six men still staring at a black screen, realizing that their conversation had been futile.

"Shall we eat?" asked Sergei to the other five, "I do believe that the chef is ready for us."

Chapter 38

It was nice to finally be out. The cool breeze was delicious as it gently passed through the open windows into the Caddy's interior.

As I navigated south on A1A, opulent beachfront homes to the right, and the dazzling sight of the Atlantic Ocean to the left, I suddenly realized that my daily existence in this subtropical paradise, was probably most people's greatest dream. It would be their ultimate vacation, so I pinched myself that I lived here. And I was still alive, which was a bit of a bonus considering recent events.

"What do these people do to own homes like these?" Layla asked, "I mean, they can't all be criminals, can they?"

"You'd be surprised," I answered, "But no, not all of them, some were born wealthy and others have just made a shedload of money in what we call the American Dream. But yeah, we have our fair share of criminals here too."

"Where are we headed, do you have a plan or are we just seeing where the road takes us?"

I smiled, as I realized that I had a free day to go wander with this lovely companion today.

"I have an idea of where we're headed to," I replied, increasingly feeling the soreness from the seat belt strapped across my abdomen, "But there's a nice little place called Hammock Beach further south, where I thought we might have a picnic."

"Cooper Hemingway, you're definitely speaking my language, I love beach picnics. Never did that when I was married."

"You were married?" I asked.

"Yes," she said, instantly reminded of the fact that she still was married, and immediately regretting her slip of the tongue. But she did feel relaxed in Coop's company, so it was easy to have accidentally mentioned it.

"How long were you married for, if that's not an impolite question?" I asked.

Layla suddenly realized that if she told Coop when she got married and for how long, he would easily do the math and come up with the answer that she was either very recently divorced or that she was still married. But she hated to lie to this man, who really was quite charming in his roguish way.

"Oh, for about twelve years or so," she replied, truthfully.

"I'm sorry, didn't mean to pry."

"I got married very young," she responded swiftly, acutely aware that she was stretching the truth. Her tone held a hint of reluctance as she continued, "It was one of those impulsive decisions, you know?"

"Any kids?" I asked, "Shut me up if I'm being too personal."

At least she didn't have to lie about this, she could be totally forthcoming on that subject.

"No, no children," she said, "My husband didn't want any."

"Okay," I replied, "That sometimes happens, and I guess for many different reasons."

"How about you? I remember you saying when we first met that you had a daughter and that your wife had left you on your own to raise her. That's pretty unusual for a guy."

"In hindsight, I guess I didn't give it much thought really," I reflected, my mind filled with a mixture of nostalgia and affection, "Molly, she was an amazing child, and now she's grown into an incredible young woman. I couldn't be prouder. Sometimes, I feel like I've hit the jackpot in the daughter department."

And I need to keep lucky and not put myself at risk as I had done the previous week…

"I'm sure she is lovely given that she has a great dad," Layla responded warmly, "Does Molly ever hear from her mom?"

"No, not a word since the day she walked out," I replied matter-of-factly, "But honestly, it's fine by me. She has no idea what she's missed, it's her loss."

"Doesn't Molly want to try and get in touch with her? She must want to know something about her mother?" Layla continued, "Is she even alive?"

"Molly's never really shown any interest in Genevieve. I've shown her some photos, but she just remarked on how pretty she was and took no further interest. As for whether she's alive or not, your guess is as good as mine. But I do hope she's out there somewhere, because she gave me something truly amazing in Molly, and for that, I'm grateful."

"Is Genevieve French? Sounds like a French name," Layla asked, trying to discover a little more about Coop.

"Genevieve was half French, half Swiss, and believe it or not, and I know it's such a cliché, but I met her at a wedding where I was best man."

"Sounds almost as clichéd as how I met my husband," she replied, laughing now.

"Tell me about him?"

"Uh… I'd sooner not, if that's okay with you? Not just yet anyway."

"Sure, no worries…" I replied, realizing that maybe I'd touched a nerve with her, "Listen, we're going to have to pull off the highway to head inland in a minute, and find a Publix with a deli counter."

"Why's that?" she asked.

"Well, if we're gonna have a picnic, then we're going to need some food," I replied.

"Of course, doh! But we don't need to pick up wine, I brought a bottle with me," she replied, pulling it from her bag, and now clearly excited about how the afternoon would unfold.

Chapter 39

Remy was all over his phone that morning. His paranoia about the coming storm that might, just might become a hurricane, had him checking the radar every ten minutes.

"I'm beginning to think you're having an affair with someone, you never seem to put your phone down these days, Mr. Washington."

"I'm sorry, Memph, I don't understand myself sometimes, I ain't scared of nothing that comes my way, but jeez, these friggin storms freak me the fuck out every year in hurricane season."

Memphis pulled down the sheet that covered him, revealing a stocky, but taught and muscled torso.

"You want some *breakfast*? Might take your mind off things?" he asked, a small glint in his blue, blue eyes.

Remy knew that hurricanes didn't scare Memphis, hell, he didn't know of anything that scared him. But it was kinda nice to know that Memphis was going to be with him, which was the first time he would be with a partner during what was always a nightmare for Remy.

"I might be tempted," Remy replied, turning from his seated position on the side of the bed and revealing his own extraordinary physique, marked only by scars from serving in the military.

"You know, it's true what everyone says," said Memphis, you do bear an uncanny likeness to Denzel, just a little meaner looking."

"If I had a dollar …." quipped Remy, as he leaned in closer to his companion. His hand slowly ventured south from his chest, beginning its tantalizing exploration.

The air was thick with a shared anticipation, the intensity of their connection palpable. Each stroke of Remy's fingertips carried a promise, an invitation to surrender to the intoxicating pleasure that was assured. As Remy began his descent, Memphis couldn't help but release a contented sigh, his nails digging deep into the fabric of his desire.

"But I love this beautiful face more than Denzel's," Memphis declared, his voice tender as he cradled Remy's face in his large, but gentle hands.

"You ain't so bad yourself, for a white boy," Remy replied, with a mischievous smile.

His fingers made their journey through the flowing strands of snow-white hair, finally resting on Memphis' lips, "And you kinda remind me of one of those old-time wild west cowboys, with your flowing locks and this cute little handlebar mustache."

"I'll take it, I always wanted to be a cowboy," said Memphis, pulling Remy closer, their desires aligned as they melted into each other's embrace.

Remy gently pulled away for a second,

"I think breakfast may very well spill over into brunch," he said.

"Good, I'm hungry…"

Chapter 40

As they walked into the Publix store, headed directly for the deli counter, Layla realized that today was the first time she had begun to feel as though her old life was a thing of the past. She was totally relaxed in Coop's company, even felt as though they were an old married couple, just out doing the weekly grocery trip.

He was so easy to be with, and he seemed genuinely kind too. She watched as he stopped briefly in the aisle to grab a can from the top shelf for a little old lady struggling to reach.

"Why, thank you," she said, stashing the can of sweetcorn in her shopping cart, "You're very kind!"

"De nada," he'd replied, smiling at the woman, *"Anytime, ma'am."*

Layla felt a sudden urge to hold his hand as they continued down the aisle, almost a compunction to do so. But then she realized that they weren't even a couple, weren't even dating, so she felt foolish that the thought had even materialized in her mind.

"This is nice," she said.

"What? You mean going to the store?" I laughed, aware that actually, I was enjoying it too.

"Yeah, just feels kinda normal, I guess."

"I'll take you to all the best places, we could go visit a Home Depot if you like," I said, laughing once more.

160

"I've never been to one," she replied, sadly realizing that it was actually true, having never needed to visit a hardware store during her marriage with Carlo.

"You haven't lived," I said, "Next date, we'll do Home Depot, Walmart and CVS, and then end the day by having dinner at an Olive Garden!"

Next date? That would actually be pretty nice…

She loved his humor and his gentle ribbing, it was incredibly refreshing for her.

We arrived at the deli counter, and I asked Layla if she was a vegetarian.

"I grew up on a farm," she replied, realizing that she had let slip another piece of her past, "So absolutely not, I'm a red meat kinda girl."

"Good to know," I replied, reaching for a ticket from the machine.

I didn't know what Layla was thinking, but it did feel so easy to be with her. I'd almost reached for her hand earlier on, but then suddenly had had second thoughts, and stopped myself, mid-motion. I wondered if she too had felt the urge.

Probably not…

"Number 47!" the voluptuous African-American girl behind the counter called out.

"That's me," I replied, showing her my ticket.

"What can I get you, baby?" the girl asked.

A bit forward, but hey ho…

"Can we get a half pound of turkey breast, and a half pound of beef to start with?"

"You got it, baby, coming right up."

Seriously?

She waltzed off and began pushing turkey and beef through the meat slicer, with speedy and alarming efficiency. Although I did notice a couple of Band-Aids on her fingers.

"She seems to like you," said Layla, nudging her elbow into my arm.

"I have to fight them off!"

"Is that all, baby?" the girl asked, laying the two wrapped packages on top of the glass counter.

"I need a few other things," I replied, "Can I get a wedge of Emmental and one of those Camembert rounds? Maybe a chunk of smoked Gouda too?"

"Course you can, baby, anything else?"

"Yeah, can you do me a mix of the Kalamata olives, the stuffed tomatoes and… maybe a bunch of those sweet chili peppers as well? Oh, and a couple of the Pan Cubanos, please?" I responded, my hunger growing as I gazed upon the wonderful array of deli food in front of me. The rule of not shopping for food when you're hungry, was instantly lost on me.

"No worries, baby, you feeding the whole beach today?"

"Nah, just have a big appetite," I said laughing, "And who can resist a girl like you with what you have on offer here?"

Layla began giggling now, realizing that I was schmoozing the girl.

"I'm polyamorous," the girl abruptly stated, right out of nowhere.

"You like parrots?" I suggested.

"No, I love more than one person."

"Me too, I'm ambidextrous."

"No, I mean I have a boyfriend and a girlfriend."

"Tricky..."

"But they know about each other."

"Oh!" I exclaimed.

"My girlfriend's coming over from the U.K. for Christmas."

"That's nice, you could toast marshmallows... the three of you."

"She likes cheese, French cheese."

"Fromage a Trois?"

"But she loves fish 'n chips too."

"That'll work..." I concluded.

Layla was now trying desperately not to burst out laughing, and had turned a one-eighty to look away, but squeezing my arm at the same time.

"That all, baby?" the girl asked, handing me my packages.

"Yes, thank you," I replied, now trying to suppress my own giggles, "See you at Christmas?"

"You got it, baby, see you then."

We hurried away toward the checkout, now unable to stifle our laughter.

"You do attract them, don't you, Cooper Hemingway?"

"Seems that way, but what can you do?" I replied, instinctively putting my arm around her shoulders. And strangely, she didn't seem to mind…

Chapter 41

The album was on the home straight now, Joe could almost visualize the finish line. Canceling the sessions at Rock City Studios and moving the band into his own studio at home, had actually not been a problem at all with them.

He'd thought he was going to be met with a whining chorus of pissiness from each band member, but the additional offer of accommodation in the house had been the dealmaker. They were loving being waited on hand and foot by Felipe, and spending the daylight hours on Joe's private beach.

Financially, this was very good news, particularly after Joe's meeting with his business manager, Angel Ramos-Juarez. Angel's first name was meant to be pronounced, *An-hel*, but no one called him that, so he was simply known as, The Angel.

But angels don't always come bearing good news, and at the end of what had become a six-hour meeting that day, the news certainly wasn't pleasant for Joe.

Angel wasn't a man to pull punches, so he laid it straight down on the line for Joe. Yes, he owned his house, albeit with a two-million-dollar mortgage from Chase Bank, and the value of the property was likely north of seven million, but the downside was that there wasn't much cash at the bank.

His cars, his guitar collection, and his artworks were all paid for, and as a whole, they were worth more than the capital Joe had in the house, but Joe had shown no intention of wanting to part with any of them. And his spending on a daily basis was off the charts, which didn't even include the rising costs with the band. And he could never fire Felipe.

Angel had then added in the prospect of Flick becoming his soon to be ex-wife, and that was going to take a huge number to pay her off. Joe had groaned at this, laying his head on the table and cursing her, cursing himself too for being such an idiot. The truth was, that although Joe was pretty wealthy in capital assets, Flick was probably going to devour half of them, so he needed cash. Soon as.

It wasn't as though Joe had never learned the value of money, because he had. He'd grown up in a working-class family, flipping burgers at fifteen and working nights in a gas station. He knew how hard it was to find the dollar.

But then, at the age of twenty-three, the band that he'd formed in his dad's garage, literally a garage band, had been spotted by a record company exec, playing a set at *Jack Rabbits Live* in Jacksonville. The venue hadn't been too difficult to get a shoe in, because it wasn't big, more an intimate comedy club with a tiny stage.

But that night, having honed their set at other small clubs up and down the coast of Florida, Joe's band, *Vile Urchins*, had simply blown the audience away. The music exec, Craig Kenny, had immediately spotted an opportunity, and was quickly inside the band's tiny dressing-room soon after they had left the stage.

To cut a long story short, they signed to WestCoastPacific, one of the big labels based in Los Angeles, recorded their debut album, began a nationwide tour and became overnight global superstars. Suddenly, Joe and his band members were rich, even though they were on a terrible deal. And Joe was the wealthiest, because Joe wrote all the songs.

"Look, Joe," said Angel, "It ain't all bad."

Joe looked up from the table where his face had been planted in despair.

"How come? All I see is the end right now."

"So… here's the good news," said Angel, "The record label made one mistake when they signed you all those years ago."

"I doubt it, they stitched us up, well and truly," replied Joe, still thinking about life without money. Well, life without money in his eyes.

"I checked back on the contracts they did back then and compared them to the ones they use today. And the royalty section of the contract is vastly different nowadays," said Angel, opening a PDF on his laptop that showed scans of every document Joe had ever signed.

"What does that even mean, Angel, you've lost me. Sorry, man."

"Well, fortunately for you, they used a template from an older contract when they signed you for writing royalties, and in the boilerplate legalese, I recently discovered that all the rights of every song you've ever written, automatically revert to you after twenty-five years," explained Angel.

"So, when is the twenty-five years up?" asked Joe, now sitting bolt upright in his chair.

"Six months ago."

"Jeez, Angel, you're a fucking genius!" yelled Joe, suddenly awakened from his haze of melancholy.

"That's why they call me The Angel."

"I could kiss you, man!"

"Whoa, hold on. There is one caveat that you need to understand," said Angel.

"Whaassatt?" asked Joe, now only dreaming of what he could spend his new-found wealth on."

"Your ownership of the back catalog isn't going to make you a whole lot of cash these days, is it? Your records no longer sell in their millions, more like in their hundreds now."

"Fuck," said Joe, his head immediately slumping back to the table, the melancholy and depression returning with a thud.

"You need a hit, something new. You remember what happened to Michael after *Thriller* was released in '82?

"It ain't something I'll ever forget, everyone who bought that record wanted to get their hands on everything he'd ever done in his whole life," said Joe, now thinking about how his own back catalog could generate enormous revenues if the new album was a hit.

"And he wasn't even able to promote it on MTV either."

"I know that, black artists were banned on that channel, right up until Michael released Thriller, and it was outselling everything, so they had to show his videos. Fuckers."

"Are you working on anything at the moment?" asked Angel.

"Yessss!" yelled Joe, "I've got a new band, *Shamenless*, they're friggin' awesome!"

"Okay… are you writing the songs?"

Angel was now thinking that perhaps Joe wasn't going to be an ex-client after all.

"Of course, man, these guys are brilliant but they couldn't write a song if their lives depended on it," Joe replied, now laughing at the idea of any of them having a single decent song in them, combined.

"Are you recording yet?" asked Angel, now realizing how suddenly enthusiastic Joe was about his music, something he hadn't seen in a very long time.

"Yeah, we've almost finished the debut album, it's friggin' smokin', Angel!"

"If we have something to market, you may be making a big comeback, Joe Jarvie, and I love the idea of the rest of the band being kids. Makes it so easy for me to get you signed."

"Why's that?" Joe asked.

"Because youth is the only thing that seems to matter in the music industry these days. But youth combined with a proven rock star songwriter is golden."

"D'you really think so?" asked Joe, suddenly getting his mojo back.

"I do," said Angel, no doubt about it. Can I listen to anything you've already laid down?"

Although Angel was no musician himself, he loved music and enjoyed being part of the industry, even if only in the managerial aspect.

"Dude! The kids are already in the studio right this minute, rehearsing the last song on the album. C'mon, you're gonna friggin' love it, man!"

But as Joe led Angel through the house to the studio, like a kid who'd just discovered candy, Angel had other more important things in his mind that would need to be dealt with quickly.

If the new album was going to be the great success that Joe was dreaming about, Flick would need to be his ex-wife before the money came rolling in again. Because from his experience with Flick, he knew she was armed with the natural ability to smell dollars from a thousand yards away.

Chapter 42

As I spread out the blanket on the sand, Layla began to unpack the deli assortment. I think that maybe I'd over-indulged because the spread of food was enough to feed six, and not just the two of us.

"Who's making the sandwiches, me or you?" I asked.

"I'll do it," she replied, "I'm thinking you're a beef and Emmental guy, maybe throw in some sweet peppers too?" she asked, already slicing a Pan Cubano.

"That'll work for me," I replied, putting down some rocks on the blanket's corners, and swiping a couple of olives from the plastic container, "I'll open the wine."

In many ways, I still couldn't quite believe that I was lying on this beach with Layla, I just don't think I ever saw it happening. My defenses were up at that moment, because it felt almost too good to be true.

"I can't remember the last time I did something like this," I remarked, sitting up on the blanket.

"I definitely can't remember, because I haven't ever done this before," Layla replied, remembering that she'd spent many a night sleeping alone on beaches in recent months.

"We should do it again…"

In that moment, I felt content, blissful, and even with the pain that still existed in my body, I was so relaxed as I lay back again, that my eyes began to close as the sun shone down on us.

I must have dozed off for twenty or thirty minutes, because the next thing I felt was Layla gently nudging me awake.

"I'm sorry, I can't believe I just fell asleep on you," I said, somewhat embarrassed.

"You've been shot, Coop, I think you need all the sleep you can get right now."

"Well, I'm still sorry."

"Don't be. More wine?" she asked, after handing me another Cubano to replace the one I'd already devoured, this time filled with turkey and Camembert.

"Are you fattening me up for Christmas?" I joked, reaching for the remainder of the wine and replenishing her glass, and half-filling my own.

"No! But this is such a perfect day that we might as well make the most of it," she replied, laying down next to me. Not touching, but close to.

~~~

The picnic had been perfect. Simple, but absolutely perfect. The beach had been oddly uncrowded, our quickly purchased picnic assortment had been fabulous and endless, and the wine was now gone. We'd even swum in the ocean. Well Layla had anyway, I just paddled because my wound was not yet healed enough.

We spent the entire afternoon, just chatting about anything and everything. But eventually, as we had grown tired from the sun, we had decided to pack up, return to the Caddy, and head back north to Palm Beach.

The drive back to the marina was spectacularly beautiful that evening, the glistening ocean lay calm to our right, and the familiar golden glow to our left was radiated by the burning orange sun, as it began to spread its rays across the horizon. I was happier than a clam at high tide, as the Caddy's engine burbled along, casually devouring the miles ahead.

"Coop, I want to tell you that I've literally had one of the best days ever. You've no idea how much I needed this, so thank you, I mean, seriously, thank you," said Layla, brimming with happiness.

"You've no idea how much I enjoyed today too, Layla, so I'm the one who should be thanking you, believe me."

"It's funny, isn't it? You know, you and I have spent so much of our adult lives living near the ocean, and we just take it for granted," said Layla, "And it doesn't take much to slip away to the beach for even a couple of hours and go home feeling like you've been on vacation."

"I totally agree, we become kinda blasé about it, almost forgetting that it's right there on our doorsteps," I added, "So, I'm guessing you've lived in Florida for a while, then?"

In all of our conversations that day, I realized that Layla hadn't really talked about herself much at all, just more about the world in general. And I really did want to find out more about her, because I hadn't been so drawn to anyone in so many years.

"Yeah, I've lived in Florida for quite a few years, but not in this area," she replied, still not giving up on anything concrete or personal.

"But if you've lived in Florida for some time, were you down in Miami?" I continued, hoping to extract a little more from her.

Layla realized how guarded she had been during their time together today, but also on their previous meetings. She decided that Coop was solid, someone she was finding she could trust, even this early into their friendship.

"Yes, I lived in Miami for around twelve or thirteen years, but I'm not from there, as I think you already picked up on," she replied.

"I noticed a faint midwestern accent somewhere in your voice, Minnesota?"

"Close, just a little further south-east, I grew up in Wisconsin," she replied, "But in a town so small, you'll never have heard of it."

"That's a beautiful state. I've been there once before," I said, "And not being American myself, it kinda reminded me of what the original America must have been like, you know, cowboys, horses, cattle, the whole Wild West."

"That's about what Wisconsin is really, not in the cities though, more out in the valleys and plains. But we do have Lake Superior up in the north and Lake Michigan to the east," she continued, clearly holding her home state in pure affection.

"Sounds beautiful," I replied, wanting her to continue opening up to me.

"You should visit again when you have a couple of weeks downtime, it's so beautiful and unspoiled, you can't imagine you're actually in America when you see those gorgeous shorelines."

"I'll take your advice… maybe you could show me sometime," I replied, smiling at her as I said the words.

"And maybe I will," she said, looking at me.

"So, what made you move to Miami?" I asked, "Was it the cold winter months in Wisconsin?"

She laughed.

"You could say that, Coop, because I don't miss the winters, they are sooo cold!"

I laughed with her because I'm a bit of a sun chaser myself, and I wouldn't survive long where Layla came from. And it was even worse further north, up in Minnesota.

"But no, it wasn't really that. I'd grown up on my parents' farm, been with horses and dairy cattle all my life, so I was used to the freezing cold of winter."

"Just wanted to see the bright lights of the big city?" I asked.

"No, it wasn't that either… my parents died in an auto accident almost thirteen years ago."

"Oh Layla, I'm so, so sorry," I said, now genuinely regretting that I had been so curious about her past.

"No, no, it's okay, I've had plenty of time to come to terms with that now, it's all good," she replied, "But I couldn't run the farm myself and it had built up huge debts for lots of reasons that I won't bore you with, so I sold up, paid the bills and headed to the sunshine."

I glanced at Layla, as she looked ahead through the windscreen, her arm trailing out of the passenger door's window, smiling the biggest smile as our journey continued.

"Well, I guess you chose something completely different in Miami, it's a beautiful place in general but it has its dark sides," I replied, now keen not to dwell on the passing of Layla's parents.

"Oh, tell me about it, Miami is not the tourist brochure it's made out to be, far from it, actually…"

~ ~ ~

Forty-five minutes after leaving Hammock Beach, we slowly pulled into my parking spot at Riviera Yacht Club.

As we began to retrieve our things from the trunk of the car, we had suddenly grown quite silent, accentuated by the stillness and quiet of the marina.

I walked Layla over to her Mini Cooper, took her bags from her and laid them on the back seat of the tiny British car.

"Thank you," I said, smiling at this now tousle-haired girl standing in front of me, "That really was an unexpected day."

"For me too, Coop," she replied, coming closer to me, "You really are an interesting man."

"Uhm… err…" I stuttered.

"And yes, I would like to see you again," she said, instantly realizing my inability to utter the words I was thinking, "But only if you'd like to?"

"Of course," I replied, "I'd love that."

And with that, she went up on her tiptoes, drew my body to hers, and kissed me gently on the lips. In what seemed like forever, but was only a moment, I felt lightheaded, almost like a dizzy teenager.

"See you soon, Cooper Hemingway," she said, climbing in behind the wheel of the Mini.

I watched on as she reversed out of her parking spot, and then drive slowly toward the exit of the marina.

A hand appeared through the open window, waving, and all I could do was to wave back at her, not really wanting her to leave, but unable to leave the spot where I stood, for maybe one or two minutes after the car had finally disappeared from view.

Chapter 43

Rainee Showers was in her Palm Beach apartment that morning, having had just four hours sleep after an evening-into-night bodyguard gig, for a newly, stupidly wealthy, teenage rapper, Mo-Nay$Neverenuff. Nine hours with the boy and his 'boys' had been a slam dunk, a thousand bucks for pretty much zero effort. But these boys did like to have a female bodyguard around, it was good for their image, *'bro'*. Particularly when that girl looked and dressed like Rainee.

She was eating a bowl of Cheerios at her kitchen table, laptop open and deeply engrossed. Her hand absentmindedly searched for the mug of black coffee to her left, found it, and she emptied half of its contents, in one swig.

She was feeling frustrated, and decided to call Nate.

"Ms. Showers, I don't see your lovely face too often these days, how are you?" said Nate when the call connected.

"Morning, Mr. Ransom, yeah, I know, I missed you last time I called in a few weeks ago to pick up some hot wings to go," she replied, appreciating how good the food was at Nate's, and how badly she ate most of the time.

"I must have been having a rare day off, sorry I missed you," Nate replied, "And stop a little longer next time, dinner's on the house."

"Haha, Nate, I only need one invitation!"

"So, Rainee, what do I owe the honor of this call today, what's up?"

"You know the chick who recently started working for you? What do you know about her?" asked Rainee, straight to the point, as was her style.

"Layla? Not much, really, but I already told Coop that. She showed up one day, asked for a job, and she seemed nice, so I started her working behind the bar. Customers love her, and besides, I'm guessing you might have already met her when you stopped by."

"Really?" asked Rainee.

"Yeah, I think she'd already started here."

Rainee thought about this last comment from Nate. She had seen a new girl there, but that night she was so hungry and keen to get to her job with Mo-Nay$Neverenuff, she hadn't really taken the girl in, except to pay for the wings and hurry out of the bar.

"Do you have a photo of her?"

"Of course I don't, Rainee!" Nate replied, laughing at the idea, "Ask Coop, maybe he has one now."

"Do you know her last name?" Rainee pressed.

'Yeah, Wray, Layla Wray," he replied, "Why do you need to know all of this?"

"Does she have a social security number?" Rainee pressed again, ignoring Nate's question.

"I never asked. You know what it's like, Rainee, I take on dozens of part-time staff here. I don't ask the questions that they don't want to answer, because usually they're gone in three or four months, often sooner."

"But what about payroll, she's on the books, right?"

"Nooo!" Nate replied, chuckling at the idea of barkeeps paying state or federal taxes, "I pay them in cash, or I doubt they'd even want to take the job in the first place!"

"Okay, so all you have is her name, nothing about where she's from?"

"As I said, I don't ask questions."

Rainee was becoming more frustrated than before she'd made the call to Nate.

"How about a car? Does she have one?"

"Yeah, she's got one of those British cars, a Mini Cooper, nice little thing," said Nate.

"That's really helpful, just a few more things I need to know."

"What is this? Twenty questions?"

"Just help me out here, Nate, it's kind've important."

"Okay…"

"Do you know the license plate?" asked Rainee.

"Yeah, I do in fact. Hold on, I noted it down on her application form when she first arrived."

"You have an application form?"

"Of course," Nate replied, "Why wouldn't I?"

"For undocumented workers who you pay in cash from the till?" said Rainee, now laughing out loud at the idea that Nate would even bother.

"I like to do things by the book," said Nate, now sniggering too, "Well, mostly anyway."

Rainee waited patiently, while Nate retrieved Layla's application from his desk files. She finished her coffee in a second swig, and started pushing the remaining Cheerios around the milk in her cereal bowl. They'd gone soft now.

"Got it," said Nate, as he came back on the line, "It's four-two-six-two-alpha-victor-romeo."

"You're a star, Nate, I owe you," said Rainee, now pleased that she had a little more to go on than she did ten minutes earlier.

"But tell me, what's the big deal about Layla?" asked Nate, "She's turned out to be a real find for me, she's fantastic actually."

"Yeah, Coop thinks so too," Rainee replied, "In fact, I know for certain that he's out with her today."

"Hmm… interesting," said Nate, "But honestly, I don't blame him; she's a great girl and I knew he liked her when he met her here, so why not?"

"I'm just checking all the boxes, and you know full well what I'm like."

"I do, Rainee, but you can't forever be looking after your old man, he's forty-six for Christ's sake, he knows what he's doing."

"See, that's the problem, Nate, he doesn't. For a tough guy, who's kinda smart, he can be a little naïve with women. I just like to have his back."

"Naïve? Coop?"

"Yeah, I know that sounds ridiculous, but really, Nate, he literally doesn't have a clue, especially if he's smitten."

"You're not jealous, are you?" asked Nate deliberately, knowing it would stoke Rainee.

"For fuck's sake no, you moron! Of course I'm not jealous, Nate, I just care about him, a lot. You know the story about us, he's kinda like a father-figure, but he's just a bit stupid sometimes."

"Methinks the lady doth protest too much…" said Nate.

"Fuck off, Nate, you're starting to sound like that Shakespeare dipshit, Talbot. I'll see you later for an order of hot wings," laughed Rainee, "And Coop's not my old man."

Chapter 44

At the same time that Rainee was searching for information on Layla, Shira Kadosh was feeling antsy, hunkered down in a hotel room, waiting on the information that Sergei Fedorov had promised would be soon forthcoming.

Sure, it was a nice place to be, the Four Seasons had a lot to offer, she'd even managed to improve her tan on a sun-lounger beside the hotel's pool. It was also on someone else's dime. And the two million she had already been paid, was hers to keep, hit or no hit. In fact, she didn't have much to moan about, if she stopped to think about it.

But Kadosh was not one for sitting around, she could have wrapped this one up, and been on to another high dollar job by now. She wasn't one of the elite assassins for nothing. And she missed her son, seven-year-old Eitan, a name she'd given him for its meaning, 'lion'. And he would grow to be a lion, just like his mother.

Eitan never knew his father, not that Kadosh had wanted that for him. Eitan was the result of rape, and his sperm donor was dead. Kadosh had eliminated the man, soon after she had been assaulted. There wasn't a man in her life, never really had been. Being in this business, and the idea of a regular relationship was never going to happen. And she didn't need anyone, most men were assholes.

But when she was on a mission, as she was right now, her routine didn't falter. Each day, she would go back to her room, disassemble and reassemble the two Israeli Army IWI DAN .338 sniper rifles along with her pair of SIG-Sauer handguns, repeatedly and often.

The sniper rifles had long been her weapon of choice. Not just for the 1,200-meter range accuracy, because the IWI DAN did possess a phenomenal minute of accuracy (MOA), meaning that it was accurate in an expert's hands at one-inch of deviancy per one hundred meters. And Kadosh was a pure and certified, expert sniper. Her kill tally in the Israeli army was testament to that.

So, armed with an IWI DAN, and over a huge distance of say, 1,200 meters, the .338 Lapua Magnum round would deviate by just twelve inches. And Kadosh liked that, because her targets were generally only at a maximum distance of around three hundred meters. One shot, stone dead.

But she also liked it for its collapsible stock, and its MIL-STD 1913 picatinny rail, that could be mounted in a variety of forms to accommodate a wide range of optics setups. And the cherry on the cake was that its skeletal frame weighed a mere fifteen pounds.

Being totally prepared with guns that would never fail her, was the mark of who she was. The mark of an elite soldier who became legendary in the Israeli army. And although she'd killed more men than she could remember, she hadn't killed any women so far.

But right now, as she set about her daily assemble-disassemble routine, she wondered why both the Russian mob and Miami Mafia were still being eluded by a girl with zero training.

She'd received all the current intel the Russians had on the girl from the Miami people, via her handler, and to be truthful, there wasn't much to go on yet. They were pretty much being outsmarted by a Miami housewife, which was comical. That is, if Kadosh had ever possessed a sense of humor. Which she didn't.

She had thought about using her own connections to track the girl down, but decided that, well, why should she? It wasn't her job, although it wouldn't be difficult, so let the idiots do the work. She'd be ready when she got the call.

Chapter 45

Rainee was once again huddled over her laptop to do some more research, given the new information she had from Nate. She'd already downed two more coffees since the phone call, but this time, she'd made triple-shot espressos to keep her mind buzzed.

Pulling up a fresh web page, armed with her new intel, she started off by running the name of Layla Wray through all of the usual social media apps. Facebook, Instagram, Twitter, all of them showed hundreds of Layla Wrays, and she doggedly ploughed through each and every profile to find Coop's Layla. Four hours later, she was still none the wiser, all of them had drawn a blank.

"Goddammit, Layla, you either don't exist, or you're the only girl on the planet who doesn't have a social media presence," she muttered to herself. Although, neither did Rainee, so maybe it wasn't so unusual.

Deciding to can the social media apps, she pulled up another web page to begin a general search on the internet, using the key words, Layla, Wray, Florida, Mini, Blonde… but another hour later, still she came up with nothing that looked like a match.

"Shit," she said, "What the fuck am I doing searching the internet for someone who clearly isn't on it?"

When Coop had first introduced her to the private detective business, he had shown her something called LexisNexis, a data tool he had been using even when he was a policeman in San Francisco. Rainee had long been accessing the LexisNexis database, and now she would find it hard not to have it at hand, it was a crucial tool for her too now. LexisNexis was also used by all of the law departments, from the State Police to the FBI and the CIA, it was their go-to database.

She pulled up the site, and began by inputting Layla's full name. Hundreds of hits came back, and once again, she trawled unswervingly through each and every one of them. The great thing about LexisNexis was that its database provided every mug-shot, every arrest, every birth, marriage and death certificate, and even every speeding ticket that a person had been given.

It was evening now, and Layla had nothing to show for her afternoon endeavors, and she was tired, even after all the caffeine shots she'd had.

But then she hit pay dirt. She dispensed with the girl's name and instead did a search on the Mini's registration. She inputted the digits, 42-62-AVR, and finally found a match. Well, kind've.

"The car is registered in fucking Mexico," she said out loud to no one, "What the hell?"

Fortunately, she was still able to trace the car via the export notes that had come up with the vehicle's Mexican tag.

"I love you, LexisNexis," Rainee muttered again to herself.

From what she could ascertain, the car was yet to be registered as an American vehicle. After scrolling through all of the documents pertaining to the Mini's recent export to the U.S. just a few months prior, she finally found a business address for the company that had bought the Mini, along with three more similar vehicles.

RandyWayneAutos Inc.

16851 S. Dixie Hwy,

Palmetto Bay,

MIAMI, FL 33176

United States of America.

"Bingo," she said, closing her laptop, before deciding what she should do with this newly found information. But there were things to be done prior to that.

Chapter 46

"Aren't you angry? Even just a little bit pissed?"

I was back in my chair on the dock, watching a new thong. Different color, and I think, a different girl. Pretty much the same scene though, so I wasn't disappointed.

"Not really, it's pretty much part of the job. It's what you sign up for, so if you can't take it, you should be doing something else," I replied.

The thong was baby blue this morning, although there was a distinct absence of the previous hirsute and heavy body mass accompanying this new girl today.

"But one day, you're not going to be so lucky, Coop, you're going to run out of luck sooner or later," Pip continued.

"Well, hopefully it'll be later. But thank you for your concern, it's nice to know that the staff cares about me."

Pip sat in the folding chair next to mine, looking splendid and radiant in her above-knee summer dress, revealing perfectly tanned limbs beneath it. My daily dose of purity.

"Well, if you die, there won't *be* a staff, will there? And Molly will be parentless, haven't you thought about that, for goodness sake?" Pip persisted.

As I have said before, I like Pip, she is an inherently good-natured and caring human being. And, to be honest, she had a point.

So, I decided that I would abandon thong-watch and be serious for a moment.

"Yes, I think about it a lot, Pip, and I know I seem to have a kind of blasé attitude to life most of the time, but I do care, very much. Particularly as far as Molly is concerned, that's for sure."

"But don't you want revenge?" she asked.

"On Tommy?"

"Yes, and Flick too, come to think of it," Pip replied.

"If I took revenge on every person I'd been wounded by, I wouldn't have time to do my job," I said, "So there would be no income, and ergo, no staff."

"Stop it, Coop, you're not even taking me seriously, are you?"

"Of course I am, Pip, but right now the police are looking for Tommy, Flick too, so what am I supposed to do?" I replied, "And I'm still in recovery mode because I'm not fully healed yet. So I say, let the police do their job."

"I'd be so angry that someone could get away with trying to murder me, I'd be seething," she said, absentmindedly twirling her hair around her fingers as she also began to watch the activities on the vessel next door.

"Well, as I said, they're probably holed up together somewhere doing the dirty, so the authorities will find them at some point."

I could see that Pip was not convinced.

"Did we get paid?" I asked.

"We did, in full, and with a $5,000-dollar bonus for the video footage Rainee got."

"Am I getting paid again?"

"Of course, I take care of my employees."

"That Joe Jarvie is a stand-up gentleman, wish all our clients were like him," she continued.

"He certainly is."

"How did your date go?" she asked, suddenly deciding on a new line of questioning.

"Ah, I knew we would get to that at some point," I replied, laughing, "You're not jealous, are you?"

"Don't be a twat."

That was the one word I would never have expected to come from Pip's mouth.

"Why the interest, then?"

"Because, of all of the females who have passed through this boat since I've been working here, Layla seems to be different, somehow."

"In what way," I asked.

"Well, for starters, you shaved and wore cologne, put on fresh clothes."

"Isn't that always the case?" I replied.

"Not really, most of the time when you go on a date, your clothes have already seen a wearing, your beard looks like that of a grizzled sailor, and you rarely wear cologne."

I was a little distraught and indignant that my staff thought I looked a mess most of the time. Although that can happen when they get too familiar.

"You guessed right, then," I replied, "Yes, Layla is different, I really like her and I'm taking it slow. She's pretty special."

"I watched through the binoculars when she arrived," said Pip, "She's pretty gorgeous, too good for *you*."

"I think so too. I mean, she's gorgeous. Not necessarily too good for me."

"So don't fuck it up."

Again, another unexpected expletive.

"I'm hungry," I said, "Do we have any pizza left?"

"Nope, I gave that to Diablo this morning, he likes the Meat Feast."

"But I'm really hungry," I countered, "What have we got?"

"I'm putting you on a new diet," Pip announced, now looking at the thong that had just walked along the boat's stern, "I've got to admit though, those girls up there are pretty hot, I'm beginning to understand why you watch."

"It's good that we're finally copacetic," I replied, now joining her in her gaze.

"Do you think I would get the same audience if I paraded about in a thong all day?"

"I'd be selling tickets," I replied, "But back to my hunger, what's on offer?"

"Remy's arriving in around twenty minutes," she replied, "I've asked him to pick up some things from Publix, I'm making Kung Pao Tofu and Roasted Cauliflower and Hummus bowls. Remy's having lunch with us."

"I should put Remy on staff," I replied, "Are we turning vegetarian?"

"You couldn't afford him," she replied, "And yes, you eat too much meat."

"Do I have a say in that?"

"Not really," she replied, rising up from her viewing seat and making her way to the galley.

Chapter 47

Rainee detested Miami. In her eyes, it was a hotbed of vice, villains and vileness. She could feel the change in her mood as she closed in on the city that morning.

She chose not to take her old Impala for the journey, instead opting for the safer option of her Ford F-150 Raptor pickup truck. The 5.2 supercharged V8, 10-speed Raptor was a brute, it was fast, and it was a girl's best protection in some of Miami's nastier areas.

As she turned off I-95 onto US-1, the landscape began to change immediately after the Interstate ended. There were enormous billboards everywhere, not just the old-style paper versions, but now live video screens that stood high above the freeway. Endless ads for all the big box companies, Best Buy, Walmart, Home Depot, Costco and BJ's.

She had always wondered why a company would call itself BJs. Hmmm...

As she merged onto S. Dixie Highway, she noted the University of Miami to her right, and the proliferation of repetitive chain stores that appeared in every American city, coast to coast, from Trader Joe's to Whole Foods, Shake Shack to Arby's.

She knew she was now in the land of automobiles, as she passed dealership after dealership, Ford, Hyundai, BMW, Genesis, Dodge-Jeep and Honda, the list went on and on.

Her Raptor's dashboard navigation showed that her destination lay a half mile ahead, at 16851 S Dixie Hwy, where the big brand dealerships ended, and the rental car businesses, towing companies and diners began.

As she arrived at the marked spot on her screen, she waited for traffic to pass before gunning the big truck across the center median and onto the forecourt of RandyWayneAutos Inc.

~ ~ ~

Across the street, two men sat in a Lincoln Town Car, watching the Raptor that had just pulled onto Wayne Randolph's lot. They didn't do anything immediately, except to note down the license plate of the truck, and stash the Post-its in their wallets.

"Lookie-loos?" asked the bigger man.

"We'll find out soon enough," said the smaller stockier one, "For now, let's just watch."

"Could be someone looking to trade their truck, maybe dealt with Randolph before," the big guy suggested.

"Eddie, just watch. Okay?"

"For fuck's sake, Don, we've been watching this place for weeks now, why don't we just go and see what's going on over there?"

"You were never good with patience, were you?" said Don.

"I'm hot, sticky, hungry and I haven't punched anyone for a month. No, I'm not fucking patient, Don," Eddie retorted, his frustration showing.

"Okay, so tell me how many times we've seen someone on the lot and it's turned out to be nothing?" asked Don, starting the Lincoln's engine, "Just enjoy the air conditioning for a minute."

"I think this individual ain't just a passer-by," Eddie insisted.

"Why not?"

"Because who trades in a 2022 Raptor?"

"Good point, Eddie."

~ ~ ~

Rainee sat inside the Raptor, engine still running, air-con on high.

"Fuck, I swear it gets more humid the further south you go," she said to herself.

She looked around the lot. What was once a busy little one-man-band used car lot, was now deserted, not a car or truck in sight.

What looked like the sales office, a thirty-foot square cabin to the left of the property, was boarded up, and when she looked behind her toward the road, she saw a For Sale sign, newly erected from the look of it.

She put the Raptor in gear, and slowly inched her way down the side of the lot toward the rear boundary.

The owner was clearly a tidy man. Although the lot was deserted, it was easy to see that during his time here, he'd taken care of the greenery and trees that circumnavigated the property. It was immaculate.

When she arrived at the rear boundary, she saw that it backed onto a Krispy Kreme.

She was hungry, maybe there would be someone working in there who knew something about RandyWayneAutos.

Rainee shut the engine off, locked the truck and bounded over the four-foot fence that separated the two properties.

~ ~ ~

"Looks like the guy is having a snoop around," said Eddie.

"Let's wait ten minutes, then take a casual look-see over there," said Don, now starting to feel that Eddie may be on to something.

It was rare, because Eddie was a dumb fuck, and he was only with Don, in case a situation necessitated the use of blunt force, often resulting in trauma when Eddie was suitably polarized.

"You want coffee?" asked Eddie.

"Nah, go get me one of those health juices from down the street," Don replied.

"A fucking health juice?" asked Eddie, "Are you serious, you turning into a fag or sommat?"

Eddie didn't see it coming, certainly wasn't expecting it, as the fist of the smaller man slammed into the side of his head.

"Jeez, man, what the fuck was that for?" asked Eddie, holding his hand to his temple, already feeling the aching throb from the chunky signet on Don's ring finger.

"You gotta look after yourself, Eddie, you should try one, get in shape," Don suggested, looking at the bulk that Eddie had around his midriff.

"Fuck me, you didn't have to do that," said Eddie, realizing now that calling Don a fag, was a big mistake.

"No, I didn't. Just watch your mouth, you moron," Don replied, "Now get yourself down to Auntie's Key to Life Juice Bar, before I do it again."

"Okay boss, waddya want?"

"They have a nice *Diabetes-Kiss Me Goodbye*, I'll take a 20oz and a Tuna Salad bowl," Don replied, now feeling hungry too, "And get one for yourself."

"What should I get?" asked Eddie, having never been in a juice bar in his life.

"Try the *Gut Punch*," Don replied, "You'll enjoy that."

~ ~ ~

As Rainee approached the queue at the counter in the Krispy Kreme, she realized that today was going to be another day of crap food.

When she was next in line, she looked up at the menu behind the counter, salivating at the photos of the doughnuts on offer.

"What can I get you, ma'am?" asked the boy, who was no more than eighteen years old, resplendent in his tan Krispy Kreme-logoed baseball hat and company t-shirt.

"I'll take the Fan Favorite's Half-Dozen and a Triple Espresso," she answered, thinking that she would have something to munch on during her drive back to Palm Beach, "And give me an Americano to go."

"Take a seat right over there by the window, ma'am," replied the kid with the permanent smile, "I'll bring it right on over."

Rainee paid the kid, took a seat where he'd indicated, and pulled out her iPhone. She did a historical Google search on RandyWayneAutos, to see if she could find images of what the dealership had looked like before it had closed down.

Fortunately, she found that Google Maps hadn't updated the street in quite a while and she was able to see, and look around the street she was on. And the place had clearly been a busy little enterprise, by the vast number of vehicles that sat three-deep on the front of the lot.

In one image, there was a man in jeans and Timberlands wearing a Stetson. Could that be the owner?

She was awoken from her thoughts when the kid arrived with her order.

"Anything else, ma'am?" he asked.

"Actually, yeah, there is," she replied, looking up and seeing the name tag on his t-shirt, "What do you know about the car dealership behind you, Mason? Looks like it's all closed down."

"Ah… yeah, closed down a few months ago, kinda sad really."

"How so?" asked Rainee.

"Well, he was a good customer, nice guy too," said Mason.

"The owner? Randy Wayne?"

"Nah, that was just the name that Mr. Randolph used for the business."

"Does Mr. Randolph have a first name?"

"Yeah, Wayne, Wayne Randolph," replied Mason, "We always delivered doughnut orders every day to him, said his customers liked them. So, every morning I'd hop over the fence with three dozen of his favorites. Always tipped well, shame he's gone."

Rainee put down a twenty-dollar bill on the table.

"How do you mean, gone."

"He's dead, ma'am."

"Really? What happened?" asked Rainee.

"Got murdered."

~ ~ ~

Eddie belched. Don sighed. There were times he couldn't help but feel utter disdain for the oaf.

"Come on, I'm not sitting in this car while you unleash your flatulence, let's go," commanded Don.

"I gotta let it out, Don, I get stomach ache if I don't," Eddie grumbled, in defense.

Don cursed him as they got out of the Lincoln, and waited for the traffic to pass before crossing the road toward the lot.

Their mob suits did little to disguise two henchmen entering Wayne Randolph's lot. Anyone who noticed them would have assumed they were up to no good.

They slowly crept down the side of the lot toward where the Raptor was parked.

Eddie tried the door handle of the truck.

"It's locked, boss."

"No kidding," said Don, wondering what the fat idiot would score on a Mensa test.

~ ~ ~

"He was murdered?" Rainee exclaimed, "What happened?"

Mason looked at Rainee, realizing that he should get back to serving other customers, but also enjoying spending the moment talking to the woman.

"Cops arrived day after it happened, he'd been shot twice. A customer had raised the alarm when they looked through the sales office window," replied Mason.

"I want to say I'm shocked, Mason, but this is Miami, and rules don't seem to apply here," Rainee responded, "Was there any talk after the cops had been and gone, about what had gone down?"

"There were lots of rumors," whispered Mason, "But his wife died too."

"What? A double murder?"

"No, she committed suicide at home, hung herself apparently on the same day."

"I'm really sorry to hear this, but you've been an amazing help, Mason, here's a hundred bucks, take that blonde girl over behind the counter out tonight, she's got eyes for you."

Mason's own eyes lit up, not just at this stranger giving him a C-note, but also because he'd wanted to ask Chloe out for months, and maybe she *was* interested, and he just hadn't realized it all this time.

Rainee stood to leave, patted Mason on the shoulder, "See you around, kid, and enjoy yourself tonight."

~ ~ ~

"Hold on, boss, there's a chick coming toward us from the Krispy," Eddie said quietly, immediately reaching inside his jacket pocket for his gun.

"Duck down," ordered Don, "She might have seen us."

Rainee had indeed seen activity by her truck. With her left hand holding the bag of doughnuts and coffee, she slipped her right hand inside the leg pocket of her cargo pants.

There was a reason why she abandoned her normal attire of gym gear in favor of baggy clothing when she was in Miami.

"What's going on over there?" she yelled, quickly marching now toward the Raptor.

Eddie and Don stayed crouched below the fence, grateful that it was covered in vine.

Rainee kept moving forward, but now at a slower pace, hand still in the cargo pocket.

She was maybe fifteen yards from the fence now, when two men suddenly stood, both raising guns and pointing in her direction.

Her hand was now no longer secreted in her pocket, and as the two goons scrambled over the fence, she dropped the Krispy Kreme sack, pulled both of her military-grade tasers and fired a 50,000-volt shot at each man.

Both men went down simultaneously, their bodies jumping epileptically as they writhed in the dirt.

She went over to them, having reloaded the tasers, and gave them a second dose of electricity, kicking away their pistols whilst doing so.

"So," said Rainee out loud, "What do we have here, fellas?"

She searched through each of their pockets and found their wallets, pulling their driver's licenses out to see who they were.

"Eduardo Falcone and Donald Faber," she said quietly, "You really shouldn't mess with girls."

Stowing the wallets in her pant pocket, she retrieved the Krispy Kreme bag, climbed into her Raptor, slowly reversed out of the lot, and headed back north to Palm Beach.

Chapter 48

Don and Eddie hadn't ever seen this version of Carlo. They knew he was one of the meanest motherfuckers in Miami, but right now, it looked as though he was about to explode.

When Don and Eddie had eventually woken up at the back of the Krispy Kreme, they realized that their wallets and guns were gone, and only had vague memories of the girl who had taken possession of them. And when Don had finally made the call to Carlo to tell him what had gone down, Galotti ordered them to his house immediately.

"Just how stupid do you think I am?" Galotti raged, "Am I supposed to believe that two of my entrusted so-called 'bad boys', packing heat, were outwitted and outsmarted by a mere girl? Do I look like a fucking idiot?"

"She wasn't just some girl, boss, you should have seen her," said Eddie, "The bitch was like friggin' Lara Croft on steroids."

"Lara Croft? I have no idea who that is, you dumb fuck, what the hell are you talking about?" growled Galotti, as he whirled on the pair who stood unflinchingly still, behind the vast ebony desk in Galotti's equally vast home office.

"She's that chick in the computer game," Don mumbled, unsure if this particular nugget of information was relevant.

"Listen up, and listen good. We ain't playing computer games here, this is real life," Galotti thundered, "The bottom line is, no matter how you want to dress it up, she was just a fucking girl!"

"I know that, boss, but she was no ordinary girl, even her wheels were stealth-like, never seen a Raptor like that one she had," replied Eddie, somewhat out of his depth now with Galotti, and clutching at invisible straws.

"And she was kinda cute too, but man, she moved like a cheetah, we had no chance," added Don, not really knowing what else to say in their defense.

"She was cute, huh?" Galotti asked, his eyebrow raised derisively.

His tone had suddenly become deceptively calm and measured, as he positioned himself directly in front of his two henchmen.

Don felt Carlo's penetrating gaze on him as the man continued, "And you claim you had *'no chance'*?"

"Boss, she'd had training, I mean, serious training," explained Don, hoping to somehow assuage the situation.

Galotti snapped. His fist came up from nowhere, hitting Don square in the middle of his face. Blood immediately sprayed across the Egyptian rug where Don now lay, his nose now unidentifiable above his mouth, a gap appearing where his front teeth had once resided.

"Boss, boss!" yelled Eddie, laying a hand on Galotti's shoulder to stop him committing more brutal damage to his partner.

Carlo stopped dead in his tracks when he felt Eddie's hand on his shoulder, and Eddie suddenly realized his mistake, an error he couldn't reverse.

You never laid a hand on Carlo Galotti.

In a split second, Galotti had produced his beloved SIG-Sauer from his shoulder holster, and rammed it into Eddie's gaping and quivering mouth, snapping a half-dozen teeth as the barrel found its end stop.

Don's eyes opened as his vision began to crystallize again, watching Galotti push Eddie down onto his desk, the gun still renting space in his partner's mouth.

"You fuck up, and then you have the nerve to lay a hand on me? Who the fuck d'you think you are?" Galotti growled, as he pushed the man's head harshly onto his desk, his pistol now seemingly surgically attached to Eddie's mouth.

Eddie's words were unintelligible, they might have been his reply or maybe screams, it was difficult to tell.

"Well, as you are unable to form your own response, let me tell you who you are. You're a fucking dead man!" yelled Carlo as he pulled the trigger and Eddie's brains blew out of the back of his skull, mixing with the ebony wood from the now imperfect desk.

"Boss…" said Don, knowing that he was next, "Please!"

Carlo languidly turned to face the still-prone Don, lying nervously on the stained rug.

"You get to live… for now," Galotti delivered with a cold, unrelenting gaze, "But the clock is ticking, Don. Find my wife."

"Yessir," gasped Don, now getting up from where he had fallen, "Thank you."

"Clear up this mess and get out of my sight," ordered Galotti, now already walking out of the dead room.

Chapter 49

There was a significant change in the air this morning, one that I had felt many times before over the years I have lived here. The wind was blowing forcefully, maybe only at about thirty miles per hour, but then with occasional gusts topping forty-five to fifty. I knew what was coming, and I knew it was going to leave a mark.

But, I was more excited than I had felt in a very long while. A week later and my pulse was quickening at the thought of seeing Layla once more. We had made plans to meet that evening, and I was looking forward to it like a kid on a first date. She just lit me from within, and I liked it.

However, Rainee had called this morning and asked to meet with me, which was a little unusual, because usually she just turned up, whether I was busy or not. So, the fact that she had scheduled an urgent meeting, had me somewhat perturbed.

But right on time, at eleven-thirty, I saw her Raptor ease into a parking bay at the end of the dock, and I watched as she jumped out of the truck and made her way urgently toward *Lost Soul*.

"You want coffee?" I asked, as she sat down in the chair next to me, where I had been momentarily perusing activities next door.

"Nope, no time for that. You're in a heap of trouble, Coop," she replied, no smile, no humor.

"I'm always in some kind of trouble," I replied, "What's new?"

"Your girl, Layla, or whatever her name is, you've got problems there."

"I doubt it," I said, grinning, "I haven't had this much fun in a very long time."

"I went down to Miami yesterday," she continued, bluntly.

"Have fun?"

"I wasn't there for fun, idiot," she said, "I was checking out Layla."

"For fuck's sake, Rain, I don't need a babysitter all the time!"

"Well, this time you might," she replied, "I don't think Layla is everything you think she is, that's all. I doubt that Layla is even her real name."

"Come on, Rainee, why ever would you think it wasn't?" I asked, but deep inside me, I now felt a certain degree of concern, because Rainee doesn't make things up just to piss me off.

"I traced her car, you know, the Mini, and it's not registered in the U.S., in fact it's still registered in Mexico."

"What?"

"Yeah, it was imported from Mexico to Miami. And not only that, I tried to find out more about her, checked all the social media, newspapers, Google, used LexisNexis too, zip."

"So she's just very private, that's nothing new these days," I said, "Anyway, what did you find out in your sleuthery?"

"Nada," said Rainee, "Absolutely nothing."

"So, there you go, as I just said, she's just one of those very private people, exactly as I would have imagined."

"I found out where the Mini was shipped to from Mexico, that's why I was down in Miami."

"Look, thousands of cars come in from Mexico, they're cheap, so dealers can make a good profit if they import in bulk and then register them in the U.S., it's nothing new," I replied, now feeling less concerned that there was nothing much to worry about.

"Give me some credit, Coop," she interrupted, her steel-gray eyes now burrowing into me, "How do you think I got the Raptor so cheaply? It ain't my first rodeo, for fuck's sake!"

"My bad," I replied, and continued to listen to my partner.

"Anyway, I tracked the car to a small mom & pop dealership run by a fella called Wayne Randolph, RandyWayneAutos Inc."

"Cute name," I replied, "What did the guy say about the Mini?"

"Nothing. He's dead."

"Okay… maybe Layla has had the car awhile, and just didn't get around to registering it yet. It's not exactly a felony, it's a small fine, at worst," I suggested, although there was clearly something more that Rainee was going to tell me.

"I did some scouting around, Randolph's place backs onto a Krispy Kreme, I talked to a kid that works there."

"Jeez, now you've got me hungry," I replied.

"Don't be an asshole, Coop, just listen, for fuck's sake," said Rainee, obviously in no frame of mind for Hemingway humor this morning.

"Sorry, go on," I replied.

"So, the kid says that Randolph's a cool guy, you know, a genuinely nice dude. Said he ran a busy little used car lot with pretty high turnover, knew his cars inside out, didn't rip off the customers. People liked him, period.

"Sounds like my type of guy," I said, "Did you find out when or why he died, or what happened with the business?"

"I did. The business is now closed down, it was like watching tumbleweed drift through the lot, no cars, boarded up windows, zip going on. Pretty sad really, when the kid said that only a few months ago, it was buzzing and they were delivering boxes of Krispy Kremes there, three, sometimes four times a day. And he'd been running that business successfully for nearly twenty years."

"Jeez, good auto businesses don't go belly up in Miami for no reason, people down there are always trading their cars in faster than their spouses, it's a cash cow," I replied, now very interested in what Rainee was saying. I was also becoming trepidatious about it all being connected to Layla.

"But Coop, here's the kicker. Randolph was murdered."

"Shit, Rainee, are you thinking the same as me? This is more than just a coincidence?"

"Yeah, I am. But there's more, Coop."

"This isn't going to be good, is it?"

"No. After I'd left the Krispy Kreme to get back to my car on Randolph's lot, I had visitors waiting for me."

"Oh jeez, Rainee," knowing that whatever my friend had stumbled upon, was not going to be good.

"Yeah, there were a couple of thugs waiting for me, showed me they were carrying."

"You took care of them?" I asked.

"They weren't a problem, just a couple of goons, maybe mob, but the tasers took care of them," she continued, "Oh, and I've got their IDs as well as their guns."

"Nice work, Rain," I said, "You make me very proud."

"But there's one more thing."

"Go on," I said, "Spill it."

"So, on the same day that Randolph was murdered, his wife topped herself at the family home, hung herself, in fact," Rainee continued, "Coincidence?"

"Unlikely," I said, "Maybe a double hit."

"Kinda looks that way."

Chapter 50

I had arranged to pick Layla up at six-thirty, and as the Caddy nosed its way into Nate's parking lot, Layla was already coming down the metal side-staircase that led from her studio apartment above the bar. She must have seen me pulling in.

As she walked toward my car, I climbed out and moved toward her to embrace her, but I was still rattled by the conversation that I'd had with Rainee only seven hours earlier.

But Layla looked so beautiful, so natural, and so radiantly happy, dressed in a simple white summer dress with matching white sneakers, her long blonde hair swept casually back in a loose plait, that my mind was quickly focused on the here and now.

"Hello, you," she said, wrapping her arms around me and kissing me on the cheek, "You look nice."

"As do you," I replied, reaching for the car's door handle, "Your carriage awaits, ma'am."

~~~

We drove north-east on what was a serenely balmy Floridian evening, because I had decided to take Layla to a special place in what I termed as old-school Florida; a sleepy little town an hour away called Jensen Beach. I also had friends from there, some of whom still lived in Jensen.

There was Memphis, of course, but also two of three friends that I'd made when I first arrived in South Florida, Talbot and Perryman. There was one other guy I'd formed a bond with years ago, Jake Delaney, but he'd relocated to San Luis Obispo, California, and we rarely got to see each other, but we still stayed in touch, mostly via email. And Jake's story is a whole other ball game.

Gaylord Talbot is a small-town lawyer, a slight, rail-thin man, who has had a lifelong penchant for Shakespeare, his conversation often littered with quotes from the Bard. Talbot is a shy intellectual, he's very bright, very smart, but he never hankered after the big city life.

So, after a spell away in England for a few years to satisfy his intense love of Shakespeare and all things English, he and his wife, Autumn, eventually decided to come back to Jensen Beach with their daughter, Ella, to spend the rest of their lives here.

Autumn, by no strange coincidence, is Jake's sister-in-law. Jake's wife, Summer, being Autumn's younger sister. Yeah, it's a long story. And Perryman, well, Perryman is a different kettle of fish.

Vaughn Perryman began teenage and adult life as a surf instructor on the beaches of Jensen and nearby Stuart and Sewall's Point. He'd been surfing since he was six years old, practically lived on the beach, and even won his first state championship at the age of eleven.

He was an amazon of a man, muscled and toned, permanent golden tan and long blonde hair. Physically, he was the polar opposite of Talbot. But Perryman is also intensely nice as well as being ridiculously handsome. So, it was no surprise to see the wealthier women of Sewall's Point, Jensen and Stuart, queuing up to book him for private surf coaching.

But what most of these monied ladies had no realization of back then, was that Perryman was asexual, he chased after neither girls, nor boys. He was one of those unique people who had every possible asset that God could pour into him, but had *almost* zero sexuality within himself. Some might say a freak of nature, others like me who knew him well, just the best human being you could possibly encounter. And if he became your friend, then it was a bond forged for life.

Perryman had almost died at the hands of three men who'd been hired by one of his lady student's jealous husbands. If the husband had known anything at the time about Perryman's sexuality, he'd have had no reason to be jealous.

The remorse felt by said husband, along with his own financial failings, led to the man's suicide. Emerson Steiner was sadly, a loss to no one.

But after Steiner's death, a lifelong relationship was created between the man's wife, Krystal Steiner and Perryman, where Mrs. Steiner pretty much adopted the boy who had been living in his old 1950 Ford 'Woody' Wagon since he first learned to drive. There was never anything sexual, just a pure connection, almost like a best friend and mother rolled into one. And it was something Perryman had never had in his life.

The friendship grew exponentially, and after her husband's suicide, when Krystal Steiner decided to relocate to Europe and live life without the reminder of her obnoxious and odious late husband, she gave her house to Perryman, along with a seven-figure sum to help with the bills. The house back then, was already a million-dollar home, and this was in the mid-1980s.

A few years later, when Perryman had taken advice from his best friend, Talbot, and invested half a million dollars in Amazon, he eventually became ridiculously wealthy, owning homes all over the globe. But he still loved Sewall's Point, and later decided to buy the two adjacent oceanfront properties, and build the biggest and most palatial home in South Florida.

With his 'ex-girlfriend' Sofia, and his new 'girlfriend' Delilah, they had adopted and had also naturally produced children, now totaling eleven and counting. So, they needed the space, I guess.

I had been recounting these stories to Layla, who sat with rapt attention and amazement at it all.

"But didn't you say Perryman is asexual?" she asked, "How did natural childbirth come about?"

"Perryman likes a drink or two occasionally, and he sometimes gets carried away," I replied, laughing.

"Interesting..."

"And even that's pretty weird, because his first partner, Sofia, is gay, or maybe bisexual, and she lives in the house with her latest girlfriend, Eloise, with Perryman and all of the kids. And we're not even sure about Delilah, but she's moved in too. It's a bit like the Brady Bunch on steroids," I said, now into full chuckle mode.

"You do have some curious friends, don't you, Mr. Hemingway?" said Layla, just marveling at the tale I'd just told, "I think I'd like to meet some of these people one day."

"And you will, that's a promise, possibly sooner than you think."

We had continued chatting for the rest of the journey, not deep conversation, because with my new knowledge about Layla, I knew that she would understandably, be very guarded about her personal life. But I still enjoyed it, and what's more, I could feel myself enjoying her even more.

~ ~ ~

We pulled up on Jensen Beach Boulevard, fortuitously finding a parking spot near to where we were eating that evening. Jensen Beach Boulevard may sound grand, but this was just the three-hundred-yard end of it, which was pretty much Jensen's Main Street, a series of mostly single-story, independent shops, restaurants and bars.

I have a real soft spot for the town, it's old-fashioned, quirky, maybe even a little worn out, but its unspoiled location situated right by the water, is becoming rarer and rarer these days.

With oceanfront property now so valuable, and highly prized by developers who would love to put up high-rise condominiums, it was amazing that the ladies and gentlemen that oversaw the town, had still managed to keep it just as it had always been.

We're here," I said to Layla, "Welcome to Jensen Beach."

"It's so cute," said Layla as she opened the door and began to climb out of the Caddy, "I'm not sure I've ever seen anywhere quite like it."

Layla was smiling the same expression that most people have when I've taken them to Jensen, it was just the peacefulness and old-fashionedness of it all, particularly now that the sun was setting and the town's lights had begun to glisten and shimmer.

"I had the same feeling when I first came to Jensen, and I'm not sure there's another town like it in South Florida," I said, relishing the gentle breeze sweeping up the street from the ocean.

"Is this where we're eating tonight?" Layla asked, pointing to the restaurant we were parked next to.

"Oh, I love this place, it's been here for longer than I can remember," I replied, "But no, that's not where we're heading tonight."

"That's a shame."

There was a look of disappointment on Layla's face as she took in the color and quirkiness of *Mulligan's Beach House Bar & Grill*. It was a unique ocean beach bar, with its small tables dotted along the sidewalk, surrounded by bright yellow chairs and protected by straw canopies to shield the customers from the sun.

"I wouldn't be disappointed if we were dining here tonight," she said.

"Another time, c'mon, it's only a short walk," I replied, reaching for a hand that was seamlessly and simultaneously reaching for mine.

We walked slowly along the sidewalk, Layla wanting to stop at, and talk to each and every street vendor selling their wares on this Thursday market evening.

The weekly market was called Jammin' Jensen, sponsored by the small town, and all along the street were artists selling paintings, inexpensive handmade jewelry, and carved and glass ornaments from the many local crafters who chose the purity and sanctity of Jensen Beach as their home.

At one point, Layla stopped and tried on a little sea glass necklace, very simple, just a thin gold chain holding a pale blue, weathered, and sea-tumbled piece of glass.

"It matches your eyes," I said, "It's very pretty."

"I love it!" she replied, fastening the chain around her neck as I slipped the seller a twenty-dollar bill.

"You don't have to do that, Coop," she said, when she saw that I'd paid for it, "I have money."

"It's twenty dollars! I'm not gonna go broke," I replied, laughing.

"Well, you're very sweet, and I accept, thank you," she said.

"You're welcome," I said, "But we need to get moving, our reservation is at eight, and it's five before already."

We turned down Maple Street, and at No.11, I announced, "We're here."

Layla gazed at the beach-cottage-style building that was covered in vines and flowers, surrounded by a small white picket fence, a blue gazebo in the center, framing the entrance.

"This is a restaurant?" she asked, "It's very cute."

"It is indeed, this is my favorite, it's called *Eleven Maple Street*," I replied, "And I think you're going to love it even more inside."

We made our way through the gazebo, up a small stone pathway and into the restaurant, stopping at the door to check in for our reservation.

"It's beautiful, Coop, it feels like one of those ski chalets you see in the movies," she said marveling at the timbers that framed the simplicity of the interior.

"You haven't tasted the food yet," I said, "The chef, Michael Perrin, who is also the owner, is a culinary artist. He opened the restaurant with his wife, Margie, in 1985, and for me, it's the most unique place in South Florida.

"Was that Margie who just checked us in?"

"No, sadly Margie died too early and unexpectedly in 2017. Everyone adored her, she was a shining light with an infectious sense of humor. We all miss her dearly."

"Oh my gosh, Coop, that's so sad," Layla replied, "How on earth did her husband have the will to continue with the restaurant?"

"Michael, as I said, is dedicated to his art," I replied, "And I think that after her death, he decided that to continue, would be the best tribute to his wife."

We were shown to our table, and once we were seated and given a wine menu, I ordered champagne for us.

When the champagne arrived and was poured, I raised a glass to Layla's, and I said, "To Margie."

"To Michael too," she replied, gently touching her glass to mine, "And to us."

Chapter 51

Now partner-less, and having paid a visit to his dental surgeon to fit a bridge across where his front teeth had been savagely expelled, Don Faber decided that if he was to gain any kind of respect back from Galotti, he'd need to do this solo. Eddie was gone now, and he didn't have time to find a replacement.

But what did he know, what could he remember about that day at Randolph's lot? He did remember the dark-haired girl, and she did bear an uncanny resemblance to Lara Croft too, regardless of the fact that Galotti knew zip about computer games.

She had to be connected to Cassidy Swain, how couldn't she be? Because why would she rock up on Randolph's lot asking questions? He knew she'd been fishing for information on Randolph, because before being ordered to go and see Galotti, he managed to find who she'd been talking to in the Krispy Kreme.

The kid, Mason, was an open book, said she was a nice lady, told Don and Eddie that he'd just been telling her about Randolph, what a nice guy he was. Mason was so full of praise for both Randolph and the girl, that Don and Eddie had almost began to like the pair themselves.

But one was dead, and the other would be dead once he'd got some intel from her about Cassidy. It cost Don a hundred bucks, but the information the kid had freely given out, was important.

Don also remembered the Raptor; how could he forget a stealth beast of a truck like that? The big problem was that he couldn't remember the whole license plate, just a few letters and numbers, because it was Eddie who'd been assigned to note down the vehicles that came and went on Randolph's lot. But after a few hours searching the DMV database, he believed that he'd tracked her down. One Rainee Showers of Palm Beach, Florida.

There was nothing to be found out about her on the web or social media, she was pretty much anonymous, except for her driver's license and property taxes. Couldn't even find what she did for a living. But there had to be a connection between her and Cassidy, same sort of age, good looking chick, and both with a connection to Randolph.

As he sat there in his home office, in his not-too-shabby and indeed, quite luxurious Pompano Beach waterfront home, he made the decision to track the Showers girl down.

"Marylou," he called out in a loud voice to his wife who was in the kitchen preparing his lunch, "Pack me an overnight bag, will you? I gotta go away for a few days."

"Sure baby, you wanna have lunch first?" a voice echoed back from the kitchen.

"What is it today?"

"It's your favorite, turkey and cranberry on rye," she replied, bringing in a plate with two hefty sandwiches sitting on it.

"Maybe a glass of Rombauer too?" he asked, gently slapping her behind.

"Coming right up, sweetpea," said Marylou, instantly pirouetting, and making her way down to the wine cellar.

Chapter 52

Tropical Storm Jacques had finally become Hurricane Jacques, and I was aware that its five radar trajectories from *The National Hurricane Center* in Miami, all predicted that it would make landfall in Miami in the next few days.

The same predictions all generally assumed that it would head north up the east coast of Florida, then head north-west building speed and strength, with the likely end game of disappearing into the Gulf before destroying much of Alabama, Mississippi and Louisiana. As if those states hadn't been punished enough by deadly hurricanes over the past twenty years or so.

"Bad timing, Jacques," I said to myself, knowing that my fledgling relationship with Layla, was about to be rudely interrupted.

But there were plans to be made with the knowledge of what was in store for the residents of Florida, and that included those people nearest and dearest to me, which now also included Layla.

I would need to meet with Molly and Billy, Remy and Memphis, and Rainee and Layla to decide a plan of action. My boat, *Lost Soul*, would be a potential victim, which saddened me, but I could always buy a new one from the insurance payout. And I was thankful that I'd just recently renewed the policy on her. But possessions could be replaced, people couldn't.

And a plan had already begun forming in my mind after the wonderful evening I had spent with Layla, just two nights ago. We had dropped by Perryman's place, after we'd had dinner followed by a romantic walk on the beach, because he'd been banging on about me visiting to see the new home he'd built on his three joined lots. So, we had taken the opportunity to pop in that evening, albeit at quite a late hour.

The house was more than spectacular. At forty-six thousand square feet, excluding the garage that housed fourteen automobiles on revolving turntables, it looked more like a luxurious Four Seasons hotel than a domestic family residence.

Gone was the huge Mediterranean style residence that Perryman had been given by Krystal Steiner, itself spectacular in its own right, now replaced by a gargantuan glass and metal edifice from the future.

One might wonder why anyone would build a home with so much glass, in the hurricane epicenter of the world? But as Perryman had gleefully pointed out on the tour of the property, the glass on this place was so toughened that it could withstand winds of over two hundred miles per hour, more than any speed ever recorded in a Florida hurricane.

It was also built with reinforced steel, unlike many homes in Florida that were 'frame'; those built with timbers, and easily punished by even a tropical storm. The only possible harm to Perryman's home, could come from the roof being torn off by the small tornadoes that circulate on the outer edges of a hurricane, which in fact, usually cause the most damage, rather than the hurricane's windspeed itself.

But Perryman believed he had that covered too, by having installed a state-of-the-art motorized roof system that could transform from an A-frame style to an inverted one. He began to explain the technology to me in his southern drawl, but he'd lost me after the first two sentences.

Layla had really enjoyed meeting Perryman and his clan, and was amazed that the whole domestic lifestyle he'd accidentally created, worked so seamlessly well. Perryman had met us at the door, ('door' is an understatement) dressed in gold lamé pants, bare-chested with a flowing white silk gown and burnt-tangerine Ferragamo Gancini sandals.

For some reason, Perryman with his golden tanned chest and still enviable physique, coupled with his ever-present flowing blonde wavy locks, could get away with it. I couldn't, but the look suited him, he wore it well. It matched the irrepressible, ice-white-toothed grin from his handsome visage.

It's impossible to adequately describe in words, the interior of Perryman's new home, save to say that opulent didn't nearly describe what his designers had delivered for him.

The art, lighting, sculptures, rugs and furnishings were the ultimate tip of the hat to the modernist movement, and although the central glass viewing area that overlooked the ocean, was itself two hundred feet wide, it took some time to walk right up to it and gaze out.

It would be hard to invite Layla back to Lost Soul after this visit.

I knew Sofia and most of the kids from years ago, but I hadn't met her new belle, Eloise, or indeed, Perryman's latest flame, the very delightful, Delilah. Sofia is a very petite and attractive ex-policewoman, and Eloise, quite the opposite, a raven-haired, tall and lithe ex-Olympian beach volleyball player.

Delilah on the other hand, is summer-kissed beautiful in the same vein as Perryman. Although, who wasn't attractive in this household? Jeez. Delilah is also a part-time actress, who has made a handful of bit-part appearances in a few recent Netflix series and movies.

Once we had all sat down in the vast seating zone that surrounded the glass viewing area, as an enormous central wall of waterfall gently splashed down behind us, the conversation eventually moved on to the impending arrival of Hurricane Jacques, and what I was planning to do.

"Y'all know, Coop," said Perryman, in his inimitable and delicious southern boy drawl, "Ma' home is your home, brother, y'all can take cover here, ain't nuttin' any 'cane can do to fret you at Casa Perryman."

"Vaughn," I replied, always using his given name instead of his last name, "We might very well take you up on that offer, so thank you, buddy, I'll let you know."

And so, with those comforting southern words from my glorious friend, my plan had already hatched.

Chapter 53

Don Faber had rented a compact car from Enterprise, he was damned if he was going to pay a large rental fee out of his own pocket for a full-size sedan. And he was doing this off his own back, off the books, so the less Galotti knew, the better.

He'd booked into a crumby little Motel 6 on Blue Heron Blvd. in Riviera Beach, an easily drivable distance to where the Showers girl lived in Palm Beach. A snip at thirty-nine bucks a night.

After he'd retrieved the key from the reception desk, handed to him by a chain-smoking, greasy and obese kid stuffing pizza down her throat, and whose life seemed to revolve around her daytime tv crap that he'd interrupted the viewing of, he made his way to his room. Even the wooden fob on the keyring felt filthy and slimy.

The un-airconditioned smell that hit him when he opened the door, almost made him gag. He held his breath, putting his hand to his face, and immediately opened the windows and switched the ancient air-con unit to maximum power, the struggling machine rattling as it came to life. The stench of recent sex in the room was no surprise, given that one could also rent rooms here by the hour.

The air immediately started to freshen with the influx of the warm air from outside, and Don did his usual routine in dumps like this one, first removing the quilt from the bed, checking for bedbugs, and then checking the entire floorspace for cockroaches.

The bathroom was vaguely clean, good enough to take a shower in anyway, and the bedroom had a coffee-maker that looked like a recent purchase. It would do for a couple or three nights.

He sniffed the sheets and pillows on the bed, and having decided that they had been recently laundered, he sat down on a chair and opened his briefcase.

Inside, were his two favored automatics, both .44 Magnums, one with a suppressor and one without. He liked the .44 because it was the same gun Clint Eastwood had used in the Dirty Harry movies, and Dirty Don had a ring about it.

Cradling both guns, he said to himself, "Time to shine, my little beauties."

~ ~ ~

In what could only be described as the opposite end of the hospitality business, Shira Kadosh was in her elegant suite at the Four Seasons, also inspecting her weapons, hers being even more deadly than Don Faber's.

She had received information about this new girl, Rainee Showers, from her handler who had had Galotti's office bugged. The fact that Kadosh hadn't heard a word from Galotti himself via her handler, seemed clear to her that he was holding back for whatever imbecile reason, and it may be another month before she was given a lead.

She was at the end of her patience now and with the growing longing to see her beloved son, Eitan, she had finally decided to take things into her own hands and get the job finished.

Chapter 54

The newly released album from *Shamenless*, was now riding high at No.1 on the Billboard charts. Its spectacularly uninventive title, *F*ck Me Shamenless,* was one of Joe Jarvie's less creative moments.

But Angel had to agree with Joe, the title may have been a better hook than he'd first thought, because the album had gone straight to the top and showed no signs of being toppled, even by Beyoncé's and Taylor Swift's new offerings. And Angel had to admit, the album was possibly the best that Joe had written.

The band didn't feature on the album's cover, instead just the image of Joe, leaning back, mane of hair waving in the wind, bare-chested, smothered in glycerin droplets, and in typical guitar hero pose, with flames flaring out of his mouth.

It was an image that would be lapped up by his army of still-adoring and aging fans, eagerly shelling out fifteen bucks to listen to Joe's latest record. And that they did, by the millions.

Angel's job now, was to ensure that Joe didn't start spending the royalties that hadn't actually arrived yet, and that wouldn't be easy.

"Joe," said Angel, as he sat down on a wicker chair by the pool while Joe was cooking up a meat feast on the barbecue, "Let me remind you why this album is so important right now."

"Fuck, yeah!" replied an over excited Joe, "We're gonna get a river of cash, man, it's gonna be just like the old days. You want ribs with your Porterhouse, man?"

"Yes, sure, that would be great, thank you. But Joe, have you already forgotten that we have a cash crisis?"

"Nah, but that'll be taken care of as soon as the dough comes rollin' in, right?"

"You're forgetting about what you have now and what you might not have soon, once Flick realizes you're suddenly going to be worth a lot more to her with the success of the new album," replied Angel, "You need the divorce to be settled quickly."

"It's all good, Angel, you got that meeting set up with the lawyers, day after tomorrow, right? We'll have everything nailed down after that and Flick'll be out of the picture. She's already agreed to everything."

"No, she has agreed the terms of the divorce, that's all," said Angel.

"So it's good to go, no?"

"Agreeing terms is one thing, signing the document on Thursday, is quite another," said Angel, knowing that deals can fall over in a heartbeat.

"Listen, compadre, you ain't gotta worry," said Joe, calmly, as he put a giant plate of Porterhouse steak and short ribs on the table in front of Angel.

Angel looked up at Joe's face, curious as to why he seemed so calm, the complete opposite of how he had reacted on their financial come-to-Jesus meeting prior to the chart-topping of *F*ck Me Shamenless*.

"Why would that be?" he asked.

"Me and Flick had a phone convo the other night, she's good to go, just wants out. She's golden, trust me," replied Joe, instantly stripping a short rib of its meat in one giant bite, "And she has no interest in music, particularly mine, so she doesn't even know about the album. Hell, she didn't even know I was recording one."

"Okay…" said Angel, unconvinced, "We'll see, I guess."

Chapter 55

"It's forecast to hit Miami late afternoon on Saturday," I said, guiding the Caddy into the driveway of an elegant, beachfront Mediterranean-style villa just outside the town of Boynton Beach.

"Hurricane Jacques, you mean?" Layla replied, sitting up in her seat, now that we'd arrived.

"Yes, that's the one," I said, keen not to let it spoil our evening together.

It was a cool evening on this Wednesday, the kind of evening that precipitates the coming of a storm, or in this case, a hurricane. The cicadas were in full chorus, now that night had fallen, but other than that, there were precious few sounds in the genteel neighborhood in which we'd arrived. Nature's animal and bird population was already aware of the coming menace.

"Where are we?" she asked, looking around at the classy homes that lined the street, "This is pretty nice, I'm guessing it's not yours?"

"You guess correctly, ma'am, let's just say that we're visiting," I said, knowing that this wasn't strictly true, as I hadn't been invited.

"Stay here for a minute," I said, climbing out of the car, and walking toward the lockbox that hung on the handle of one of the entrance doors.

I typed in a six-digit code, and the light went green. Opening the box, I retrieved a set of keys for the house, inserted one of them into the door's lock, and opened it to switch on some lights.

Walking back to the car, I pulled some bags of groceries from the Caddy's trunk, opened the passenger door and took Layla's hand.

"Welcome to Cooper's Cooking Evening," I said, leading Layla into what was indeed, a very nice home.

"Why does it have a For Sale board up in the driveway?" she asked.

"I'll get to that later, now come on in."

Layla stood in the open-plan lounge/kitchen, marveling at the intimate beauty of the home, as I went around switching on the table lamps and other dimmable lighting in the area.

"So, this place doesn't belong to you?" she asked.

"Confirmed," I replied.

"Who does it belong to, a friend?"

"In all honesty, I'm not entirely sure who owns it," I said, truthfully, as I began to unpack the groceries and wine I'd bought earlier that day.

"Oh, come on Coop, spill it, are we breaking and entering?" she asked, laughing at my secrecy.

"Not quite… it's on the market, but the couple who own it are snowbirds, so once they realized a hurricane was coming, they upped sticks and went back home to New York as fast as they could get there."

"So how do you have access, it looked like you knew the code for the lockbox?"

"I have a buddy, Stevie Newell, he's a well-known realtor in these parts. He trusts me, so when I occasionally get stir-crazy on my boat, he lets me *use* one or two of his listings that aren't occupied," I explained, "And usually it's in times of freak weather when my boat might be taken out by a hurricane."

"But what if the owners come back unexpectedly?"

"Let me explain, these people are extremely well-heeled, they spend maybe three months of the year in their vacation home, and the other nine months in their 5th Avenue apartment, or even overseas. There's absolutely no way they'd be coming back during a hurricane," I replied, but realizing that Layla wasn't entirely comfortable with the situation.

"You're absolutely certain?" she asked.

"Certain as the sun is gonna shine in the morning," I replied, "And anyway, we have a get-out procedure."

"What would that be?"

"Well, real estate has changed these days, and the sellers have had to come on board. Oftentimes, a potential buyer will like a house, but would ask for a weekend to try it out, spend some time in it," I explained.

"Really??" she said, incredulous that this even happened.

"So, if the owners did come back, I would just get Stevie on the phone and he'd explain to them that you and I were selected potential buyers who had asked to spend time in the house to see if it worked for us, and he'd forgotten to let them know. Simple."

"Okay, sounds good, I just hope they don't return, that's all," she replied, now somewhat mollified with the arrangement.

"Also, when Stevie gives me a date for when the owners return, I go back to whatever house I've been using, do a thorough clean, and stock up the refrigerator. It's a win-win," I replied.

"Cooper Hemingway, the rascal with a heart of pure gold," remarked Layla, seeing the funny side of a vaguely criminal situation.

"And honestly, you know that Nate is already shuttering up the bar, so I'm not sure what you'd want to do if you were left alone there, because Nate won't be staying to ride out Hurricane Jacques," I replied.

"Gosh, I hadn't even thought about that," she reflected, knowing that when she was with Carlo, his home was like an impregnable fortress, capable of withstanding a war, let alone a hurricane.

"So, you can always stay here until the storm is on its way out," I suggested.

"Are you having mischievous thoughts, Mr. Hemingway?" she asked, coming up to me and putting her arms around my neck.

"Not at all," I replied, unconvincingly, "I'm a gentleman, didn't you know?"

Layla then kissed me full on the lips, a kiss that lasted maybe four or five seconds, before she pulled away.

"Now, Chef Cooper, what are you making for me?"

Chapter 56

At four-fifteen in the morning, and after another two-thousand bucks a night gig, babysitting her new teenage rapper client, Mo-Nay$Neverenuff and his equally teenage 'crew', Rainee was once again eating a breakfast of questionable nutrition, in a 24-hour McDonald's down the street from her apartment. And on this morning, she was hungrier than a woodpecker with a headache.

She had already dispensed with a Double Sausage & Egg McMuffin, a Bacon Breakfast Roll with hash browns, and she was now halfway through a plate of pancakes & syrup. Two flat whites had already gone, and now she sucked on the straw of an iced latte.

"Man, I should get me a diabetes check," she muttered to herself, always surprised that she never put on a pound in weight and still maintained an enviable figure. Although, she did work out twice a day, and when Rainee worked out, it was more akin to a boot camp than a quick fling in the gym.

On the table in front of her, intermingled with her finished and unfinished breakfast items, lay the wallets, driver's licenses and credit cards of Donald Faber and Eduardo Falcone.

"Faber & Falcone, sounds like a pair of lawyers," she muttered again to herself, "Pair of mutts, more like."

Her laptop was open, ready to do a search on them. She hadn't had much spare time with her recent, nocturnal and time-consuming Mo-Nay$Neverenuff job, and she wasn't sure how relevant the two men were in the grand scheme of things. But Rainee never left a stone unturned.

As far as she could make out from the links that came up on LexisNexis, they were connected guys, so there were mob ties. But they also seemed pretty lightweight compared to the typical mafia thug. Faber lived in a nice, and pretty damned expensive home on the water in Pompano Beach with his wife, Marylou, and Falcone appeared to still live at home with his mother in Boca Raton.

"Typical Italian boy, can't leave his mom," she said.

But digging deeper, she finally found a real connection that revealed a lot more.

Both men, Faber the older one at forty-nine, and Falcone the kid at twenty-eight, worked for a well-known mafia don in Miami. One Mr. Carlo Galotti, a man not to be messed with, according to the newspaper archives she was scrolling through.

On seeing the newspaper photographs of Galotti, the man was easily six-three in height, slim, but definitely built too. He was a pretty good-looking older guy, derived from what Rainee guessed were Italian genes.

He always dressed impeccably, whether it was a day suit or evening attire, but always a suit, except for a few photos of him aboard his yacht where he was dressed more casually. But even then, immaculately turned out. If he weren't a Mafia man, he'd probably be a catch, if you liked silver foxes.

Galotti had never done time for any of the murders he'd been accused of, or for any of the fraud, drug deals, prostitution, protection and intimidation rackets he had been connected to. The man was like Teflon, every charge slipping effortlessly off his deeply tanned and permanently oiled skin.

"That kind of criminal activity going unpunished, only means one thing," Rainee said to herself, "He has complete control of the ruling elite as well as the Miami Police Department and what looks like, the city's whole fucking judicial system. He knows he'll never do time, he can just do whatever the fuck he wants, when he wants, how he wants."

She began again to scan the myriad of press photos of Carlo Galotti attending galas, banquets, official city events and marquee balls. In almost every photograph, Galotti was accompanied by tall, stunning, young, model-figure girls, replete in revealing and gasp-worthy gowns. But each girl was different from the last, except for one.

She scanned every single image, blowing the photos up to see as much of the face of this one particular girl, who appeared to accompany Galotti on maybe six or seven occasions in the past couple of years. And in all of these photos, it was at a particularly prestigious event.

The girl was blonde, not so tall as the rent-a-chicks, but really quite striking and fundamentally different from the other girls in just about every way. She actually seemed to be a genuinely nice, hometown girl.

And checking the byline under each picture, Rainee could see that the girl's name was Cassidy Swain. And Cassidy Swain, she discovered, was Galotti's wife, and someone who was clearly only wheeled out for his very special engagements.

Rainee had never seen the girl before, but digging deep into her memory of the night she'd collected take-out from Nate's, she realized that maybe her vague recollection of the girl she'd briefly met then, could be Galotti's wife?

She still couldn't be sure though, the one in the photos was dressed immaculately at high-end events, looking really quite stunning, and the girl in the bar had been dressed in what… t-shirt and jeans?

"Damn, if only I had a photo of you, Layla Wray."

Chapter 57

The nominal remains of our meal rested on the dining table, such were our appetites tonight, that we'd eaten almost everything I had prepared. I'd bought two dozen oysters, and prepared them on a huge platter of ice with lemon for squeezing, Tabasco sauce, and my own recipe mignonette, a kind of shallot vinaigrette, but with added gin and jalapeños.

I hadn't thought to ask Layla if she liked oysters, hadn't even asked her if she had allergies, which could have been a bit of a disaster. Fortunately though, she loved them as much as I did and we devoured the entire platter. I did however, remember to ask if she had any particular food allergies before we began eating, and like me, she didn't.

As an entrée, I'd prepared beef filets with jus au Hemingway, a reduction of dates, raspberries, balsamic, pinot noir and brown sugar. It went down well, so well in fact, that my key lime pie became surplus to requirement.

We had relocated to the lounge area and Layla had taken control of my Spotify app on my iPhone and played one of her own playlists. I was pretty used to my own selection of music and it was interesting to see what Layla had chosen. The playlist was mellow, slow songs, kind of romantic really, and the music set the tone for the end of a wonderful evening with her.

"You like?"

"I do," I replied, "I like very much. Not what I would normally choose, but it's nice to hear something different."

"I like you, Coop."

"The feeling is more than mutual, Layla."

"But even though we've only known each other for a short amount of time, I like *us*," she continued, which was music to my ears.

"Lo stesso," I said, "Potresti essere la ragazza che stavo cercando."

"You speak French?"

"A little," I replied, "But that was Italian, just some pretty words I picked up."

"What does it mean?"

"It means, I feel the same way, *lo stesso*," I replied.

"You're the original romantic rogue, aren't you?"

"I have my moments," I said, now looking into her striking, pale blue eyes.

And then, out of the blue, she moved effortlessly from her position on the sofa to straddle me, and placed her long and slender hands on my chest.

She then leaned into me, caressed my face with both of her hands, and paused to look deeply into my eyes, our faces only inches apart.

"This is not something I've done for a very long time," she whispered, "But you're different, Coop, you make me feel like a woman again."

"I have to be honest with you, Layla, I've dated in the past, but you are so different to anyone I've ever met before," I whispered back, "And I feel like I've known you forever, if that makes any sense?"

"Lo stesso," she murmured, remembering my words.

She ran her fingertips across my face, and then across my lips, before finally leaning in and finding my mouth with hers.

It was a kiss that I had often dreamed of having with Layla, her lips were like small pillows, her tongue like chocolate velvet, as we kissed long and deeply.

After what seemed like an hour, but was only a minute or so, I cupped her face in my hands and pushed it very gently away so that I could see the beauty of her visage again. I slowly slid my fingers through her silk-like blonde hair, riveted once again by those pale, but intensely blue eyes of hers, before pulling her back in hungrily, for another long kiss.

Eventually, she began to unbutton my shirt, pulling it wide to reveal my chest, and began to delicately kiss me there.

She looked up at me, "I want you, Coop, is that so bad of me?"

"I want you too, Layla, I have done since the moment I first saw you. It feels right, no?"

"It feels so right," she replied.

I began to lift the white linen dress she was wearing, my eyes silently asking if it was okay to do so. She nodded her consent, and as the rising dress began to reveal her golden tanned skin, I almost gasped when her body was finally revealed.

She finished the disrobing for me, tossing the garment to one side, and began to pull my shirt from my body, knowing that she didn't have to ask me now.

I cupped both breasts, more perfect than I could even have imagined, and bent to kiss them, circling each areola teasingly, before taking one of her now hard nipples between my lips, sucking and gently biting, before moving to the other, as she closed her eyes and leaned back.

I felt a small shudder as she moaned something, and then she leaned in hard to find my mouth again with hers, the kiss more frantic now.

Putting my hands on her bottom, I slowly began to stand, as her legs wrapped tight around me, our lips still locked together in what seemed a never-ending kiss.

The music playing now was so apposite, Savage Garden's *Truly, Madly, Deeply*...

I walked to the master bedroom, and laid Layla down on the huge Californian King bed, letting my chinos fall to the floor to match Layla's own virtual nakedness, and lay down next to her.

Our faces were just inches apart again, and under the cool of the ceiling fan, I slid my hand from her shoulder, down the inward curve of her body to her rear, hovering for a moment before caressing the top of her thigh.

She turned from her side onto her back, and beneath the briefest of white thongs, I imagined what lay under its silk, her pubis so rounded and sensual that I needed to touch her there.

I kissed her, gently this time, and rose up to move further down her immaculate body.

Leaning down, I put my lips to the silk and kissed her so softly. Layla's body instantly arched and she emitted a low moan again as I explored the areas to the side of the silk triangle that hid her jewel, biting them softly and licking and kissing the entire area.

"Oh God, Cooper, now I really need you," she gasped, and I realized my growing manhood desperately needed her too.

I put my fingers under the fine silk straps of the thong, and gradually began to pull it down, Layla's body arching with the need to be rid of it.

My eyes could barely believe the beauty of what lay within, and my lips went to it, kissing it lightly, desperate to explore with my tongue. And she let me…

Her taste of honey was aphrodisiacal, as my tongue probed and circled and teased her tiny jewel, putting it ever so gently between my teeth, sucking on this minuscule pearl of orgasmic power.

"Aaaaaah," she moaned, indicating to me that I had found her exact spot. I felt as though she could achieve climax quite quickly in the way her body was not only quivering, but was now almost shaking.

"Come here," she said, "I can't come yet, because this is too good to be over in what might be seconds."

I did as she bade, sliding my torso up between her legs and hovered above her breasts, as she pulled my face in to kiss me again.

I felt her hand slide down my back, feeling the curve of my own derriere, before exploring around my abdomen to touch my burning engorgement.

Her slim, long fingers wrapped around it, knowing that my desire was reaching the very limit of control, and she guided me into her, a feeling of the most intimate connection I'd not felt before.

We couldn't rush this, it was not just a physical volcano burning between us, but an emotional and passionate one too.

As I gradually found myself fully immersed inside Layla, I began a slow rhythm, her pubis meeting mine on each measured and languorous thrust. It was becoming so hard to contain myself, when unexpectedly, Layla turned me on my back, and sat astride me. Pushing me back inside her, the thrust of the rhythm was now becoming more and more intense, as our soaked bodies moved in a synchronized harmony.

She swept down to me, our lips locked, a river of passion crashing through us.

"Can you hold on?" she asked, desperate for the climax not to arrive just yet.

"I can… but not for much longer…"

She gently withdrew from my raging hardness, and turned around on her knees, her hands clutching the headboard, and I instantly knew what she wanted.

I moved in behind her, mesmerized by the slimness of her back, the symmetry and beauty of her cheeks, and then in a moment, we were physically, passionately joined together once more.

In our new position, an almost animal instinct seemed to ignite between us, and each thrust got harder and harder, until Layla's body went completely rigid and she suddenly yelled loudly, "Fuck, fuck, fuck!"

She closed tightly around me now, as she reached what seemed an eternal orgasm, and only moments later, the beast within me roared, my climax ripping through me as I gasped with pure sexual and sensual emotion.

It was the longest, deepest and most muscle-deflating feeling I'd ever encountered, as the two of us, as one now, collapsed giddily onto the now sweat-dampened sheets.

We couldn't utter a word for over a minute, each of us so breathless as we sucked in every piece of available air.

Layla nuzzled into my chest, her breathing, and mine, finally beginning to return to normal, as our heartbeats slowed to a normal rhythm. I wrapped my arms around her, never wanting this moment, this night, this life, to end.

I had never before experienced such pleasure, such emotion and passion. Nuzzling the top of her head, and realizing that I'd fallen for this girl, she looked up at me, smiling that smile that I loved so much.

"I'm hungry," she said.

"I've got key lime pie?"

Chapter 58

The quickening sound of her pale-yellow Jimmy Choo's clicking along the sidewalk on Northlake Blvd in Palm Beach Gardens, was testament to her need to get this over with quickly. She'd parked the Jag in a red zone in front of a fire hydrant, as close as possible to the law offices of *Dibrino, Shea, Hurst & Nakamoto Inc.* and Flick didn't really care if it got ticketed or towed.

She could easily buy a new one with her payout today, and just let Joe take care of the problem. Today would likely be an Uber day if the car was gone once she'd emerged back out onto the street again. She seriously didn't care, she just wanted her money, and she wanted out of their sham marriage. Although she had to concede that she was the one who had orchestrated it back in Vegas. She chuckled to herself.

Flick pushed open one of the huge glass doors of the building that housed multiple law firms and insurance companies, and walked directly to the elevator, her heels now echoing loudly on the polished limestone floor of the lobby.

"Miss? Can I help you?" one of the receptionists called after her, as Flick bypassed the reception area and was already pushing the 'up' button by the elevators to take her to the eleventh floor.

"Nope," Flick replied, "I won't be here long."

"But miss, do you have an appoi…"

The words were lost on Flick as the elevator door closed and she began her victory rise to floor number eleven.

~~~

Joe and Angel had arrived early, both keen to read through the details of the provisional divorce agreement that Joe's lawyer, Haruto Nakamoto, had drawn up. It had already been agreed on in principle by Flick and her lawyer, Bertha Marin, one of the more unscrupulous and vicious attorneys in Palm Beach.

The firm's conference room, where all four were now sitting, was typical of a successful corporate law office. The wraparound-glassed corner room, showing a panoramic vista of Palm Beach, was center-pieced by a long maple conference table, with a central glass oval inlay. Seven Polycom Trio designer telephones dotted equally along the center of it. The twelve mocha leather Vitra Eames chairs that surrounded the table, showed a company at the very top of its game in the legal profession.

"May I offer you a coffee, Ms. Marin?" asked Nakamoto of the woman who had arrived a few seconds earlier.

"Is it drinkable?" she replied.

"We pride ourselves on our many varieties here, what may I get you?" asked Nakamoto, his formal but impeccable host nature, the ice cube to Marin's inferno.

"Black, no sugar…," Marin replied, "Please."

~ ~ ~

With the refreshments ordered for all four participants, the shuffling of paper began.

The door abruptly burst open, as Flick, in a yellow and black polka-dot summer dress entered the room, her stiletto heels loudly announcing her approach.

"Not planning on starting without me, are we, fellas?" she sneered, ignoring Joe and Angel.

"On the contrary," Nakamoto said serenely, rising from his chair to greet the woman, "We're just getting ready for you. Would you like a refreshment, Mrs. Jarvie?"

"You can quit with that name, Haruto, and I won't be here that long, so thanks, but no thanks, let's just get to it."

"As you will."

"Hello Joe, I see you have reinforcements with you," said Flick, pointing one of her newly manicured fingers at Angel.

"I'm just here on a professional level," replied Angel, "This is only between you and Joe, so please don't mind me, Flick."

"Ha! I'm kinda surprised that your private-dick buddy and the bitch ain't here too," she replied, now looking at Joe, who'd sat silently since Flick had arrived.

"Coop's a good friend, Flick, so is Rainee, so let's not get into it," Joe replied quietly.

"He's a fucking pussy, is what he is, *and* that cunt who works with him," sneered Flick, her mouth engaging before her brain. But then realizing, that if she kept opening her mouth with torrents of abuse, she'd never get out of there.

"Let us begin," said Nakamoto, "I trust that all items and all procedures in the document have been fully agreed and understood, now that we are at this point in the process?"

It was Bertha's turn now, and she took it.

"Well, there are a few changes I'd like to make for my client, on issues that I'm not overly happy with…"

"Shut up, Bertha, let's get this over and done with, for fuck's sake," said Flick, shutting her attorney down before the woman could finish her sentence.

Bertha Marin was not used to being addressed in this way, although Flick had pissed her off monumentally on several occasions during the divorce proceedings.

"Flick, slow down, let's not be impetuous…"

"Fuck you, Bertha, I'm parked in a red zone, just get on with it," Flick replied, shutting the formidable woman down once again.

Nakamoto's words, in his own Japanese fashion, brought an end to the squabble.

"Ladies, gentlemen, let us proceed. In essence, bearing in mind that all parties have read, acknowledged and understood all terms listed in the document, let me summarize in layman's terms, everything that we are planning to sign off on this morning."

"Good," said Flick.

"Right," agreed Joe.

Bertha remained silent, seething at the disrespect from her abominable client.

Angel kept quiet too, hoping that Flick was still unaware of the information that nestled inside his and Joe's minds.

Nakamoto continued.

"As far as property goes, Joe will retain the family home, and Flick will have full ownership of the house in San Diego, are we in agreement?"

All parties voiced a chorus of agreement.

"All motor vehicles will be divided up equally, as stated in the document," Nakamoto continued, "And all art, furnishings and jewelry that exists in each of the two residences, shall belong to the newly sole-designated owners of said properties. Agreed?"

"Yep," said Flick.

"Cool," agreed Joe.

"Now," continued Nakamoto, "We can move on to the financials."

"Quickly, please, Haruto," said Flick to the only individual in the room that she actually liked, even had respect for, "I'm still parked in that red zone."

"Of course, Flick, no problem at all," said Nakamoto, feigning obsequiousness.

After a moment's silence, and acknowledging that there were to be no further interruptions from the other three, Nakamoto continued.

"Bertha and I have drawn up a document that shows all current available funds in all bank accounts, here and overseas. These funds total a rounded-down figure of 8.3 million U.S. dollars, which will be divided equally between both parties, giving you Flick, and you, Joe, 4.15 million dollars each. Can both of you confirm that you are happy with these figures?"

"I'm okay with that," said Flick.

"Yeah, me too," confirmed Joe.

"In that case, these were the only items, the largest financial ones, that is, that I needed confirmation on from both of you, so if you're happy to bilaterally sign the agreement, we can conclude this meeting.

"Ms. Marin, do you have anything else to add at this point?"

"I don't think so, but…"

"Shut up Bertha, just gimme a pen, Haruto," said Flick, "Let's get outta here."

Marin's rage was intensifying exponentially, but even she wanted to get out of there now, as soon as possible, so she said no more.

"Of course," replied Nakamoto, handing her his Montblanc Meisterstück Glacier Doué fountain pen, that he'd been given as a leaving gift from his previous firm in Zurich, Switzerland.

Flick scribbled a signature, tossed the pen to Joe, who followed quickly with his. Both signatures were seconded and witnessed with the addition of the signatures of both Marin and Nakamoto.

Nakamoto retrieved his beloved pen, drew both sets of papers together, handed one set to Marin, and inserted the other set inside Joe's folder.

"Thank you, ladies and gentlemen, Nakamoto announced, "I can now confirm that this meeting is now concluded, and that your formal divorce will be finalized in Palm Beach County Court in the morning at 10am. May I wish you all a pleasant remainder of the day."

But Flick was already heading to the door to find out whether she needed an Uber or not.

And Joe and Angel, they just looked at each other and grinned.

Chapter 59

Rainee Showers just couldn't let it go. She now believed that she had confirmed Layla's real identity. And after eight hours of much needed sleep since coming back to her apartment from the McDonalds, she was again making coffee, to fire up her brain and begin putting the pieces together.

She was back on the LexisNexis website, now that she had what she thought was, a true identity to go on. The search this time was not quite so mysterious, and in a way, it was pretty much like an open book as far as Cassidy Swain was concerned.

Cassidy was born in 1987, in the town of Elk Mound, Wisconsin, population 927, according to the 2020 census. The town was mostly a farming community in Dunn County that lay in the Chippewa Valley, between Eau Claire and Chippewa Falls.

Cassidy had attended Elk Mound High School, the sole school to service all of the small towns in Dunn County, with a total enrolment of 347, until graduation at eighteen years old. After high school, Cassidy began her degree at the largest and most respected in-state college, University of Wisconsin-Madison. The much-reduced fees for attending an in-state university, hugely outweighed the costs of going out of state, which no doubt would have pleased her financially-struggling parents.

"So how the hell did this small-town girl suddenly become the wife of a notorious gangster like Carlo Galotti?" Rainee asked herself, "None of this makes any sense at all."

Digging deeper, she found the names of her parents, Eugene and Myrtle Swain, who owned and ran a cattle and dairy farm, Swain Farm.

The farm had prospered over the years, until corporates had moved into the area, building vast new office and commercial buildings on what was always deemed to be farmland for eternity, the most significant of these companies being Menards.

This, Rainee knew, was the colossal rebate-coupon company, whose products were snipped from newspapers and magazines in their millions, by indefatigable coupon-clippers across the nation, secreting their vouchers for huge numbers of discounts in retail stores nationwide.

She also learned that Eugene and Myrtle Swain, had died in an auto accident in January of 2009, presumably when snow conditions were at their worst in Dunn County.

Rainee had only ever seen snow once, when she was badgered by friends into going on a ski vacation in Aspen, Colorado. That wouldn't ever happen again, that was for certain, she'd hated it. But she could understand how deadly the deep snow and avalanches could be, and how even the most seasoned veterans of treacherous snow conditions, might find themselves in peril.

Cassidy was thirty-six now, so she would have been maybe twenty-two years old when she lost her parents, either before, or shortly after graduating from University of Wisconsin-Madison, where she had studied agronomy and soil science on a three-quarter paid scholarship. Rainee thought that the scholarship would have been manna from heaven for her parents, who could barely keep the farm going.

But when Rainee looked at Swain Farm's historical tax returns, she could easily see that once Cassidy's parents were gone, there would be no reason for her to continue running the farm at what had become a loss-making business.

So, the farm had been sold, and then Cassidy just kind of disappeared. And there appeared to be no known relatives that still remained in Elk Mound, none that she could find, anyway.

When Rainee looked at the DMV register on LexisNexis, she could find only one vehicle that had ever been registered to Cassidy, a 1979 Jeep CJ-7 Renegade in the extremely popular Firecracker Red of the time. Pretty much what Rainee might have expected for a farm girl in the mid-west; the CJ-7 Renegade was almost a rite of passage for a young girl in these areas.

Now tracking through the history of the car, Rainee discovered that its last known sale had been in 2010, to someone whose name Rainee immediately recognized. Mr. Wayne Randolph of RandyWayneAutos Inc.

"Gotcha," said Rainee, exhaling, realizing that she'd been right all along.

This was the missing piece of the jigsaw, and Wayne Randolph was the link. He'd supplied the Mini to Layla, having previously bought the Jeep from Cassidy. Layla Wray was Cassidy Swain.

Another search in the records database of the Miami-Dade County Marriage License Bureau, confirmed that Cassidy Swain married one Carlo Galotti in November, 2010.

So, everything was now beginning to make sense for Rainee. The only question remaining, was how she had come from packing up her

Jeep in Elk Mound, Wisconsin, and only six months later, becoming Mrs. Carlo Galotti? And further examination provided one more fact. There had never been a divorce.

Chapter 60

Hurricane Jacques had gathered momentum quickly. After leaving a trail of death and destruction across the prone, vulnerable and defenseless islands of the West Indies, and then on into Cuba, its treacherous projected course as predicted by the National Hurricane Center, had taken a sharp detour north from Havana.

Jacques was already shredding homes and resorts to shattered pieces of debris in the most southern part of Florida, from Key West up through Marathon and on to Islamorada. South Florida residents and businesses already knew what the outcome for them was going to be. They'd witnessed it far too many times. It was the same old, same old.

Never-ending queues had formed around every hardware store, with lines running around the entire perimeters of the larger ones; Home Depot and Lowes, and even smaller stores like Ace Hardware.

Everyone wanted to buy generators in case of a power outage, and everyone wanted them now. Self-salvation and self-centeredness became the new mantra for the masses.

Instead of the usual mixed array of cars and contractors' trucks in the car parks of these stores, just about every vehicle now was a pickup truck, low-loader or van, while other desperate customers with saloons and hatchbacks, were struggling to ram their hurricane supplies inside their cramped cargo spaces.

Sales of plywood, plastic sheeting, electric saws, and screws and nails, were going through the roof, fueled by residents and businesses that didn't have the benefit of metal hurricane shutters; these unlucky ones nailing ply or chipboard to window frames as a cheap solution in order to withstand the impending impact.

The rooves of these buildings though, were a whole other problem. All anyone could do on the eve of a major hurricane, was to check roof-tiles and shingles were secured and just simply say a prayer.

Batteries, flashlights, solar radios and first aid supplies were flying out the doors, with harangued and abused store assistants trying their hardest to restock the shelves, before impatient customers were dragging them back off them to load into their carts and scurry to the checkouts.

Outside, the triumphant customers who had snared their treasures by camping outside the stores throughout the night, raced their swollen carts to their cars, often having to stop and go back to retrieve items that had fallen off in their incessant hurry to get home and lock down.

Gas stations saw lines of cars stretching down the highway, for voracious customers eager to fuel up their vehicles, most of whom had also brought dozens of gas cans and containers with them, to take home in case the gas stations ran out of unleaded or diesel after the storm had left.

In the supermarkets, it felt like the end of the world was coming, Armageddon itself, with once again, multiple lines of shoppers, some with two shopping carts apiece. They raced inside, literally clearing shelves in their wake, grabbing anything that wasn't perishable, and actually, even everything that was.

Canned items, such as beans, tomatoes, fruit, juice and meat were the top prizes for every shopper that swept them from the shelves into their waiting carts. Spam had never been so popular. But pasta, rice, cereal, dried fruit, alcohol, candles, matches, and toilet rolls soon followed once the deli counters had been cleaned out.

Some shoppers, those with two carts, wearily exited the supermarkets, haphazardly steering their supplies to their cars, one cart loaded with food, the other balancing dozens of one-gallon containers of water, should there be a water cut as well as a loss of power.

Even banks were under siege, account holders packing the foyers, coupled with the insatiable queues waiting for the drive-thru.

For some inexplicable reason, many of these customers were drawing out all of their cash, deciding that it was better kept under their mattresses, rather than trust the banks who in recent times had been failing and closing, with customers losing their savings, if they weren't FDIC-insured. People no longer trusted the banking mechanism. And they had a point.

At homes and businesses across the length and breadth of South Florida, the unrelenting buzz of chainsaws drowned out the omnipresent sound of the cicadas, as men and women chopped down the branches and felled the trees that could be perilous to rooves and windows.

Trees that had been lovingly planted and grown for decades, disappeared in the vicious cut of a vituperative and malevolent chainsaw. They would be replaced afterwards, of course, but this was man against nature.

Those who had small sail boats or motor cruisers that were habitually taken out as weekend pleasure crafts, anxiously stowed them in their garage if they had one.

And yards and pools were cleared of any items that would be collected by the hurricane. Floridians knew that airborne menaces could not only take out windows, doors and rooves, but they were also a deadly threat to humans who had unwittingly decided to prematurely venture outside.

Even a storm-detached and weightless piece of tin soffit, flying so fast through the air, could literally decapitate a person who hadn't seen it coming.

So, anything that avoided the catastrophe of owners losing their precious and hard-worked-for properties, with many unable to afford the tens of thousands of dollars required to insure them in the first instance, saw neighbors helping other neighbors, with particular regard to the older and more incapacitated ones who couldn't help themselves.

This was one of the most beautifully human and humane aspects seen in times like this, whether pre-hurricane or later in the aftermath, when the storm had finally left, when the debris had to be cleared and repairs made.

It was a feeling of the very best form of camaraderie. There was an exhalation of gratitude that they, the survivors, had been spared. That moment would literally be the quiet *after* the storm when people came together and acted as one, almost joyful amidst the destruction in which they stood.

And right now, in the days before the impending impact of the hurricane, a never-ending supply of flasks of coffee, ice-coolers brimful of beer and sodas, and home-baked cakes and muffins, flooded out of neighborhood homes to be shared around to all of the workers, men, women and children alike.

But as Remy Washington bore witness to the chaos that was happening right in front of his eyes, beads of sweat formed on his forehead as he navigated the Escalade back toward Riviera Yacht Club, his colossal frame shaking in trepidation as his hands gripped the steering wheel.

Chapter 61

Tommy Burns knew that he couldn't ever go back to the house now. He didn't really much care, it was a rental anyway, and he hadn't paid the rent in three months. And it wasn't like he had much in the way of possessions either, so he guessed whatever there was, would go out in the trash once the landlord re-rented the place.

Since that night, that had seen him running naked down the street, with a gun in his hand, he had been sofa-surfing at a few friends' places. He'd been given clothes, a place to sleep and had stolen food from the local markets. His lifestyle had done a complete one-eighty since Flick, and he resented the bitch now.

Tommy had in fact, spent one more night with Flick at a seedy dump of a motel on Okeechobee Blvd, which turned out to be Flick's final hurrah with him. When he had arrived there, she was already naked in the bed, so he thought that maybe, he could still skim a few bucks from her for the foreseeable future.

But that hadn't turned out to be the case. She'd fucked him raw until two in the morning, and then upped and left while he was sleeping. Although she had left an envelope with a couple of thousand dollars in it on the bedside table with a note,

It was fun while it lasted, but gotta run now. Good luck, baby xx

And the two grand wasn't going to last long, he thought, as he sat there on a stool at the counter in a friend's kitchenette. Rolling a dollar bill into a 'straw', and snorting two more lines of coke up his nose, he realized that he was doing that three times a day now, at forty bucks a pop.

He had a little shy of three hundred dollars in his pocket, and he needed to find another payday like Flick. Sooner, rather than later.

Chapter 62

Sitting in the tiny and cramped Toyota Yaris, Don Faber lifted his binoculars to his eyes when he saw a familiar Ford Raptor pulling into a parking spot outside the apartment building. As he crouched down in the seat, he watched as the same girl who'd taken him down in Miami, slid out of the truck, clicked her key fob to lock it, and strode toward the entrance door of the building.

"Lara Croft," he smirked, "I think your tomb-raiding days are over, sweetheart."

There was little to be done in broad daylight, but he needed to confirm that Rainee Showers actually lived here, and hadn't rented her apartment out as an investment property as many Palm Beach owners did. It would be a terrible shame to kill the wrong girl.

He knew exactly which apartment she lived in, from information on the Palm Beach County Property Tax register, and he was pretty certain that the key-coded doors wouldn't be an issue for him. His handy little fifty-dollar ECM Jammer would freeze the code for twenty seconds, allowing him to easily gain access.

"Too fucking easy," he said to himself.

But with the knowledge that Hurricane Jacques was going to arrive in the next forty-eight hours or so, time was not on his side. He would need to get information out of the girl, without having to kill her straightaway, and then send it to Galotti, who was probably already hunkered down in his mansion.

After that, he'd hightail it back to Pompano Beach, and weather the hurricane at home with his beloved Marylou.

~ ~ ~

Almost by reflex, whenever Rainee came back to her apartment, she habitually picked up her own set of binoculars, hers being US military-grade AGM PVS-7 NL1 thermal imaging binoculars, that she could also strap to her head if needed. And that was often a requirement in her job.

She scanned the car park, looking for particular heat variations everywhere, but primarily focused on the parked vehicles.

Usually, the task was uneventful, but she had become acutely aware since her discovery of Layla's connection to the mob, that she probably ought to be extra vigilant for the time being.

As she scanned the cars, she paused on a blue Toyota Yaris, the deep red thermal image indicating that someone was sitting in the vehicle. The fact that the binoculars were not registering any engine heat, indicated that the occupant had either just got in the car or they had been sitting there for some time.

Rainee suspected the latter and swapped her thermal binoculars for a pair of Steiner M830 laser rangefinder field glasses, and focused in close on the occupant of the Toyota. She recognized the man immediately.

"Ah, Muppet number one," she said quietly, "You've finally decided to come out and play."

~ ~ ~

In the far corner of the parking lot, mostly hidden by a metallic window sunshade, Shira Kadosh was still able to focus her own scope on the girl whom she now knew as Rainee Showers. Kadosh, like Faber, had also rented an anonymous vehicle for surveillance. The beige Toyota Camry EV was perfect for the job, because beige Camrys were practically invisible.

Kadosh had assumed that a girl like Showers would be fully and tactically armed, which was confirmed when Kadosh identified the thermal imaging binoculars at the window. Fortunately, the purchase of a metallic-silver sunshade at Walmart had diminished Kadosh's own body heat in her car, which at a cost of twenty bucks, was a steal in her mind.

But then she saw Showers switching to a pair of laser binoculars, having clearly focused on something she didn't like the look of. Kadosh turned her head to the left, raised her field glasses again, and saw a Japanese compact with a man inside.

"What the fuck?" she exhaled, stunned that someone else might be tracking the girl.

Showers had now switched to a digital SLR with a very long telephoto lens, and seemed to be taking photos of whoever it was that occupied the vehicle.

And then suddenly, the car's engine started and the driver was heading quickly to the exit and out onto the highway.

Certain that she was still 'invisible' to Showers, Kadosh looked back at the apartment window and saw that the girl was gone.

274

Chapter 63

"Do you ever get scared of hurricanes?"

"It's not my first rodeo, so no, not anymore," I replied.

Layla snuggled into me, as I continued talking.

"Although my buddy Remy will be jumpier than a rattlesnake in a pickle barrel by now, so we'd better go and check on him shortly.

"Tonight?" she asked.

"No, but first thing in the morning," I replied.

Layla and I had spent an idyllic couple of days and nights in our 'adopted' home, and we were about to spend our third night together. I felt happier than a tick on a dog.

"Coop?' she asked, her elegant naked form hidden partially under the sheet, "Can I trust you?"

"I sure hope so, Layla," I said, dipping my head down to kiss her head, "What's wrong?"

"There's something I need to tell you, but it's a big thing and you might have second thoughts after I tell you."

I remembered what Rainee had told me in her discreet investigation into Layla, so although I had no idea what her secret was, I felt prepared for just about anything right now.

She sat up in the bed and turned to face me, and I could see a tear trickling down her face.

"What's wrong, Layla?" I asked, shocked to see how upset she had become so quickly.

"My name's not Layla," she replied, her voice breaking now.

"Okay," I said, "Then what is it?"

"It's Cassidy, Cassidy Swain."

"Well, it's a pleasure to meet you, Cassidy," I said, trying to diffuse what was clearly an upsetting moment for her.

"And I'm not divorced either, I'm still married."

This was a bit of a shock to me, but it still didn't change how I felt about her.

"Is there anything else you want to tell me?" I asked gently.

"Yes,' she blurted, "But you're not going to like it."

"Well, I've seen and heard a lot of things in my life, and I'm at the point now where nothing much fazes me anymore," I replied, "So whatever it is you need to tell me, nothing is going to change between us."

"I killed a man."

I did my best to remain calm as Cassidy was quickly falling apart, moving close to her and hugging her tightly.

"Look, baby, I've killed a man too, several in fact. Do you want to tell me what happened?"

"I do, Coop, I want to be completely honest and open with you. I'm not a bad person, please believe me."

She was trembling in my arms and I needed to calm her.

"Would you like a drink, something strong?" I asked, "I think you might need one, your whole body is shaking."

"Yes... please... I'd like that, I think."

I quickly got out of the bed, leaving her in the bedroom, and brought back a bottle of brandy and two crystal glasses that I'd found behind the house's home bar.

Pouring a generous amount in each glass, I gave one to Cassidy, who took a big gulp, and I downed half of mine in a second.

"You should know you can tell me anything, Cassidy, I'm not easily shocked," I said quietly after a moment's silence.

"I know, Coop, and I will."

Chapter 64

"Fuck me, she's finally out of my fucking life, and we completely fucked her."

Joe Jarvie was not one to omit an expletive if the opportunity merited one, and today was no exception to that rule.

"I'm as shocked as you are, Joe, that she somehow, *completely* missed a critical fact," said Angel, "Astonished really, given the woman you married."

"Does she not even pay attention to the music scene these days?" asked Joe, pacing around the spacious lounge, chain-smoking Marlboros, "Or d'ya think she was so intent on gettin' her settlement and disappearing, that it just didn't occur to the bitch?"

The debut *Shamenless* album, *F*ck Me Shamenless* had sat in the top position on the Billboard charts for two weeks so far, and with current worldwide sales, it was unlikely to be toppled anytime soon.

"It's not just the album sales she missed out on, Joe. Think about the money we're going to make from the tour and all the merchandise," said Angel.

"Man, I love merchandise, you don't have to do a fucking thing and the cash just keeps on rollin' in, like waves on the shore," said Joe, lighting another Marlboro with the cigarette he'd just finished.

"I'm guessing that residuals and royalties from the album alone could get to maybe forty million bucks, as a conservative estimate," replied Angel, "But the tour profits are going to double that figure, and well, the merch is the gift that keeps on giving."

"How will we earn so much from the tour?" Joe suddenly asked, inquisitively, "We've never really made much from touring, I remember you saying that, and you always told me it was pretty much a loss leader, but we just had to do it to promote a new album."

Angel laughed out loud.

"Look, it's been, what, twenty years since you last toured?" asked Angel.

"Probably," said Joe, "I've forgotten what it was like to play gigs now."

"Then, let me educate you about touring in 2023," Angel replied.

"Okay… have at it," said Joe, now studiously curious, his pacing coming to an abrupt stop.

Angel sat back on the sofa, as Joe finally sat down and stubbed out his latest cigarette.

"When you last toured, when you were with your band back in the late nineties, you played venues that held maybe three thousand fans."

"But they were awesome gigs, man, don't you remember, it was fucking wild at the after-parties, I never did so much blow in my life!" Joe chortled, laughing at the memory.

Angel also remembered it far too well, because he was the one that had to pay for the coke and the parties, as well as all the damage the band routinely did to every hotel room they stayed in.

"How much was a ticket back then, for a show?" asked Angel.

"I dunno, man," Joe replied, "Fifty bucks?"

Angel smiled once again at his very talented, but somewhat naïve client.

"Ticket prices usually averaged around twenty dollars, believe it or not," said Angel.

"Whaaaattt?" yelled Joe, clearly shocked at what Angel had just told him.

"And that never even covered the cost of the gig with all the trucks, equipment and payroll," Angel continued, "I remember what the bills were, it was sickening to think we were making such a loss."

"Fuuuuuck!" exclaimed Joe, "I never knew that, man."

"You didn't know a lot of things, Joe, I made sure of that. And merchandise was only about break-even, we just had to have it at the gigs to get promotion from the fans when they wore the stuff in public places. It was a pain in the ass, to be honest."

"I'm fucking confused, Angel, how we gonna make so much dough then this time?"

"Things are different now," said Angel, "The mark-up on the merch is around six hundred percent, and that's online and in stores, as well as at the gigs."

"Got it," said Joe, "But is that seriously gonna pump up the bucks that much, to the numbers you've just been talkin' about?"

"No," replied Angel, "But it's one humongous hike in dollar bills compared to the 1990s, trust me."

"Yeah, I guess, and I've always trusted you, Angel, I wouldn't be where I am without you."

"Thank you. But the big difference now, is that you're not going to be doing a nationwide tour of venues holding two or three thousand people," Angel continued, "Your next tour is worldwide and we've moved into the big time now, you're going to be playing stadiums."

"Stadiums?" asked Joe, "But they hold fifty, maybe a hundred thou."

Angel stirred his coffee that Felipe had just placed on the coffee table in front of him.

"And," said Angel, "Ticket prices aren't twenty bucks anymore, more like a hundred and eighty, minimum."

Joe slumped back on the sofa, completely astonished at what Angel was saying.

"And Flick," Joe realized, "She ain't gonna get a dime."

Angel took a sip of the cappuccino, and reclined back once again.

"Now you get the picture, my little rock god, welcome to my world."

Chapter 65

"It's why I had to run, to escape. If I hadn't left when I did, I'd be dead already."

Cassidy had calmed a little with the aid of a second shot of brandy, but I didn't push or interrogate her, I just wanted to let her tell me everything at her own pace.

"Why don't you just start at the beginning, and take your time, we have the whole night, don't worry about anything. Seriously, Cassidy, you're safe here."

"I made a stupid and terrible mistake," she continued, "But I was young, a dumb and naïve girl suddenly finding herself in the dazzle of a big city."

"Miami?"

"Yes, but it was exciting at first, it was all so new to me, and I guess... well, I was just enjoying being completely free of the farm life, living in a major city for the first time, and meeting some really amazing young people."

"What happened to change that feeling?" I asked.

"I found myself alone at The White Party, have you heard of it?"

"I have, yes, I've even been to one of them when I first moved to Florida from San Francisco. I was staying in Miami, but the city wasn't really my bag, so I came further north to make Palm Beach my home."

"Oh, okay, so you know how lavish and amazing those parties are?"

"Yes, and they raise a lot of money too, for a good cause," I replied, "But what happened at the party?"

"I was sitting alone at a bar; my friends had left me there while they tried their luck in the casino."

"Fool's game," I replied.

"I know, I would never gamble," she continued, "And suddenly, a handsome and charming man was sitting next to me, offering to buy me a drink."

"Really?" I asked, "That's weird because the drinks are complimentary at the White Party."

"So I found out," said Cassidy, "But from the moment I met this guy, he literally swept me off my feet."

"What happened then?"

"We began dating, you know, in a really nice and proper way, and he made me feel so good about myself, something I had never experienced before in Wisconsin."

"A bit of a sharp contrast, I'd guess?"

"Totally. He would send a limo to my hotel to collect me and take me to a restaurant or to the opera or a show, and he would always be there to greet me when I got out of the car," said Cassidy, "He was pretty amazing really, and I began to fall for him."

"I can definitely see that happening, so what went wrong?"

"After only two weeks, he proposed to me."

"You didn't say who the man was, would I know of him?"

"I think so," said Cassidy, "I became Mrs. Carlo Galotti."

"I know who he is, most people in South Florida would recognize that name," I replied, "But you had no idea that he was mafia?"

"No! Why would I? This was a world I knew nothing about," Cassidy replied, clearly feeling embarrassed that she was having to tell me about the mistake she'd made.

"It's okay, Cass, I get it, honestly."

"And to be honest," she continued, "For the first year or so, it was pretty good. I lived in this huge home, a luxury compound really, and I had everything I wanted. Drove fancy cars, wore designer clothes, and Carlo showered me with gifts, mostly expensive jewelry."

"So what went wrong?" I asked.

Carlo would often go to big events, show openings, banquets, balls, you know, all that kind of stuff," she continued, "And I was always on his arm. Until I wasn't."

"Why was that?"

"He began to take other girls to these high-end gatherings, mostly models I think, and I stayed home on my own. I felt like I was no longer relevant."

"I can't imagine anyone ever thinking that way about you, Cass," I replied, "You're not like most girls I've met, you're very special."

"Thank you, Coop, I really appreciate that," she replied, pulling my hand to her chest and squeezing it tightly.

"It kinda feels like you had become surplus to requirement, could you not have just filed for divorce?"

"Oh Coop, that would have been my best option, but you just don't get to divorce a man like Carlo Galotti," Cassidy continued, "They either divorce *you*, or they kill you, there's no middle ground."

"So, you just had to wait it out?"

"Pretty much, but I became so depressed about what I'd stupidly gotten myself into."

"Did you have any close friends in Miami, you know, people that you could turn to?"

"Yes, I did, still do, but obviously I haven't seen them since I've been on the run," she replied, "A wonderful couple, Wayne and Greta Randolph, I met them when I sold my Jeep."

My stomach churned at the thought that Cassidy was completely unaware of the couple's fate, and in this moment, I had to decide whether or not I should be the bearer of terrible news to her.

"I would spend a lot of time with them, their home was like my sanctuary, and Carlo barely knew they existed," she continued, "Wayne even made it possible for me to escape with absolute anonymity, and I miss them both so much, but I can't even tell them where I am, or what I'm doing as I don't want Carlo getting to them."

Cassidy broke down at this thought, and she was inconsolable, her tears streaking down her face, as I took her in my arms and cradled her. And right now, wasn't the best moment to tell her about the Randolphs' fate.

After a few minutes, Cassidy once again became calmer, and her tears began to stop flowing as her breathing returned to a more stable rate.

"Do you want to tell me more, or should we take a break?" I asked.

"I need to tell you everything, Coop," she replied, "I can't keep this inside me any longer. You've become important to me, and I don't want there to be anything left unsaid. Do you understand?"

"Okay, but just take it easy, and tell me one piece at a time."

"The years went by, and my depression worsened. Carlo was no longer a husband to me, or someone he even cared about. All I was, was a bauble, an attractive trinket to have in the house when he threw parties or dinners."

"I can only imagine," I said.

"But then, around six months or so ago, he had some powerful new business associates come to the house for a party he was throwing for them, to celebrate their new business relationship. You know, a beautiful sunny day, barbecues and spit-roasted pigs, lots of very young girls in bikinis, mostly topless. I'd seen it all before, but this time, the businessmen were Russian."

"Go on," I said in a quiet voice.

"I remember exactly what Carlo said to them in front of me, she continued, "He said, "This is my wife, Cassidy, please enjoy her, she is at your disposal, and she's a decent fuck on her good days.""

Her voice quivered, heavy with the weight of humiliation of what she was telling Coop.

"A real charmer," I said, anger building up deep inside of me.

"But they all seemed to take it as a joke, and I'd already had enough of the party, and decided to go up to the bedroom just to get away from it all."

"I'll bet you just wanted to get out of there and disappear?"

"I did, but there was no way that was going to happen," replied Cassidy, "And then everything changed while I was in the bedroom."

"You thought about escaping?"

"No. It wasn't that. It was much worse."

I didn't even know what she was going to say next, but I couldn't believe that this girl had ever found herself in this predicament, although even I knew that it wasn't unusual.

"I was lying on the bed, just enjoying the breeze that was coming through the French doors, when suddenly, the bedroom door opened and one of the Russians came into the room, a younger man I recognized."

I wasn't sure I was ready to hear what might have happened next, but I remained silent and just let Cassidy talk.

"He said, "So you're the pretty girl I can fuck, yes?""

"Jeez, Cass," I said, kissing her on the top of her head and pulling her closer.

"I told him to get out of my bedroom and find someone else. But this guy was intent, he wasn't used to ever hearing the word 'no' in his world. He leapt onto the bed, grabbing at my bikini top and ripping it from me. He was going to rape me, Coop."

"Oh Cass, I can't even begin to contemplate what you were going through, it's horrific."

"I knee'd him in the balls, which stopped him for a few seconds, and then I saw the look on his face and I was terrified. There was no way he was leaving the room until he'd done what he came for."

I felt sick, not for myself, but for Cassidy, and for every girl who has to experience an assault like this.

"He was wearing a pair of board shorts, and he stood at the end of the bed and removed them. I knew there could only be one of two outcomes, so I yanked open the bedside table drawer and pulled out Carlo's gun and aimed it at the bastard."

I wanted to wrap her up and protect her forever, as I squeezed her tightly.

"His face was just a salacious smile now, and he ignored the gun pointing at him, and advanced toward me. At that very moment, I made a huge decision, and shot him three times, until he finally slumped down on the bed, dead."

"That was too close for comfort, Cass. Did anyone hear?"

"Oh yeah, everyone heard, which is why I made another decision. To escape. And I've been on the run ever since."

"Who was the guy?"

"That was the biggest problem, he was the twenty-six-year-old son of one of the Russians at the party. The boy's name was Anatoly Sokalov.

On hearing this new information, my gut didn't just churn, I felt fear for her, and me. Cassidy wasn't only on the run from Carlo Galotti, which was bad enough anyway, but she was being hunted by one of the most powerful and ruthless Russian mafiosos ever to make America his domain.

"The son of Nikita Sokalov," I said, in a very quiet voice.

Cassidy gasped, "How do you know?"

"It's a long story, baby."

Chapter 66

Rainee hadn't told Coop about anything she'd recently found out about Layla. Two reasons really, firstly because her calls and messages had gone unanswered, his phone probably turned off, and when she'd paid a visit to his boat, it was locked up, battened down. Pip, she already knew, had taken Diablo and gone to her parents' home, so there was little point in Coop being at the marina. And Kinky had probably already made other plans.

Rainee wasn't unduly worried either. If the romance between him and Layla/Cassidy was going better than ever, she knew that Coop would want to have some alone time with her. So, for the moment, even though he was ignorant of a potentially lethal situation, there would be no way for anyone to find him. She knew that from past experience.

In fact, Coop had admitted to her that occasionally when he just wanted to have time out from living on the boat, he would 'babysit' a vacant home. She never did find out how he came to babysit, but she did know that when he left these houses, he cleaned them, ran the vacuum round the whole place, and left food and wine in the fridge. The courteous criminal.

She also knew that with the imminent arrival of the hurricane, Coop would soon be gathering his troops, including Molly and Billy, Remy and Memphis, probably Layla too, and of course, Rainee herself, to hunker down at a suitable location. He would turn up right on time, never failed. When the shit hit the fan, Coop was clockwork.

She'd finished up working for Mo-Nay$Neverenuff until the hurricane had passed, and so she now had some time on her hands.

And to be honest, with the sudden appearance of Don Faber outside her apartment today, she didn't want to be a sitting target. She liked things to go down on her terms, not on anyone else's.

All she had to do was to keep moving and wait for the call.

Chapter 67

Don Faber watched as the Rainee exited the apartment building, and climbed into her Raptor. This time, he was parked across the road in a no-parking zone. And he really didn't give a fuck if he got a ticket.

"Fool me once," he said to himself.

Once her truck peeled out onto the highway, he put the Yaris into gear, pulled out and began to follow at a safe distance. It was getting dark now and he doubted she would spot him tailing her, and he could hang back five or six cars, because the Raptor was so easy to see, it stuck out like a clown at a funeral.

But Faber was unaware of the car that had peeled out twenty seconds later, the Camry staying at a two-hundred-yard distance behind his Yaris.

Rainee was hungry again, and had decided to get some supper at a local Outback restaurant. She could have gone to Longhorns Steakhouse, which was closer, but she loved the Bloomin' Onions at Outback, and their prime rib was pretty damned good too. And inside the Raptor, she could almost taste the Aussie chain restaurant's Gold Coast Coconut Shrimp. Rainee was hungry.

The rain was battering Faber's windshield now, and it was getting harder to see the Raptor, so he moved past a couple of slower moving cars to get a better line of sight on it. He touched the reassuringly cold hard steel of the Magnum that nestled in the body holster beneath his jacket.

"Not long, sweetheart."

When Kadosh had seen the Yaris moving closer to the Raptor, she waited forty-five seconds before closing the gap on the car. The rain was making the task of following a little more difficult than she had planned. However, on a well-lit and busy highway like Southern Blvd, it was pretty much like driving in daylight in the rain.

Faber wondered where the girl was heading, but eventually, he saw the Raptor's turn-signal blink on ahead, as Showers took a right at the Outback, two hundred yards in front of him. He slowed down before also making the turn, but noting the enormous brightly-lit sign of the other businesses situated there, he ignored the Outback parking lot and headed toward the Costco building that lay behind the restaurant.

Kadosh also slowed down as she saw first, the Raptor turning off, and then the Yaris following, although the car continued toward the Costco. She pulled over on the side of the highway for exactly one minute, before edging out and slowly turning right, and made her way to the Outback parking lot.

It didn't take long to spot the Raptor truck, and Kadosh parked the Camry forty yards away at an angle where she could surveil.

Five minutes passed, before Kadosh eyed the Yaris turning into the Outback lot, making a slow tour before spotting the truck, and then parking eight cars from it.

~~~

"What can I get you, ma'am?" asked the young man behind the bar.

"Ma'am?" asked Rainee, "Do I look like I could be your mom?"

She had clearly embarrassed the boy who was maybe twenty-two, because his face had reddened very quickly. Rainee thought that he might suffer from rosacea.

"Sorry, miss, bit of a habit here, most of the customers are retired."

"I'm fucking with you... Ben," she replied, taking a look at his name badge, "But you know what, I'm friggin' hungry."

"Name it, I'll get it pronto," Ben replied, clearly relieved that he hadn't offended anyone in what was only his second week working there, "I'll get you a menu."

He was a nice kid, probably still at college, but he presented well, in his crisp white shirt and black waistcoat.

"No menu required, Ben, I already know what I want," said Rainee, "I need a Bloomin' Onion as soon as you can get it, a half dozen Coconut Shrimps and a prime rib. Oh, and can I have a big glass of Dr. Pepper, please?"

"You got it, ma'... miss, coming right up," said Ben, scurrying off to the kitchen to make a rush food order, before running back and placing a pint of Dr. Pepper on a coaster in front of Rainee.

"Nice work, Ben, you're a keeper."

Rainee never sat at a table in restaurants, she always preferred to eat at the bar. In part, it was because she never usually had a proper boyfriend to go with her, so in her eyes, she'd look like a sad person.

When she had occasionally found someone she kind of liked, they rarely lasted more than a couple of weeks when they found out what she did for work. Rainee also thought that she somehow scared men of her age. Might also have been the arsenal of weapons she kept at her apartment.

The food order arrived quickly, and Rainee began tucking into the crispy deep-fried onion, finishing it in a few short minutes and washing it down with half the Dr. Pepper, before she began devouring the shrimp.

"You got a real appetite going on there, miss, ain't never seen someone of your size pack that much away," remarked Ben, as Rainee tore into the prime rib.

"Don't always believe what it says on the tin, Ben," replied Rainee, "And quit with the 'miss', it's Rainee."

"Can I get you another Pepper, Rainee?"

"Yes, you *can*," said Rainee, not even looking up from her plate.

~ ~ ~

Don Faber's stomach was rumbling, he wished now that he'd eaten before he came out. The chips and confectionary items that he'd snagged from the Motel 6's vending machine, were not entirely what he was used to.

If he were at home with Marylou, he'd be eating a steak, probably a nice T-bone. He was so hungry that he was half-inclined to order a burger at the take-out window at the end of the Outback building.

Shira Kadosh, on the other hand, had no hunger pains whatsoever, having already dined at the Four Seasons hotel on garlic mussels, followed by Dover sole and charred broccolini. She was good to go.

Thirty-five more minutes went by before Faber couldn't take it any longer. He jumped out of the Yaris and headed quickly over to the take-out window, ordering a double cheeseburger and two servings of fries.

Kadosh watched in amusement at the man. She had no idea who he was by name, but it was clear that his stomach ruled his life.

~ ~ ~

"Where you from, Ben," asked Rainee, hoping it didn't sound like a come-on. In reality, if she'd started very, very early, she actually might be old enough to be his mom.

"Kenosha, Wisconsin originally," Ben replied, as he began to clear the last of Rainee's dishes.

"Ha, I know a girl from Wisconsin," said Rainee, thinking about Layla, "Why are you in Florida?"

"I got a full-ride scholarship to Florida State, I'm in my senior year now."

"How'd you get a full ride?" she asked.

"I played running-back for the football team, used to anyway before I got my leg broken."

"Ah, that's a real shame, Ben, I'm sorry," said Rainee, truly sympathetically, "What are you studying?"

"Marine biology," Ben replied.

"Smart choice, you'll always be employed in Florida."

"Thank you, ma'a… Rainee, that's good to know. Can I get you anything else?"

"Nah, I'm good, just the check, please."

"You got it, and it was really nice to meet you, Rainee, you're cool."

"You too, Ben."

~ ~ ~

Faber came running back to his car, dropping French fries and ketchup sachets in his wake. He struggled to open the door, as he tried to balance his food order in his arms, but once inside, he bit deep into the burger and immediately followed it by stuffing a handful of fries into his mouth.

Shira Kadosh watched through her telephoto scope in amusement. She couldn't believe that this rotund little man could eat so much, so quickly. How does a man care so little for his body, she thought?

Meanwhile, inside the restaurant, Rainee left a twenty-dollar tip for Ben, grabbed her jacket and made her way to the exit.

~ ~ ~

Faber had already gobbled down the cheeseburger, but instantly threw the remainder of his fries down onto the passenger seat when he saw Showers exiting the Outback. She stopped, took a good look around the parking lot, scanning every vehicle as the rain hurtled down, before slowly making her way toward her truck.

Kadosh had also seen the same thing that Faber had spotted, albeit just a little earlier, because Faber was still shoveling fries into his huge and insatiable orifice.

She slipped out of the Camry, keeping low, her beloved suppressor-fitted IWI DAN rifle in her hands, and stealthily made her way forward. There was no way that she would let the fat man question her first, this was her job and no one else's.

Don Faber pulled his jacket sleeve across his still munching mouth, and then wiped his greasy hands down the front of his now stained shirt. He opened the door of the Yaris, tugged his jacket hood over his head, pulled the Magnum from his inside pocket and strode straight into the path of Rainee, as she was just fifteen yards from the Raptor.

"Rainee Showers?" he yelled at her, as Rainee came to a sudden and complete stop, the man's face partially hidden by his rain hood.

"What's it to you?" she yelled back, the noise of the rain making it difficult to hear what the man was saying, "And who the fuck are *you*?"

"None of your business, missy, I just need some information from you, that's all, ain't gonna hurt you."

"Well, you got that straight," replied Rainee, who remained completely calm, standing in the pouring rain.

Kadosh remained hidden behind a big Chevy Silverado, as she tried to listen to the exchange between the man and the Showers girl.

"What do you know about Cassidy Swain?" barked Faber.

"No idea who you're talking about, dickweed, now get out of my way, before I put you down."

Faber closed the distance between them.

"You remember me, don't you, girl, because I remember you. You're the bitch who tasered me down in Miami."

"How can I forget Dumb and Dumber?" taunted Rainee, "How's your partner?"

"He's dead, just like you'll be soon if you don't get smart," yelled Faber, "I know you've been digging into the Randolphs so you must know Swain. Now spill it, where is she?"

Rainee's hands had been in her pockets throughout this entire exchange, so the feeling of the Glock in her right hand was allowing her to almost enjoy the moment.

"I have no clue who you're talking about, fatboy, so get out of my way before I have to make you," Rainee replied.

Faber began to raise his gun, the barrel three-quarters the way up as Rainee also pointed her Glock at the man's midriff, her finger resting patiently on the trigger.

Almost simultaneously, Faber's gun fell from his hand as a .338 Lapua Magnum hollow-point ripped through his throat, blood showering from it like a crimson geyser. As he fell awkwardly to the tarmac, no more words came from his mouth, just a horrible gargling, choking sound that would precipitate his imminent death.

At exactly the same moment that Rainee had ducked for cover behind a trash can, Shira Kadosh had slithered snake-like back to the Camry, quickly got herself inside and used the electric motor of the hybrid car to silently leave the parking lot.

Unaware of Kadosh's recent presence, and shocked by what had just gone down, Rainee ducked behind the garbage bin enclosure to make sure she wasn't the next target. She quickly dialed 911 on a burner phone to report Faber's death, equally aware that the Outback's cameras would have recorded the entire event.

She was grateful that she had pulled up the hood of her own rain jacket when she had exited the restaurant, relieved that her face wouldn't have been recorded on camera.

From her secluded position, she watched through the metal slats of the enclosure and saw that forty or fifty customers and employees had now rushed out of the restaurant to see what was happening. Some were already vomiting when they saw the freshly throat-less corpse lying on the asphalt, but no one paid particular attention to Rainee.

Rainee realized that with the crowd of people now standing outside, she could easily slip away without anyone noticing.

And the last thing she wanted was to have her name in the papers, that would connect her to Faber and Layla, and ultimately, to Galotti.

But the shock of the murder had shaken Rainee, and she wasn't quite in the right state of mind to drive just yet. She needed to clear her head and take a moment, before the parking lot would be overwhelmed with the red, blue and white lights of police cruisers.

So, as the clamor around her turned into white noise, she sat back against one of the garbage bins for a moment, pretty dazed, not even realizing that her ass was getting soaked, and just stared at the dead man, now lying prostrate in a pool of rain-spattered blood, and minus a good proportion of his neck.

And then her adrenalin suddenly kicked in, realizing that she might be next, and made a swift beeline to the Raptor.

Chapter 68

Hurricane Jacques had now hit mainland Florida, having already devastated the Florida Keys. It had made landfall in Miami and that meant, given its projected northern path, it was time to get the hell out of Dodge. Palm Beach, even.

Cassidy and I had woken up to the sound of intense and pummeling rain battering the bedroom window's glass at seven in the morning. We'd instantly gotten out of bed, made coffee, and I finally switched my phone back on.

There were a lot of messages and missed calls, but before I checked them, I opened up the radar app and saw that Hurricane Jacques was maybe twenty-four hours from hitting Palm Beach.

But looking out the window, it felt like it had already arrived. It was time to get everyone together.

First on the list was Molly, and I immediately dialed her number.

"Hey Dad," she said, "What are we doing?"

"Are you with Billy?" I asked.

"We're at the apartment."

"Okay, listen. You know where Perryman lives, don't you?"

"I do, new house in Sewall's, yes?"

"Exactly. I want you and Billy to get in the truck and head straight down there now. He's expecting you."

"Okay, but what are you gonna do?"

"I'll be right behind you, see you soon."

"Love you, Dad."

"Love you more."

I hung up and then dialed Memphis's number.

"How's he doing?" I asked when he picked up.

"You know Remy, Coop, he's a bag of rags."

"Yep, figures. Where are you right now?"

"We're at my place in Jensen."

"Well, your cottage is timber, could be carnage there if Jacques becomes a category five."

"Don't I know it, man. But some of my wealthy patrons in Palm Beach would probably offer shelter…"

"Forget that, Memphis, Remy won't even survive the drive up here," I replied, "You know Vaughn Perryman, right?"

"Sure do, I've taken care of his bikes for years, great guy."

"Good, get on over to his place right now, he'll be expecting you. I'll see you there."

"On it," said Memphis, "Take care on your drive down here."

I hung up, as Cassidy sipped her coffee and watched me working my phone.

I called Rainee.

"You still fucking?" were her first words to me, "You know there's a hurricane coming, don't you?"

"That's why I'm calling," I replied, ignoring her crudeness, "I want you to drive up to Perryman's place, and I'll be joining you soon."

"Yessir," she replied sarcastically, "I'm assuming he's expecting us?"

"He will be," I replied, realizing that I needed to warn Perryman of the imminent arrival of my tribe at his house, "And before you ask, I'm bringing Layla with me."

"Coop, Layla is trouble, big trouble, you need to forget about her."

"We'll talk about that later, just get in your truck and hightail it up there," I said, hanging up.

"Who was that?" asked Cassidy.

"I'll tell you about it on the way, Cass," I replied, "Now let's load everything into the Caddy and get on our way."

I then called Joe, to see if he was okay and had made plans. He was in high spirits so early in the morning, which for Joe, really wasn't that unusual. What was surprising, was that he was even up. But he said he was cool and not to worry about him, he was sorted.

The final thing I needed to do before we locked up, was to call Perryman and tell him that I'd taken him up on his offer. He was delighted, of course, even seemed to be planning a party, the Hurricane Party, he called it. Perryman, he's different.

Chapter 69

We joined I-95 with thousands of like-minded people heading north. I figured that it was best to avoid the coastal A1A road, because it would likely already be flooded in places, due to the initial progress of the hurricane.

The road was slow moving; a huge amount of traffic, of course, but also because the Interstate itself was beginning to flood. Any fast driving now could result in fatalities from high-speed aquaplaning.

"I found that pretty sexy," said Cassidy, taking my hand in hers.

"Sexy? What was sexy?" I replied, clueless as to what she was referring to.

"How assertive you are in a situation," she said, "I was impressed."

"Oh that, I think it's just the police training in me, Cass," I replied, "We were taught to handle situations like this, calmly, coolly and quickly. I don't think you ever lose it."

Cassidy and I had agreed that for the time being, she would remain Layla to everyone we met, although I knew I had to be careful as I was already using her real name when it was just the two of us together.

"Last night," she continued, "You mentioned something about Nikita Sokalov back in the day? Was that when you were with the police?"

"Yes, it was. But it wasn't a good experience."

"Do you want to talk about it?"

"Sure, I don't have any secrets, Cass, you know that, although it's not a pleasant story."

"Well, it looks like we've got at least a couple of hours in this traffic, I'd like to hear about it."

"Well… okay…" I said, but continued, "I was stationed in San Fran in the SFPD as you know, started as a rookie. I'd been a patrol cop for the first six years or so, before making detective. So, when I changed grade, I also changed partner, because my new role was going to be totally different."

"How so?"

"Instead of being first on a crime scene in my cruiser, I was one of a pair of lead detectives who would arrive once the perimeter had been set up and the CSI crew and coroner had begun their work."

"I've watched the shows on television, I get the picture," said Cassidy, "Go on."

"My new partner was a guy called Danny Zenko, and I had partnered with him for almost five years. He seemed a pretty stand-up guy and we worked well together. I liked him, he was funny too. He'd been a detective for a couple or three years longer than me, so I was junior to him. It's always the way, and to be honest, I learned a lot from him."

"But obviously something happened, yes?"

"It did, and in a really bad way, Cass," I replied, suddenly recalling events of my life that I hadn't ever really wanted to revisit or share.

"I'm listening, Coop," she said, squeezing my hand.

"There was this one time when Danny and I were investigating a newcomer to San Francisco, a certain Nikita Sokalov, and we'd been hunkered down in an unmarked car down the street from where we knew Sokalov had set up his offices. We also knew that San Francisco didn't need a new crime lord, particularly a Russian one like that man."

"I've met him, sent shivers down me," said Cassidy.

"Of course," I replied, "So, I'm getting restless and say to Danny that we should go in, you know, take a look at what was going down. For some reason though, Danny was very reluctant and I couldn't understand why. But I was feeling antsy and I'd had enough of watching with nothing coming from it, so I eventually persuaded him to come in with me."

"Why was he so reluctant?" asked Cassidy.

"I'll get to that," I replied before continuing.

"It was nighttime, early evening but it was already dark up in San Francisco. They have seasons there, believe it or not. But anyway, we were armed, and Danny, being the senior officer, led the way, and I followed. We knew Nikita Sokalov's offices covered the entire second floor, and we took the freight elevator to approach from the rear of the building."

"And you weren't scared?" asked Cassidy, "I'd have been terrified walking into that gangster's den."

"Sure, fear was an unwelcome part of the job, but we were cops, we were armed, and to be honest, they would've been unlikely to shoot us, more likely they'd want to have some kind of in with us," I replied.

"Okay…"

"Now, we were carrying, because we didn't want to have to reach for our guns if anything went off. Much better to have them in your hands, safety off, but still hidden in your overcoat," I said, "But Danny made a big mistake."

"Oh my, what did he do?"

"He opened the first door he came to, with his pistol showing in his hand, and there's a bodyguard who must have heard us outside the door who pulls his own gun and fires."

"Did Danny die?" asked Cassidy.

"No, he didn't, although in retrospect he should've, I guess. But my own immediate instinct was to dive and push him out of the way."

"Playing the hero," she said, smiling at my dumb bravery.

"Not really, Cass, I got shot protecting my partner and spent the next month in intensive care at the hospital."

"Jesus!" said Cassidy, "Is that the scar I've seen, was that when you lost a kidney?

"Yeah, but I've still got the other one."

"Did Danny take control of the situation and call for an ambulance?"

"No, Danny fled the scene, it was actually Nikita Sokalov who called it in, would you believe?"

"What??"

"It turned out that Danny had been on Nikita Sokalov's payroll for three years, he was dirty, but Sokalov wanted to maintain a relationship with the judiciary. Initially, anyway, until he had control of it."

"Did Danny confess, did he go to jail?" asked Cassidy, completely shocked at what I'd just told her, "The bastard might have gotten you killed."

"No again, Danny Zenko just completely disappeared without trace, never to be seen again," I replied.

"Really??"

"Crazy, right? Yeah, so that was my one and only experience with Nikita Sokalov, and after that, I was offered an early disability pension, so I took it and got the hell out of San Francisco. I had a daughter to protect and I no longer felt safe up there."

"Jeez, Coop, that's a helluva story, but I'm glad you're still around," said Cassidy, leaning across the Caddy's bench seat and snuggling up next to me.

"I've been in worse situations, but yeah, I'm happy I'm still around myself, but happier that you are too, Cass."

Chapter 70

Carlo Galotti was grateful that Nikita Sokalov and Sergei Fedorov had decided to take the opportunity provided by Hurricane Jacques to head back to Russia, where they had an important meeting with Vladimir Putin, a close friend of Sokalov.

Although both Sokalov and Fedorov were known by the CIA and FBI as two of the most lethal and powerful gangsters in the whole of the USA, Galotti knew that the two Russians traveled freely, because no criminal charges, and there were plenty of them, were ever made to stick.

But Carlo also knew that when the Russians arrived back in the US, and hopefully not for a couple of weeks at least, they would want to hear the news that Cassidy Swain was indeed, dead. And although Sokalov had seven children from three different wives, Carlo had been crucially aware that Anatoly Sokalov was the favorite son, the one he'd been grooming to head his empire, once Nikita was gone. And that ship had sailed now.

Carlo also realized that he himself, didn't appear from the outside to be the feared mafioso he once was. And it didn't help that this was compounded by the fact that the men who worked for him, although near and distant relatives inside the mafia organization, were becoming more and more useless. Soft, even.

He had made a mistake by putting Don Faber and Eddie Falcone on a mission like this one, he knew that at the very moment he'd realized Shira Kadosh had been hired. His two men weren't even in the same poker game as Kadosh.

Galotti knew Faber was experienced, and had mostly been up to the task in earlier years, pretty good in fact, so he figured that partnering him with muscle like Eddie, could work out. The kid might have even learned something from Don. He didn't, of course.

But Eddie was now buried with the alligators in the Everglades, and the obligatory flowers and a check had been sent to his mother, with the news that Eddie had died bravely in service.

The big problem now was that he hadn't heard anything from Don, nothing, zip, ever since he last saw him during Eddie's final demise. And that was strange.

He'd sent a couple of his boys over to the Faber house to see if he was there. But all they found was Marylou with a bunch of guys putting up the hurricane shutters on the Faber residence, and Don, he was nowhere to be seen.

They grilled Marylou, who Carlo actually liked, a nice lady in his opinion, but all she could tell his guys was that Don had had to go away on a business trip, but he hadn't said where he was heading. She'd just packed a bag for him, and he had said he would be home in a few days. And Marylou was straight up, wouldn't even know how to lie.

So, one of two things had gone on. Either Don was doing business outside of Carlo's remit, or… he had taken it upon himself, and gone rogue, deciding to track down and kill Cassidy himself.

Knowing Don's allegiance and respect for Carlo, he doubted it was the first option.

So, it was probably the second, because Carlo knew that Don, being the stalwart mafia man that he was, would want to make amends. And having checked his company credit cards, there hadn't been a single charge made on them since Carlo last saw him.

~~~

"It will be nice to see Moscow in the autumn," said Sokalov.

"*Da*, and to finally enjoy some time at the dachas, *Na Zdorovie*," replied Sergei, clinking his champagne flute with Sokalov's, relishing time at his palatial home by the water in the countryside just outside Moscow.

The two men were speaking in their native language, aboard Sokalov's brand new, seventy-five-million-dollar Gulfstream G800, traveling at a high-speed cruise rate of Mach 0.9, 700mph. It meant that the journey would take only nine hours, and negated stopping in London to refuel.

Sitting on the table in front of Sokalov, was a pretty, hand-painted, carved Matryoshka doll nest. His fingers gently stroked the shiny lacquer of the symbol of Mother Russia. He lifted the doll and carefully laid it aside as another smaller, but differently painted doll was exposed beneath.

"Galotti," said Sokalov, once the stewardess had finished placing an iced, caviar dome and two glasses of Kors 24K vodka in front of them, "I think we need to deal with him. Permanently."

"I agree, Niki, he has been very useful to us over the years, but his continued presence appears to hinder us now. I think there is an expression that they use in America… "his boots are too small", no?"

Sokalov laughed at his great friend's dry humor, but it had become clear to him in the preceding couple of years, that Galotti was no longer the king of Miami, as he once had been years ago. The Galotti empire was crumbling. He lifted the doll again to reveal another different, but smaller doll.

The two Muscovites had been friends and comrades since they were five years old, attending the same schools and universities. They did not come from poor origins, though. On the contrary, in fact, they grew up in two of the most elite families in Moscow. And Sokalov's father had been a great friend and business partner of Yuri Andropov, the short-term President of the USSR, for whom Putin had enormous admiration.

"Perhaps," said Sergei, leaning back in his opulent, Nappa leather airplane seat, "We will have Kadosh take care of the details for us."

"Only after her current work is done, my friend," replied Sokalov, downing a second tumbler of vodka, and casually revealing the fourth doll in the Matryoshka nest, "However, Sergei, in the intervening months, I have had time to reflect."

"How so," queried Sergei, "Are you having second thoughts, Niki?"

"*Nyet*, it's not that," Sokalov replied, "As my eldest son, my Anatoly was destined to take our empire much further, but you and I both know that he wasn't... what is the expression they say in English... "not the brightest light in the harbor"?"

"I agree, Niki, but he was young too, he was still maturing," replied Sergei.

"Of course, yes. But I had met Galotti's wife on a couple of occasions, and you yourself knew her much better," continued Sokalov, lighting a cigar and removing another doll that revealed the fifth and final doll, "And to me, she seemed... decent, no?"

"*Da*, I agree with you on that, Niki, she was always pleasant to me."

"But I still have a recurring nightmare of hearing the shots fired, and rushing up the stairs to find my son naked, and dead."

"So… are you saying that we are going to pull Kadosh off the hit?" asked Sergei.

"*Nyet*, Anatoly was my beautiful son, the future, and he has been taken from me, from us," Sokalov replied.

"As you will, Niki," replied Sergei.

Sokalov stared at the remaining doll on the table for a moment, before casually flicking it to the floor, watching as it skittled down the aisle of the aircraft.

"Do svidaniya, Mrs. Galotti, Izvinite."

Chapter 71

Everyone had finally arrived at Perryman's luxurious home on the water, and the appearance of seven new temporary occupants didn't even make a dent in the property's square footage. With sixteen bedroom-suites, everyone would be comfortable and safe during the coming hurricane.

"Y'all know it's party time tonight," said Perryman to me, before Cassidy and I had even put our bags down.

"Your whole life is a party, Vaughn, tell me something I don't know," I replied.

Perryman guffawed at that, his infectious laugh ringing out loud in the foyer, as he put me into one of his infamous bear hugs.

"And lookee here, Cooper, I see you've brought the divine Miz Layla with you, now ain't you a beautiful sight, honey child?" he said, also hugging her, but this time with extraordinary gentleness.

We tried to say hello to everyone in the near vicinity, including my daughter, who I embraced for what felt like an eternity. I had never felt happier to see my Molly than I felt that afternoon.

But I suddenly realized that I had arrived with Cassidy, and Molly didn't yet have a clue who she was, or that we were dating.

"Molly, I'd like to introduce you to Layla," I said, "She's someone I met a while back at Nate's and she's going to be taking shelter with us here."

Cassidy stepped forward, putting out her hand towards Molly, and Molly reciprocated.

"I've heard so much about you from your dad, Molly, you have one incredibly proud father."

Molly dealt with this sudden new friend of mine in exactly the way I had hoped, and added in a tiny fib.

"Pleased to meet you too, Layla," she said, taking Cassidy's hand in hers, "Dad's mentioned you before."

"Then I feel honored!" Cassidy replied, smiling at my daughter.

"Have you met Billy yet?" asked Molly.

Molly turned around to where Billy was standing a few yards away.

"Billy," she said loudly above the music, "Come meet Dad's new friend."

More introductions were made between Cassidy and Billy, and after a minute or so of chatting amongst the four of us, Molly and Billy decided to go off and dance for a while. But not before Molly gave me a hug, and whispered,

"She's lovely, Dad, she might be a keeper."

And then she was gone before I could reply.

We needed to drop our bags off, so we made our way upstairs to our assigned bedroom.

"Wow, this is pretty grand," said Cassidy, looking around at the vast suite in which we were standing, "In fact this whole house is insane!"

"I know, right? So, I guess we could treat this time as a luxury vacation for the next few days," I replied, also astonished at the level of luxury that Perryman had installed, "It beats living on my boat, I guess."

"I want to see your boat, Coop, I'll bet it's much nicer than you say it is."

"Huh, don't get your hopes up," I replied, "It's seriously unimpressive."

Cassidy collapsed down on the Californian King bed, as I unpacked our bags and stowed everything in the closet.

"Coop, we even have a wine fridge here, do you fancy a sneaky glass?"

"Oh, I think I could manage that," I replied, "Something red, perhaps?"

Cassidy poured a couple of generous glasses of Pinot Noir, handing me one as I joined her on the bed.

"Damn." I said, "This beats my bunk on the boat."

"I'll be the judge of that," said Cassidy.

"Yes, ma'am," I said, whilst opening up my phone to check on the radar app.

Jacques had picked up speed once it had made landfall, and was estimated to be with us within twelve hours, far earlier than I had expected. I was grateful that we all had made the journey this morning, rather than waiting until later today.

"Holy fuck!" I exclaimed, staring at my phone.

"Coop, what is it?" Cassidy said, worry now writ large on her face.

"Damn!" I said, "I can't believe this!"

"Coop! You're scaring me."

"I'm sorry, Cass, it's nothing bad, I promise, in fact, wow, it's pretty incredible."

"Tell me, please," said Cassidy, a look of mild relief on her face now.

"It's Joe," I replied, Joe Jarvie, my friend, he's just wired $40,000 into my account, and he sent a note."

"What? Why?" she exclaimed, "What does the note say?"

I handed her my phone, "Read it yourself, it's incredible."

Cassidy began reading…

Dear Coop, I've sent you a little token of appreciation for what you and Rainee did for me. The new album has gone platinum already, and I'm going to make a fortune with that and the stadium tour coming up. And the best of it is that I'm now officially divorced, and Flick doesn't get any of it, so thank you, buddy.

PS… I sent a similar wire to Rainee, she earned it too.

Love you, brother,

Joe xxx

"It's really generous, Coop, but don't forget, you nearly died," said Cassidy, handing the phone back to me, clearly unmoved.

"But it's not been a bad month financially," I replied, laughing now, "I get tranquilized by thugs on the next-door boat, and then a bullet from the kid, that's fifty-grand for a couple of injuries, nice work if you can get it."

"It's not even funny, Coop, stop it," snapped Cassidy, clearly upset now, "If anything like that happens again, there might not be an 'us' in the future, is all I'm saying."

"I'm sorry, Cass, was just trying to make light of everything," I responded, holding her hand, "I love us, and I never want to lose you either."

"I guess we're going to have to deal with that problem when it comes," she said, clearly wanting to change the subject, "Now, writer man, what are you going to do once the hurricane has gone and you're back on your boat?"

"Make love to you?" I replied, hopefully.

"No, seriously," she replied, punching my shoulder.

"Well, I do have a novel to finish that my agent has been whining about, but I've kind of put it on the back-burner since I've been working for Joe."

"So?"

"So, I thought I'd give the PI business a break for a few months, I'm still not even fully recovered anyway. And with my new-found wealth, I'll still be able to pay Pip now. Thought I'd try and get the book finished," I said, truthfully.

"Does it have a title yet?" she asked.

"Writers tend to change their titles as their novels evolve, so often they might go through four or five working titles," I replied, "But right now, yeah, the title is *To Kill or To Love,* although it started life as *Book 3*."

"So, this is your third novel, then?"

"It is, but I'm trying something new."

"Sounds like it could be interesting. How much more do you need to write?" Cassidy asked, "Good title by the way."

"My novels are usually around the eighty-five-thousand-word mark, so I'm guessing from memory, I've got maybe thirty thousand more words to write."

"What's the novel about?" she asked, as we'd never really discussed the books that I'd written.

"It's a crime thriller," I replied, "It's not my usual genre, but I'm actually enjoying writing it, something I never dreamed would happen. It's got a touch of 'boy meets girl' aspect to it too, I like a little love story to throw in the mix."

"Well, this girl is glad she met this boy," she replied, "Now come here…"

Chapter 72

Joe Jarvie's home was built from concrete block like many of the faux Mediterranean-style homes in his upscale neighborhood, so it was already well protected. And Angel had already brought in a team of guys to install the hurricane shutters to all of the windows, knowing that Joe wouldn't leave his place because of any natural phenomenon, least of all a Cat-5 hurricane.

Angel still wanted to protect his favorite and most lucrative client, particularly now, with the album the hottest one globally, and a huge worldwide tour coming up. He cared for Joe too, loved him like a son, maybe in part because Angel had never had children, childless like Joe.

But Angel couldn't keep Joe company during the storm, because his wife was his primary focus, and she was going to need all the comfort Angel could give her. So, having checked all areas of the property, happy that it was pretty much bombproof, he gave Joe a parting hug and said he'd be back in a couple of days as soon as Jacques had moved north.

Once Angel had left, exiting through the recently replaced hurricane-proof main entrance doors, Joe had gone to the kitchen to make something to eat. And Joe was famished. He had already sent Felipe on a flight back home to his mother's house in Richmond, Virginia earlier that day, so as he looked around the kitchen, he was suddenly aware that he had never actually cooked anything in it himself.

In fact, he realized that he had never cooked a single meal in a kitchen his entire life on planet Earth. It had always been his mother who'd cooked when he was young. And then after he'd gotten famous, every meal had either been made for him by his longstanding butler, Felipe, or he'd eaten in restaurants or fast-food joints. Felipe had shown him how to use the barbecue, but that was outside on the patio, and he sure wasn't going to be venturing outdoors today.

So, right at this minute, and still looking bemusedly around the vast kitchen, he had no clue where to start.

"What would you do, Felipe?" he said to himself, opening a dozen cupboard doors before finally arriving at the refrigerator.

He peered through the glass door of the massive Sub Zero Pro-48 to see what was inside.

"What do we got here?" he said to no one in particular, "Chicken, sausages, bacon, eggs. Steak, cheese, an' a whole bunch of veggies."

He opened the door.

"Man, I could kill me some faa-heetas, but how the fuck d'ya cook chicken?'

After rifling through the refrigerator's entire contents, Joe settled on eggs and bacon. He pulled out a large potato too, because he'd seen Felipe cook one in the microwave and Joe knew how that worked. He put the potato in the microwave and guessed a cooking time of twenty minutes.

Reaching for a skillet that hung with other pots and pans above the nine-ring stove top, Joe added a heap of butter and turned the control to the maximum. He threw in six bacon rashers and three eggs and watched as the pan began to sizzle. He didn't know how to flip the eggs and also realized they were cooking far more quickly than the bacon. And the potato still had another twelve minutes to go.

"This is why I have you, Felipe, it's gonna be a lonely coupla days here," said Joe, suddenly realizing how much he relied on his dear friend.

~ ~ ~

The man had skirted around the property, looking for any kind of access, but eventually conceding that it was locked up tighter than the White House. At least he'd been able to disarm the alarm by isolating the feed.

The hurricane was practically on top of the property now, as he glanced at pieces of unsecured tin soffit slicing through the air like giant razorblades. Dozens of palm trees were already lying on the ground, the force of the wind ripping them effortlessly from the earth.

There wasn't much time if he was to survive this alive, he thought, quickly scurrying back to his truck to retrieve some tools.

~ ~ ~

The eggs were burnt, but it didn't faze Joe in the slightest. The bacon was actually good and he'd loaded the baked potato with butter, sour cream, and salsa. In fact, Joe Jarvie was pretty proud of what he'd managed to cook, as he shoveled the last of the bacon into his mouth.

He got up from the sofa, having cast his plate to the floor, and walked over to the bar to ponder his options, before he put the TV on for the night.

Deciding to celebrate Flick's exit from his life with the drink that had brought her into it all those years ago in Vegas, he reached for a bottle of Wild Turkey, poured three fingers and downed it in one gulp.

"Nice," he said, "Tastes better now than it ever did."

So, he poured four more fingers this time, took the bottle with him, and hit the couch.

~ ~ ~

The noise of the hurricane was deafening. Terrifying.

The man was worried that his truck would be whipped up into the air and come back down to earth, crushed. But so far, the vehicle had miraculously stayed its ground.

Keeping close to the wall of the house as he skirted around it, he looked up and spied an external vent, not ten yards from where he was standing. He deduced that this must be the laundry room, but the door was secured tight, with locked accordion shutters.

However, the window to the right of it was fortified by a single panel, with just four bolts securing it. The socket wrench he'd just retrieved from the truck should fit nicely.

~ ~ ~

Joe sat sprawled on the giant pink sofa, watching YouTube videos of his band performing on his equally gigantic flat-screen on the wall above the fireplace. It occurred to him, that he'd never actually had Felipe light a fire in all the time he'd lived there, although it was always stacked with logs in the thought that there might be a cold day in the year.

The Wild Turkey bottle was now half empty and Joe decided to find something non-alcoholic, before he got so loaded he'd never get up the stairs to his bedroom. And he wasn't ready to sleep just yet, he was enjoying watching the YouTube videos too much, thinking how many more of them there would be after the tour had ended.

He stumbled up from the sofa, realizing how dark the house was, with only the television lighting the room. It didn't help that the windows were all shuttered, giving the whole house a kind of eerie feel to it.

In another of those thoughts that seemed to be constantly flooding his mind right now, he also realized that he had never switched the lights on and off, it had always been Felipe.

"Damn, I'm gonna give that man a pay rise when he gets back."

He groped his way through the hallway toward the kitchen, not knowing where each light switch was situated for each room, stumbling in his quest to find some cans of Pepsi in the kitchen's soda fridge.

The man froze when he saw Joe enter the room. He had thought that Joe would have evacuated and that the house would be completely empty, no one home. The man was dressed completely in black, including a balaclava, and was mostly hidden from Joe by the wall that divided the kitchen from the laundry room, so he waited.

But as Joe made his way toward the soda fridge at the other end of the kitchen, the man panicked.

In a split second, rather than let Joe retrieve what he was looking for and leave the kitchen, the man made an unwise and reckless move.

He crept silently out from his hiding place and began to move quickly to where Joe was now kneeling in front of the cooler. He knew he could put Joe to sleep with just a couple of well-timed punches, so he could get on with finding what he came for.

The clatter of the carving knife that skittled across the limestone floor was enough to alert Joe that he wasn't alone. In hindsight, had Joe not accidentally knocked the knife onto the floor whilst cooking, the outcome may have been wildly different.

Joe stood up and whirled around, astonished to find who was standing in his kitchen.

"You?" he said, "What the fuck are *you* doing in my house?"

The man, ignoring Joe's question, suddenly realized that he'd been recognized, even with the balaclava on, and in that one fleeting moment, he made a terrible decision.

Reaching down quickly, he grabbed the kitchen knife from the floor, and lunged at the helpless Joe.

Joe's eyes were wide, and in a state of utter shock, as he felt the cold steel of the twelve-inch knife, burrowing its way into his kidney. He just stared at the man, their faces only a few inches apart now, as the knife withdrew and plunged once more inside him.

Joe slumped to the floor, itself now pooling in an increasing crimson circle, and Joe's life ended in that final remorseless and callous stroke of metal. There would be no stadium tour, because now, there was no Joe.

Chapter 73

That evening, on the very night that Hurricane Jacques was going to envelop and potentially destroy the area around us, Vaughn Perryman, true to his word, was throwing the ultimate hurricane party.

He had invited a dozen extra guests, and as usual at Perryman's parties, one of those guests was in control of the music for the event. Our mutual friend, Gaylord Talbot.

When Cassidy and I had finally emerged from our suite, the party was already in full flow, Lou Reed's *Perfect Day* ironically pounding from the multiple Definitive Technology loudspeakers littered around the house.

"Y'all decided to get out of bed, after all," said Perryman, grinning at the two of us.

Perryman definitely had his own style. This evening, the huge man was dressed in pink skinny-fit leather trousers, coupled with a turquoise and gold-trimmed silk shirt that was slashed open to his navel. He had finished the look with a white, floor-length fur cape and gold and diamante sandals. I kind of envied him.

"Have I ever missed a Perryman festivity?" I asked, feeling a little dowdy in my cream-colored chinos, jean shirt and tan loafers.

"No, you haven't, my brother, and I'm delighted that's still the case," he beamed, "Now let's go and get your precious little lady a drink from the bar."

When Perryman instructed, one tended to obey, so we followed him to the bar which was located fifty paces away on the other side of the room. All of the guests and family members, immediately made way for him as he strode forward like Moses parting the Red Sea.

"Champagne, Layla?" he asked, as soon as we were seated at the bar.

"I'd love that, Vaughn, thank you," she replied, clearly falling for the man that everyone who met him also fell for.

"Crys-*taaal* for the lady, my sweet Kinko," said Perryman to one of his older sons who was barkeeper for the evening, "And a couple of whiskey sours for me and my good friend, Cooper, here."

It was interesting that Perryman never asked anyone what they wanted, he already knew their particular favorite tipple. As I said, Vaughn Perryman is an interesting man.

We chatted about the gossip of Sewall's Point, the small town where Perryman had lived most of his life, where everyone's business was everyone else's business, period. There were no secrets amongst the wealthy in this high-net-worth enclave, and Perryman's tribe was always the story on everyone's lips.

After fifteen or so minutes had passed, Perryman's new lady, Delilah, wafted toward us, as though she traveled on air. She was lean, tall, maybe six feet, with a Vogue-cover body, and was dressed identically to Perryman.

"Oh my, Coop, Vaughn has told me so much about you, it's just so nice to meet you properly," she intoned in a southern accent that was alarmingly similar to Perryman's, "You must lead *such* an exciting life!"

"Er… not really," I replied to the vision, looking for rescue from Cassidy.

"And, you're the de-*lightful* Layla," Delilah purred, turning to my date, "We met briefly that time when you visited after dinner. You're stunning."

The woman was like something out of Photoshop, a vision from every angle, and for many women, and men, I guessed she could be quite daunting, but not to Cassidy, who responded perfectly on cue.

"Thank you, Delilah, you're pretty spectacular yourself," she replied, "And I absolutely *love* both your outfits, do you think Coop and I could rock that look?"

"Not gonna happen," I said, laughing at Cassidy's humor, "and anyway, we're jeans 'n T kind of people… aren't we?"

"I'm not so sure," chimed in Perryman, "Reckon I got a spare pair of these pants that would fit you nicely, Coop."

The room and the music were once again overpowered by Perryman's bellow of a laugh.

"We should mingle," I said, taking hold of Cassidy's hand, clearly needing to avoid trying on a pair of pink leather pants.

"Just make sure you have fun, boy, and make sure you go see Talbot behind the mixing desk, he'd love to see you's both," Perryman replied, in between more bellows of laughter.

We wandered over to the sound desk, where Talbot was indeed at the controls. *Common People* by the British band, Pulp, was playing which was kind of ironic, given the wealth of most of the people here tonight, present company excluded, of course.

No one really knew how it came to be that Talbot organized the music for these shindigs, because it really didn't suit him to be that man. Talbot was pretty strait-laced, a bibliophile of higher literary, and quite the opposite of most lawyers in America. He actually cared more about his clients than he did about what he earned. In short, Talbot is a very nice man.

"Forsooth, yonder sunset glows!" he said, as he looked up from his desk and saw us approaching.

Did I tell you that Talbot is Shakespeare's number one fan? He idolizes the Bard, so much so that quotes from the greatest writer the world has ever seen, litter Talbot's everyday conversation. He's what you call, a Bardolator.

"It's good to see you, buddy," I said, reaching out my hand for his.

"Goddess, nymph, perfect, divine!" he continued, aiming his words directly at Cassidy, and partially ignoring my outstretched hand.

"That man that hath a tongue, I say, is no man, if with his tongue he cannot win a woman," Cassidy replied without a beat, making both Talbot and I grin.

"Ah, you're a fan of the great man too, I see," exclaimed Talbot, coming around from behind the desk to kiss both Cassidy's cheeks.

"Well, I'm guessing not quite in the league that you're in, Talbot, but I've read a few of his plays and some of the sonnets. Yeah, I'd say I was a fan."

He finally acknowledged my presence and turned to embrace me.

"Some are born great, some achieve greatness, and some have greatness thrust upon them," he recounted from *Twelfth Night*, a play that even I knew.

I grappled for a suitable but uninspired response, "If music be the food of love, play on."

"Ah, well said, Orsino, nice save!" he replied.

"I try."

But then he leant forward and hugged me, whispering in my ear, "You're a lucky fella, Cooper, she's quite lovely."

"I know, she's a keeper," I whispered back, "And thank you."

Chapter 74

Rainee had been on high alert, ever since she'd arrived at Perryman's house. I hadn't seen much of her, but that's not abnormal with us, although I suspected we needed to have a catch up with each other.

I had introduced Cassidy to Talbot's wife, Autumn, and they were getting along really well, so I took the opportunity to take my leave for a few minutes to go and seek out Rainee. Cassidy was fine with it, and she seemed to have melded easily with everyone she had met so far at the party, so I was dispatched and told not to worry about her.

Thus far, I hadn't spied Rainee among the guests, so I decided that I would look in places she would instinctively gravitate to. It's not that Rainee doesn't like a party, far from it, she really enjoys them except when there is something on her mind, and right now, there was.

I took the elevator to the third floor, which was more of a viewing deck than a living area. The house was big so it took some time to circumnavigate the glass-balustraded walkway at the top of the house. But eventually, I found her, crouched low at a window where she was watching the whole street from what felt like a perfect birds-eye vantage point.

"Hey stranger," I said, kneeling down next to her, "What's going on with you?"

"It's a long story," she said, glancing momentarily at me before resuming her lookout, "You got a minute, lover boy?"

At least she still had her sense of humor, which was a relief.

"Always," I replied, "But I know you're not happy, so why don't you tell me what's bugging you?"

"I think you're in a whole heap of trouble, Coop," she said, finally turning to face me, "And I think I am too."

The hurricane was at the height of its power now that we had reached midnight in Sewall's Point, so I was grateful that Perryman's house was such a fortress, because what I saw through the window was breathtaking. It was like WWIII outside, many of the neighboring homes already torn apart, rooves having been ripped from their rafters, and the bedrooms inside that were once beautiful, now ravaged and scattered carnage.

"We had better talk," I said.

Rainee then replayed the entire story of seeing Don Faber literally explode in front of her at The Outback, and I grimaced at the thought of how close I had come to losing my partner.

"But the thing is, Coop, he wasn't going to be a problem for me, I already had my gun on him," she continued, "My real concern is that whoever took him out was the ultimate professional, because I have no idea where the shot came from or even who fired it. They were out of there before I could get eyes on them."

"And I guess it's safe to say that this is all connected with Layla," I replied, thinking about the possibilities going forward.

"It's not Layla, Coop, it's Cassidy," Rainee interrupted, "She's gonna get you killed."

"I know it's Cassidy, Rainee, she told me her whole story," I said, "And it's not a pleasant one. But for right now, as far as everyone is concerned, she's still Layla. It's safer that we don't use her real name."

"Really?" she said, somewhat surprised.

I then related to her, everything that had gone on during the past few weeks, sparing no detail, except for what was private between Cassidy and I.

"Jesus," gasped Rainee, "I've now got a whole different take on that girl, she's one brave lady."

"Yeah, and she's become pretty special to me," I said, "And I'm assuming that right now, your main concern is that whoever the shooter was at The Outback, may have tracked you here."

"Yep, that's why I'm up here, we're dealing with some serious shit."

"Do you really think they're going to try something during this?" I asked, pointing out the window at what was happening outside.

"I doubt it, but I think we're dealing with an assassin, and those guys don't care about hurricanes, they just get the job done."

"Okay, I agree with you, so we need to make a plan for when this hurricane has passed, probably no later than midday tomorrow," I said, looking at my watch, "Midday today, in fact."

Chapter 75

The party went on until three in the morning, by which time, most of the guests had either gone to bed or collapsed on sofas and chairs around the house. Cassidy and I were already in bed, and before we went to sleep ourselves, I told her what had happened with Rainee, and then outlined the plan that Rainee and I had put together.

"Coop, I am so, so sorry that Rainee could have been killed, I feel terrible, I should leave," she said, tears flooding her eyes, "I should never have got you involved."

"Too late for that now, we're in it and we're going the distance, don't worry."

"But I am worried, Coop, we're sitting targets, for fuck's sake."

I'd never heard Cassidy use an expletive before, so I understood the panic rising within her.

"Not completely, Cass, we still have a card or two up our sleeves."

"How?" she blurted, "They're not going to stop until I'm dead, and you and Rainee with me."

"Here's the thing, Cass, whoever the killer is, knows who you are, and now knows who Rainee is, but they don't know I even exist. That's where we have an edge."

"In what way?"

"Somehow, and I haven't thought this part through yet, but because I'm currently the unknown part of the equation, I need to draw the shooter out."

"You're going to use yourself as bait?" Cassidy asked, "No, you can't do that, Coop, I won't let you."

"Well, right now, I have a little time on my side, so I'm safe, but I'm also guessing that it won't take long for Galotti, or whoever else is involved, to work out Rainee's connection to me, and that's when it will get dangerous."

"Jeez, I hadn't even thought of that," Cassidy agreed.

"So, here's what we're going to do," I continued, "I'm thinking that by around midday, the worst of the hurricane will have passed, and we can leave. The roads are probably not going to be a pretty sight, but we'll deal with that at the time."

"Where will we head to, out of Florida?" she asked.

"No, quite the opposite, in fact, that's what they'd expect. We're heading back down to Palm Beach, I've got a place in mind."

"Is it just us going?"

"No, we'll be traveling in a convoy, You and me, Molly and Billy, Remy and Memphis, and Rainee too. After we've settled in, I'll run by Joe's house to check in on him, thank him for his generosity too."

"I'm scared, Coop, this is my worst nightmare."

"I know, Cass, but right now, we have a plan, everyone now knows about it, including Perryman and Talbot, so now we just need to get some shuteye so we're ready to go by midday, latest."

"I trust you, do you think we're going to be okay?" she asked.

"I hope so, sweetheart, I really hope so."

Chapter 76

By dawn that morning, hundreds of Mexican, Puerto Rican and Guatemalan workmen were already beginning the task of cleaning up Sewall's Point. The sound of chainsaws, nail guns, drills, leaf blowers and wood chippers, was so loud outside that it would have been difficult to have a conversation out there.

Most of these immigrant workers were undocumented, paid in cash by their equally immigrant foremen, but without these extraordinarily hard-working people, much of America would be on its knees, society ground to a complete halt.

In wealthy enclaves like Sewall's Point, the property owners paid quickly, cash in advance, to get their lives back to serene normality and harmony. They didn't like disruption in paradise, and they had unlimited supplies of cash to ensure that any interruption to their daily lives, was brief and short-lived. And it kind of made sense to me. If you've got the money, then why not use it?

From what I could see from my position in our bedroom on the second floor of Perryman's home, most of these wealthy owners were continually bringing out trays of cold drinks, coffee-urns, sandwiches and pastries for their tireless workers. It was pretty compelling to see. Natural disasters have an amazing way of bringing people together, no matter the class into which they are born.

I had only had five hours sleep, but it was long enough. I don't need a lot of shuteye, just so long as when I do sleep, it's a deep one.

I had crept out of our bedroom, got dressed in the hallway, and let Cassidy sleep on, because the less time she had to worry about the coming days, would be better for her in the long run.

Rainee had been up the entire night, but still managed to look like she'd slept for eight hours straight.

"You tell Cassidy the plan?" she asked, as I put down a tray of croissants and coffee beside her at her lookout point.

"I did," I replied, "And she's understandably terrified, wanted to just go and give herself up to Carlo and face the consequences."

"She'd be dead as soon as he saw her," said Rainee, as she bit hungrily into a croissant, and she wasn't wrong.

"Have you seen anything, a new vehicle, any movement out there?" I asked, peering out the window at all the workers' trucks parked in the street.

"Nada," she replied, "Although I didn't expect to. I can't see a shooter camping out in a hurricane, more likely he'd be enjoying his time at one of the hotels in Palm Beach. They're gonna get paid, whatever happens, so why take any risks?"

"Yeah, I agree, which is why we need to be on the road this morning as soon as the guys out there have cleared a path out of Sewall's," I replied, "Now, drink your coffee, you're gonna need it."

Chapter 77

We had parked our cars in Perryman's endless garage when we'd arrived the previous evening. It ensured that no one would know we were there, whilst more importantly, also protecting the safety of Perryman and his extended family.

Inside the garage, after loading the cars and trucks, we bade farewell to Talbot and Perryman, promising updates on what was now an extremely volatile and dangerous situation.

"You take care, man," said Perryman, wrapping me in a bear hug, "Just holler if you need me and Talb, okay?"

I hugged Talbot too, the man whispering in my ear as only he could do, "Discretion is the better part of valor, my friend, the best safety lies in fear."

All four garage doors rose together, and closed as soon as our vehicles had left. With hope, no one would ever have known we'd been there.

South Sewall's Point is a four-mile spit of sand that juts out into the Atlantic Ocean, and by midday, the road had been mostly cleared and we were able to continue our journey to join Florida's Turnpike back to Palm Beach. On this morning of all mornings, I didn't want to delay in getting everyone to safety, as I gripped the steering wheel, praying for a clear road out of there.

We were lucky, the Turnpike had been mostly spared by Hurricane Jacques, and by one in the afternoon, I took the exit for the

804, and continued on to S. Military Trail, before finally pulling in at the gates to the oddly named Gator Run Beach Club. Odd, because the club was five miles from the nearest beach.

All three vehicles were still behind me as I watched the guard get up from his seat in the sentry box.

Cassidy looked at me, but said nothing as the guard approached the Caddy, and I wound down the window.

"I'd recognize this car anywhere," said the guard as he bent down to my open window, "What the heck are you doin' in this neighborhood, Coop?"

"Just visiting, Jerry, a little r&r with the family," I replied, pressing a C-note into his palm, "But you haven't seen me."

"Seen who?" he replied as he walked back to his box and raised the barrier.

"Thanks, Jerry," I shouted to him, as our four vehicles filed quickly through the entrance to the club

"You know him?" asked Cassidy.

"Old friend, don't see him too much these days, but he's one of the reliables."

Cassidy fell silent once more as our entourage slowly navigated its way through the country club. For obvious reasons, there were no golfers out playing today as one might normally expect, and looking at the devastation of fallen trees on the fairways, it would be a long time before play resumed.

Eventually, I turned left into a cul-de-sac, and headed toward the house at the top of the circle, right at the end of the street. I'd chosen this particular house because it gave us a full view of anyone approaching from the other end of the street.

It was a large property, with room for four cars in the garage, once I'd removed the golf buggy from its charging point inside. I'd decided that we would put the Caddy, Rainee's Raptor and Remy's Escalade in the garage, out of sight, and leave Billy's Toyota Tacoma pick-up truck on the driveway. It was fairly beaten up, so neighbors, if any had stayed to ride out the hurricane, would think it belonged to workmen doing a clean-up at the property.

Once the cars were stowed, we walked around to the rear of the property, where I found the back-entrance key in the filter trap of the swimming pool's automatic cleaner. Once inside the house, we all breathed a united sigh of relief.

"Everyone good?" I asked, as the group sat down on the barstools and chairs in the property's large kitchen-diner, "Shall we get some food going, who's hungry?"

There was an immediate change in everyone, as they relaxed down as a group, happy to finally be safe.

"You want me to help, Dad," asked Molly, "You know you're *shit* at cooking."

And there it was, humor suddenly prevailed in that one line, and the laughter and jibes toward me began.

"Hey! I may not be Martha Stewart in the kitchen, but I'm godlike at the supermarket," I replied, opening a well-stocked fridge, "Who wants steak and who wants chicken?"

"I'll do the salad," said Cassidy.

"Gimme the meat, Coop, white boys got no clue how to cook it, hah!" laughed Remy, "'Cept Memphis, he got it down pat."

I was grateful that my family was safe and that normality had resumed once more, but I was already thinking about how the next few days would play out, and I hoped that no one was able to read the maelstrom of thoughts hurtling through my mind.

Chapter 78

Shira Kadosh had spent a pleasant and uninterrupted night in her suite at the Four Seasons, and felt replenished and ready for what she hoped would be her final days in Florida, so she could quickly return to her son at home in San Diego.

During the previous evening, she had had time to do some homework on Rainee Showers. It was clear to see that after the debacle at The Outback restaurant, the girl had obviously gone to ground after the interruption of Galotti's oaf, so she realized she would have to find a new way to discover Showers' current whereabouts, and then quickly, that of Swain.

The beauty of the IRS was that it was easy to search anyone's tax returns, and it didn't take long to discover that Rainee Showers worked as a freelance investigator for one Cooper Hemingway, the proprietor of Hemingway Investigations. And it seemed that the girl was a model citizen, filing and paying her taxes promptly. It would be such a shame to have to kill her.

After checking the company's mailing address, Kadosh had discovered that it was registered to a mailing box, but further digging discovered that her boss resided at Riviera Yacht Club, which was a start.

However, any mail would have been left at the marina's manager's office, so she had a little information but not enough.

What she really needed, was the name and location of Hemingway's boat, and there were many to choose from.

From her perch on the roof of the parking structure on the corner of Flagler and Quadrille, she was able to scan the activity of the entire marina through her powerful binoculars, but so far, all she had seen were maybe a dozen people dropping by to inspect the potential damage to their vessels.

~~~

On my way to Joe's place, I had decided to stop off at the marina to check on my boat. I didn't hold out too much hope that it had survived the storm, but I thought I might as well satisfy my curiosity anyway.

I parked Billy's Tacoma in one of the marina's guest parking bays, careful not to use my own assigned spot. Before I got out of the truck, I scanned the area to see if anyone stood out, a stranger in a strange land, if you will. Although, to be fair, a hitman would hardly advertise himself.

With the worrying knowledge that if someone was watching, I would be unlikely to see them, I eased out of the Tacoma and walked toward the dock where *Lost Soul* was berthed, not knowing what I might find there.

I'd taken four or five steps onto the wooden dock itself, when I was interrupted by my phone buzzing. I stopped, pulled the phone from my jacket, and looked at the caller ID. It was Colin Caine.

Why would he be calling me?

I answered the call, and immediately heard his voice.

"Coop?"

"Yeah, what's up, Coke?" I replied.

"I've got some bad news, brother," he said, grimly.

I can't explain the fear that jolted through my body like a lightning bolt finding earth, and in the humidity of the afternoon, I was suddenly as cold as ice.

"Tell me," I said.

"It's Joe, Joe Jarvie, he's dead."

I breathed a selfish sigh of relief. Although on the one hand, I was grateful that he wasn't calling about Molly, on the other hand, I was also deeply shocked at his words.

"What's happened, Coke? I just spoke to him yesterday, he was hunkering down at his house to wait out the hurricane. Did the property get hit?"

"Hurricane didn't get him, but someone did," said Caine, "He was murdered."

"Fuck, Coke, who would want to kill Joe? Everyone loved Joe, except Flick."

"Don't I know it, Coop. And it was savage, brutal."

"How did he die?" I asked, not really wanting to know the answer because I hadn't even been able to absorb the fact yet, that Joe was dead.

"Stabbed twice, quick death," Caine replied, "I'm at the scene now, you wanna take a look?"

My boat could wait until later, I thought to myself, automatically turning around and heading straight back to the Tacoma.

"On my way, Coke, see you in ten," I said to my friend as I ended the call.

~ ~ ~

Kadosh had continued her surveillance of the yacht club, to the point where she was becoming bored with the repetitious lethargy of owners slowly coming and going, until suddenly she spotted something that was far from lethargic.

A man was slowly walking onto one of the docks and had stopped to answer a phone call. As she focused in extreme close-up on the man's face, using her military binoculars, she realized exactly who he was. She'd seen a photo or two of him in her search of Showers.

After what seemed a brief conversation, the man suddenly began running back to the parking area where he hopped into a pickup truck, spun his wheels in reverse and hightailed out of the marina.

She tried to see the make and model of the vehicle, believing that it was a Toyota, but the dust that the driver had kicked up in his haste to get away, prevented her from making out the license plate.

"Damn you!" she screamed, but then immediately her assassin calm kicked in, when she realized that there couldn't be many black Toyota trucks in Palm Beach that had sprayed-on flames down the side. Shouldn't be hard to track.

And, in all honesty, there was little point in trying to follow the truck because Kadosh was three hundred yards away and it would take her over a minute just to drive her rental down to the ground level of the parking garage. The man would be long gone before she even got to the yacht club entrance.

"But I know it's you, Cooper Hemingway, and I know what you're driving. And now you're a dead man too."

Chapter 79

I eased the Tacoma into the sweeping driveway of Joe's house, finding a space where the Palm Beach Coroner's van had just pulled out from, realizing that at that very moment, my friend was lying inside the vehicle. Emotions suddenly erupted from deep within me. I've lost people in my life before, friends and colleagues alike, but somehow, this was hitting me hard. I wiped away my tears, and took a couple of deep breaths before I felt able to get out of my car.

I had never envisioned Joe's house being the center of a crime scene, with police cruisers with their blue and whites lighting up the area, a couple of PBPD Forensics trucks parked immediately outside the portico, and Colin Caine's unmarked electric Ford Mustang Mach-E on the other side of the driveway.

Yellow police tape had cordoned off most of the area, and I climbed out of the Tacoma and approached the two officers standing guard near the entrance. I didn't recognize either of them, both were young, maybe mid-twenties, but just as I opened my mouth to explain why I was there, Coke appeared at the doors.

"Let him through, guys, he's with me," he half-shouted from where he stood, "This way, Coop, and put some baggies on your shoes, buddy."

One of the officers lifted the tape and I walked over to the stone steps where I donned a pair of blue plastic shoe coverings, and continued up the steps where Coke put me in a bear hug.

"I'm sorry, man," he whispered in my ear, "I know he was your friend."

I thanked him, but was still feeling numb, almost in denial that I'd never see Joe again.

"They've already put his body in the coroner's van, so thankfully, there won't be too much to see," Caine continued, "But I could use a second pair of eyes on this to tell me what I'm missing."

He was right, coming here was the best thing for me, it would occupy my mind, instead of me asking myself a hundred questions a minute. I could grieve later, but right now, maybe I could shed some light on Joe's death.

"Has Angel been here yet," I asked.

"No, he's dealing with all the immediate fallout, you know, canceling the tour etcetera, but I made the call to him, replied Caine, "He's devastated. I don't think he'll ever be able to visit this house again."

"Yeah, I get that, Joe was like the son Angel never had, this is going to rip him to pieces," I replied, looking around me and realizing how silent it was with everybody working the scene.

"C'mon, Coop, let's take a look around, you want some coffee?"

"No man, I'm good," I replied, "Let's get started."

Colin Caine had brought me in on a number of crime scenes in the past, well, murder scenes to be accurate, because he knew I had been a pretty decent detective in San Francisco. But this, well this was deeply personal and he wanted anything I saw today that didn't make sense.

As we walked to the laundry room, he pointed out where the intruder had got in. A window was open, a hurricane shutter lying on the ground outside.

"This place was locked up tighter than a drum, except that panel on the window which was held in place by four bolts from the outside," Caine said, "It's the only shutter that isn't key-locked, so I'm guessing that the perp just lucked out."

I was already deep in thought, still nothing made sense to me yet.

"Why would anyone want to murder someone during a Cat-5 hurricane?" I asked.

"Beats me, why would anyone be dumb enough to be outside in a 'cane like Jacques?" he replied.

We left the laundry room and entered the kitchen, where I suddenly spotted the enormous pool of blood in front of the soda cooler. I've attended some pretty gruesome murder scenes in the past, without reacting too badly, but a wave of nausea hit me when I realized it was my friend's blood on the floor.

"You okay, Coop?"

"Yeah, gimme a sec," I replied, "Wasn't quite ready for that."

I took a deep breath, held it for a few seconds, and let it out.

"I'm good, man, let's continue."

"See, I'm not sure, but d'you think it was a robbery gone wrong?" asked Caine.

"You mean, the perp thinks, rich dude's house, must be empty, grab some high-end items, quick in, quick out?" I replied.

"Exactly, an opportunist."

"But the guy gets a big surprise when he finds the owner still there, panics, pulls a knife and bolts."

"Yeah, but right now, I'm not seeing a motive," said Caine.

"Let's have a good look around the place," I said, "Something might leap out that your guys have missed."

We continued up the grand curving staircase towards Joe's bedroom, oddly in complete disarray because Felipe hadn't been home to tidy up.

"If Felipe had been here…" I said, haltingly.

"You think that might have made a difference?" Caine asked.

"I do, Coke, Felipe wasn't just Joe's butler, he was his bodyguard too."

"Jeez, I didn't know that."

"He was skilled in martial arts," I continued, "Although you'd never have known it. But that was one of the reasons Angel hired him for Joe. If Felipe had been home, I truly believe that Joe would still be alive."

Caine ran his hand down the front of his face, as he himself contemplated why on earth Joe had been killed.

"It still doesn't make any goddamned sense, Coop, can you think of one person who would want to harm that man?"

"Nope, not even Flick," I replied, "I mean, sure, she's a bitch, but not a murderous one."

The bedroom showed nothing much out of the ordinary, a typical rock 'n roller's pad, unkempt black satin sheets on a giant bed, cigarette packs and ashtrays strewn across a thick, electric-blue shag-pile carpet, and the obligatory bottles of liquor and glasses on the nightstands. Loud and colorful art covered the walls, while sex toys and unused condom packets littered the area around the bed.

"Anything?" asked Caine.

"Nothing to see here," I replied, and we left the bedroom to explore the other suites on the second floor.

Finally, having discovered nothing that I thought was unusual, we made our way downstairs again, where most of the police officers and crime scene investigators were working. We navigated our way around the abundance of little yellow, numbered cones that littered the floor, being careful not to disturb them.

I stood in the center of the room, as forensic technicians, hidden under their white hazmat suits and face-masks, worked diligently and meticulously. Using Olight Marauder flashlights, they carefully extracted tiny items from the floor and furniture, before placing yet another cone beside what they'd put into evidence collection bags.

My mind was still whirling, too much was happening in my life that I couldn't control. I'd never ever before found myself out of my depth, but Joe's murder, along with the jeopardy that my own family found itself in, was becoming heavy on my shoulders.

And then I saw it.

"Coke, I think I know what happened."

He stared at me, seeing that I was absolutely motionless, staring at one particular spot on the lounge's wall.

"What are you seeing, Coop, what am I missing?"

"It's not what you're missing," I replied, "It's *what's* missing."

"You've lost me, buddy."

"There used to be a guitar hanging right there in that unoccupied spot between the other guitars on the wall."

"Okay, so there's a guitar missing, maybe it's elsewhere in the house, might be in the studio?" he replied.

"No, you won't find it, Coke, that guitar was a rarer-than-rare two-million-dollar guitar," I replied, "And now you've got your motive."

Chapter 80

I said goodbye to Coke, and once again made the short journey back to the marina. After re-parking in a guest bay, I repeated my previous reconnaissance of the surrounding area, climbed out of the Tacoma and made my way to my berth.

When I arrived, my heart sank when I realized that *Lost Soul* was no longer there. In fact, it wasn't only my boat that was missing, because from the look of other owners talking on their phones on the adjacent docks, it seemed that Jacques had taken maybe a half a dozen other vessels.

The superyachts though, remained intact, including my neighbor's carbon-fiber behemoth. And as I stood there, slowly absorbing the scene, my eyes finally rested on *Lost Soul*. She was fifty yards out from the dock, capsized and belly up, her hull broken up like splintered driftwood.

I knew immediately that she was unrepairable, a total loss as far as the insurers would be concerned. I felt sad, not so much because of the damage, but more so that she had served me well when I was at my lowest. And I don't have many possessions either, but the few that I once had that were important to me, were also now gone.

The insurance company would pay out pretty quickly, maritime brokers move much faster than home insurers, and I would have a new replacement boat soon, but all of that was irrelevant for the moment, because I had more important things to deal with. And I had made an important decision.

Running back up the dock to the Tacoma, I fired up the motor and hastily made my way back to Gator Run Beach Club.

Chapter 81

Carlo Galotti was already preparing for the worst. He had spent the last forty-eight hours alone at the mansion, until this morning when a crew had arrived to remove all of the hurricane shutters on the mansion. They were still working at it and would likely need to come back in the morning to finish up, such was the size of the property.

But he wasn't really thinking about that, his thoughts dwelled more on his own immediate future.

In reality, the Russians were right, Carlo no longer had the status that he had once had in Miami, there were younger guys who had come up through the ranks, already making inroads to making Miami become their town. And he knew that with the loss of the real talent in his employ, and the reliance on idiots like Eddie and his type, it would be impossible to stave off the inevitable.

He had screwed up on the cocaine distribution deal with Sergei and Nikita, to the point where he thought it unsalvageable. It didn't help either, that thus far, he had been unable to track down Cassidy and kill her as a mark of respect to Nikita.

He knew exactly how Sergei and Nikita viewed him, weak and ineffective, and he also knew that in their eyes, as the effective clients, he was easily replaceable.

He didn't even really care about Cassidy either. In all honesty, it would likely be Kadosh who would find her, because Carlo had basically run out of ideas, and good men too. Cassidy had meant nothing to him for a long time, sure she'd been a good lay at the beginning, but he grew bored quickly. In his current view, he thought, out of sight, out of mind. Good luck to her.

So, he had to formulate an exit strategy.

Money wasn't an issue, he had hidden at least two hundred million dollars in Swiss numbered accounts and in other offshore accounts in Monaco, Lebanon and the Cayman Islands.

His mansion, although valued north of sixty million dollars, could wait to be sold, because he figured that with so many prestigious properties left damaged after the hurricane, the rental price on his place would command maybe a million bucks a month. Of course, in a year or so's time, he'd have it put on the market, but it would have increased in value by then. Win win.

So, when the shit hit the fan, Carlo would be ready. His Bombardier Global 7500 would be fueled and crewed twenty-four hours a day at Miami Executive Airport from now on, and he could leave the country in under an hour.

Maybe he should head to Europe? He hadn't been for such a long time. Carlo knew he wouldn't be able to set up in Monaco, London, Milan or even the French Riviera, too many photographers and paparazzi. Too much publicity if you're on the downlow.

But he could see himself eating Kalamata olives and sipping ouzo on a Greek beach, or cozying up with a beautiful girl in a Portuguese beach town, or maybe even discover his roots back in Italy. Who knew? So many wonderful quiet spots with so many fabulous European beauties. The world would become his oyster once more.

But whatever he did, if the situation necessitated his disappearance, he knew that he'd need to exist in the shadows for some time. Because the Russians never let it go.

Chapter 82

I parked the Tacoma on the driveway, aware that my crew would have already seen my arrival, and quickly made my way around to the back of the house. As I opened the door, the inimitable aroma of paella hit me, and I realized how hungry I had just become.

First to greet me was Molly, and I could see the worry etched on her porcelain pale face, as she buried her head into my chest.

"Hey," I whispered, "You don't have to worry about me, I'm here, sweetie."

"Can't lose you, Dad, it's too much to even think about."

Molly rarely shed tears, and even now, although I could feel her emotions, she refused to let it out.

"Nothing's going to happen, I'm figuring it out, trust me."

We walked on through to the lounge, where Memphis and Rainee were stationed on lookout at each end of the window facing the street. Remy, Billy and Cassidy were sat on the floor around the coffee table playing Monopoly.

"Who's cooking paella?" I asked.

"That would be yours truly," said Cassidy, rising from the floor to come and hug me once Molly had sat back down to the game in progress.

One of the things that I like about Cassidy is that she reads situations very easily, and picks her moments with a great deal of thought and empathy. It might have been a natural reaction for her to be the first to greet me when I walked through the door, just as I would with her, but she knew that Molly would want to see me first, so she just waited in the background until it was the right time.

"I'm famished," I said, "How soon will it be ready?"

"That would be right about now, give me a minute and I'll dish up."

Cassidy walked into the kitchen, and I motioned for Rainee to come into the den with me.

"It's been a morning," I said, flopping down into one of the leather loungers facing the giant television, "Something I never want to go through again."

Rainee knew me like no one else, saw the gravity finally show in my face, and sat down next to me.

"Coop, whatever it is, it's bad, isn't it?"

"Yeah, about as bad as it could get," I replied.

"I'm guessing that *Lost Soul* has gone?" she asked.

"Yeah, completely totaled, but that's not the worst of it," I replied, "Joe's gone too."

"He's gone? Where?"

"He's dead, Rainee, Joe was murdered at his house during the hurricane."

"Jesus, Coop!" she exclaimed, "What the fuck happened?"

Rainee wasn't close with Joe in the way that I was, she liked the guy, but he wasn't a personal friend. However, she knew my relationship with him, and she could feel my loss.

"Coke called me when I was at the marina, told me what had happened, asked me to go to the house."

"I don't know what to say, I know you loved the guy," she said, "But hell, why would anyone want to kill him, he was harmless."

"I found out why, when I was at his house. Seems like it was someone who saw a chance of robbing the place whilst the hurricane was in play. Didn't realize that Joe would be home, panicked, killed Joe."

"Fuck. Poor Joe."

"And the only thing I could see that was taken, was the Dave Gilmour Stratocaster that I told you about, so that must have been the target," I continued, "Joe was just collateral damage."

"I can't believe this, Coop," she replied, "You know he wired me forty grand only yesterday morning, don't you?"

"I do, Joe was one of the good guys," I replied solemnly, "But listen, don't tell the others about any of this, we need to concentrate on our own predicament for the moment. I'll tell Cassidy tonight, but ask that she keeps it under her hat for the moment. We'll think about Joe and raise a glass to him sometime soon, but not right now."

"Got it," said Rainee, "You feel like eating?"

"Yeah, come on, let's join the others and then, after dinner, we need to have a sit down with everyone to plan our next moves."

Chapter 83

It hadn't taken long to find the truck. Shira Kadosh smiled at how dumb people were in this age of technology. They just never learned.

Pouring a glass of Rochioli Pinot Noir, a wine she favored from Northern California's Russian River Valley, she took it to the chaise longue and examined her MacBook once more.

With only the names of Showers and Hemingway to go on, Kadosh had easily connected them to Hemingway's daughter on Facebook. Molly Hemingway.

It didn't take her long to discover that the girl's boyfriend was one Billy McGrath. And Billy loved his truck. The boy must have posted more than a hundred photos of it on Facebook. She now had the make, model and license plate, and pretty soon after, she also had the kid's address. It was like taking candy from a baby, as the Americans said.

The problem that still remained though, was that if she didn't find the truck at Billy McGrath's apartment building, she was still no closer to finding Showers or Hemingway, so she realized that she still had a problem.

However, after digging deeper into his Facebook posts, she discovered that Billy worked at a nightclub in Palm Beach, the ridiculously named, Viper Den.

And one thing that Kadosh knew, is that nightclubs never closed, maybe for a hurricane of course, but as soon as it passed on through, The Viper Den would be open for its insatiable clubgoers.

And that might even be this very evening, so Kadosh would dress up tonight and go pay a visit. In the meantime, she might have just one more glass of the very delightful Rochioli.

Chapter 84

"Listen up," I said, once we had finished eating just about every morsel of Cassidy's delicious paella, "I need to talk to you all."

"I wondered when you were going to enlighten us on your plan, Coop," said Remy, pushing the last of the ciabatta into his mouth.

"Okay," I said, "Rainee and I had pretty much planned in advance for a situation like this, so here's the deal."

No one responded, they just sat waiting for my next words, but it was Rainee who spoke next.

"Coop and I have a shitload of hardware in my truck."

"Hardware?" asked Molly.

"Guns, honey. Sorry, but we need firepower or we'll be sitting ducks for whoever is coming after us," I replied.

It was at that point that I interrupted the thoughts that were clearly running around everyone's minds, and began telling the entire story of Cassidy, her time on the run, and the recent attempts to kill Rainee.

"Fuck!" said Molly, when I'd finished, "Sorry Dad, but that's a lot to take in."

"I know, and that's why I came to a decision this morning that it's no longer safe for you to be here."

"What??" she protested, "I'm not going anywhere, I'm staying with you, Dad."

"No, Molly, you're not," I replied firmly, "I'm getting you out of here to somewhere safe."

"No Dad! Please!"

"It won't be for long, maybe only a couple of days," I replied, "But I won't be able to function properly if I'm terrified about what might happen to you. It's a decision that's been made. I'm sorry, Molly."

There was no way I wanted her to be out of my sight at the moment, but I knew for her own safety that I had to be realistic about the current predicament.

"Where am I going?" she asked, sullenly, "And can Billy come too?"

"I have to work at the club tonight," said Billy, interjecting, "If I don't turn up for work, I'll get fired."

"That's good, Billy," I said, "Go about your life as usual, no one knows you're involved anyway."

"Should I take my Tacoma tonight?" asked Billy.

"No, I'd sooner you don't drive it for the moment, I'll keep using it for now," I replied.

"Can you drop me off then?" asked Billy, "I can get an Uber back."

"Hey Remy," I interjected, "Okay if Billy takes the Escalade tonight?"

"No worries, partner, have at it, Billy."

Billy's eyes widened, he loved Escalades.

Rainee spoke again.

"Molly, I have a friend in Georgia, she's flying down in the morning in her plane, and then she's taking you back to her farm with her."

Molly's face brightened.

"You mean I'm going on one of those private jets?" she asked, "That's cool."

"Not really," Rainee replied, "Lauren's taking you back in her crop-duster. Sorry, baby."

Molly's face fell.

"And for the time being," I added, "Can I ask everyone here to still call Cassidy, Layla, and not to use her real name, just for the moment anyway?"

"Who's Cassidy?" asked Remy, laughing as he gnawed in vain hope, on the last remaining partially stripped chicken bone on his plate.

"Exactly," I said.

Chapter 85

The Viper Den was buzzing that night, the club-starved party-animals' thirsts overflowing, having missed one night of merriment during the hurricane. They say that New York never sleeps, but the same was true for Palm Beach's teen and twenty-something crowd.

Billy had worked the door for the first four hours since the club opened at eight that night, but his first shift was taken over by his buddy, Gianni, at midnight so that Billy could take a fifteen-minute break and grab a burger and a Sprite.

Seated on a stool at the bar, Billy surveilled the crowd, which was in full unbridled revelry. At the end of the bar where he sat, he watched as punters queued six people deep to refuel their alcohol system, desperate to get wasted. And as soon as possible.

Billy could never understand why there was this need to get so shit-faced and then feel like garbage the next morning, because Billy didn't drink. He had had a few glasses of wine over the years, but mostly they had been at weddings or funerals. He just didn't much like alcohol, particularly liquor, and the effects that came with it.

On the positive side though, because The Viper Den had become so popular so quickly, the bar and admission receipts were manna from heaven for the club's owner, Peyton Gambler, Billy's ultimate boss. And Gambler paid his crew well, with Billy earning a hundred bucks an hour for his time spent working there.

Pretty soon, he was going to be able to buy that 2023 Ford Ranger pickup truck he'd always dreamed about. The only thing he didn't like, was having to work all night and sleep for much of the day, which meant that he didn't get to spend as much time with Molly as he would have liked.

And Billy utterly adored Molly. He would kid her about her style of dress, but he wouldn't want her to change. Although recently, he'd noticed that she'd begun to abandon her Goth look, in favor of a somewhat more stylishly casual wardrobe. He had guessed it was because she had met with Colin Caine about joining the Police Department. And Billy liked that idea very much.

Biting down on his burger, something caught his eye in the far corner of the club on the other side of the dance floor. He spotted a kid that he hadn't seen in a while. And the kid, a pretty good-looking boy, had a bevy of girls surrounding him in the roped-off VIP area, and just to get access to that section wasn't cheap.

Added to that, the kid was ordering what looked like Crystal champagne, like it was five-buck mineral water.

"Tommy Burns," Billy said to himself, "What the actual fuck?"

Billy knew that Tommy didn't have two nickels to rub together, because he didn't work, had never really worked a day in his life. In fact, Billy vaguely already knew Tommy, because they'd attended the same high school briefly, before Tommy had dropped out at sixteen.

"So, how have you suddenly got so much coin, Tommy boy?" he pondered aloud.

~ ~ ~

Shira Kadosh, resplendent in her form-hugging maroon leather catsuit and stiletto heels, watched Billy from afar, as she sipped on a dirty martini. Ordinarily, when she was on a job, she wouldn't be drinking, but tonight was merely a task of observation.

The boy she was watching was ripped, truly a fit young man, his muscles almost popping out of the tight, black polo shirt that was evidently the club's uniform. And he was a looker, she actually found him quite attractive. And whenever Kadosh took a lover, she favored the younger types, the ones who looked like models, but also had the required stamina.

The boy had been quickly eating his hamburger, had maybe eaten half of it, when he had clearly spotted something going on out of Kadosh's view. She watched as he pushed the plate away and then began to casually circumnavigate the dance floor at a slow pace, taking in each and every clubber as he passed them.

Kadosh waited until Billy had walked twenty yards or so, finished the remainder of her martini, and slowly began to follow him.

She danced a little on the periphery of the dance floor, mingling in with the crowd, but simultaneously watching and moving toward the VIP area where Billy seemed to be heading for.

By the time he had reached the roped-off zone, she was ten yards away, in earshot, even above the deafening sound of the music.

"Tommy boy," yelled Billy, keen to make his voice heard, "That's a heck of a tab you've got running, fella."

"What's it to you?" Tommy yelled back, "Just here having some fun until you came along."

Kadosh inwardly smiled at the pluckiness of the boy behind the ropes, because although a looker himself, he was no match for Billy in the brawn department. He was probably a bit drunk and didn't want to lose face in front of his five girlfriends who were huddled around him, slurping champagne like it was Sprite.

"I hope you've got the cash to pay for all of this," yelled Billy, "Because the last time I saw you here, your cougar was paying the bill."

"Fuck you, Billy, I've got money," Tommy replied, "Now why don't you get your ass back to the door like a good little boy?"

Billy wasn't fazed by Tommy, never had been. If he wanted to, he could squash him like a bug. But Billy wasn't going to do that.

"I hear you're a wanted man," he yelled again, "I heard you shot someone."

"Fuck you," Tommy replied again in his unique and somewhat limited vernacular, "I didn't shoot no one. Now fuck off and stop messin' up my night."

Those expletives were the last he uttered, as Billy hurdled the rope, pulled Tommy from the couch, and punched him square in the face. Lights out.

Billy was lightning quick to pull a nylon cable tie from his pocket, throw Tommy on the ground stomach down, and lash his hands together behind his back.

Kadosh was impressed, the boy had moves.

Several other bouncers in the club had quickly arrived at the scene as Billy dragged a bloody-faced Tommy across the nightclub floor, headed for the exit.

Kadosh decided that staying put for the moment was probably her best option. For the moment, anyway.

~ ~ ~

"I believe there's a bunch of people looking for you, Tommy boy, and I think they'll be super pleased to see you."

Tommy was now coming around, still full of piss and vinegar, as he spat blood at Billy.

"Untie me, you piece of shit, I didn't do nuttin'."

"I think there are people who might disagree with that," said Billy, punching Tommy's lights out for a second time.

"The first one was for Coop, dipshit," said Billy, "And that one was for Molly."

As Tommy lay prone and unconscious on the wet tarmac, Billy pulled out his phone and called a number.

When the call picked up, he asked politely and calmly, "Colin Caine, please, if he's in tonight?"

He listened as the voice on the other end of the line said something.

"Sure, I can wait," said Billy.

Once again, the line went dead for a minute or so, until a new voice came on the line.

"This is Caine," the voice said.

"Hey Coke, it's Billy, Molly's boyfriend."

"Hey Billy, what's up? You just caught me about to leave for the night."

"I think I have someone you might want to talk to, a certain Tommy Burns," said Billy, "I'm with him at The Viper Den."

"You got him locked down?"

"Don't worry, Coke, he ain't goin' nowhere."

"Be right there, son, good work," Caine responded before hanging up.

~ ~ ~

Shira Kadosh had discovered a table that had just become vacant, and waited patiently for one of the wait-staff to take an order.

"What can I get you, ma'am?" asked the girl who had finally come over to her.

"I'm thinking I'll try the burger and fries, I saw someone eating one earlier, and it looked good."

"Sure, no problem, anything to drink?" asked the girl.

Maybe another dirty martini," Kadosh replied, "I think I might be here a while longer."

Kadosh realized that she might be at the club for another three hours or so before Billy finally finished his shift, but she'd slept for much of the afternoon that day, so she wasn't tired in the slightest.

And she had time on her hands, before she would follow Billy to wherever he was staying. And as always, she was hungry. Loved a martini too.

Chapter 86

At eight the next morning, my phone rang, punching out the unmistakable Apple melody.

Must change that…

I looked at the screen and saw that it was Coke again, which had me immediately concerned.

Who'd died now?

Apart from Billy, who had worked until the early hours, the remainder of us had taken shifts on lookout duty, so that at any one time during the day or night, we had eyes on the street outside. Fortunately, I had gotten to bed by two in the morning so I had had more than enough rest.

"Coke," I said, "I sure as hell don't need more bad news this early in the day."

"Not today, buddy," he answered, "I'm the bearer of maybe some better news this morning."

"Oh?"

"Yeah, I got a call from Billy in the early hours, and I think you'll be interested in what he had to say."

"Billy? Why would he be calling you?" I replied, "He was working most of the night, I think he's sound asleep right now."

"Yeah, he *was* working, but when I got the call from him, I went straight to the club. Your boy Billy was standing over Tommy Burns, had him hog-tied on the street outside, and Tommy was a little worse for wear," he said, laughing now.

"Tommy Burns? I didn't think we'd see that boy again, thought he'd gone to ground."

"Well, Billy spotted him flashing a bunch of cash in the club, spending like there's no tomorrow, the kid got in Billy's face, so Billy got in his. Only gonna be one winner there," said Caine.

"So where is Burns right now," I asked.

"He's in an interview room, wailing like a baby," Caine replied, still laughing, "I left him there to stew while I went home to get some shuteye for a few hours."

"Are you charging him?"

"You bet," he replied, "I'll be charging him for attempted murder, you being the victim."

"You said he was flush with money?" I asked, "Because Tommy Burns has never had money, never had a job either. He say where he got it?"

"Not yet, but you know as well as I do, that we've got him for a minimum twenty-four hours to question him," he replied, "You wanna come join me?"

The wheels were suddenly turning in my mind.

"Yes, definitely, I have to drop Molly off at the airfield first, but I'll come right on over after that."

"Molly's going somewhere?" Caine asked, inquisitively.

"Yeah, she is, I'll explain why when I see you," I replied.

"Okay then, what time you coming down?"

"I'll be with you no later than eleven," I said, "And one thing, does your coffee at the precinct still taste like piss?"

"Indeed it does," he replied, laughing once more.

"Good, I'll bring a couple of lattes."

"Soy milk for me, please."

"Of course."

Chapter 87

Interview Room No.3 at West Palm Beach PD was not dissimilar to any other that one might see on television. The walls were painted in mid-gray, the metal table and chairs also in a matching metallic gray. The ceiling was characteristic of any government building, suspended with interlocking white mineral fiber tiles. Although the ones in this room were punctuated by yellow nicotine-stained circles above both sides of the table. For some reason, smoking is still permitted in these rooms.

As I watched through the one-way mirror that covered the entire side of one of the small room's walls, Tommy Burns was chain-smoking his way through a pack of Marlboro Gold, as Coke leaned back in his chair, taking the occasional sip of station coffee, and laconically asking question after question. It felt like the appropriate time for me to gate-crash the party.

I walked out into the corridor, opened the interview room's door and kicked it shut, placing one of the lattes I'd been carrying, in front of Coke. The smoke-filled room hit me as soon as I walked in, and I grimaced at spending more than thirty minutes in the smog of it.

I ignored Tommy, sat down in the vacant chair next to my friend, took a sip of coffee, and then looked up from my cup to see the terror written on the kid's face.

"Long time, no see," I said, taking a second sip of my brew.

"I dunno what you're talking about," replied Tommy, avoiding my eyeline.

The noise of Caine's fist smashing down on the table, saw Tommy fall back off his chair from the sudden shock. Caine's station coffee was also a victim as it crashed to the ground and spattered across the dull gray, painted floor.

"Don't fuck with us!" yelled Caine, standing up quickly and getting into Tommy's face, before retaking his seat and calmly taking another sip of latte.

"Now," I said to the kid, who had partially recovered from the shock and had struggled back up into his seat, "As you can probably gather, my friend here, Detective Caine, is the good cop. I'm not."

"Fuck you," spat Tommy.

"Now, Tommy, don't be like that. Because very soon, I think that you're the one who's going to be fucked. Well and truly, in fact," I replied, asking approval from Caine.

Caine nodded.

"You got nuttin' on me," he spat again, "I'll be outta here tomorrow."

"You won't," I replied, "The only place you're going is Railford Prison up in Bradford County, and I can tell you now, a pretty boy like you ain't gonna enjoy your stay there. Probably best to avoid the showers too."

"Ain't goin' to no prison, I ain't done nothin'," Tommy blurted, although this time, he lacked the confidence from his earlier expletives.

"Okay," Caine interjected, "Let's take a step backward for a moment, Tommy. Do you know who my friend here is?"

"Never seen him before in my life," Tommy replied, but actually with some conviction, meaning that he might be telling the truth.

The boy plucked another cigarette from the fast-dwindling pack on the table, and lit it as Caine took another sip of latte. I was grateful that I'd picked up Ventis, because my buddy was going through his java fix, quickly.

"Well, Tommy, he knows who *you* are."

Tommy sat silently, clearly having no idea who I was.

"Tell me about Flick," Caine continued, "I'm guessing you're old history to her now that she's got her divorce money? She's probably moved on to new meat by now?"

"Ain't seen her in a long time," Tommy replied, "And besides, she was just a cash cow to me, paid the bills, good fuck but she's gettin' old."

"Such a gentleman," said Caine, not even bothering to look at the boy, "But your next paramour won't be a cougar like Flick, it'll be your new boyfriend in Railford, probably one of the big guys, I'd guess."

I watched Tommy's face and I could see the cracks appearing quickly. I would have to be the good cop for a while if we wanted to reel him in.

"Tommy," I said, calmly, "I'm the man you shot, at your house. Do you remember running away in your birthday suit on the night my partner and I discovered you and Flick?"

Tommy began to open his mouth, but then thought better of it, so I continued on.

"Now, the thing is, Tommy, you hit me good. Real good, in fact, and had it not been for my partner, I wouldn't be sitting here right now. Do you understand what I'm saying?"

This was the deer-caught-in-the-headlights moment that I wanted.

"And the thing is, Tommy," said Caine, as he continued the two-string interrogation, "I could charge you right now with any number of offenses... assault with a deadly weapon, attempted manslaughter, leaving the scene of a crime... the list is pleasingly endless."

Tommy once again returned to his feigned ignorance of what Caine was saying to him.

"Ain't nuttin' you can charge me with, I ain't done nothin'. Let me outta here!"

"But you see, Tommy, that's where you're wrong," Caine replied, "Ballistics show that the gun you used to shoot my friend here, is registered to you personally."

"Coulda been anyone," Tommy blurted, "Y'ain't got no proof it was me."

The interview room was kept at a constant air-conditioned temperature of sixty-two degrees, not uncomfortable, but cool enough to keep a prisoner alert. But even with the frigidity of the room, Tommy was sweating buckets.

"Ah," said Caine, "Now that, young Tommy, is where you've got it all wrong."

All the boy could say was, "Huh?"

"You see, if you had been really smart when you went to Walmart to buy your handgun, you would've bought a revolver, rather than your little Beretta," I interjected, while Caine pulled a cigarette from his own pack and lit up, blowing a cloud of smoke in Tommy's direction.

Once again, Tommy had nothing.

"Huh?"

"Revolvers don't eject spent shell casings, but guns like my Glock and your Beretta do," I continued.

"So what?" he replied, "Still coulda been anyone."

"Rule of thumb, if you'll pardon the pun," Caine interjected, blowing another waft of smoke toward Tommy, "If you're going to kill someone, you should always load the gun with gloves on."

"I don't get it," said Tommy, clearly missing the point.

Man, this kid was Dumb & Dumber rolled up into one…

"Your prints were all over the casings that you left on the tarmac in your hurry to leave the scene," said Caine, matter-of-factly, "And the second point, is that we have an eye witness in my friend here, the victim. You're going down, son."

In that moment, Tommy suddenly realized the reality of the moment, and as his brain slowly ticked, he knew that he was done for.

I was fighting hard to keep the anger within me from boiling over, but I knew I had to contain it because I wasn't done yet. On my way from dropping Molly at the airfield, I'd made a stop to check on something, and my hunch had backed up my theory. And in this moment, Tommy had no defenses left in him, all he could think about was doing time at Railford.

Caine was putting documents back into the manila folder that sat in front of him on the table, ready to take Tommy to a holding cell.

"How many times have you been to the Jarvie house with Flick?" I asked Tommy.

My question had caught him completely off-guard, he wasn't expecting it at all. But my eyes never left his, and then I saw the moment as his eyes looked left. He was about to tell a lie.

Caine stared at me, wondering where this new tack was going, but like the professional he is, he quietly laid the folder back down on the table, and leant back in his chair.

"I only been there once when her husband was on the west coast," Tommy said, lying, "The guy had a place in San Diego, I think."

Had, not has…

"Is that right?" I asked, "So you haven't been there recently?"

Tommy twitched, and that was all I needed as confirmation.

"Course I ain't been there recently, Flick only took me there once," he replied, lying once again.

"Where did you get all the money you were spending at the club last night," I asked, "Did you suddenly have a windfall, Tommy?"

"I got money," he replied, but knew that no one would believe a guy who'd never had a job in his life.

The guillotine was dropping.

"What did Flick tell you about that guitar you stole from Joe Jarvie's house?" I asked, still remaining calm, still concealing my rage.

"Dunno what you're talking about," he replied, as I saw Caine suddenly get the picture on where I was going.

"Did she tell you that it was worth north of two million dollars?" I asked, "Is that why you broke into Joe's house? Is that why you murdered him? Did Flick put you up to it?"

Tommy Burns was not only on the ropes now, he wasn't even capable of getting up off the canvas, but he wasn't going out without a fight.

"You got nuttin' on me! I ain't been to that house, fuck you!"

"And there you have it, Tommy, you just caught yourself in another lie. Again," I replied, "You see, before I came here this morning, I made a stop. Sorry for being late, Coke."

"No worries, partner," Caine replied, "Tommy boy and I had plenty to talk about. Please continue, my friend."

"So, as I was saying, Tommy, I made a stop at a house that's maybe, six or seven hundred yards up from Joe's house. Do you want to know why I made a stop there?"

The boy knew the game was up and just stared down at the table, having no idea what was coming.

"A couple of months ago, when I was driving down that street to visit Joe, I happened to notice something that is quite rare. You know the neighborhood, Tommy, you know that people who live there are pretty wealthy, right?"

Tommy remained silent, motionless.

"Right?" I yelled at him, this time with my own fist slamming down on the table.

Tommy nearly fell back off his chair again, but managed to grip the table so as not to fall. His fall was also avoided by the fact that both Coke and I held on to the table from our side. But Tommy was hanging on by a thread now, mentally and physically.

My next words were calm again.

"Now, the house that I visited has this automated surveillance system, using twelve permanently panning cameras," I said, "Must've cost the guy a fortune to install, but these homes are full of valuable items, aren't they, Tommy, so you can understand why the owners would invest in such systems, right?"

Tommy's eyes never left mine, but nodded in agreement, if only to avoid another outburst from me.

"And the owner of that house, a very nice man called James, allowed me to look at the back-up drive for the night of the hurricane. And Tommy, these aren't your average security cameras, these are full color, high definition 4K babies, that record everything in the most extraordinary detail."

Caine continued to sit this one out, swigging on the last of his latte, whilst pulling another cigarette from his pack.

"So, as I was saying, I watched your truck arrive, I saw you get out and walk onto Joe's property, I saw you go back to the truck for tools, and I saw you eventually leaving the house with Joe's extremely valuable guitar in your hand."

"Oh my," said Caine, "Tsk tsk, Tommy."

"How much did you get for it, Tommy? Five grand maybe, at a local pawn shop?"

Tommy Burns looked like he wanted to puke.

"The thing is, Tommy, that Strat was valued in excess of two mil," I continued calmly now, "So even if you'd been smart enough to get ten cents on the dollar, you could have satisfied your coke habit for a couple of years. But that's the problem, isn't it, Tommy, you're just not very bright, are you?"

"Tommy, Tommy, Tommy…" said Coke, pulling yet another cigarette from what was now, a quickly dwindling pack.

"And I would bet the farm on it," I continued, "That when Detective Caine here, searches your truck today, he'll find the murder weapon, complete with Joe's blood on it that you hadn't properly wiped away."

"It wasn't me!" yelled Tommy, as Caine got up from his chair and pressed the stop button on the video camera that was recording the interview.

"Interview over," he said.

And once I knew that the camera was no longer recording, I calmly got to my feet, walked around the table and punched Tommy full in the face with every ounce of strength in me, sending Tommy crashing to the ground once more.

"That's for Joe, you murdering scumbag," I said, as I made my way to the door, "I can wait for my own revenge when I visit you up in Railford."

Chapter 88

Carlo Galotti had just gotten word from Sergei that he and Sokalov had cut short their visit to Moscow, and wanted a meeting with him when they arrived back in Florida, in four days from now.

On one hand, Carlo had pure fear running through him that he was about to be terminated by the Russians, if they had their way. But on the other, and Carlo had always been a greedy man, perhaps they wanted to cement the relationship with more business in the future?

The Clash's punk song immediately sounded in Carlo's mind, *"Should I Stay, Or Should I Go?"*

Carlo had always loved that whole British punk-rock scene from the late seventies, having spent three years in London during his early teens, before he moved with his family to Miami. The Sex Pistols, The Jam, The Undertones, Siouxie, and of course, The Clash, were his personal favorites.

He walked across the Great Room, the sumptuous centerpiece of his Miami-Modern home, and thumbed through the electronic display on the wall, that controlled and delivered sound to every part of the home, whenever and wherever he wanted it.

He found the desired track selection and hit 'play' and immediately, the unique anger and emotion of the song began, that always took Carlo back to his teens.

Some people might say my life is in a rut,

I'm quite happy with what I got...

Carlo was happy that there was no one in the house because no one would have expected to see him, Carlo Galotti – Mafia Don, utterly entranced by this song, and lip-synching every word as it sprang from the loudspeakers with raw, guttural anger. But Carlo didn't care, Carlo didn't give a fuck now...

I'm going underground, going underground

Well, if the brass bands play and feet start to pound

I'm going underground, going underground

Well, let the boys all sing and let the boys all shout for tomorrow...

The song had made Carlo's decision for him. He'd take the meeting with the Russians out of courtesy, but if the shit hit the fan, he was going underground, far, far away.

Chapter 89

Before I'd gone back to the house that evening, I'd stopped off to pick up Chinese take-out, and while the restaurant prepared my order, I'd taken a minute to check on Molly.

Surprisingly, she was having a great time, which made me happy, and she and Lauren had just come back to the farmhouse after an evening ride. I knew Lauren from way back, she was a hardworking and successful farmer in a mostly male world, so I have the deepest respect for the woman.

Lauren owns her own place that sits on three hundred acres, and there is nothing she can't do on that farm. And most things she could do better than most men. She had even learned to fly and had bought a plane so she could fertilize her crops herself, quickly and efficiently.

Lauren never had children, and most men she met just didn't fit the bill, so she breeds Palominos as her one great passion and love. She would be over the moon that she was having Molly staying for a few days.

But right now, as I made my way back to Gator Run Beach Club, the intoxicating aroma inside the Tacoma was making me realize that the last time I'd eaten, was the paella we'd all had together on the previous evening.

I'd stopped at the gate of the country club to have a chat with Jerry, but he'd called in sick and there was another guy manning the entrance whom I'd never met before.

Fortunately, I had found the gate remotes in the house the night before, one for me, one for Rainee and one for Billy. It meant that I didn't have to explain anything to the guard, and after a brief chat, I clicked my remote and drove through.

~ ~ ~

I made my way to the rear of the property, careful to avoid the trip-wires, caltrops and shotgun-blank traps that Rainee had installed when we'd first arrived at the house. The house, being in a quiet and suburban gated community, would be an unlikely candidate for urban warfare in normal circumstances. But right now, this was not a normal one. We also had the benefit of motion detector cameras, which one of our crew was monitoring throughout our time there.

I entered the house via the kitchen, where I found Cassidy pouring some glasses of wine, as she monitored the camera feeds.

"Hello stranger," she said, giving me a quick hug, "Whatever you've got in those bags, I want it now."

"I've missed you today," I said, realizing that the longer I knew her, the more I wanted her as a permanent fixture in my life, "It's Chinese, by the way, and it's still hot. Let's get some plates and cutlery out, I'm starving too."

We took the food and place-settings into the dining room, and sure enough, Rainee and Memphis were on lookout. They both briefly nodded to me, but then continued their gaze toward the end of the street.

Billy had already gone to work at The Viper Den, so he would be eating at the club, but Remy leapt up from his chair in the TV room as soon as he smelled the arrival of food.

"Oh brother, I am so damned hungry," said Remy, which wasn't unusual, given his endless appetite, "Lemme help there."

"Rainee, Memphis, come eat," I said, "I'll take watch for now."

"Not gonna refuse that," said Rainee, "I'm famished and this is getting kind of old, looking at a street that feels like the Mary Celeste."

"You sure you don't wanna eat first, Coop?" asked Memphis, "Happy to wait."

"Nah, come on, take a break, man, food's gonna get cold."

"Don't need to ask me twice," he replied, handing me the rifle.

"I'll put a plate in the oven for you," said Cassidy looking at me, "You need to eat too, baby."

"Baby?" said Remy, laughing his big cackle, "You two are like a honey-pot!"

That brought a much-needed break to the tension in the room, and pretty soon, I felt buoyed and comforted by the laughter in the house, but I was also particularly happy that Molly was safe in Georgia.

Cassidy brought me over a small plate of spring rolls and sesame shrimp toast to tide me over while the others ate.

"How did it go with Colin at the police station?" she asked out of earshot of the others, with half an eye on the portable monitor she had in her hand.

"It's probably something I should share with everyone here," I replied, "So maybe we should wait until everyone's eaten. But yes, it's all good, Tommy is being charged with murder and attempted manslaughter."

"Murder?"

"Yeah, he killed Joe,"

"Jeez, Coop."

"That boy is going straight to the penitentiary," I said, "He's an ex-problem now."

I went back to watching through the window, as night had now fallen and it was when the streets were dark, that I felt the most vulnerability.

Twenty minutes had passed when Rainee got up from the table, her plate already empty, and came over to me.

"You wanna go eat?" she asked, "I can take over for the next couple of hours and then Remy can relieve me, while Memph and I get a few hours' sleep."

"Sounds like a plan," I replied, "But listen in on my conversation, there have been some updates today."

"Will do, now go, eat."

When I'd taken a seat at the table, it was Remy who spoke first though.

"I've actually got some good news for you, Coop, you're getting a new boat in the morning."

"What??" I exclaimed, "How do you figure that?"

"Had me a long chat with the marina insurance company this afternoon."

"But they don't insure my boat, Rem, I do," I replied, "And I'm dreading making the call to them."

"Well, brother Coop, you ain't gonna be making that call, it's all arranged."

I sat silent, completely nonplussed, so Remy continued.

"See, the marina makes a shed load of money on all the slips there, and because they have a lot of high-net-worth clients, it insures itself up to its ass. So, when I told the guy at the office that a couple or three boats had been lost in the 'cane, and those weren't superyachts of course, he agreed to pay for the replacements on the marina policy."

Remy then stuffed a huge fork of Singapore noodle in his mouth, which rendered him unable to form new words, and I was recovered enough from my bewilderment to say something.

"I'm kind of speechless," I said, "I don't know what to say."

"Don't need to say nuttin', brother, it's what I do."

"Thank you, Remy, I owe you."

"No, you don't, now eat."

I tucked in, I was ravenous and needed sustenance before I told them the latest news, but I was still incredulous at Remy's news for me.

"Anyway, where you been today," asked Remy, before devouring two huge tempura shrimp in one savage mouthful.

"I was coming to that," I replied, "I've got some pretty terrible news to tell you all."

No one said anything, they just waited for me to continue.

I related the whole sorry story of how Joe had been murdered on the night of the hurricane.

"Oh fuck, man," said Memphis, "Who the hell would want to do that?"

"It's the question everybody's asking," I replied, before continuing with the events of my meeting with Coke today.

"I know that little dipshit, Tommy Burns," said Remy, "Ain't worth a lick 'a spit."

Cassidy said nothing but just listened, and it was clear to see that she felt my pain, even just talking about Joe.

"Let's raise a glass to Joe," she said, "I didn't know the guy, but I sure wish I'd had the chance to meet him. I'm so sorry, Coop."

"And let's raise one to Billy too," I replied, "Without him, we may never have known who took Joe from us.

Chapter 90

In the early hours of the previous morning, Shira Kadosh had tailed the Escalade in which Billy had left the club, back to where he was heading for the night. But if she had been surprised to see him get in behind the wheel of a seventy-thousand-dollar Cadillac SUV, instead of a gaudy, hand-painted Tacoma, she was even more surprised that he hadn't headed home to his apartment building. But she followed, regardless.

So, when Billy had signaled to turn in to a gated development, she had extinguished her car's headlights, pulled over onto a verge by the trees on the opposite side of the road, and watched as the guard came toward his vehicle.

It seemed that the guard had immediately recognized the Escalade, and he had chatted a minute with Billy before the barrier raised and the Escalade drove through. She had watched for a little longer as Billy slowly continued driving, until the SUV eventually took a left turn.

"Target acquired," she'd said to herself, silently performing a U-turn before switching her lights back on.

She had headed directly back to the Four Seasons, where she would sleep for a few hours, have breakfast, and then sleep for another ten.

~ ~ ~

And right now, Shira Kadosh was wide awake.

Lying in the brush, opposite Gator Run Beach Club's gated entrance, she waited. She needed to gain access without causing alarm to anyone who came and went. She also figured that anyone entering the country club this late in the evening, was likely a resident who would simply use their remote to raise the barrier.

Her sniper rifle was set up, with the target being the security guard who was working that night. So far though, it had been incredibly quiet, and she hadn't spotted the guard yet. But she was pretty sure he'd want to leave the confines of the small hut at some point, if only to stretch his legs for a moment or two.

Twenty more minutes elapsed, and just as Kadosh had predicted, the door to the hut slid open, and the man stepped out onto the tarmac, stretching his arms out above his head, and slowly paced around the area.

Kadosh locked in on him through the telescopic sight, and gently pulled the rifle's trigger, firing a single, silent shot.

The man fell to the floor in what seemed to Kadosh, like slow-motion, uttering not a single word, as his brain immediately closed down, while the muscles in his body continued to retain life, twitching throughout his whole body. Until they didn't.

Target down.

She quickly stowed the rifle and tripod in the trunk of the Toyota, climbed in behind the wheel, and soundlessly drove up to where the man's body lay. He wasn't dead, just incapacitated with a tranquilizer dart. She could have killed him but opted not to leave a trail of blood on the tarmacadam at this moment.

Kadosh stepped out of the car, the door jamming slightly on the rotund stomach of the dead man, pulled the dart from his chest, and looked around.

Nothing stirred tonight, not even the cicadas. It was an eerie feeling with the lack of humidity after the hurricane, and complete stillness all around.

She opened the nearside rear passenger door, dragged the man to it, and bundled him in, closing the door gently as she walked to the guard hut.

She pressed the button inside the hut to raise the barrier, climbed back into her car, and drove through, the Toyota's electric motor making no sound at all.

Retracing the route Billy had taken, she eased to a stop at the top of the road he'd turned into, a cul-de-sac, and immediately recognized the Escalade parked in front of the house right at the end of the street.

"Excellent," she said, before driving onto the golf course, and dumping the guard's body in a bunker.

"Going to be hard to rake that one," she said, amused at her own infrequent humor.

Driving silently back to the street, she was amazed that there seemed to be only one or two lights showing in the windows of the moderately expensive homes. But she guessed that most of the owners here, were probably what the Americans called, 'snowbirds', old, retired, and tired of the cold in the north, seeking permanent sunshine in the state of Florida. They were probably all in bed by nine after 'happy hour' had been and gone.

She parked the Toyota in a guest bay further up the street, got out of it, and popped the trunk to retrieve her backpack, rifle and tripod, before noiselessly closing the trunk's lid. She decided not to lock the car, as it made a loud beep when doing so. No one was going to steal it tonight.

Keeping to the tree line that backed onto the golf course, she walked back to the clump of trees and bushes in the precise area that looked directly down the street where Billy's truck was parked at the end.

She buried herself deep within the foliage, and had her tripod and rifle set up in just a few minutes.

Lying down on her stomach, her entire body outstretched on the still-warm earth, she looked through the telescopic sight, focused it, and smiled.

In it, she saw a partial image of the Showers girl at the window, a couple of guys in the background, and one of them was talking to another girl… it was Cassidy Swain.

"Not long, Eitan, I'll be home soon, my beautiful lion."

Chapter 91

"I'm more than grateful to Remy for what he did in getting me a new boat," I said to Cassidy, "But I don't see us being able to christen it anytime soon."

"Don't be so gloomy, we'll have all the time in the world to break a bottle of champagne across her bow when this is over," Cassidy replied, "And then we can christen her properly."

"Methinks the lady doth speak in tongues," I replied, "Shall I stray lower, where the pleasant fountains lie?"

"Is that Shakespeare?" she asked, laughing, "Sounds kinda mischievous."

"Mmm, not really, a bit of my own adaptation from the man," I replied, "And Talbot would kill me for the horrible misappropriation."

We both laughed, relishing the humor in what remained a stressful time.

But it was in that very moment, while we were still laughing, that I heard a small cracking noise and simultaneously saw the blood that was now flowing from Cassidy's arm through her shirt.

"Lights out!" I yelled, as I crashed into Cassidy, throwing her to the ground, Rainee simultaneously running to the light switch to blacken the room.

"Whatever it is, it's here," I shouted, "Everybody keep low, Remy, go wake Memphis, Kevlar on, now!"

As I ripped the shirt off Cassidy to see the damage, she just stared up at me, fear coursing through her entire body as it shook beneath me.

"Baby, you're gonna be okay, it's just a nick, I'm going to clean and bandage the wound."

Everyone had gone into full combat mode now, Memphis and Rainee had switched to night-vision headgear and were guarding the window and doors, Remy had pulled a first aid kit from his gear bag, all three now suited up in Kevlar vests.

"Coop, I got it man, lemme fix her up," said Remy.

"Okay, but keep your head down," I replied quietly, already suiting up as I uttered the words.

~ ~ ~

As Shira Kadosh peered through the rifle's scope, she saw that the Swain girl had gone down, but in her heart of hearts, she thought her shot was a little off. She'd recalibrated the scope that morning, but also realized that the distance she was currently working at, seven hundred yards or more, had the potential to be minutely unreliable. She assumed she was dealing with civilians here, so it wasn't going to be a difficult job, and she was eager to make this the last night of her assignment. But was her desire to get home to Eitan making her careless?

As the house suddenly became dark, she waited before attempting another shot, with the knowledge that time was still on her hands. At some point, if she had caused enough damage with the first shot, there would be activity at the front of the house, if only to go to a hospital. Then she'd eliminate Swain.

But even with her night-vision binoculars, it was hard to make out what was happening inside the house. She figured that there were maybe four individuals inside, although in the last few seconds, it had become still and lacking movement of any kind. And so, she sank lower into the brush, her breathing deliberately reduced to almost non-existent, and waited, listening for any sounds around her.

~ ~ ~

The three of us, Rainee, Memphis and myself, crept low on all fours toward the rear of the yard, knowing that we couldn't risk showing ourselves at the front of the property. Remy was tending to Cassidy, and was fully armed himself, should there be a frontal attack on the house. I'd left a pistol with him to give to Cassidy, once he'd dressed her wound. In our many conversations recently, she'd told me that her father had trained her in the use of weapons when she was a teenager on the farm.

"Jesus," said Rainee, "If this is the same person from the Outback hit, he's not just a pro, he's a full-blown assassin."

"Shit, Coop, we're dealing with a real professional here," whispered Memphis, "We got no room for error, buddy."

"Right on both counts," I said, "So stay sharp, got it?"

"What's the plan?" asked Memphis.

"We only have one choice," I replied.

"Fan out from the rear?" asked Rainee.

"Exactly. We'll need to cross over the surrounding neighbors' yards, and circle back toward the end of the street, which I'm guessing from the angle of trajectory, is where the shot came from."

"The golf course is behind the tree line at the end of the street, you wanna double circle?" asked Rainee.

"You good with that?" I asked Memphis.

"Got it," he replied. "What about radios?"

"I've brought them with me," I said, handing one to each of them, "But critical use only."

Both nodded back at me.

"Suppressors?" Rainee asked.

"Yes, confirm suppressors on all guns, we don't want it sounding like a war out here, innocent people could get killed."

"Check," came back both voices in my earbuds.

"Let's go, but keep your pace measured," I instructed.

The three of us began our journey, all of us taking different routes over fences to make as wide a circle as possible to get to the area at the end of the street. We had already donned the night-vision helmets, so the darkness swiftly became green, but with the sudden added ability to see everything that moved.

As I crept over the neighboring fences, I was careful to remain at an undetectable distance from the yard sensors that would turn on intruder spotlights. I'd done this before, and had worked out that most sensors would only be activated within around twenty feet. Rainee knew this too, and had briefed Memphis.

It was breathtaking to see the amount of wildlife that existed, fully awake in the darkness of the night. Cats lounging on sunchairs, owls, lizards, toads, and the occasional iguana crouching motionless beside a swimming pool. I watched as I continued my slow progress, but was suddenly distracted by my namesake, a Cooper's Hawk, swooping down to snatch up an unsuspecting Gecko lizard. With the lizard's bright green color giving no protection from the hawk's laser-vision eyes, I realized that if we weren't careful tonight, the hunter might become the hunted, but in the human predator form. Nighttime is another world.

I was making good ground, and hoped the others were too. After around four minutes, I had made my way onto an open lot that hadn't yet seen a new home construction, and the grass had grown to around four feet in height there. With my rifle strapped to my back, I progressed slowly through the thickness of the grass on all fours, until I finally emerged at a bend in the road where I wouldn't be seen from the end of our street.

I rested for a few seconds, the sweat trickling down my body, pausing to reconnoiter. As I did so, I was immediately aware of a black, and almost soundless drone moving through the air above, approximately fifty yards from where I lay, buried deep in the undergrowth.

Through my earbuds, I heard a familiar voice.

"In position," said Rainee.

"Me too," said Memphis.

"The guy has a drone up, searching our area," I replied, "I need to lay low for the moment, can't risk moving yet, but make sure you're covered."

"Check," came back both voices.

I had taken the more difficult and longer route to our target, because I knew the lay of the land better than the other two, but my journey had taken another three hundred yards and much more time.

A couple of minutes later, I had finally arrived at my position, which completed the triangle with Rainee's and Memphis' locations, the tree line at the end of the street being the center.

I was certain that I had escaped the view of the drone, but not completely. And then, I heard a familiar pop, and the muted sound of glass being penetrated.

"Rainee, Memph!" I whispered into my mic, "He's taken another shot at the house, we need to close in quickly."

"I heard it too," replied Rainee, "I'm on the move."

"Right with you," said Memphis.

The three of us began our journey, creeping from three sides of the course toward the tree line.

A minute later, I heard another pop, and a grunt.

"Hit," said Memphis, "Leg wound, I'm down."

That was enough for me, I picked up the pace until suddenly, I saw the shooter, crouched low in the brush, and shivered when I saw Rainee, practically in the assassin's sight at the other end of the tree line.

"Rainee!" I whispered loudly, "To your left!"

Rainee spun around and ducked, saw in a fraction of a second what I was seeing, and let loose four Magnum shells at exactly the moment my own trigger finger was dispatching lethal rounds at the assassin's back, the gunshots immediately followed by a howling scream.

And then there was no movement anywhere. No sounds either.

I put a finger to my lips when Rainee saw my position, and she crouched beneath a dip in the earth.

I pulled a second gun from my jacket, and duckwalked toward where the killer had been hiding, my eyes never leaving the guy's gloved hands. His body lay motionless in the undergrowth, his rifle a foot away. I waited for a full minute, fifteen feet away, before crawling to the man's lifeless body. Checking that he had no weapons in either hand or within reach, I checked for a pulse, but the man was dead.

"It's over," I said to Rainee, "It's safe now."

Rainee joined me as I was bending down over the body of the man, already pulling off the black balaclava that covered his face.

"Jeez!" exclaimed Rainee, "It's a chick."

We had hit the woman hard, seven of our ten shots finding their target. If she had been wearing Kevlar and a helmet, she might have made it, but she was probably already history on the third wound.

"Memphis, you okay?" I said into my microphone.

"Takes more than a flesh wound to get rid of me," he replied through the radio.

"Okay, buddy, don't move and stay where you are, we'll be with you in a few."

"Any ID?" asked Rainee, still shocked that the assassin was a woman.

"Unlikely," I said, rummaging through the dead woman's pants and jacket, "Assassins don't normally advertise who they are."

I was correct in my theory, she had nothing on her, which I had expected, but as I shone my flashlight on her face for the first time, I realized what a visually striking woman our assassin was.

"Someone's daughter," I said, "Maybe someone's mom too."

"Not now, she ain't," said Rainee, "We gonna call the police?"

I noticed that several lights had come on in surrounding homes, residents who must have faintly heard the multiple shots of our suppressed guns, and now a couple of entrance doors had opened, with people looking out to see what was going on.

"Let's give it five minutes, wait for everyone to go back to sleep," I replied, "Then I'm going to call Coke and tell him what's happened tonight."

"You get him?" came Memphis' voice on the radio, "I sure as fuck hope so."

"We did, Memph," I replied, "But here's the kicker, it's a her, not a him."

Chapter 92

Sergei was accustomed to getting brief and concise updates from Kadosh, but as he sat in the comfort of the Gulfstream jet, his concern was mildly raised in that he hadn't heard from her in the last twenty-four hours.

"Don't concern yourself, Sergei. She is likely completing the elimination as we speak," said Sokalov, watching as Sergei checked his KGB-sourced encrypted messaging app.

"You're right, Niki, of course, she has a one hundred percent success rate, I'm not concerned. It's just that she is extremely punctual in her updates, every twelve hours, and I haven't heard from her in a day."

"Let us concentrate our minds on our upcoming meeting with Galotti, we have some decisions to make, no?" pronounced Sokalov.

"Your question is more… should we keep him, or should we terminate him?"

"Exactly, my friend, because he could still be useful to us alive."

"How do you mean?" asked Sergei.

"Galotti has been useful to us in the past. Particularly with his comrades on the West Coast when we first went to California," continued Sokalov, "And even though I believe he's become a deadweight in some ways, it's partly because of him that we now control all of the cocaine that enters the United States through Los Angeles and San Francisco."

The cocaine that the Russians imported onto American soil, was pure, 'uncut', sourced from Colombia, Peru and Bolivia. But by the time it had been cut with baking soda, powdered milk or laundry detergent, the weight of the imported product was usually three to four times what the pure version had started out as.

"I agree, but the reason for retaining Galotti was to secure the Miami and New York routes also," replied Sergei, "And thus far, he has failed. How much rope do you give a man, Niki?"

"The meeting on the yacht will be the time to decide, Sergei," replied Sokalov, pushing the call button for the stewardess, "Now, what shall we have for lunch, my friend?"

Chapter 93

Back at the house, we found Remy and Cassidy, both unscathed, apart from the wound to Cassidy's arm which Remy had expertly disinfected and dressed. I'd called them on my cell phone, immediately before calling Coke, and told them that the danger was over. But the sudden thought that hurtled into my mind was that I may have lost Cassidy if the shooter had been just a little more accurate. The guilt of leaving her was now engulfing me.

Cassidy looked pale, considering she was so tanned.

"Hey you, come sit down, you're probably still in shock."

"I'm fine, Coop, it was only as you said, a nick."

"We'll get you and Memphis to the ambulance when it gets here," I replied, "But I still think you might be in shock. Brandy's a good leveler, and I think I need one too now. Stay here, I'll be right back."

Outside, at the end of the street, there was a blaze of police lights, the street already being cordoned off, and the usual array of vehicles blocked all three ways at the intersection. It wouldn't be long before Coke came knocking at the door.

Rainee and I had helped Memphis back to the house, where Remy was now giving first aid to the tough little guy's left leg. In the meantime, Rainee had gone back to where the body was, to wait for Coke to arrive and apprise him of the evening's events.

"Is it bad?" I asked, looking at Memphis' leg and then at Remy.

"Nah, for him it's just a graze, might have ruined a tattoo, but I'll tell you something, Coop, we got lucky tonight with Cassidy and Memphis."

"Tell me about it, brother, I guess we used our quota of luck for the year."

"You sure you're okay, Memph?" I asked.

"I've had worse wounds falling off my bike," laughed Memphis, "Now go on in there, see to that girl of yours."

I grabbed the brandy and two tumblers and went back into the lounge, where Cassidy was sitting cross-legged on the sofa.

"Do you think it's over now?" she asked, as I sat down on the floor next to the sofa.

"I can't say for sure, because I don't know your husband," I replied, truthfully, "But the shooter was an assassin, and from my experience in the force, they don't come cheap."

"What are you saying?"

"I'm saying that I don't think Carlo is behind this, because I'm pretty damned sure he wouldn't be funding what would be a staggering cost to hire her," I replied, reaching for her hand and placing a glass of brandy in it, before taking a slug from my own glass.

"You think the Russians are behind it, don't you?" she whispered, "Maybe they became impatient with Carlo and decided to take my demise into their own hands?"

"I don't know, Cass, I just don't know," I whispered, feeling my own inadequacy, and realizing that I had no answers for her.

Chapter 94

Coke had called me late that evening, but said that he wouldn't come to the house and bother us all at such a late hour.

"Get some rest," he said, "I'll be round in the morning to get the whole story, I already know it's going to be a good one, but I haven't slept myself in twenty-six hours. Have coffee ready."

By ten o'clock the following morning, Coke was at the door, clearly in need of his first caffeine fix of the day.

"You got soy here?" he asked, brushing past me as he entered the house.

"Of course, what did you expect?" I replied.

"Any bacon?"

"Remy's fixing breakfast in the kitchen," I replied, "Come on in, say hi to everyone."

Coke went straight to the kitchen where he greeted Rainee and Remy, and introduced himself to Cassidy and Memphis. He had already snagged a rasher of crispy bacon, even before introductions were made.

"Two injured," he said, "Could've been a whole lot worse, going by the intel I found on your shooter."

"You got an ID on her?" I asked, as I finished preparing his soy latte and handed it to him.

"We got lucky, I guess," Coke continued, greedily slurping on his latte, "No ID on the body, but the techies did a check on surrounding hotels in Palm Beach, compared her face with security footage using facial recognition software, and we got a hit at the Four Seasons on South Ocean Boulevard."

"So, you got a name, Coke?" asked Remy.

"We did. She's ex-Israeli military," Coke replied.

"Mossad?" Rainee asked.

"No, she's from the super elite special force, Sayeret Matkal, said Coke, "They make Mossad look like amateurs."

"Well, she wasn't a super-elite tonight, thank God," she replied, knowing that we'd come too close to losing our lives.

"A name?" I asked again.

"Oh yeah, Shira Kadosh, a highly paid, and very much in demand assassin. She's wanted by almost every three-letter agency in the world, except that they've always been looking for a man, never dreamed it would be a woman."

"Sexism still exists then," said Rainee.

"Not from me, Rainee, but yeah, I guess it does. Sorry," replied Coke.

And then, after listening to all of this new information, Cassidy finally spoke.

"Am I still in danger, Detective Caine?"

Coke was fully up to speed on Cassidy's situation, and he turned to her, gripped her hand, and gently replied.

"Right now, Cassidy, I would say not. What we don't know at the moment is whether it was your husband who hired Kadosh, or the

Russians who sent Galotti on the mission to track you down in the first place."

"I have no clue how much hitmen cost to hire, but I'm guessing it's a lot of money," Cassidy replied, "And as Coop said, I'm not sure Carlo would part with that kind of cash. But as you know, he's been doing business with Nikita Sokalov and Sergei Fedorov for the last four years, and they have deep pockets."

"I was going to get to that, Cassidy," said Coke, "Right now, we have both of them on our radar. They arrived at PBI on Sokalov's jet this morning."

Cassidy's face fell.

"We can't arrest them for anything at the moment, because in the eyes of the law, they haven't committed a crime, to our knowledge," he continued, "But we have both of them under surveillance, so don't fret."

"But you know that those guys are drug smugglers and murderers," I interjected, "Surely there's got to be something you can arrest them for?"

"We probably could, Coop," said Coke, "But they have an army of lawyers who would ensure those two would never spend even one night in county lockup. So, my role now is to stay out of it, and let those agencies do their work."

"So, they can just carry on living life as they please?" asked Memphis, incredulous at what money could do.

"They're both US citizens, Memphis, legally residing in this country," Coke replied, "But don't worry, from what I've found out this morning, it won't be for too much longer."

"I trust your judgment, Coke, so thanks for the update," I interjected, "Is it safe to go back to the marina, d'you think?"

"We have eyes on them, so yeah, I'd say give it a couple more days and I think you'll be fine."

"I'll be sure to keep a good lookout myself, not that I don't trust your boys," I replied.

"Smart man, Coop. Now, is there another mug of that soy latte in the offing?"

Chapter 95

Cassidy and I had spent the next couple of weeks on my new boat at the marina, courtesy of Remy's deal with the owners. It was actually a nicer and larger boat than *Lost Soul*, and in truth, even with all of the turmoil we'd been through, I felt grateful to be finally back and enjoying my new home.

Cassidy did too, and she alternated between staying on the boat with me and going back to Nate's to work shifts, occasionally staying above the bar when she felt too exhausted from her working day.

I had waited for the moment when I would tell Cassidy the awful news about her friends, Greta and Wayne Randolph, something that I had dreaded for weeks. She collapsed in tears and horror of what Galotti had done, disbelieving that the Randolphs were now gone, and it had taken two days and nights of soothing her to the point where she could finally begin to focus again. But it was something that would remain in her mind for the rest of her life.

Molly had stayed with Lauren for another week, which had come as a surprise to me. But she had loved being on the farm, and had fallen in love with Lauren's palominos. But eventually, she came home and began the task of deciding what she was going to do as a career.

She was now back home, living harmoniously again with Billy, and Billy had really missed her. I like Billy. But when he had had the idea to pop the question and ask Molly to marry him, she had declined. For the moment, she'd said.

Billy was a little upset at being turned down, but I had taken him out for lunch one day, told him that it was maybe too early for them to get married, and that Molly did indeed need to concentrate on her career path at the moment. I'd also said that I would look forward to him becoming my son-in-law in due course, and that seemed to appease him. As I said, I like Billy.

So now, and with a great deal of assistance from Coke, Molly has joined the FBI for training, and although it's only been a week, she is absolutely loving it. My daughter, a Feeb. Who would've known?

I had asked Coke if he was still going to run down Flick, but the truth was, he'd said, she hadn't committed a crime, except for being a lousy wife. The divorce from Joe had been pretty uneventful, considering how acrimonious their marriage had become, and it was Tommy who had committed murder, not Flick. As far as Coke was concerned, there were no charges to press, so she had disappeared into the wind. And she wouldn't be missed.

We had had a belated low-key funeral for Joe, and all of us had attended, as well as his bandmates and Angel. After the funeral, we had had a private memorial for Joe at Nate's, where everyone who had known Joe, got to say a few words about the man. I kept my own eulogy reasonably short, knowing that others had wanted to share their own experiences with Joe, but also because my words were emotionally faltering as soon as I began to speak.

But when I had spoken to Angel after the service, I got the feeling that he would never get over losing Joe, the man was just a shadow of his former cheery self. And I'm not sure I would get over losing Joe either. But life must go on.

Chapter 96

Now, I have a fascination with the exotic species of birds that inhabit Florida, my favorite being the elusive Cardinal. Its color is a vibrant red and they are hard to photograph, because they don't stay still for long, and they are gone before you can grab a camera to snap them.

So not long after we had returned to the boat, imaginatively named *Lost Soul II*, I had bought some bird feeders and an array of food they liked, milo, safflower, peanuts and suet, and I had finally managed to get some shots of the stunning little creatures.

"Your bird feeder's run out of nuts," said Cassidy as she came up onto the deck.

"I know," I replied.

"You've still got fat-balls, though."

"Thank you."

Her humor had really come to the fore since we had returned to the boat, and I guessed it was because she no longer felt that she was on the run. We had become a real couple, looking after each other, sharing jokes and stories, and we had settled into a kind of nautical domestic bliss.

I hadn't ever dreamed I would be in this position again, and the longer we were together, the more I wanted it to never end. Cassidy was the yin to my yang, and I was in love with the girl. I think she kinda liked me too.

"Would you like some breakfast?" she asked, "I'm famished."

"Eggs and bacon?" I suggested.

"Deal," she replied, "I'll get it started, you make the cortados, mister."

~ ~ ~

Pip, my staff, was no longer my employee. The hurricane had had a profound effect on her life outlook, not in a bad way, but more that she had decided that she needed to see more of the world.

So, a week ago, and I'm still not sure if she just thought that three was a crowd, with Cassidy spending most of her time on the boat, she handed me a letter of resignation.

"What's this?" I had asked, as she busied herself in the company files.

"I'm leaving," had been her reply.

"Why? What have I done wrong now?"

"Nothing, nothing at all, but I've decided to go on my travels, spread my wings, as you might say."

Diablo suddenly looked distressed and went to lie down by her side. Dogs just know, don't they? Kinky, however, was nowhere to be seen.

"But what am I going to do without you?" I had asked.

"You'll be fine, Cooper Hemingway, you'll always be fine."

"Where are you spreading your wings to?"

"I'm going to Africa, to work in an elephant sanctuary."

"They're gonna love you, I'm jealous."

An hour later, having gotten my banking and work files systematically labeled and up to date, Pip was gone, and I shed a few tears as I watched her saunter down the boardwalk to begin her new life with some lucky pachyderms.

Chapter 97

Sergei and Nikita had gotten word that Shira Kadosh had failed in her mission to eliminate Cassidy Swain. Not only had she failed, she'd ended up dead too. Currently, since landing back in the USA, they had failed in their attempts to discover exactly how she had died, which for them, was inexcusable.

The fee that they had lost was immaterial, two million dollars was pocket change. But the intel that they had received, was that the FBI and CIA were watching them, so clearly, they had connected the Russians to Kadosh.

They had therefore decided to delay the meeting with Galotti until things had become more stable. A few more weeks wouldn't make any difference to them anyway. They had plenty of other business to attend to in the interim.

Galotti hadn't shown any signs of nervousness when they had called him to arrange the meeting on the yacht, in fact, he seemed decidedly upbeat, considering that there might be a fateful outcome for him after the meeting.

Galotti hadn't heard the news about Kadosh, and he had actually asked if they wanted him to step up his task of finding Cassidy. Which was odd, considering that all of his, and his men's efforts to find the girl, had come to nothing.

Sergei had told Galotti that his services as far as the girl went, were no longer required. But they were keen to meet with him on the yacht to discuss the Miami and New York cocaine routes.

Galotti seemed buoyed by the fact that the Russians were back with the aspiration of doing business again, so a date was set.

Chapter 98

It was another picturesque and sultry evening on *Lost Soul II*. I had spent the day with Cassidy, but she had to work the evening shift at Nate's, so I was on my lonesome. It didn't really matter, because I knew that Cassidy would be back in the morning and she also had two days off from work.

I planned to take her to the Rapids Water Park in the afternoon, because although I knew she had a mild fear of water itself, the seven-story water slides and quarter-mile Lazy River were pretty breathtaking, and I knew that she was a bit of a thrill seeker at heart.

I say I was on my lonesome, which wasn't really true. After the events of recent weeks, Rainee and Cassidy had really hit it off. I was pretty pleased about this, because Rainee didn't have female friends, so to see these two getting along so well, was pretty damned sweet for me.

Rainee had spent the late afternoon and early evening on the boat with us before Cassidy had gone to work, and then she'd crashed in the guest cabin after having done a stint with Mo-Nay$Neverenuff's crew until 5am that morning. Once Cassidy had left, I knew that I wouldn't see Rainee surface until dawn the next morning.

So tonight, I was grilling a couple of burgers on *Lost Soul II*'s stern, with the aid of my new grill that I'd recently bought at Ace Hardware. I was hoping that Remy might join me for a burger and a couple of beers, but he was snowed under with paperwork from the aftermath of Hurricane Jacques. It wasn't only boats that had been damaged, but parts of the marina's dock had been wrecked too.

It was getting on for ten o'clock, and I watched hungrily as the beef patties and onions sizzled on the grill. I split the burger rolls and lay them beside the patties to toast them a little, before removing them and adding ketchup and mustard.

Next door, on the behemoth superyacht, there seemed to be a lot going on this evening, people coming and going, and not a single fruit-colored thong in sight.

I had also purchased one of those new-fangled air fryers that everyone seems to be buying these days, and was keen to try out cooking French fries to go with my burgers. I'd bought one on Amazon at the lofty price of thirty-nine bucks, too good to be true, no? But the truth is, and very much to my surprise, they're like magic machines. No grease, no clearing up dirty oil, just perfectly cooked, golden fries coming out of the thing.

But as I was taking my first bite of my second burger, my stomach feeling much happier, I nearly choked.

Sitting in my chair, burger in hand, I froze as a man walked quickly past my boat, seemingly eager to get out of the marina. He didn't recognize me, never actually noticed me, but I recognized him from a photograph. Carlo Galotti.

"Sonofabitch."

I couldn't believe what I was seeing. Why would Galotti be here? Where had he come from? I somehow thought that he must have been visiting with people on the superyacht, but I couldn't be sure. Thirty lost seconds had already elapsed, until my instinct kicked in. The man had traumatized Cassidy, and he wasn't going to get away with it this time.

I rushed into my cabin, retrieved the first weapon at hand, my trusty Louisville Slugger baseball bat, jumped off the boat onto the boardwalk and gave chase. I yelled after him, which probably wasn't the smartest thing to do, because he began to run and he was already two hundred yards away.

I was closing the gap, had it down to a hundred yards or so, but by the time I reached the car park, Galotti was already in a giant Humvee, racing toward the exit.

"Fuck, fuck, fuck!" I said out loud, although no one was listening.

I'd missed a golden opportunity for a little payback on the bastard. I was so pissed with myself for not reacting sooner because this man, and I didn't care about how he was connected, was my number one target.

I began walking back to the boat, still furious with myself. But as I got closer, I could see more activity next to the superyacht. It seemed odd, because they had been very quiet neighbors all the time the yacht had been moored there, and as I approached and had gotten to within twenty yards, three faces turned toward me, and the commotion suddenly ended.

Still angry with myself, and not thinking too much about self-preservation, I foolishly walked toward the group.

Chapter 99

It wasn't really a fair fight, was it? I mean, three against one and the youngest of them must have had fifteen years on me. So, what do you do? There's only one thing you can do in a no-win situation like this, you fight. There are many things that go through your mind in a moment like this one, because let's be very clear here, it was only going to be a moment before I did my final shuffle.

Death by knife is a far slower process than the instant finality from a bullet to the head. It's drawn out, sometimes it can take several minutes. But all three of these assassins had knives, not a gun to be seen. A gunshot or ten would be heard far and wide in the stillness and quiet of the marina, and these killers killed by stealth, because there was no unnecessary advertising in their type of business.

And I had a baseball bat. Not great against three men with knives, but I guess it would have to do. But as they encroached on my position, they skillfully encircled me so that if I actually managed to land a blow on one of them, I'd be taken out in the next second by one of the other two.

But that was all that was on offer to me. Their savage voices that spoke in a language that sounded like Russian, were blood curdling and I felt something that I haven't often felt. Abject fear, utter terror.

I decided to go for the biggest one of the trio, you know what they say, go big or go home. I arched my bat behind my right shoulder and took two steps forward, feeling every muscle and sinew in my arm, shoulder and back expanding in anger, before smashing the maple wood into the side of his face.

I heard the eerie and sickening sound of broken bone, which likely included jaw, eye socket and a partial caving of the left side of his skull. There wasn't much blood to speak of, except for the remains of part of his head on the end section of my bat.

One down…

A split second later, as the giant fell to earth, unlikely to ever get up again, I felt it. I'd felt it before so the recognition was instant. The second of the three had plunged the seven-inch blade of his stiletto knife deep inside the area between my left shoulder blade and my back.

It's a very strange thing when you're stabbed. If you see it coming, if you watch as the blade enters your body, the pain you feel is like an instant inferno because your mind escalates the conscious understanding to a new level of horror.

But when you don't see it coming, it is almost unnoticeable, more of a cold sensation of numbness. I was only mildly aware of being stabbed, and I knew it was a deep incision because I felt the knife's hilt forcibly stop in my back because it had run out of blade.

The second wound was one that I was far more aware of, because I could see it coming. I might have even avoided it with a sidestep, but I hadn't, therefore leaving me somewhat poleaxed and incapable of avoiding the equally lethal, oncoming blade from the third man.

As I said earlier, I knew I was going to feel immense pain because I could see how this was playing out in front of me. And as I describe this to you, it really does feel as though everything is in slow motion, a thousand-frames-a-second event that in reality, is only a few seconds, and maybe just four or five.

I grimaced, not in immediate pain, but in anticipation of it, as I watched the blade arcing through the still air, its trajectory on a collision course with my still-beating heart. It was right at that very moment that I knew my life was about to come to a crushing end, and again, all in that fabulous and gory slow-motion film of a high-speed camera.

But it was at that very moment when the blade was only milliseconds from slicing my heart, ventricle to ventricle, that my oncoming assailant slipped on something. Crazy, huh? But that was indeed what had happened.

It was simply a small pool of spilt oil, from when I had been filling my boat's emergency oil canisters the previous morning. Which goes to show that I'm correct in my thinking; never do today, what you can put off until tomorrow.

However, the downward fall of the man caused the blade's motion to increase in speed until it found its resting place in the vastus lateralis of my left thigh. In English, my anterior quad muscle.

Oh, and did I feel that pain, the blood now erupting through the rip of my jeans where the knife had entered and then immediately been pulled out again as the man clattered to the ground.

Again, all of this still felt like a slow-motion scene, like when you watch a boxing match on television and see the crushing blow from glove to face as the boxer's head seems to wobble like jelly, each drop of sweat and blood identifiable and navigable in their expulsion from the victim's broken face.

And in that same moment, as my assailant began to fall, I gripped both ends of my bat and slammed it with all of the strength left in my dying carcass, onto the soon to be deceased man's head. Once again, I felt the crack of skull.

It would be nice to think that I had inexplicably, against all odds, defeated my assassins with the aid of my trusty baseball bat. But sadly, for me, and for a few others I suppose, that was not to be the case. You remember, there were three of them at the beginning of this scene?

The remaining member of the killing crew was unfortunately still unhurt. I only knew that when he whirled around to face me, the stiletto now free of my shoulder, and watched as he plunged the bloodied blade up through my ribcage.

I felt my lung begin to deflate as he withdrew the lethal weapon and plunged it for a second time into my dying pulmonary organ.

When you're about to meet your maker, the last thing you're going to be thinking about is whether you fed the cat or not. Kinky wouldn't starve, that's for certain. No, the actual things you think about are far more obvious. It becomes serious, this wasn't a laughing matter, even for me.

The biggest realization for me in these last few moments, is the fact that I wouldn't have that last embrace with Molly, never wanting to leave her on her own in this messed up world that was getting messier by the day. All I can hope, is that she remembers the good things about her dad, and not his many failings.

And you think about your loved ones who are still living, Molly, Rainee, Remy, Nate, and of course, Cassidy, all of whom would continue to go about their lives with me no longer existing in them.

But at the point of death, I won't know much about that, because I will be no more. I would like to say that I'll miss Diablo too, and of course I would, if my brain still received electric pulses, but I won't because my mental and emotional hard drive will have been disconnected. But right now, while I still breathe, I know that that beautiful dog will be in good hands after my expiration.

And as I lie here on a bloodied boardwalk, I feel a sudden surge of sadness and regret engulfing me. Images of Molly crash into my head... her first steps, her first day at school, her graduation, her twenty-first birthday.

Memories relentlessly flood my mind, and I momentarily find myself back in Corona Heights Park in San Francisco, when Molly was just five years old. Her arms outstretched as she twirls around, her long blonde hair flying behind her like a golden halo. *"Did you see me, Daddy, did you see me?"* she shrills, as she envelops herself in my arms, her infectious giggle and beaming smile melting my heart.

And then I'm in our little kitchen, cooking her favorite supper, chicken fajitas, with my now teenage daughter, her hair dyed a deep shade of purple with a few streaks of pink thrown in for good measure. She rolls her eyes at my latest dad joke, and I laugh anyway.

And then abruptly, new glimpses of the future memories that Molly and I would never make, are savagely tearing my heart into pieces. I would never see her get married, I would never get to hold my grandchildren, and I would never get to tell her one more time how much I love her and how very proud I was to be called her dad.

But as my eyes begin to close, and I realize my heart has finally stopped beating, this was no longer the slow-motion attack I'd previously been describing. It was now a murder scene.

Chapter 100

Remy had been working late that evening, trying to get every boat owner's accounts up to date for invoicing. He actually enjoyed the peace and quiet of the approaching midnight hour, with only the constant thrum of nocturnal cicadas breaking the marina's silence.

But that silence was broken when he heard distant shouts coming from the far end of the marina, not the inflamed voices of an argument, but instead what felt like the beginning of a fight breaking out. And whatever that fight was, the sound was coming from where Coop's boat was berthed. And if Coop was involved, after all that had happened recently, his friend might be in trouble.

He grabbed his Smith & Wesson from the gun safe bolted to the wall, and ran out of his office toward the boardwalk to Coop's boat.

~ ~ ~

Rainee had passed out quickly after her long night and day. But after only a few hours or so into her slumber, she had awoken, jerked awake by the shouts of strange voices in close proximity to the boat. As she lay in the guest cabin, she didn't know what time it was or whether she had just been dreaming.

She pulled on her pants and t-shirt and stepped onto the wooden dock, just as a small tender fired its engine and began speeding away from the dock next door. She almost collided with Remy, who was running at full pace toward where three bodies lay stricken on the ground just a hundred yards away.

"Come on!' yelled the big man, brandishing a pistol in his hand, "Coop's in trouble, call 911."

She ran barefoot, following him until they pulled up to what looked like a small massacre, blood seeping everywhere on the dock's wooden planks. And then she saw him, her best friend lying still and prone, eyes closed and no sign of life in his body.

Remy went straight to him, as Rainee pulled her phone out and called the emergency services. He knelt down by his friend, checking for a pulse, listening for breathing. There was none.

"He's not breathing," he yelled at Rainee, "Go get me the defibrillator on that post over there!"

Rainee momentarily felt sick, she couldn't move at the sight of Coop lying there. She wanted to throw up.

"Move Rainee, dammit!" yelled Remy once more, his one good arm ripping away Coop's clothing to see the damage on his friend's body, "He's not breathing, he's gonna die!"

Instantly, Rainee was jolted out of her paralysis, ran to the defib box and pulled the kit out, immediately taking it back to where Coop lay.

Having seen three knife wounds on Coop's lifeless torso, Remy began ripping his own shirt into pieces, using his knee and his hand to do so, taking each one and stuffing them as hard as he could into Coop's wounds. It was a natural thing to do, he'd done it on the battlefield, even when he knew there was no point, but that was his medic training kicking in.

Rainee unpacked the defib kit, checking that there was battery life. Although she knew how Remy ran the marina, nothing was ever left unchecked.

Meanwhile, Remy had taken a Swiss knife from his pocket and unpanicked, had made a small hole in Coop's trachea. He then inserted the tube from a biro into the hole and blown into it, hoping that it would clear any clots of blood.

"Hold this in place," he instructed Rainee, "Make sure the tube doesn't come out."

Rainee sat next to Coop's head, holding the biro casing in place as she cried, stroking his head, her tears falling down onto his weathered features. She felt powerless, a feeling that she wasn't used to, unable to help Coop in the moment he needed it most.

Remy had set up the defibrillator by now, two sticky pads now placed on Coop's chest.

"Stop sobbing, Rain, I need to listen."

She grimaced as the first electrical current jolted through Coop's body, and Remy felt for a pulse and a breath.

Remy pressed the button for a second try as Coop lay unresponsive to the current's surge.

In the distance, Remy could already hear the sirens approaching.

Too late, he thought, administering another shock to Coop's lifeless torso.

"He's going to die, isn't he!" cried Rainee, sobbing uncontrollably now, and for the first time in a very long time, she felt utterly helpless.

"He's already dead," said Remy.

Chapter 101

Carlo Galotti had read the room well. The meeting with the Russians on the yacht, had been almost too cordial. But Carlo knew from his own experience of being 'friendly' toward someone whose life he was about to end, that the Russians had a similar endgame in mind for him.

And once he had bolted out of the marina, he had driven directly to Miami Executive Airport, boarded his Bombardier jet, and flown out of the United States for the very last time.

He had heard nothing more from Sergei and Nikita, assuming that they had probably ceased searching for him once he had disappeared. And Carlo was good with that, he had all the money he required, and realized how much he needed not only a change of scenery, but also a change of life.

And life in the tiny beach town of Polignano a Mare in Puglia, on Italy's southern Adriatic coast was idyllic. Each morning, he would walk down from his house to the little cove, the Ponte dei Lapilli, to have a cappuccino or two, along with fresh, warm Sfogliatellas and Cannolis.

This morning, having said a brief farewell to one of his girlfriends, the delightful and energetic Bianca Bianchi, he arrived back at his sea-view home on the Adriatic, for another afternoon of sun and wine, before his favorite girl arrived, the sultry and perpetually sexy twenty-five-year-old, Luna Amato.

~ ~ ~

The man handed his passport to the State Security guy behind the plexiglass, and waited while he examined it. After maybe two minutes, the man looked up and asked,

"Prima visita in Italia, signore?"

"Prima visita ovunque, immagino," he replied.

Another minute elapsed, until the security guard finally stamped the passport's blank visa page, and said,

"Benvenuto in Italia, signore, goditi il tuo soggiorno qui."

He quickly found the Europcar rental desk, signed the waivers, paid the fee, and received the key for an Opel Mokka.

Having located the car, he set his iPhone's navigation with the address of a good friend of his, a longtime client, in fact. And approximately forty-five minutes later, that same friend was welcoming him with a big smile and an even bigger hug.

"Long time, no see, my friend," said the friend in his native Italian accent.

"I've missed you, buddy," said the man, "You need to come back and visit again in the good old US of A."

"I do indeed, I need more stock anyway, so that's a very good reason to come and see you."

"I've always got stock, you know that, and I want to spend a couple of days with you," replied the man, "But right now, I have to make a brief stop somewhere else, do you have it?"

"Certo, è in garage, vieni."

In the garage, the man's friend produced a rag bundle from a locked cupboard, and handed it to him. He unwrapped the bundle and revealed a handgun with a suppressor already attached.

"Perfect, is it loaded?"

"It is, six shots, and the safety is on," said the Italian, "And the serial number has been filed off, so it is completely untraceable."

"Wonderful. How much do I owe you?"

"Niente, consideralo come un regalo da un amico a un altro."

"You are very kind, Alberto, you'll get a big discount on the next order."

"Grazie, mi amico."

"But now I have to go, I'll see you in a few hours."

"Buona fortuna."

~ ~ ~

Carlo Galotti was watching television, enjoying his favorite sport in the world, soccer. And his team, Inter Milan were destroying their arch rivals, AC Milan, by three goals already with only thirty-five minutes of the match played so far.

Luna was a little late arriving this evening, but he didn't care, as it meant he could probably watch the whole match in peace. Luna wasn't a soccer fan, but she was sensational in bed.

Just before half-time, he heard the entrance door open and realized that his dream of seeing his beloved team thrash the old enemy was about to come to an end.

"Is that you, bella, I'm in the lounge watching Inter play," yelled Galotti, "Come on in, make yourself at home, and open a bottle of Chianti, please?"

Luna didn't reply, which was odd. Instead, a tattooed man he'd never seen before, walked into the lounge and stood before him.

Galotti almost choked on the beer he'd been swigging.

"Who the fuck are you, and what the hell are you doing in my house?"

"My name? I'm not sure it's really going to be relevant to you in a few moments, Mr. Galotti, but as you asked so politely, the reason I'm here, is to give you a permanent lesson."

"You know who I am?" spluttered Galotti.

"Indeed I do, I'm a friend of your wife."

"Cassidy?"

"Well done, at least you remember her name."

"As far as I'm concerned, she's not my wife anymore, she's a fucking whore!"

"Wrong answer," said the man, pulling the gun from his leather jacket, and firing a deadly round through Galotti's heart.

"That one's for Cassidy," he said, pointing the gun at Galotti's head, "And this one's for a friend of mine."

If Galotti's life hadn't been ended by the first shot, the second one confirmed his death.

As the man walked out of the house onto the street, he nodded politely to the pretty girl coming toward him,

"Una bella giornata," he said as she passed.

"Lo è, divertiti!" the girl replied.

"Yes," thought the man, "It really is a beautiful day now."

In Galotti's lounge, AC Milan had staged an incredible comeback, they were now 4-3 up, and would go on to beat their rivals, 6-3.

Fortunately for Galotti, he would never have to experience the pain of that famous victory.

Epilogue

Six months later…

Friday, March 10th, 2024

So, you see, I had been murdered. I was medically dead for around ten minutes until the paramedics arrived, restarted my heart, given me oxygen and taken me straight to the Emergency Room. If Remy hadn't been staying late at his marina office, you'd be hearing nothing more from me, so once again, I owe that man my life.

Oh, I almost forgot, what with all that's been going on in the previous months. That thing about me being murdered? I had indeed been physically murdered, but I'd also been judgmentally murdered more recently, and Nora didn't help too much with that. Although I still might keep her.

You see, my book, *To Kill or To Love*, which during my recovery and enforced medical house arrest, had actually gotten written, which surprised me more than anyone. On its launch, it was utterly panned by those bastard critics but strangely, not by the public, that wonderful institution I now refer to as my readership. It would seem that they kind of adore me, well, the book anyway.

"*Cooper Hemingway, Literary Genius, New York Times #1 Best Seller for his 3rd Novel, To Kill or To Love.*"

That was the headline from The Times that Nora had grudgingly emailed me. I'm not sure why she's still such a curmudgeon with me, she takes a nice cut from my royalties. Anyway…

Now, here's the big news. Rainee has been dating someone. And it's become long-term, six months now and counting. And it was because I had 'died', that she had met Victor Martineau. Victor is a surgeon at Good Samaritan Medical Center, and he became my doctor, not long before he became Rainee's paramour.

I've never seen Rainee smitten before, but this was true love. A couple of months ago, they purchased a pretty upscale apartment near City Place, and to my astonishment, they are living together as one very loved-up couple. Victor is exactly who Rainee needed, he's smart, tall, hunky, good looking, half French and half English, and he takes care of her boss too. It's a win-win, as far as I'm concerned.

My Molly has been with the FBI for almost seven months now, and the career she has chosen is made for her. They seem to like her and she's even going out in the field now, but more as watcher than as an active agent for the moment. Personally, I have two feelings about that. One, that I feel immense pride for what she is achieving, but two, that the FBI can be a dangerous career choice. Meanwhile, Billy is still waiting for the moment to pop the question again.

Memphis and Remy's relationship continues on an upward spiral. Remy persuaded Memphis to sell his flimsy Jensen Beach cottage because it was no place to live during a hurricane. Memphis liked the idea of he and Remy making a home together, although he's never lived with another man before. But once Remy's place was also sold, they moved to a brand-new hurricane-resistant ranch home at Bear Lakes Country Club in Palm Beach. Domestic contentment seems to suit them.

The Shamenless tour, much to my surprise, is actually going ahead, albeit with a long and respectful delay since Joe's death. The band decided, in memory of Joe, to finish up recording eleven more of the unfinished tracks that Joe had written before his death. Needless to say, the new album, entitled, *Joe Jarvie – Gone, But Never Forgotten*, is outselling *F*ck Me Shamenless*.

So, with the clamor from fans wanting to see the band play live, Joe's bandmates persuaded Angel to come out of retirement and make it happen. And, Joe appeared on stage with the band. Not as a living human being, of course, but instead as an AI-generated 3D hologram.

Having seen rehearsals myself, it's eerily real to see Joe performing once again like the maniacal stage performer he always was. There was also talk that Axl Rose was going to guest on the tour, in place of Joe, although I'm not sure that rumor holds much truth.

We had heard the news from Coke, that Interpol had confirmed the death of Carlo Galotti. It was understandably, an incredible relief to both Cassidy and myself. But when I'd asked Coke what had happened, he said that the Italian police had informed him that it was a home invasion, and that Galotti was found alone on his sofa, his death the result from two gunshot wounds. The Italian police also confirmed that they currently had no suspects, and were unlikely to continue the investigation for much longer, as it was assumed that the hit was Mafia related.

I suspect with all of the news I'm telling you, that you're probably wondering what happened to Cassidy? Well, we live in blissful harmony on *Lost Soul II* and I couldn't be happier. She says she feels the same, but I wake up every morning, pinch myself and wonder why? It can't be the royalties I'm now getting as I begin my sequel to *To Kill or To Love*, maybe it's my charm, or my intelligence? Probably not, though.

But I can't quite foresee Cassidy and I forever living on the boat, so we're saving up to buy a home on terra-firma sometime in the future. If my follow-up to *To Kill or To Love,* sells in vast numbers, I'm hoping that a new home might be sooner, rather than later. But as I've mentioned before, I'm a little lackadaisical when it comes to getting my head down in front of my laptop, so it might be later.

"Coop?" asks Cassidy's melodic voice from inside the cabin, doubtlessly eager to experience more of my endless humor and intellect.

"When are you making my morning cortado?" she queries, now appearing like a vision of loveliness in my gaze.

It's the coffee, isn't it? It's always the coffee.

"That's the least I can do, my love," I said, getting up to go to the galley.

"What's the most?" she asks, a grin appearing across her face.

Hmmm…

Author's Note

I was once staying in San Diego, over from England and looking for a house for my family's impending relocation to California. I had some time on my hands, and so I made my way to the local Barnes & Noble bookstore to find some new novels to read during my stay. I'd never heard of Dan Brown before, but I chanced upon four of his novels, and having read the synopses, I greedily snagged them and took them back to my hotel.

I was mesmerized by the writing style and the storytelling and devoured all four books within my two-week stay in Del Mar. I didn't realize it then, but those four books became part of my inspiration years later; to begin writing novels myself. But I should mention my other favorite authors who were equally important in that decision, and who contributed enormously to my deciding to jump off the ledge and inspire me to write, their own immaculate and unique styles one can only aspire toward.

Those wonderful people are John Sandford, Michael Connelly, Jonathan Kellerman, John Lescroart, Nelson DeMille, David Baldacci, Tami Hoag and of course, John Grisham. Thank you so much for every entertaining word you write for us.

My own background is in film and television, so when I wrote my first novel, *The Sea Glass*, I found myself writing scenes, instead of chapters. My love and passion for film, drove me to try and put the reader in the scene, rather than watching it from the outside. I want to immerse you in my stories, to be part of them. I have no idea if my style works, but I sincerely hope it does.

As I grow older, I cherish the things I learn from young people. My daughter, **Lucy Robson**, teaches me new things all the time, far more than I could ever teach her now. We've spent the last couple of years working together on renovating her home, a wonderful thing for a father and daughter to experience together, and in that time, we have become closer and closer. But she is a beautiful and ever-shining guiding light for me, forever encouraging me to achieve the unachievable. I love you, Lulu.

I also want to thank my ex-wife, **Jayne Robson**, for bringing Lucy into this world, and for being the greatest mother Lucy could ever wish to have. I also want to thank her for her continued support, love, and friendship, something that is rare but crucial and wonderful after marriage. Jayne is one of those amazing human beings, who will do anything for anyone, and I love that.

My partner, **Amanda Everett**, is not only the girl who can make me look presentable in the photos in this book, but she is also my manuscript editor who has driven me, sometimes unmercifully, to achieve the best I can be, and to make this story a far better one than it would have been without her invaluable, incisive and brilliant input. I feel incredibly fortunate to have someone who shoots from the hip, with the only intention of making me push harder. But it's always delivered with love, and a belief that everything I write can be made better.

My friend, **Craig Dallas**, is one of those men that every man should have as a friend. I feel incredibly fortunate to have met this man twenty years ago, when we began a friendship that is more akin to having the best brother you could ever have. He is eternally optimistic, utterly loyal, with a heart made from pure gold, and I greatly appreciate his presence in my life.

I've known **Matt Forrest** for over forty years. We first met on the production of a music video, and a friendship began that has never faltered. During the writing of *Tick Tock*, he read everything I wrote, making copious notes as he went through the manuscript.

Sometimes, I would dread receiving his notes, knowing that they might be brutal, but also understanding that he wants me to achieve everything possible. Without Matt's input, this book wouldn't be what it has become, so thank you so much, my friend.

Finally, I would like to thank you, the reader, for taking the time to read *Tick Tock*, I feel enormously, and gratefully honored, to have you onboard.

Printed in Great Britain
by Amazon